Cathy Williams can remember reading Mills & Boon books as a teenager, and now that she's writing them she remains an avid fan. For her, there is nothing like creating romantic stories and engaging plots, and each and every book is a new adventure. Cathy lives in London. Her three daughters—Charlotte, Olivia and Emma—have always been, and continue to be, the greatest inspirations in her life.

USA TODAY bestselling author **Natalie Anderson** writes emotional contemporary romance full of sparkling banter, sizzling heat and uplifting endings—perfect for readers who love to escape with empowered heroines and arrogant alphas who are too sexy for their own good. When not writing you'll find her wrangling her four children, three cats, two goldfish and one dog…and snuggled in a heap on the sofa with her husband at the end of the day. Follow her at www.natalie-anderson.com.

D1144279

MARRIAGE BARGAIN WITH HIS INNOCENT

CATHY WILLIAMS

PREGNANT BY THE COMMANDING GREEK

NATALIE ANDERSON

MILLS & BOON

First Published in Great Britain 2019
by Mills & Boon, an imprint of HarperCollins*Publishers*
1 London Bridge Street, London, SE1 9GF

Marriage Bargain with His Innocent © 2019 by Cathy Williams

Pregnant by the Commanding Greek © 2019 by Natalie Anderson

ISBN: 978-0-263-27340-3

MIX
Paper from
responsible sources
FSC® C007454

This book is produced from independently certified FSC™ paper
to ensure responsible forest management.
For more information visit www.harpercollins.co.uk/green.

Printed and bound in Spain
by CPI, Barcelona

MARRIAGE BARGAIN WITH HIS INNOCENT

CATHY WILLIAMS

CHAPTER ONE

GEORGINA LOOKED UP at the imposing Georgian mansion in front of which she was standing. Well, she would have expected nothing less.

She raised her hand to the doorbell. Her brain was saying *Might as well get it over and done with* while her feet were yelling *Hang on just a minute...let's think about this*.

She went with the brain and pressed the buzzer before her feet could start winning the argument.

She was here now. She'd travelled hours to be here and she wasn't going to slink away without telling the owner of this over-the-top mansion in Kensington—a man she had known since childhood, a man on whom she had had a very inconvenient crush when she'd been a kid of sixteen, —that, *Hey...guess what...? I bet you never thought that you and I would be in a relationship after all!*

Matias had no idea who could be ringing his doorbell, but whoever it was deserved a Medal of Honour for the most timely interruption in history.

The icy blonde perched on his white leather sofa hadn't stopped screaming for the past thirty-five minutes. She carried on screaming now, as she followed him out of the vast sitting room towards the front door.

'I refuse to let you break up with me! I've told *every-*

one that you'll be coming to the anniversary party next weekend! I've bought a *dress*! There's someone else, isn't there? Who is she? Do I know her? How could you *do* this to me? I love you! I thought you loved *me*!'

Matias had stopped answering her questions ten minutes ago and he wasn't going to start again now.

He pulled open the door and stopped short.

'Matias.' Georgina peered around him to the source of the high-pitched screaming. 'I'm guessing I've come at a bad time?'

The feet were desperate to take to the hills, but she wasn't quitting now that she was here. That said, she wanted to do nothing more than run away, because it didn't matter how much she braced herself for Matias's ridiculously stupendous good looks, every single time she saw him she was floored all over again.

Dry mouth, thudding heart, clogged brain…and a crashing reminder of what it had felt like to be an adolescent, with her hormones wildly out of control, in thrall to a guy who had never been short of his own personal fan club full of adoring hot babes from the age of thirteen. She'd kept her idiotic crush under wraps, but she could still burn with shame at the memory of it because she'd always been the last sort of girl he would ever have looked at.

'Georgie, what the hell are you doing here?'

'That's not a very nice way to greet an old friend, is it? I'd rather not come back, Matias. I've spent hours on a train and I'm hot and tired and my feet need to rest.' *Or to take flight*, she thought, willing her nerves to go away and thinking, yet again, how much she disliked the man. So stupidly sexy, and yet with a set of values that *so* got on her nerves.

'Is my mother all right?' Matias demanded.

'Who are *you*?'

A blonde had materialised next to him and Georgina wondered whether Matias ever got bored of dating women who were clones of one another. Towering blondes with catwalk figures and a racy sense of fashion that was based on wearing as little as possible even in the depths of winter.

This particular blonde was wearing a tiny red miniskirt and a tiny red top and some very high sandals because it was the height of summer.

'Time for you to go, Ava.'

'We could still make this work, Matias!'

Matias cast a sideways look at Georgina and raked his fingers through his hair. 'No chance,' he said grimly, rescuing her tiny tan designer bag from the table in the hall and handing it to her while channelling her towards the doorway. 'You deserve better than me.'

Georgina rolled her eyes. She stood aside while the blonde walked past her, at least eight inches taller in her heels and as skinny as a runner bean.

'That was considerate of you, Matias—softening the blow by telling her that she could do better than you,' Georgina remarked, stepping inside the mansion and getting a glimpse of his departing back as he headed towards some other part of the house—probably the kitchen, because he looked as if he could use a stiff drink.

Charming, she thought, walking briskly behind him. What on earth did all those women see in him? Yes, he was rich. Yes, he was good-looking. But beyond that… There was nothing that appealed on any level. Which made it quite ironic, considering she was here to tell him that they had secretly been seeing one another, falling in love and getting embroiled in a hot and heavy relationship that was destined to lead…*who knew where?*

She felt queasy at the revelations about to be put on the table.

'Well?'

Matias didn't bother looking at her. He went straight to a cupboard, pulled out a bottle of whisky and poured himself a glass, offering her one as an afterthought, but obviously not really expecting her to take him up on the offer.

'Your mother is fine. In a manner of speaking.'

'I've had a hellish day, Georgie, so spare me the riddles. Not that it's like you to beat about the bush. Bludgeon it into the ground is far more your style.' He raised his eyebrows and didn't look away when their eyes tangled. 'I spoke to my mother two days ago and she sounded well, so what's the matter with her?'

'Nothing. Her health hasn't deteriorated. I mean, she's still weak after the stroke, and her speech isn't quite back to normal, but she's doing all the exercises the doctor recommended.'

'Good.'

'You have a wonderful house, Matias.' She didn't feel that the subject waiting to be broached could be broached quite yet. She needed to feel a bit more comfortable. Right now, her nerves were at breaking point. 'And I *will* have that drink you offered, actually.'

'Whisky?'

'Wine, if you have any. Thank you.'

'I'm warning you it's not organic. It's incredibly expensive, though, so please think twice about pouring it down the sink because it fails to meet your high standards.'

Matias strolled towards the fridge and withdrew a bottle of Chablis. He looked at her over his shoulder. She was dressed as she was always dressed, in some sort of flowery concoction that was designed to do absolutely nothing whatsoever for the female form. Long skirt, loose top... A veritable riot of colours, none of which flattered a woman who was small, round and had bright red hair.

Was it *so* hard to make an effort? he wondered.

'Very funny, Matias.'

'We both know how much you like to bang the drum for organic farming. I wouldn't want to get in the way of your social conscience.'

'You can be really horrible, do you know that?' she asked. But her voice was neutral, because she was busy looking round the spectacular kitchen with its shiny gadgets and space-age feel.

'You'd miss it if I wasn't,' Matias murmured without batting an eye, and he held her gaze for a few seconds longer than strictly necessary before lowering his eyes, letting his lush dark lashes shield his expression. 'What would you do with a nice, *polite* Matias?'

Georgina blushed—much to her annoyance—and glared. 'I've spent hours travelling here to see you. The least you could do is to be nice to me.'

'Yes, you have,' Matias said thoughtfully, 'and I'm wondering why. In fact, I'd go so far as to say I'm burning up with curiosity. I don't think you've ever come to this house, have you?'

'You know I haven't.'

'In fact, I didn't think you ever got out of deepest, darkest Cornwall.'

'You've always been so scathing about Cornwall!'

Don't you have *any* loyalty to the place where you were brought up?'

'No. So, moving on, Georgie…' He circled her the way a shark might circle a minnow, slowly, thoroughly, and with keen, watchful interest. 'If you're not here to talk about my mother, then what exactly *are* you doing here? Not that your arrival wasn't opportune.'

He sat on the chair facing her and tugged another chair towards him so that he could stretch out his long legs.

Georgina opened her voice to give him a piece of her mind. His mother despaired of him. His women came and went with barely a pause for breath in between, because Matias Silva had the attention span of a toddler in a candy shop when it came to women.

She caught the veiled amused expression in his dark eyes and abruptly shut her mouth. He wanted to get a rise out of her and that was the last thing she needed.

Instead, she met his gaze steadily and coolly. It took willpower, because he was, without doubt, the most drop-dead gorgeous man she had ever seen. Blessed with the exotic genes of his Argentinian father and the spectacular beauty of his English mother, Matias had emerged into the world with the sort of physical advantages that made people stare and then turn around for a second look, because surely no one could be quite so spectacular.

She had long ago forgiven herself for her girlish crush. She just wished that her disobedient eyes could stop drinking him in the way they were doing right now.

His features were chiselled to perfection, but his bronzed colouring and raven-dark hair, which he always kept slightly too long, rescued him from being just another good-looking guy.

'I *am* here to talk to you about your mother,' Georgina said into the lengthening silence. 'But could I just unwind for a bit? I'm exhausted.'

'It's seven o'clock. Have you eaten?'

'I had some sandwiches on the train.'

'I'll take you out to dinner.'

'I doubt I'm dressed for the sort of restaurants *you're* likely to patronise,' Georgina said wryly.

'How would you know what sort of restaurants I'd be likely to patronise?' he asked.

But he was smiling crookedly at her, reminding her that beneath their obvious, glaring and insurmountable differences, there were times when they were eerily tuned in to one another. Longevity and history, she presumed.

'Because I'm smart like that.' She was beginning to feel overheated. 'Thank you. It's very nice of you. But... er...no, thank you. Why don't you show me round your lovely house? I'd far rather that.'

The plan Georgina had sketched out had been a hurried one—a response to circumstances, formulated on impulse and put on the table before she'd had time to think through the details and, more to the point, the glaring, inescapable downsides. By the time she'd sat back and thought about it, it had been too late to take it all back.

Rose Silva believed that her son was finally on the verge of settling down, if not with the girl of *his* dreams, then certainly the girl of *hers*. She adored Georgina.

She finally had something to live for. She would have a daughter-in-law she loved. Her son would be settled, as he should be, with no more of his silly cavorting with women who weren't suited to him at all. There would be grandchildren. All would be right in the world.

In the space of five minutes, Georgie's suggestion of

a relationship with Matias had turned into a full-blown *when-shall-I-start-looking-for-a-hat?* response. Georgie had squashed that enormous leap as firmly as she could, but here she was, supposedly having a serious relationship with the guy looking at her now with those fabulous dark, dark eyes.

What had begun as an ill-thought-out but well-intentioned little white lie had taken on a life of its own faster than a rocket soaring into space. An entire future had been planned before Georgina had had time to draw breath—and now here she was.

'Please don't say a word to Matias,' she had begged Rose, horrified at the thought of a congratulatory phone call to a guy who would have no idea what his mother was going on about. 'We…er…planned on breaking it to you together… Just that we're going out, Rose… Who knows where that will lead…?'

The feeble utterances had actually brought her out in a cold sweat and prompted her immediate departure to London. As his newly acquired girlfriend, didn't she need to know the layout of his house? She still felt queasy.

'You want to see my house? Why?'

'You're so scornful whenever you come down to Cornwall… I want to see what you have here that's so superior.'

Matias tilted his head to one side and looked at her carefully. 'Why am I getting the feeling that something's going on here that I don't know about?'

'You don't have to show me around if you don't want to.'

'Bring your drink. Maybe after a bit of alcohol you'll tell me exactly what's going on, Georgie.'

'Why are you so suspicious?'

'Because I wasn't born yesterday. I also *know* you. Some might say better than I've ever known any woman. You're here for a reason, and if it's not because my mother needs me to come down to Cornwall for health reasons, then you're here for something else and you're too scared to come right out and tell me. Is it money?'

On his way to the sitting room to begin the grand tour, Matias stopped abruptly and looked at Georgina through narrowed eyes. He positioned himself so close to her that she could pick up the faint whiff of whatever expensive aftershave he wore. She automatically edged back.

'You think I'm here to…to ask you for *money*? And you claim to *know* me?'

'It's not that far-fetched.' Matias shrugged. 'You'd be surprised how many people come crawling out of the woodwork to ask for money when they find out that I'm in a position to bestow it upon them.'

'Why would I have to ask you for *money*, Matias? I have a job! I'm a food photographer! By your lofty standards it may not pay much, but it's more than enough for me to live on! So why on earth would I have to come to you for a loan?'

'No idea. Who knows what sort of financial trouble you might have got yourself into?'

He spun round and Georgina stared at him with outrage. No one had ever been able to rile her as much as Matias Silva. Or challenge her. Or generally send her nervous system into frantic overdrive. He was right. They *knew* one another—whether she cared to admit it or not.

From the side-lines she had watched the way he had turned into a forbidding and coolly remote adolescent after he had won a scholarship to a boarding school in Winchester. All pretence of having any interest in his parents' organic farm had been dumped. Ambition had become his constant companion.

It was little wonder that he was now wondering whether she had shown up on his doorstep out of the blue because she needed a hand-out. For Matias, money was the only thing that made any sense. He'd never had much growing up, and he'd made it his life's work to compensate for the lack.

Was it any wonder that they rubbed one another up the wrong way when they were as different as chalk and cheese? She was argumentative. He was intransigent. She was uninterested in money. Money was all he cared about. She loved where she lived. He hadn't been able to wait to escape from it. She admired his parents. He privately scorned them.

'Well? Spit it out, Georgie. Do you need a loan?'

He looked her up and down, head inclined to one side, his dark eyes coolly speculative. She didn't think there was a man alive who got on her nerves more.

'Have you been living beyond your means?' he murmured with exaggerated interest. 'Nothing to be ashamed of. Oh, wait… I can see why you *might* be ashamed, bearing in mind your holier-than-thou outlook on life which you've spent the past ten years droning on about.'

Georgina gritted her teeth and balled her hands into fists. 'I'm not here to ask you for money, Matias.'

'Didn't think you were.' He moved off to begin their tour, pushing open doors without bothering to explain which room was used for what.

'Why's that?' she asked.

All white. Minimalist. Big, expensive abstract art on the walls. A lot of chrome. The best money could buy. Again, no surprise there. Matias had gone to university a year early, studied Maths and Economics, and left with a job at an investment bank in his hand. Within five years he had made his first million and then he had started flying solo, buying up sick companies and turning them around. He'd invested in property on the side. By thirty he'd had an empire under his belt and more money than anyone could use in a lifetime. Every room she glimpsed bore witness to how rich he was.

No wonder Rose was intimidated by her billionaire only child.

'He's always been something of a genius,' she'd once confided wistfully. 'That's why he's never liked the simple life. It isn't enough for him.'

'Georgie,' Matias was saying now, 'it doesn't take a genius, looking at you, to realise that you have *no* interest in *anything* that could possibly get someone into debt.'

'What's that supposed to mean?'

'You're not the typical picture of someone leading a raunchy life beyond her means. If you have a predilection for designer clothes, fast cars and jewellery then you're doing a damn good job of keeping it under wraps. Besides... I remember you showing me your piggy bank when you a kid. You were very proud of the eight pounds sixty you'd managed to stockpile over six weeks. It would beggar belief that you'd go from parsimonious and proud saver to wildly extravagant spender. Now, do you want the tour to carry on upstairs?'

He looked at her and she wondered whether he realised just how offensive he could be.

'Or have you relaxed sufficiently to tell me why you're here? You may have had sandwiches on the train, but I'm hungry. I'll get some food delivered. Let me know if you want to see the rest of the house and I'll order when the tour is done.'

'No—no need to go upstairs.'

She thought *bedrooms* and backed away from the thought fast. Despite loathing the man, it had always been way too easy to associate him with bedrooms—partly because he was so sexy, and partly because, even though time had moved on from that girlish infatuation, age had failed to completely extinguish the remnants of her crush. She still occasionally caught herself daydreaming about him. Fortunately she'd learnt how to avoid getting too embroiled in that kind of pointless fantasy.

'Good.' He headed back towards the kitchen, phoning for food on the way. 'Where were you planning on spending the night?'

He looked at the battered khaki backpack which she had dumped on the ground in the kitchen.

'B&B.'

Matias frowned. 'That's ridiculous,' he said shortly. 'Didn't you consider staying here? Don't you think I'm not appreciative for everything you do for my mother and have done over the years? A night in my house is the least I could offer in return.'

Georgina flushed. 'I shouldn't be the one doing stuff for your mother, though, should I?' she muttered, fidgeting.

'When it comes to that old chestnut—been there, done that. I've heard every variation of criticism from you over the years, so let's drop the topic and move on.'

Matias felt a flash of guilt dart through him like quicksilver. He had no reason to feel guilty. None at all. He supported his mother financially, made sure she wanted for nothing. It took hard work to make the sort of money that he did, and without his money life would not be nearly so rosy for his mother. When things went wrong in her house he made sure to replace them with top-of-the-range equivalents. Over time, her kitchen had been so expensively kitted out that any professional chef would have been happy to ply his trade there. And as for the farm...

The organic farm she'd insisted on hanging on to brought in peanuts and she couldn't have begun to handle it without his help. He made sure that everyone who worked there reported to him—just as he made sure that any headaches were sorted before they became full-blown.

And organic farming—as he had discovered years ago—was nothing but one long, grinding headache. Crops had a nasty habit of falling victim to the wrong type of insect. The chickens, which had made a brief and optimistic appearance for a year and a half, had fallen prey to foxes or else wandered off hither and thither to lay eggs that couldn't be located and therefore never made it to the shelves at the local greengrocer.

Although, in fairness, it was better than the Reiki treatment, the donkey sanctuary, the creative workshops and the gem-selling crackpot ideas that had preceded the farm when he'd been a kid.

So guilt? No, he had nothing to feel guilty about. He and his mother might not be close, but how many relationships between children and their parents were trouble-free? He was a responsible and dutiful son, and if his mother thought that he came up short in the personal stakes then he could live with that.

He shook his head free of inconvenient introspection and surfaced to find Georgie apologising.

'*Sorry?*' His eyebrows shot up. 'You're *sorry* about criticising?' He grinned. 'Now I'm *really* getting worried. Since when have you ever made apologies for getting under my skin?'

He watched as she noticeably didn't answer but instead devoted her attention to inspecting the rooms they had previously walked past.

Just when he was about to break the ever-lengthening silence the doorbell went. When Matias returned, it was with a spread of food from a top London restaurant.

'I've ordered enough for two,' he said, dumping the lot on the table and hunting down two plates and some cutlery. He poured them both wine and sat facing her.

'Most people have Indian or Chinese take-out,' Georgina remarked.

She shouldn't eat. She had had those sandwiches and she could do with shedding a few pounds. But her mouth watered at the sight of fluffy white rice, beef in wine, vegetables…

'Dig in,' Matias encouraged drily. 'But save room for the chocolate fondant.'

'My favourite.'

'I know. I recall going to that restaurant by the sea years ago, with my parents and your family, and you made them bring you three. Eat—and tell me exactly what you're doing here. I'm bored with going round the houses.'

'It's about your mother, but not about her health as such. Like I said, she's doing as well as can be expected, and I know you've paid for the best consultants, the best hospital, the best of everything… But health isn't just a physical thing. It's also a frame of mind, and your mum's been depressed for quite a while.'

'Depressed?' Matias frowned. 'Why would she be depressed when she's on the mend? She didn't sound depressed when I spoke to her last.'

'She wouldn't have wanted to worry you, Matias,' Georgina said impatiently. 'She's been making noises about her mortality. She's waiting for some test results—perhaps that's been preying on her mind—but she could be in a mental slump.'

'Test results? What test results? At any rate, they can't be important or the consultant would have mentioned them to me. And thoughts of her mortality? She's not even in her mid-sixties!'

He relaxed. If this was a simple case of hypochondria then an informal chat with her consultant would soon make her see sense. She was on the road to recovery. Mortality thoughts were only appropriate for people in their eighties and nineties, anyway.

He had a couple of big deals on the go, but as soon as he was through with those he would go down to Cornwall. He might even consider staying longer than a weekend. It could work… He had had the fastest possible broadband installed in his mother's house years previously, because he couldn't function without the Internet. In short, he could spare a little time down there without it affecting his work schedule.

'She's got another thirty years in her,' he said, noting that for someone who had refused the offer of a meal out Georgie had certainly done justice to the food on her plate. No one could ever accuse Georgina White of having a feeble appetite. It was a refreshing change, in actual fact.

'She doesn't see it that way.'

'*She* doesn't have a medical background. The consultant has no worries about her health or I would know about it. That's what he's paid to do—keep me in the loop. It's just a question of convincing her of that. If she's concerned that there's a risk of this thing happening again, then I can get Chivers to show her the charts and scans.'

'It's not just a question of that, Matias. She feels…' Georgina sighed and gazed at him, then wished she hadn't because she couldn't seem to tear her eyes away. He was so ridiculously good-looking. 'She feels that she's been a failure as a mother. She feels that there's a chasm between you two and it's one that will never be breached. All she wants, she tells me, is for you to settle down…have a wife and kids. She tells me that she's always wanted to be a grandmother and that she feels there's nothing to look forward to. When I say that she's depressed, it isn't because she thinks she might be pushing up the daisies in six months' time. It's because she's been looking back on her past and questioning where she is right now—in the present. I've had a word with Mr Chivers… I hope you don't mind.'

'It wouldn't make any difference if I said I did, would it? Considering you've already contacted him.'

Matias scowled. The guilt was back and with a vengeance. It seemed it had been buried in a very shallow grave. His mother had never been impressed with his lifestyle or his money. Nor had his father, when he had been alive. Neither had ever said anything, but their silence on the subject had spoken volumes.

'What did he say?'

'He says that under normal circumstances he wouldn't be worried. Rose is young. But because of her anxieties, and the subsequent stress, there's a chance that her health might be jeopardised. She's lost interest in all the things that used to occupy her. She doesn't seem to care about the farm any more. She's not going to the gardening club. Like I said, she's talking about having nothing to live for.'

'You could have just called to fill me in on all this. Leave it with me. I'll have a word with Chivers. I'm paying the man a small fortune. He should be able to do *something*. There might be a course of medication my mother could go on...there are tablets for that sort of thing.'

'Forget it. It won't work,' Georgina told him bluntly.

Matias frowned, his brooding dark eyes betraying the puzzlement of someone trying to join dots that weren't quite forming a pattern.

'Then what will?' he asked, with an elaborate show of patience that got on her nerves.

'You'll probably need something stiffer than a glass of expensive white wine before I tell you my solution.'

'Spit it out. I can't bear the suspense.'

'I may have told her a couple of tiny white lies...' Georgina stuck out her chin at a pugnacious angle—an angle that said that she was a woman about to dig her heels in and was ready for a fight if he wanted to have one.

Now that they were getting to the heart of the matter, her nerves were kicking in big time.

'You *may* have told her a couple of tiny white lies...? Now, why does that admission send a shiver of apprehension racing down my spine?'

'I love your mother. I've always been close to her, as you well know, and more especially now, since my parents decamped to Melbourne for my dad's three-year secondment to the university there. I've been with her throughout this awful business, and you can trust me when I tell you that her spirits are sinking lower and lower by the day. Who knows what could happen?'

'Yes, I'm getting the picture. You've known my mother since the dawn of time and you're worried about her, despite hard evidence from the experts that everything's ticking along nicely. So, Georgie, just say what you have to say—because my apprehension is still there. Why don't we dump this meandering, getting-nowhere-fast route and stick to the main road? In fact, why don't we just return to those little white lies of yours?'

'Okay, Matias... I *may* have encouraged your mother to feel that she has every right to look forward to the future...'

'Bracing advice.'

'Because you're involved with someone, and happily it's not one of those women your mother disapproves of.'

'The more I hear, the more I ask myself whether you and my mother have any topic of conversation aside from me.'

'We *never* talk about you!' Georgina snapped, momentarily distracted by the sheer egotism of the man. 'It's only because of the situation that she's taken to confiding in me... Naturally I'm not going to tell her to keep her worries and fears to herself... Trust me when I tell you that I *don't* encourage her to talk about you!'

'Let's leave that to one side for the while. So, I'm involved with someone my mother approves of? I suppose, as fairy stories go, that one could work—provided I'm not called upon to introduce this paragon to her. Because if I am, then it's going to take a lot more than creative spin to cover up the cracks in your plan.'

'Well, you see, this is where it may be less difficult than you imagine…'

She cleared her throat. She couldn't carry on—especially when he was staring at her narrowly, his clever brain whirring away to make sense of what she'd just said. She inhaled deeply and reminded herself that this was why she was here—this was why she had made this inconvenient trip to London to see a man who had always managed to rub her up the wrong way.

She was here to do a *job*, so to speak.

Yes, she had acted on impulse—but impulse was not a dangerous thing because it was a *good* thing. All she had to do was look ahead to the good that could come out of it. And not be deterred by those bitter-chocolate-dark eyes staring at her with off-putting intensity.

'I'm all ears.'

'I've told your mother that you and I are an item,' she said in a challenging voice.

It came out in a rush and left behind a silence that was thick and dense and so uncomfortable that she could only stare down at her sandals while wishing that the ground would open up and swallow her whole.

Oh, how different the whole thing had seemed when she had told Rose. She had watched how the older woman's thin face had lit up. Rose had actually clapped her hands with delight, and Georgina had had a wonderful moment of basking in the warm glow of having made someone she loved very happy.

Before common sense had set in. By which time it had been too late to retract what she had said and the warm glow had been replaced by an icy, clammy dread.

Right now, right here, she wondered what had possessed her. How on earth could she have thought that this might be a good idea? She had travelled up to London prepared to stand her ground and fight her corner, but she had forgotten how intimidating Matias could be.

Why had impulse galloped ahead of common sense?

'Sorry?' Matias inclined his head with an expression of rampant disbelief. 'I think I may have misheard what you just said…'

CHAPTER TWO

'YOU HAVEN'T,' GEORGINA said flatly.

'Okay. So let me run this past you and you can tell me if I've got anything wrong. My mother is feeling a bit low...'

'With all the signs of depression...'

'Which could probably be taken care of with a course of tablets, because—believe it or not—tablets *do* exist for conditions like depression. But you've unilaterally, and without bothering to consult me, decided to rule that practical solution out.'

'You're making it sound so black and white and it's not. Which is something you would see if you were around a little more often!'

'Let's leave the criticisms to one side for the time being, Georgie. In a nutshell, my mother is down, wishes she could hear the pitter-patter of tiny feet, and to oblige her and raise her spirits you've decided to tell her a whopper about you and I being involved.'

'You should have seen the expression on her face, Matias. She hasn't looked so overjoyed in... Well, I would say *years*. Not since your dad died. Even before the stroke!'

Matias looked anything but overjoyed. His expression

was a mixture of outraged incredulity and simmering anger. Of course she hadn't expected immediate capitulation, because that would have been too good to be true, but she saw she was going to have to use all her powers of persuasion. She couldn't bear the thought of his mother fading away into a chronic depression.

Even after Antonio's death Rose hadn't sunk into the sort of dull-eyed, low-level despair Georgina had begun to notice in her recently. The fact that tests were still ongoing was simply feeding into her acceptance that the road she was travelling was heading sharply downwards. She was ill, she was down, and nothing was ever going to change.

Until now Georgie hadn't really appreciated just how much of a surrogate mother Rose had become for her. Her own mother, whom she loved dearly, was worlds apart from her, wrapped up in academia—a world with which Georgina was unfamiliar. She had never got her intellect going, never been able to follow in her parents' intellectual footsteps. Her father lectured in economics, her mother in international law.

She, on the other hand, even from a young age, had been a lot happier being creative. It was to her parents' credit that they had never tried to push her towards a career she would have had no hope of achieving, and while they had busied themselves with university stuff Georgina, growing up, had drifted off to Matias's house, bonded with his parents and adored their wacky creativity.

She *loved* his mother, and that thought put a bit of much-needed steel in her weakening resolve.

'If I didn't know better,' Matias said, 'I would be inclined to think that you've finally cracked. And here's a little question, Georgie—*why* would my mother believe that you and I are an item? Every time we meet we end up arguing. I don't like women who argue. My mother knows that. For God's sake, she's met enough of the women I've dated in the past to know that chalk and cheese just about sums it up when it comes to you and the kind of women I'm attracted to!'

Every word that left his beautiful mouth was a direct hit, but Georgina refused to let him get to her. However, she was distracted enough to ask, with dripping sarcasm, 'So…you don't like women who argue? Or do you mean you don't like women who happen to have an opinion that doesn't concur with yours? In other words, does your attraction to the opposite sex begin and end with towering blondes whose entire vocabulary is comprised of one word…*yes*?'

Matias folded his arms and burst out laughing. 'Now you're making me sound shallow,' he drawled. 'But, just for the record, I've never had a problem with towering blondes with single-syllable vocabularies. When you live life in the fast lane the last thing you want is a sniping nag reminding you that you're back five minutes late and asking where's the milk you were supposed to buy.'

'I doubt you've ever done anything as mundane as buy a pint of milk, Matias.'

'Not recently, I haven't. Not since I was a kid, running errands down to that woefully badly stocked corner shop next to Bertie's place. Of course there was only the occasional need for milk to be *bought*,' he continued, his voice hardening, 'after my parents decided to try their hand with a pet cow. But back on point, here. If my mother has bought this story of yours then she's suffering from more than just mild depression. I mean…when exactly are we supposed to be conducting this raunchy, clandestine relationship that's only now come to light?'

This was the longest one-to-one conversation they had had in a while, and Georgina was mesmerised by his dark, compelling beauty. She was noticing all sorts of details that had only before registered vaguely on her subconscious.

Like the depths of silvery grey in his eyes—at times as icy as the frozen Arctic wastes, at times almost black and smouldering. Like the sensual curve of his mouth and the aquiline perfection of his lean features. Not to mention the dramatic lushness of those black lashes that were so good at shielding what he didn't want the world to see. He oozed an unfair amount of sinful sex appeal, and the longer she looked at him the more addled her brain became and the faster she lost track of what she wanted to say.

As if from those faraway days when she had dreamily fantasised about a relationship that had never stood a chance of materialising, the impact he'd always had on her came rushing back, as though no time had intervened...as though she'd never seen first-hand the type of women he enjoyed and the type he definitely didn't. In short—*her*.

She dragged her disobedient eyes away and focused on a point just past his right shoulder. 'I'm close to your mother, but she doesn't know my every movement, Matias. I told her that we'd been meeting in secret for the past few months but didn't want to bring it out into the open because it was still quite new...'

'Ingenious. But now that's all changed because we've...what? Had an epiphany? Fill in the blanks here, would you?'

'I just said that it was…you know…in the early stages but definitely serious…'

'And I'm guessing that you skirted over the details because you trusted that old adage that people will always believe what they want to believe?'

Georgina blushed. Her green eyes flashed defiance, but she was finding it hard to win him over, and with a sinking heart she knew that he wasn't going to jump on board with this. She would have to return to the village with her tail between her legs and break the news that their so-called serious relationship had crashed and burned.

So much for impulse being a good thing. So much for the ends justifying the means.

'Not going to happen, Georgie,' Matias delivered with finality. 'It was a ludicrous idea and, whilst I appreciate that you lied for the best of reasons, I'm not going to sucked into giving credence to your little charade.'

Defeated, Georgina could only look at him in silence. She tucked her hair behind her ear and sat on her hands, leaning forward, her body rigid with tension.

'Furthermore, I dislike the fact that you saw fit to drag *me* into this poorly thought out scheme of yours. Did it never occur to you that I might have a life planned out that *doesn't* include a phoney relationship with you to appease my mother?'

'No,' Georgina said with genuine honesty, because at the time there had been one thing and one thing only on her mind, and that had been the fastest way to bring Rose back from whatever dark place she was getting lost in.

'Well, perhaps it should have.'

'I just thought—'

'Georgie,' Matias interrupted heavily, standing up to

indicate that the conversation was at an end, 'you've always been like my parents. Warm-hearted, but essentially lacking in that practical gene which can sometimes appear harsh but which is the one that makes sense at the end of the day. Now, do you want some fondant?'

'I've lost my appetite. And if by *practical* you mean hard as nails and cold as ice, then I'm very glad that I was born *without* that particular gene.' She stood up as well. 'You may pride yourself, Matias Silva, on seeing the world from your *practical* point of view, but that doesn't necessarily make you a *happy* guy, does it? Yes, it might make you a *wealthy* one, but there's a great big world out here that is rich and rewarding and has nothing to do with how much money you have in your bank account.'

'We'll agree to differ on that one.'

Georgina swerved past him and strode, head held high, towards the front door.

'For God's sake, Georgie, you can still stay the night in my house.'

'I'd rather not, as it happens.'

'Well, where's the B&B?'

'Somewhere in west London—but I'm happy to make my own way there.'

'Just give me the address and I'll get my driver to drop you. It'll be a damn sight more comfortable than trekking on the Underground or trying to work out which bus goes where.'

He didn't give her time to object. He flipped his cell phone out of his pocket and positioned himself in front of the door so that she couldn't run away.

Matias had said what he'd wanted to say but he still felt guilty. He knew that she would see his lack of co-operation in her hare-brained scheme as a lack of concern for his mother. Nothing could be further from the truth. He had never had much in common with his parents—had always seen their idealistic, holistic, hippy approach to life as charming but irresponsible—but that didn't mean that he hadn't loved them in his own way.

His biggest regret was the fact that he hadn't been able to make it back for his father's funeral. He'd been abroad, and it had all happened so damned fast. The flight connections to get him back to Cornwall had not been quick enough. He'd been too late. He'd never had the chance to fix the relationship he'd had with his father—a relationship that had been broken over a period of years as Matias had become ever more distant from his tree-hugging parents, whose ideologies he had never been able to grasp.

He'd failed as a son and, even though he'd spent his adult life trying to make up for it, by assiduously making sure his mother was taken care of, Matias knew that there was a yawning chasm between them for which the small, round, feisty copper-haired woman in front of him had judged and sentenced him a long time ago.

But as far as Matias was concerned involving him in something like this without first consulting him just wasn't on.

'My driver will be here in five minutes.' He looked at her and she squirmed resentfully under his piercing gaze. 'What will you tell my mother?'

'Do you care? Maybe I'll tell her that I showed up here and sadly found you in bed with a blonde.'

She sighed. She had no one but herself to blame for the mess she found herself in. Matias had every right to refuse to go along with her. He had his jam-packed life to lead, after all.

'I won't say that.'

'I didn't think you would.'

'Because I'm so predictable?'

'Because you're not the sort.' He paused. 'I *will* come down to Cornwall,' he murmured thoughtfully. 'Maybe next weekend, and I'll stay for a little longer than I usually do.'

'I'll make sure to keep out of your way,' Georgina inserted politely. 'It might make for fireworks if we're supposed to be in the throes of a hostile break-up.'

Matias looked at her and reluctantly grinned. 'Tell me why you've always been able to make me laugh even though we fight like cat and dog? No, scrap that. You'll probably end up fighting with me again. What story will you spin for my mother when you break the disappointing news that we're no longer a hot item?'

'I don't know. I'll think of something.'

'This was *your* idea,' Matias mused, 'but I'll shoulder the blame for the break-up of a relationship that never was. It'll be far more believable that I'm the baddie in this scenario anyway. I won't be letting my mother down too much.'

He saw the flash of curiosity in her eyes and sidestepped it adroitly.

'Fair's fair, after all. Now… Safe trip back, Georgie.' He hesitated. What else was there to say?

Georgina didn't hang around. His chauffeur-driven Mercedes was waiting by the pavement, engine idling, and she didn't look back as she ducked into the back seat.

Mission Impossible had turned into Mission She Must Have Been Crazy. She consoled herself all way to the bed and breakfast by telling herself that she had done her best and there was nothing more she could have done.

The bed and breakfast was not in the most salubrious of locations, but it was reasonably priced and it was clean. Her room was so small that everything seemed to be squeezed in, with only just enough free space to allow passage from bed to bathroom without minor injuries occurring en route.

She had a shower and stuck on the little tee shirt and skimpy shorts she always wore to sleep. At night, in the darkness of the bedroom…that was the time she felt most self-confident about her body.

She could have been married by now. She could have had a child! It was bizarre to think it, but it was true. Lying there in the dark, something about seeing Matias's dark, beautiful face brought to mind thoughts of Robbie and the marriage that had never been.

They were memories that she kept locked away in her head, but now, like imps released from captivity, they stretched and decided to have a little fun at her expense. Memories of being engaged, planning her big day, only to be told a handful of weeks before they were due to tie the knot that he just couldn't go through with it.

'It's not you!' he had declared magnanimously, in what had to be the most over-used craven expression in any break-up. 'It's me. I just don't feel the same way about you that I used to… I don't understand it…'

They had parted ways and she had had to endure months of sensing the whispered pity behind her back every time she entered a room.

Robbie had stopped being attracted to her. Had he *ever* been attracted to her? Maybe not. Maybe he had been carried along on a tide of wanting to please her parents, because he had been her mother's star pupil.

In her darkest, deepest thoughts she had sometimes wondered whether a part of her hadn't simply been drawn to a guy who was diametrically different from Matias—a guy on whom she could pin all her hopes, finally snuffing out that silly, girlish flame that had continued to burn long after she should have grown out of it.

She cringed when she'd remembered the way Robbie had tried to encourage her to lose a bit of weight. Afterwards, when the dust had settled, she had discovered that he had met and married someone else in record time. Someone long and thin. Ever since then Georgina had made even more of an effort to conceal the body that had let her down.

Yes, it was silly—and, yes, it was nonsensical. But since when did feelings make sense?

She drifted into a restless sleep and had no idea how long she had been asleep when she heard a knocking on her door.

She surfaced, feeling drugged and disorientated. It didn't occur to her to be careful when she tentatively pulled the door open because the bed and breakfast was securely locked against intruders. Which meant that the owner, a lovely woman in her fifties, could be the only person knocking.

And it wasn't that late. Only a little after eleven. But she had been so shattered after her pointless visit to Matias that she had climbed into bed and fallen asleep almost immediately.

Her eyes started at the bottom. Loafers—expensive ones. Black jeans—low-slung. Black close-fitting jumper. Muscular body.

Georgina knew that it was Matias before her eyes collided with his silver dark gaze.

'Let me in, Georgie.'

'What are you doing here?'

'We need to talk.'

'How did you get in? Who let you in?' She peered angrily past him in search of the culprit. 'Whoever let you in had no right to do so!'

'She sensed I wasn't going to steal the family heirlooms. Let me in.'

'Do you know what time it is?'

'*Not* bedtime on a Saturday evening for most people under the age of forty-five. And time for me to tell you that there's been a slight change of plan.'

Matias raked his fingers through his hair and shot her a look of brooding unease.

'Whatever you have to say will have to wait until morning.' Her heart beating like a sledgehammer, and feeling acutely aware of her lack of clothing, Georgina made to shut the door. In response Matias neatly wedged his foot in the open gap before he could be locked out.

'I realise this is not the most convenient place in the world for a conversation, but what I have to say can't wait. My mother called.'

Georgina hesitated. With a sigh, she reluctantly opened the door, then told him to sit at the dressing table so that she could at least get dressed.

She knew the sort he went for. Tall, leggy blondes who weighed next to nothing. She knew that what she had on was no more revealing than what most girls would wear to the park on a hot day. But she still had to swallow down a sickening feeling of self-consciousness as she scuttled into the bathroom clutching jeans and a tee shirt.

She'd disappeared in under ten seconds. But that was all it had taken for Matias to realise that the body she had always been at pains to keep hidden away was voluptuous, with curves in all the right places, and a derriere as round and as perfect as a peach. She wasn't overweight. She was *sexy*.

His libido, which had been sadly tepid during the last few weeks of his tempestuous relationship with Ava, roared into shocking life, forcing him to conceal a prominent bulge by sitting on a stool by the window.

'You were saying…?' Georgina asked bluntly, when she reappeared in a more acceptable jeans and tee shirt outfit.

She made sure the overhead light was on its brightest setting, so that the room was now as brightly lit as the changing room in a department store. She perched on the edge of the bed, because there were no other available chairs, and rested her hands on her lap.

'You should have dumped your pride and stayed at my place. It's ridiculous what some people call a B&B in London. There's not enough room here to swing a cat.' It was proving impossible for him to get into a comfortable position.

'The owner is lovely. It's cheap. It's clean. And I'm not being ripped off. What did your mother have to say?'

'First of all, I was caught off-guard. It was late, and my mother seldom calls me.'

'That's because she doesn't like to think that she might be disturbing you.'

'More conversations about me, Georgie? Before I could break the disappointing news that we'd decided to call it a day, she launched into a long, excitable congratulatory speech and told me that it was the best thing that had happened to her in a long time. She said that she was under strict instructions not to call me, to wait until we both came down to Cornwall, but she knew that you'd headed to London and couldn't contain herself. Said she felt she finally had something worth living for...'

'Didn't you believe me when I told you that?'

'Hearing it from the horse's mouth made a difference.'

He stood up, strolled to the window, peered out at an uninspiring view of the back of the building, where tall plastic bins were arranged like soldiers against the wall.

He slowly spun round to look at her, half sat on the broad window ledge. 'You were right. She's the happiest I've heard her in a long time. I couldn't get a word in edgewise.'

'So,' Georgina said slowly, 'what you're saying is that you didn't tell her that it's off...?'

'How could I?'

'That's a bit of a problem, then, isn't it? Considering you told me in no uncertain terms that you weren't going to pretend anything for the sake of your mother.'

Matias flushed darkly. 'Don't think that I *approve* of the way you auditioned me for a role I hadn't applied for,' he reminded her abruptly. 'But here we are. I didn't have the heart to break the bad news down the phone so we'll play this game—but the way I see it this will be a temporary situation. It beggars belief that my mother has fallen for your outrageously improbable scenario, but if it's aiding her recovery then it's something I will have to accept.'

Georgina didn't say anything. She had thought so far and no further when it came to this charade. Now a shiver of unease rippled through her and she looked at Matias from under lowered lashes.

He was the king of urban, sophisticated cool and he was supposed to be going out with *her*. She, too, marvelled that his mother hadn't fainted with disbelief at the improbable scenario.

They were supposed to be an item. Boyfriend and girlfriend. Lovers...

Her stomach lurched, because her imagination threatened to veer off in all sorts of uncharted directions.

'So...' Matias picked up the thread of the conversation. His voice was clipped and businesslike, 'I'm here to briefly discuss the mechanics of this situation. What have you told my mother about us? How much winging it have you done?'

'Can't we discuss this another time?' she replied vaguely.

'Another time?'

'Next week? On the phone, perhaps?'

'Are you living in the real world, Georgie? My mother thinks we're going out with one another in some happy-against-all-odds scenario and you want to discuss the details of our so-called relationship on the phone *next week*? *Maybe*?'

'What are you saying?'

'I'm saying,' Matias imparted coolly, 'that we'll both be leaving for Cornwall in the morning. My mother is expecting us. When we get there, having our stories match up might be an idea.'

'You say that you see this as a temporary situation... do you have a timeline in sight?'

Georgina regretted every second of whatever crazy impulse had plunged her into this mess. It had been a lot easier dealing with a fictional situation. Even when she had boarded that train to London she had not really thought about facing Matias in the flesh. He'd been much easier to deal with in her head. Less intimidating, less forbidding, pretty much less…*everything*.

'I have—and it's not a long one. We go down…we indulge in this charade for a few days… Sooner rather than later things can begin to go downhill. I'm happy to carry the can for the inevitable. There are too many differences between us… It's only become apparent now that we're spending a lot of undiluted time with one another… Put it this way: I can spare a couple of weeks and then I have meetings in the Far East. It would be preferable if all this is sorted before I go.'

'A couple of weeks…' She felt as though she'd hopped on a rollercoaster only to find that it was spinning a lot faster than she'd anticipated.

'I don't see a problem with that.'

'But your mother might be down in the dumps again at the rapid demise of our relationship.'

'Which is something you should have considered before you had your light bulb moment. We could hash all this out on the drive down tomorrow, but I think it better if we cover the basics now. I'm going to have to work for the majority of the trip, bearing in mind I'll be leaving the office without warning.'

'You're going to *work* while you drive?'

'Of course not, Georgie! My driver will take us and I'll work in the back. You can bring a book, or some knitting, or whatever you need to occupy your time. We can fine-tune our stories just before we reach my mother's house.'

He fixed his amazing eyes on her and Georgina had the curious sensation of free falling. Her stomach lurched and swooped as her eyes drifted down to his mouth and then immediately skittered away. She licked her lips and croaked some nonsense about having some work to do for her next job.

'Right,' he said, as her voice tapered off, 'how is it that we've gone from war zone to bedroom in such a short space of time?'

'I haven't thought through the details,' she admitted. 'I suppose we can say it was just one of those things. Opposites attracting. It happens. I mean, *you* have a long history of being attracted to women who are nothing like you.'

'Nor are they like *you*,' he inserted smoothly. 'Aside from which, I've never had a serious relationship with any of them—not like the one we're supposed to be having...'

'I acted on impulse,' Georgina said in a muted voice. 'I would never normally think of deceiving anyone, but before I could think things through—work out how it's even credible that the two of us could ever have anything going—I'd come right out and spun a story. I'm sorry about that. You've been cornered into doing something you don't want to do, and I don't blame you if you're seething.'

'Forget it.' Matias looked at her.

'I never even stopped to think that you might actually be going out with someone...one of your ditzy blondes...'

'You were so wrapped up in cheering up my mother that rational thought took a back seat?'

'Something like that.'

'So, it's a very good thing that I'm going to be in charge of making sure that that doesn't happen again. We will do what is necessary and make sure that the boundary lines are firmly in place.'

'Meaning...?' Georgina automatically bristled.

Matias didn't say anything for a few taut seconds.

Out of the blue he was thinking back to that luscious body—a body he would never have guessed lay beneath the layers of unattractive flowing sacks she was so fond of wearing. His libido kicked into gear again and he scowled.

'Meaning we don't forget that this is a convenient charade...'

There was no way Matias was going to give in to that sudden, inexplicable surge in his libido. When it came to relationships Georgina White was after the real thing. Once upon a time she'd been engaged, and she'd been stood up at the last minute. That didn't mean she'd shut the door on her dreams. That wasn't her nature. But she'd been hurt once. There was no way he would ever be responsible for hurting her again by taking what his libido had wanted when he'd seen her in those next-to-nothing pyjamas.

'I won't forget,' Georgina returned stiffly. 'And once again I apologise for landing you in this mess. Your life is so well ordered—this must be a nightmare for you to take in.'

'Now, why do I sense an implied insult behind that butter-wouldn't-melt-in-your-mouth remark?' Matias drawled, glancing at her full lips and absently noting how perfectly defined they were. Like rosebuds the colour of crushed raspberries. Funny he'd never noticed that before...

He lifted his dark eyes to hers. 'I really wouldn't waste time regretting what you've done. What's the point? The fact is that we're here now...in this together for better or for worse, so to speak.'

'I didn't stop to think things through.' Georgina chewed her lip and shot him a worried glance. 'I never considered the ramifications of how your mother would feel when it all…you know…collapsed…'

'That's a bridge to be crossed when we get to it. You're projecting ahead. She'll be fine.' He looked at her, his dark eyes brooding. 'At least once it's over she'll be able to think that I'm capable of holding down a relationship with a woman who isn't obsessed with her physical appearance.'

'Until you return to your catwalk model blondes,' Georgina pointed out absently.

He shot her a crooked grin that did all sorts of annoying things to her heart-rate. Had she spent her entire life oblivious to just how spectacular Matias was? she wondered. No, that wasn't it. She'd always known just how spectacular he was. It was just that now the situation between them was leading her to think thoughts that were taboo—wicked thoughts about what that lean, muscular body might look like underneath his clothes.

A Pandora's box was opening and she knew that she had to make sure it stayed shut. She wasn't an impressionable teenager any more! And, as he had coolly pointed out, this was a charade—a piece of fiction with no basis in reality.

'Maybe I'll go for a different type next time round,' he drawled, standing up. He stretched, flexed his muscles and strolled towards the door.

'What about all these details you want to put into place before tomorrow?' Georgina remained where she was. 'I thought you rushed over here to iron everything out because you're going to work in the car on the way down?'

His hand was on the doorknob as he turned to look at her thoughtfully. 'Question: did you ask for the house tour because you needed some background information to consolidate the myth that we've been meeting secretly, and it would have seemed odd if my mother had asked you about my house and drawn a blank?'

Georgina reddened, and then nodded sheepishly, at which Matias burst out laughing.

'You're one of a kind, Georgie,' he mused, rocking on his heels and looking at her in silence for long enough for her to start feeling hot and bothered. 'And one of a kind is certainly going to be a novelty for me.'

He opened the door. 'I'll text you before I leave tomorrow to come and fetch you. And then our little adventure will begin...'

CHAPTER THREE

HE'D PHONED TO SAY he would be there at two sharp, and right on time Matias arrived to collect her. He didn't leave the car, instead choosing to phone her mobile and then wait, working in the back seat of the Mercedes, while she settled the bill and exchanged a few pleasantries with the owner.

It was another lovely day. Summer was promising never to end and Georgina wished that she had brought something other than the long skirt she had worn the day before and a change of top.

Shielding her eyes from the glare of the sun, she walked briskly towards the one and only car on the road she knew had to be his because it was the one and only car that had tinted windows and looked as though it had been driven straight from a showroom. She stepped into air-conditioned cool and shut the door behind her.

Knowing that her plan was in danger of being put into action, she had spent what had remained of the night tossing and turning and projecting into the future. Matias had made it sound easy. They'd appear together, they'd begin to argue, they'd break up and lo and behold everything would be done and dusted in two weeks, leaving a saddened but more upbeat Rose who would no longer be prone to depression.

Georgina was uneasily aware that she might have bitten off more than she could chew, and that the easily digestible scenario Matias had painted might turn into a horrendous nightmare. But he had come on board and it was too late to back out now.

She met his eyes as she shuffled to find a comfortable position next to him while strapping herself in. Suddenly she was lost for words, and shy in a way she never had been before in his presence.

'I've had a few hours to think about this,' he opened without preamble, snapping shut his computer and fixing her with his amazing silver-grey eyes.

He slid shut the partition separating his driver from them for privacy.

'Have you had a change of mind?' she asked,

'On the contrary,' Matias drawled. 'If you knew me at all, you'd know that once I make my mind up on a certain course of action I stick to it. Which brings me to what I was thinking about after I left you.'

'Which was what?'

The car had slid silently away from the kerb, and with the tinted windows and the lack of noise she felt cocooned in a luxurious bubble. The outside world had ceased to exist. From his house to his car, every single aspect of him oozed extreme wealth. No one would ever guess that he came from a working class background where luxuries had been few and far between.

'However weirdly unquestioning my mother has been about the details of our so-called relationship, she's not stupid. She does know me, and she knows that it's unlikely that I would suddenly be attracted to someone who doesn't at the very least make an effort to dress properly.'

A slow wash of colour rushed to her cheeks and Georgina felt a swell of rage. 'What are you trying to say?'

'You know what I'm trying to say. Flowing skirts? Baggy tops? Shoes made for hiking in rough terrain?'

'Do you have *any* idea how rude you're being right now?' she said tightly.

'You have my sincere apologies—'

'I'm a food photographer.' She ignored the token lip service he had paid, trying to placate her. Her voice was cold and steely. 'I'm freelance. There's no need for me to have a wardrobe of power suits and cocktail outfits.'

'Which is exactly why we won't be heading for that section of Selfridges.'

'What are you talking about? Why would we be going to Selfridges?' The rollercoaster sensation was back with a vengeance. 'I'm not following you.'

'If we're going to do this, then we're going to do it properly, Georgie. No half-measures. We need to be convincing. The alternative is that my mother suspects it's all a crock of lies and her health is set back even more than before. She will lose trust in both of us.'

Georgina didn't say anything because he was painting a graphic picture. He was also making her realise just how sketchy she had been when she had told that first little white lie.

'We might be able to gloss over the little technicality that we've previously spent most of our time together engaged in a series of low-level arguments… We might just be able to pull off that old chestnut of—as you've said—opposites attracting. But beyond that the details have to carry some verisimilitude.'

And after a long line of catwalk models, Georgina thought furiously, *it would beggar belief that he would go for someone who didn't think twice about snapping up bargain buys in the clothes section of a supermarket.*

'Well, what about *you* dressing down?' she fired back.

'For example…?' he returned smoothly, with an undercurrent of amusement in his voice.

'Well, less of the designer cool and more of the beach bum!'

'Interesting thought.' He sat back, leaning against the car door, his legs sprawled apart, one hand resting loosely on his thigh. 'What would that be? Ill-fitting flowered shirt? Cheap shorts? Flip-flops? Is that the kind of look you would go for?'

Georgina blushed and looked away. The man was so good-looking that he would pull off a bin bag and he knew it. Hence the smile that made her want to grind her teeth together in frustration.

'No one would ever believe that you would wear anything as casual as flowered shirts and flip-flops, Matias. Even when you're relaxing you give the impression that you'd really rather be working.'

'I had no idea you could be so accurate when it came to reading me. Maybe there's more substance to our relationship than meets the eye…'

'We don't *have* a relationship—and I won't be dressing like that woman you dispatched yesterday.'

'I'm shocked you're not kicking up more of a fight over this,' Matias admitted with honesty.

'Is that what you think I do? Kick up a fight over everything?'

That stung for some reason, because there was an element of truth in it. She knew that she picked at him, but she quickly told herself that he deserved it. He hardly ever came down to visit his mother...he always made it abundantly clear that he had moved on and was bored with the place he came from...he hadn't even shown up to his dad's funeral!

And yet so much about him refused to be corralled into neat little boxes.

'Not everything,' Matias conceded. 'At least not in the company of other people. I've seen you laugh, so I know that when it comes to picking fights I'm the special one in your life. I get the folded arms and the scowls.' He grinned, watched her colour rise, perversely enjoying it.

'We've had our differences...' Georgina could feel her cheeks suffused with colour. 'But it's only because I've always been close to your parents.' She hesitated, then found herself confiding, 'I adored mine, of course, but I didn't have loads in common with them. I liked art and taking pictures and rummaging in the undergrowth. And you know my parents, Matias...they were all about intellectual pursuits. I think they pretty much packed it in with me when I hit my teens.'

This was something Georgina had never confessed to anyone, and she was surprised that she was confessing it now—especially to Matias—but then wasn't that part and parcel of his compelling personality? So cool, so controlled, so *annoying*. And yet...and yet...he could engage with her on levels no other man she had ever met had been able to.

'Meaning...?'

Georgina laughed, and that did something to Matias's libido again, reminded him of those sexy, unexpected little curves he had glimpsed the night before.

'I stopped getting big, thick books for birthday presents,' she said drily, 'and my mum stopped slipping law, international politics and university into the conversation.'

'I never knew you were bothered by that,' Matias murmured, an element of surprise in his voice.

'A bit. But they were great when it came to supporting my decision to go into photography.'

'Taking pictures of my parents' produce…?'

'It was a start, Matias. I have a steady stream of work now, but I can't afford to splash out on a new wardrobe of clothes I'll only be wearing for two minutes.'

'I wouldn't dream of letting you put your hand in your pocket to buy *anything*,' he said flatly.

Their eyes collided and her heart skipped a beat. Heat rushed through her body and her mouth went dry. He really was so very beautiful. That raven-black hair curling at the nape of his neck, the sensuality of his mouth, the lazy intensity of his eyes…

'And if,' he continued, 'my mother suspected that you had, she would know for sure that this is a sham—because no woman of mine has ever been expected to pay for anything when I'm around.'

But I'm not your woman, Georgina thought confusedly.

'And she would know that you'd bought your own clothes because you wouldn't be able to resist buying items that are two sizes too big.'

'That's out of order!'

Matias laughed. 'Entirely,' he murmured, 'but what's the point in tiptoeing round the issue? Sexy, but refined is the image I'm thinking you should go for.'

Georgina blanched. In what world could she go from homely to *sexy, but refined*?

Aghast, she realised that while they had been talking the driver had been skilfully manoeuvring through the London traffic and had now pulled to a smooth stop at the back of the expensive department store.

She was channelled out of the car and shepherded to the designer floor where, somehow, a personal shopper had been summoned to assist them.

'I'll sit in on this,' Matias said, *sotto voce*. 'If we're going to do this then, like I said, we're going to do it well. And it starts with clothes.'

He sat on a velvet-upholstered sofa with every semblance of keen interest. He didn't even open his computer. He watched in silence as clothes were brought out for inspection—clothes that she would, presumably, wear for him.

He watched as she resentfully paraded in them, chucking aside anything that looked too small, too short or too tight or showed off her boobs too much. Because *he* might go for that look, but Rose would know in an instant that *she* never would.

She opted for *refined* over *sexy*, and she did her utmost to ignore those lazily inspecting eyes as she tried to douse the hot fires of her embarrassment.

Eventually, when the pile of clothes had grown to a ridiculous amount, she put her foot down and resurfaced in her original outfit, hands on her hips and grim determination on her face.

'That's it,' she said flatly. 'I'm not getting anything else.'

'Why not?'

The assistant had vanished to start the business of packaging all the clothes, and Matias patted the space next to him on the sofa—which Georgina ignored.

'I thought women enjoyed nothing more than buying clothes.'

'Not me.' Georgina stood in front of him, arms folded.

'So you hated every second of the experience?'

Georgina hesitated. She refused to admit that a part of her had rather *liked* the business of trying on stuff she would never normally have worn, a lot of which hadn't looked half bad. And a forbidden part of her whispered that trying on stuff *for him* had made the experience even more exhilarating.

'It was a necessary ordeal,' she offered in a clipped voice.

Matias laughed shortly, unfazed. 'Liar. Well, you're going to have to up the appreciation levels,' he drawled, 'and eliminate the sniping rejoinders if we're going to be playing to the gallery.'

He stood up just as the assistant reappeared, obediently waiting in the background for his imperious beckoning finger.

'But you're right. There's enough there to be going on with. It's not as though this little play-acting game is destined to be a never-ending charade.'

Georgina followed his eyes to the expensively ribboned, tissue-wrapped pile of packages on the table by the assistant.

There were clothes and shoes for every conceivable occasion. For expensive meals out…for casual dining in his mother's garden—he had informed her that he would be getting a top caterer in for the duration of his stay with her—for walks along the beach, with his mother doubtless tripping along with them as witness to their rosy relationship.

Before, presumably, it all began going sour.

Georgina wondered whether they should have got a few special *it's all going pear-shaped* outfits. And then she thought that at that point she would just slip back into her normal gear and that would say it all.

'You'll have to show up wearing one of these outfits we've bought,' he said, without glancing at her as he paid for the pile of clothes. Transaction done, he turned to her. 'I'm thinking that your mystery visits to London, under cover of darkness, would have entailed something of your new persona being presented as my new and exciting love interest. In short, would you have turned up in London wearing comfy work clothes and shoes designed to take on rough terrain and stamp it into submission?'

'I honestly don't know how I'm going to look as though you're the light of my life,' Georgina muttered through gritted teeth, but she did as told, peeking into one parcel and then disappearing into the changing room.

She had made sure, during the clothes parade, to keep some of her own baggy clothes on—the flowing skirt twinned with a smaller top, the loose-fitting top twinned with slim-fitting trousers... But now, when she appeared a few minutes later, she was wearing a complete outfit, and she looked...

Matias tried not to gape. The woman looked stunning. The girl next door was gone. In her place was a woman any red-blooded man would have wanted to haul off to the nearest bed, caveman-style.

He sat forward. Slowly. He knew he was staring but he couldn't help himself. She was wearing pin-striped silk culottes and a small silk top, and the ensemble managed to leave everything to the imagination while sending his libido into the stratosphere.

She had had her hair scraped back before, but now it was loose, tumbling over her shoulders in colourful curls. The practical sandals had been replaced with soft leather flats.

'You look…pretty good.' Matias stood up with fluid grace and nodded at the assistant to bring the bags, while keeping his eyes riveted to Georgina for a few seconds.

'Thanks.'

She knew that she was blushing. He was looking at her, for the first time, in the way a man would look at a woman. So *pretty good* might not the compliment of a lifetime, but then this was a game they were playing. It wasn't as though he was really attracted to her. But she was no longer invisible…

She reached for her backpack but he swept it up before she could fetch it.

'We forgot about a handbag.' He turned to the assistant and told her to get something in tan, price no object. 'There's no place in this charade for…' he dangled her backpack from two fingers '…*this*.'

Georgina thought that was more like it. A brisk, businesslike approach to the situation foisted upon him. *Bye-bye scruffy backpack—hello co-ordinating designer handbag.* It was a timely reminder that when he had stared at her, sending her blood pressure soaring, it hadn't been because he was *seeing her*—not really. He had been evaluating her, to work out whether or not she fitted the bill for the part she was playing.

She had felt a frisson, the feathery brush of excitement as those fabulous eyes had rested on her, but there was no need to hear any alarm bells. He didn't fancy her and she certainly didn't fancy him. And even if she did—if she found her eyes straying and getting a little lost in those sinfully exotic good looks—then her reaction was perfectly normal, driven by her hormones and not her head. He was stupidly sexy and she was, after all, a normal healthy woman.

But he'd never been her type and—especially after Robbie and the way she'd been dumped—she had sworn off men. If someone came into her life—someone solid and stable, with a dash of creativity…someone she could envisage sharing her life with—then all well and good. But she would never again be drawn to someone inappropriate.

Robbie had been inappropriate. He had always expected her to bow to his greater knowledge and compliment him on his achievements. He'd been smart and well-read and intellectual, and she hadn't stopped to look any further because she'd been in love with the idea of being love.

The drive down to Cornwall was not the awkward situation she had anticipated.

Matias, confirming what he had said to her, worked for much of the journey, only surfacing when they were a matter of twenty minutes away from his mother's house, at which point he briefly quizzed her on what, exactly, she had told her mother.

'Not a huge amount,' she admitted. 'It was a spur-of-the-moment thing and I came to London almost immediately to see you.'

'I still find it difficult to credit that you could have made such a monumental decision on the spur of the moment,' Matias murmured.

'Don't you do anything on impulse?'

'What do *you* think?'

'I think it's really strange. Your parents must be the

most impulsive couple I've ever known, especially compared to mine, and yet you're completely the opposite. Look at the way they embarked on their organic farming…and the way your mother took up Reiki…and then there was the whole horses for the disabled business… such a shame that crashed and burned.'

'And yet anyone could have predicted that that would be a mistake.'

His knew his voice had cooled somewhat. He could remember his mother passing round her cut-price *Reiki at Home* business cards to some of the parents at his boarding school at the end of term, having rocked up in their brightly painted camper van, much to the hilarity of all the boys in the entire school.

'I certainly did and I was barely out of my teens at the time. As for doing anything on impulse? They're a successful argument for *avoiding* impulsive behaviour.'

What Georgina saw as romantic and glamorous, he saw as a regrettable handicap.

'Maybe,' Matias continued, 'if they'd started with the organic farming from the very beginning and specialised in it, it might have gone further than it did. But instead they got waylaid by anything and everything, and naturally a Jack-of-all-trades-and-master-of-none will always be destined to fail.'

'They were *happy*. They didn't *fail*.'

Matias grunted, disinclined to continue a conversation that was going nowhere. 'So, no stories we need to tally?' He brought the conversation back to the matter at hand. 'No eyes meeting across a crowded dance floor? Good. The fewer lies, the less room for complications.'

'And the quicker the inevitable end to our relationship?'

Georgina marvelled at his ability to see everything in black and white. No surprise there, but once again it made her realise how different they were. For some reason that was a reassuring thought, and she held on to it because it stopped her disobedient imagination from getting out of hand.

'Should we plan that out now?'

'No need to muddy the waters just yet. You can leave that to me. Like I said, I'll take the hit.'

They were approaching Rose's house, much to Georgina's surprise, because the drive seemed to have been completed in the blink of an eye. They had already passed the turning that led to her parents' house, which she was looking after and living in rent-free while they were in Australia. The houses had given way to open fields on one side and on the other a distant view of the sea.

Rose's house sat on a hill, and Georgina felt as if she was seeing for the first time just how little enthusiasm the older woman now had for the fields she and Antonio had spent years cultivating. The crops looked vaguely straggly and ill-kempt. There was even a feeling of dilapidation about the house, as they approached it, although that shouldn't be the case because a lot of money had been spent on it over time, thanks to Matias.

'It looks tired,' Matias pointed out, reading her mind. 'I've tried persuading my mother that it would be in her interests to move to something more manageable but she won't be budged.'

'Many happy memories within those four walls,' Georgina murmured, surprising Matias, because that emotional explanation would never have occurred to him.

His brain just didn't function along those lines. He

didn't see the house in the same way at all. He'd been out of it for such a long time that when he looked all he saw was concrete and glass and a bunch of problems waiting to happen.

Rose was waiting for them when they pulled up outside. A semi-circular courtyard fronted the property and the front door was open, framing Rose, who was beaming from ear to ear.

She was a slightly built woman, with soft fair hair that she was allowing to turn grey. She had enormous blue eyes and the sort of delicate features that had once made her startlingly pretty but now made her look fragile and breakable, as though a single gust of wind might blow her off her feet and whip her away.

But she was still smiling as she hurried forward, peppering them with questions, then standing back to look at them both with excitement and satisfaction. She moved to embrace Matias—a proper tight hug of an embrace—and Georgina noted the way he stiffened before returning the embrace with awkward sincerity.

He's not used to such shows of affection, she thought, startled. But then she wondered why she was surprised, when she knew how distant the relationship between them was—when she had seen with her own two eyes the awkward way they circled one another, almost as though they had forgotten how to interact as mother and son. It seemed, with that spontaneous hug, that it was a chasm Rose was trying to close.

Matias had moved to stand by Georgina, and then he did something both expected and unexpected at one and the same time.

He slung his arm over her shoulders.

Just like that her breasts were suddenly heavy, her

nipples pinched and sensitive, scraping against her cotton bra. She wanted to squirm, to *move*, because she was gripped by a sudden restlessness. But instead she remained as still as a statue, barely able to breathe as he absently stroked just below her collarbone in small circles, finding bare skin beneath the light silk top.

She knew that Rose was chatting animatedly as they walked into the cool of the house. She was aware of Matias responding. But the details were foggy because all she could think of was Matias's arm still around her, so close to her breast, his fingers so close to her rigid, aching nipples.

'I think,' she heard him drawl in that deep, dark, velvety voice of his, 'that I'll leave Georgie to answer that one…'

'Huh?' Georgina blinked vaguely and accepted the cup of tea that had appeared in front of her. She looked at Matias and her heart banged in her chest. Her pulses raced and her pupils dilated.

'How did we meet? My mother wants no details spared.'

Georgina had not taken any physical contact into consideration. But to all intents and purposes they were here together in Cornwall, a couple, doing all the things most normal couples did.

Like putting their arms around one another.

Like *this*…she thought, with sluggish fascination as Matias lowered his head.

Her eyes closed and her mouth parted as his lips ever so lightly brushed against hers.

The kiss was over in a heartbeat, but the effect was devastating. She blinked and made a huge effort to get her brain to engage. His attention was back on his mother, and Georgina was furious with herself for letting the kiss get to her. But it had been thrilling. She didn't know whether that was because it was forbidden or because he was such a good kisser that he'd managed to blow her self-control to smithereens.

She edged away from him and sat down in front of the cup of tea which she had deposited on the table. Rose followed suit while Matias strolled through the kitchen, inspecting stuff.

'So?' Rose was pressing. 'How *did* the pair of you meet? Silly me! I know you've known one another since for ever, but when did you first realise…? Oh, I would never have guessed!'

She was tripping excitedly over her words and thankfully not pausing for breath, which meant that Georgina hadn't been cornered into answering any direct questions yet—although she knew that it was just a matter of time.

'You've certainly kept it under your hat, Georgie! I had no idea you were going up and down to London, seeing Matias!'

'The train service is so efficient, so quick…' Georgina said faintly.

'And I can understand,' Rose exclaimed, 'when Matias says that neither of you wanted to say anything yet *just in case…*'

'Ah…er…yes…' Georgina's eyes skittered towards Matias, who raised his eyebrows, sipped his tea and left her floundering in her own panicked witlessness. 'Well, you know…relationships can be so unpredictable…'

'Of course, my darling. And you of all people would know that after Robbie. I'm sure you were ultra-cautious…'

'Yes, ultra-cautious,' Georgina parroted weakly.

'But you did the right thing,' Rose mused thoughtfully.

'Instead of rushing into a replacement relationship you took lots of time to come to terms with what had happened before dipping your toes back into the dating pool.'

She gazed at her son with affection.

'Darling,' she addressed him, 'I can't begin to tell you how I hoped…' Her voice threatened to break and she gathered herself. 'But you still haven't told me how all this *happened*. Was it as romantic as it sounds?'

Matias fixed his fabulous eyes on Georgina and said precisely what she'd hoped he wouldn't say.

'Darling—would you like to do the honours?'

He was such a good actor, Georgina thought with some of her usual spirit. The warm voice, the light touch, the easy proximity… He was probably thinking of the next big deal he had to complete while playing the attentive lover, but no one would ever have guessed—least of all his mother, who looked as though Christmas had come early.

She gathered herself and smiled brightly. 'Of course… *darling…*'

Busying herself pouring another cup of tea killed a couple of minutes, during which time Matias sauntered towards the kitchen table, where she had sat down, and rested his hands lightly on her shoulders. He gently massaged the nape of her neck, then lifted her hair to feather a kiss where his massaging thumbs had been.

Breathing became difficult. This was totally out of order, she thought furiously. Some semblance of affection might be permissible, but *this…*?

'What was it,' he murmured, thankfully straightening, although he kept his hands on her shoulders, 'that made you fall head over heels in love with me?'

'No idea.' Georgina lightly covered his hands with hers and gently but firmly prised herself free.

In response, Matias circled around to take the seat facing her, slightly behind his mother so that he could watch the expression on her face without Rose being any the wiser.

Georgina ignored him to the best of her ability. She smiled at Rose, although her jaw was beginning to ache from the effort of pretending that this was just a normal conversation.

Out of the corner of her eye, she registered Matias's lazy gaze resting on her. Was this his way of punishing her for having put him in a situation he hadn't invited? Watching her having to flesh out the little white lie that had propelled him into sitting here in his mother's kitchen, pretending to be someone he wasn't?

Rose was looking at her with eager, interested eyes and Georgina felt a flash of anger towards Matias. Couldn't he see that he was making their inevitable break-up all the harder by laying on the touchy-feely stuff in such abundance?

She gathered herself. 'I mean, it certainly wasn't his engaging humility or his sweet-natured, easy-going personality! You know your son, Rose! He's challenging, to say the least! And sometimes...' she smiled brightly at Matias '... I'd go so far as to say there's an arrogant streak there...'

Matias watched, amused, and then he returned with a wicked smile, 'Well, my darling, if it wasn't my soft, soppy nature and my ambitious streak, it must have been my scintillating and exciting personality...wouldn't you agree?'

How, she wondered irritably, had *sweet-natured and*

easy-going turned into *soft and soppy*? How had *arrogant and challenging* become *ambitious*?

'Let's just say,' he continued, much to his mother's delight—this was obviously just the sort of familiar banter she enjoyed hearing—'that I made her heart race and it hasn't stopped racing since. Wouldn't you say, my darling, that that just about sums it up...?'

CHAPTER FOUR

'THAT,' GEORGINA SAID less than an hour later, once Rose had retired for a brief rest before dinner—which she had prepared even though Matias had told her not to bother, that he would make sure a caterer was on board when they arrived, 'was awful.'

'You look as though you could do with a drink.' He poured them both a glass of wine and then stood back to look at her coolly. 'I had my doubts about this hare-brained idea of yours, but I have to admit that my mother is a different woman to the one I visited three months ago.'

Georgina accepted the proffered glass of wine and stared moodily into the clear liquid as she swirled it round and round and wondered how a couple of hours spent with a woman she dearly loved could end up being as wearying as if she'd run a marathon up Mount Everest carrying weights.

But the questions had been exhaustive and had called for a repertoire of invention she had not foreseen when she had embarked on—as Matias had called it—her *hare-brained scheme*.

When did they first know…? Where did they go when they met…? Had they met in Cornwall on the sly…? What about getting engaged…? Summer wedding or winter…? What sort of rings did she like…? There was an excellent jewellers not too far away—she knew the one… Oh, don't mind me…you probably think I'm getting ahead of myself…

By the time the conversation had settled into something resembling normality Georgina had been wrung out. And Matias hadn't helped matters.

'I didn't appreciate your hands all over me,' she bristled now, sipping her wine and hunching into herself as she looked at him severely over the rim of her glass. 'I know it's important that we maintain a…a…realistic…er…front, but you don't have to touch me all the time!'

'Point taken,' Matias said piously. 'Although I thought you might welcome the way I've thrown myself into this situation without grumbling.'

'And is there really any need for us to go exploring tomorrow?'

'What do you suggest we do, as a loved-up couple with stars in their eyes?' Matias returned coolly. 'Go our separate ways and communicate via email while I'm here? Don't forget that I didn't *ask* to get embroiled in this situation but here I am. Rather, here *we* are. I propose you go with the flow and cut back on the steady stream of objections.'

It still got on his nerves that he was doing something he hadn't banked on doing—especially something he hadn't generated himself. But Matias had enjoyed himself this evening. His mother's attitude towards him had been subtly but noticeably different. Less…*wary*. It surprised him how much he had liked the unexpected thaw when he'd always considered himself as hard as nails when it came to accepting the shortcomings of his relationship with his mother.

He'd always known that she judged him for the life choices he had made and, crucially, for not being able to attend his father's funeral. But, despite that, their relationship had meandered along, with neither party doing the other any harm. He'd fulfilled every obligation when it came to supporting his mother financially. Whatever she wanted, big or small, he did not hesitate to provide. And if there was a certain distance between them, then Matias accepted that it was simply the way it was. Irreversible and inevitable and not that unusual when it came to family dynamics.

Except it wasn't.

His mother had embraced him. She had teased him. Had laughed with genuine warmth. Her guarded affection had been replaced with an open show of love and it had felt like the reconnection he had never imagined possible.

And as for the touching that Georgina had talked about... He'd liked that as well.

She wasn't bony, like the catwalk models he was accustomed to dating. Her skin was soft and smooth, and those intermittent touches had put him in mind of what it might feel like to touch a *real* woman—which was a phrase he would have scoffed at only days ago.

He *liked* the smallness and the roundness of her...he liked the way her breasts were generous and lush...he liked the shapeliness of her legs. Touching her had *definitely* not been a hardship.

'Your mother doesn't expect us to be all over one another!' Georgina was protesting now, heatedly.

'She didn't look distraught at the sight.'

'Well, I won't be joining you for dinner tonight.' She

stood up and primly smoothed her hands over her trousers. 'I have stuff to do.'

'Stuff? What *stuff*?'

'None of your business.'

'Oh, but *everything's* my business now that we're a couple…'

'You're enjoying this, aren't you?' Georgina gritted.

Matias delivered a cool, mocking smile. *'Enjoying?'*

Georgina flushed, because of course he wouldn't be *enjoying* anything. He'd been shoved into playing a part with a woman who got on his nerves most of the time and whom he didn't fancy at all. He would rather steer clear of her. Instead, where was he? Having to put on a show of physical affection for the sake of his mother.

'I have a job coming up,' she said, opting for a conciliatory tone. 'I'm photographing some food for an up-and-coming young local chef. It's a good job because she's going to be using some of your mother's produce—that should be free advertising for the farm. I need to start working on my templates.'

Matias grimaced. 'I've never seen your work,' he mused. 'I'll have to put that right. And, for the record, while I'm here I'm going to use the opportunity to try and persuade my mother to leave this house. It's too big. Naturally there are memories, but isn't that what photo albums are all about?'

Georgina shot him an incredulous look from under her lashes. 'You're *impossible*, Matias. How can you be so cold and unfeeling? Not that anyone would guess with that touchy-feely show you put on for your mother. You're a brilliant actor. But… I'm really glad you can see a difference in your mum. I know you got dragged into this, and it helps that you can see why I ended up doing what I did. Anyway…'

She stood up and hovered for a few minutes.

'I'm going to head off now, before Rose comes down. She'll understand. She knows that I have a lot of prepping to do before the shoot the day after tomorrow.'

She hovered some more. She hesitated for just a little too long. Watching him. Paralysed by the surreal nature of events, torn by weird, conflicting emotions that she couldn't rationalise.

The sound of Rose's voice made her start.

'You're going? But, my darling, *where* are you going?'

It took a few moments for Georgina's brain to sluggishly register that Rose, who should have been safely tucked up having a nap, was now looking at her and waiting for an answer.

The only thing Georgina could stammer out in response was, 'Home. You know…work… But of course I'll be back tomorrow…'

'What Georgie is trying to say…' Matias neatly stepped into the breach, moving to gather her against him '…is that she's going home to finish up what she has to do but she'll be joining us for dinner.'

'Er…' Georgina's voice trailed off.

'Darling,' Rose intercepted briskly, 'I'll have none of this nonsense about you two being apart while you're down here. Never you mind my sensibilities! I wasn't born a century ago! I do realise that young people in love actually share beds! You could have Matias's bedroom here, but I think you might enjoy the privacy of staying at *your* place, Georgie.'

She beamed and Georgina tried hard to beam back and appear delighted.

'You don't want a middle-aged woman getting underfoot.'

'Er…but… Matias…? Didn't you say that the whole point of you coming down here was to see your mum?'

'And I will,' Matias soothed with infuriating calm. 'But of course my mother is right. It makes complete sense for us to be in the same place.'

He moved to give his mother a peck on the cheek. She looked delighted. While she, Georgina, contemplated a scenario she hadn't banked on in a million years.

Share a house? With Matias?

On the one hand at least she would be able to dispatch him to the furthest bedroom from hers, because his mother wouldn't be there keeping tabs on the loving couple, but still…

Share a house?

'You look a little anxious, Georgie.'

Rose stepped forward to reach for Georgina's hands, which she clasped warmly. Her sharp eyes reminded Georgina that recoiling in horror at the prospect of sharing her space with the guy she was supposed to adore wasn't going to do.

'But I do understand that you want to finish some work tonight—and, yes, give Matias some time to be on his own here with me.' She looked at Matias with a smile. 'That's the sort of lovely, understanding girl Georgie is. Always putting other people ahead of herself.'

'An absolute angel,' Matias murmured, tightening his hand on her waist and giving it an affectionate little squeeze that made her stiffen in response.

'Perhaps tomorrow you two can go off and do something exciting together. It's so beautiful around here at this time of year! I know you probably think you should drag me along wherever you go, but please don't.' Her face shadowed for a few seconds, but then the smile returned. 'Why don't you head to Padstow and explore? I could even make you a picnic to take to the beach. When was the last time you were at a beach, Matias?'

She looked at her son, tentative and affectionate at the same time, breaking new ground, making Georgina feel that it would be a sin to rain on the older woman's parade.

'A century and a half ago...' he drawled.

So it was decided. The details of this wonderful day out floated around Georgina's head. She tried to think *It's all for a good cause—just look at how great Rose looks compared to a few days ago...* Instead, the only thing she had in her head was an image of Matias in her house, in a bedroom, in the shower...sharing her space. An intruder in her life and one *she* had invited—an intruder who could make her break out in a cold sweat and remind her of a time when she had idolised the ground he walked on.

Eventually Rose left the room, and the first thing Matias said, dropping his arms and walking away from her, was, 'Do I make you nervous? Because you were behaving like a cat on a hot tin roof just then.'

'Of *course* you don't make me nervous.' Georgina cleared her throat and let loose a brittle laugh, very conscious of the burning patch of skin he had touched and of those amazing eyes now pinned to her face. 'I just didn't expect your mother to...to...'

'To suggest we actually do what most people would do, given they were in a serious relationship? Inhabit the same bedroom?'

Georgina squirmed and reddened. 'I thought she would be...might be...relieved not to have to confront that…er…reality… Plus, how are we to demonstrate the decline in our relationship if your mother isn't around to witness it?'

'Did you think the occasional woman I've brought here over the years was primly shown to a bedroom on another floor when I came to visit? And as for my mother seeing first-hand all the differences between us… Well, there will be time enough to demonstrate those. In the meanwhile, this is a tonic for her and I have no intention of whipping it away just yet.'

'You're not exactly being helpful, Matias.' Georgina drew in a sharp, impatient breath and he raised his eyebrows.

'Nor are you,' Matias responded, without skipping a beat. 'If concern for my mother is top of your agenda, then you should be embracing her enthusiasm for us to spend all our available time down here together, instead of trying to figure out how fast you can disillusion her.'

'That's a far cry from you refusing to even get involved in this whole charade!'

Matias opened his mouth to dismiss her snide but perfectly understandable interruption. Instead he found himself saying, *sotto voce*, and with a sincerity that cut right through all his usual weary cynicism, 'I've lost touch with my mother over the years. Taken care of the essentials and visited only as a matter of duty. Time has wreaked destruction over the years…and my values are so different from my parents'… *Hell*.' He raked his fingers through his hair and flushed darkly, for once caught on the back foot. 'Reconnecting with her, even in these utterly fake circumstances, isn't something I'm plotting to destroy before it's even really begun.'

'Matias…'

'I'll see you tomorrow.'

The conversation was closed. She could see it in his shuttered expression and hear it in the finality of his voice. He'd opened up and already he was regretting it. She was filled with such an intense craving for this moment of shared confidence to be prolonged that it terrified her.

'I'll make sure a guest room is prepared for you,' she muttered—a reminder more to herself than anyone else of the boundary lines within this little game of theirs.

He returned a clipped nod.

Being out of his suffocating company for a handful of hours should have come as blessed relief, but instead Georgina spent the evening unable to concentrate on anything. She prepared one of the guest rooms for Matias, realising as she did so that she hadn't actually been into this particular bedroom since her parents had left. It was dusty and smelled airless.

She aired it all. and then had to fight down thoughts of Matias in the bed. How could these disturbing feelings still have lodgings inside her? Was it the oddness of their situation? Were there still embers of those flames that had been ignited all those years ago that had never been entirely doused? What had she unleashed with this ill-conceived plan of hers?

Following that thought through to any kind of conclusion made her quail with apprehension. So instead she sat at her desk and brought her computer to life, scrolling through the extensive archives of food photos that had inspired her in the past and making rough notes on what sort of vibe she wanted to get for her young chef.

But her mind was a million miles away. Things were

no longer reassuringly black and white. There was an ocean of grey in between and she was realising that she was a very poor swimmer...

The following morning she chose her outfit carefully. Casual cotton, ankle-length khaki trousers and a simple white ribbed tee shirt which she tucked into the waistband of the trousers. The same sandals she had worn the day before. Cool, easy to wear clothes put together in a way that gave her shape, brought out the best in her. Clothes that afforded her some measure of the control which she felt she needed—because the minute she was with Matias, playing this stupid game, control seemed to slip through her fingers like water through the holes of a colander.

She heard the buzz of the doorbell and a surge of nerves washed over her, but she was as cool as a cucumber when she pulled open the door to see Matias, lounging against the doorframe, finger poised to ring again, even though she'd answered the door in seconds.

It was another brilliant day and he was in a white polo shirt and a pair of low-slung faded jeans that lovingly hugged the muscular length of his legs. Her eyes drifted helplessly to the dark hair on his forearms and the way that dark hair curled around the dull matt silver of his watch strap.

She dragged her eyes away and said abruptly, 'You don't have to do this. Rose would be none the wiser if you go to the next town and work to your heart's content and then return at a respectable hour for us to join her.'

'Strangely, I'm uncomfortable with such large-scale lying. Your one whopper is bad enough without adding to the tally by telling a few more lies. Now, let me in. I'd really like to see some of your work.'

He straightened, and after a few seconds' hesitation Georgina stood back.

He brushed past her into the hall. 'I haven't been here in a long time…'

He looked around him at a house that was homely and large but in need of some TLC. He could count the number of times he had stepped foot in this house on the fingers of one hand. For some reason gatherings had always been held by his parents. Or maybe he just hadn't been around for the ones that had taken place here.

'Why?' he asked with genuine curiosity.

Why do you continue to live here…? Why not spread your wings…? You're young and sexy…

The house was typically the residence of middle-aged people who had no real interest in décor. The wallpaper harked back to an era of flowers and birds and was faded. The wood was shiny, the rugs attractive but threadbare. Everything looked tired and old-fashioned. David and Alison White, from memory, both had the academic's typical disregard for their surroundings, and for the first time he could understand why their creative daughter had been so enchanted by his parents' flamboyance.

'Why what?'

Matias shrugged, letting it go. 'Where do you work?'

Georgina hesitated, then led him to the conservatory at the back, which she had converted into a studio. Her portfolio of work was neatly stacked on shelves and in a metal filing cabinet, and some of her photos hung on the wall. Her camera equipment was extensive.

Matias was seriously impressed. He peered at the photos on display, standing back and then examining them in detail while she described the ins and outs of food photography and what it entailed with some embarrassment.

Eventually her voice tapered off and she hovered, arms folded, by the door. 'You honestly don't have to say that you like them,' she blurted out.

'They're…amazing.'

He looked at her in silence for a few long seconds and she could feel her face getting hotter and hotter and redder and redder.

'Who are your clients?'

'Some chefs…obviously…' She spun round and began heading out of the conservatory. Having him look at her work had made her feel exposed and vulnerable for some reason, and the sooner they headed off the better. 'Usually up-and-coming ones, because I'm relatively cheap. Also I've made a name for myself in the restaurant trade around here. That's my bread and butter, really. There are always new dishes they want photographed. And I've had a couple of commissions from publishing houses for recipe books…'

She blathered on witlessly and followed him out to his car. His driver had clearly vanished back to London.

'So…' Matias switched on the engine and the powerful car roared into life, but he didn't drive off, instead choosing to lean against the door to look at her. 'A day doing what loved-up couples apparently do. My mother was up at the crack of dawn preparing a picnic for our trip to the seaside. Now, I may have lived here for years, but you'll have to provide directions. I can't tell you the last time I went to a beach down here.'

'Not even with one of those blondes you've sometimes brought down?' Georgina said, disobeying her own mantra about steering clear of anything remotely personal and reverting to the comfort zone of bickering ex-neighbours.

She briefly gave him a series of directions, but her curiosity about him had been unleashed and she was finding it hard to stuff it back into its box.

'I don't do beach trips with women,' Matias drawled, glancing at her sideways as he began driving away from the house. 'And I certainly don't do home-made picnics.'

'Why?'

'Because I like keeping it light.'

'Why?'

'You're very curious, aren't you?' Matias murmured. 'Do you find me as fascinating now as you did all those years ago?'

Georgina went beetroot-red. 'I don't know what you're talking about,' she said woodenly.

'No? I remember you used to follow me with your eyes…always curious about my life at boarding school… always taking pot-shots at the girls I sometimes brought home…'

'Polite,' Georgina corrected in a strangled voice. 'I was *polite* when I asked you about school. You were the only person I knew at a boarding school! And I didn't take pot-shots at those girls. I may have sniggered a bit because they were all so empty-headed, and gazed at you as though you were the next best thing to sliced bread, but it certainly wasn't because I found you *fascinating*.'

Matias shrugged, but a half-smile tugged the corners of his mouth.

Mortified, Georgina could barely appreciate the splendour of the beach when they finally got there, and although she made all the right noises about the hamper his mother had prepared she was barely able to think straight.

She'd been so careful all those years ago! She'd watched him from the side lines, safe in the certainty that her silly crush was something no one knew about—least of all him. She'd downplayed the jealousy she'd felt when, over the years, she had noted all the wafer-thin models who had hung like limpets on his arm, gazing up at him with adoring eyes. She'd told herself that she was far happier with her photography and a sense of direction in her life.

To know that he had seen through all that made her squirm with shame and embarrassment. Made her realise how sharp his instincts were when it came to the opposite sex. Made her see just how dangerous this little game could become if she allowed her eyes to stray. If he noticed... If he jumped to conclusions...

They'd hit the beach at peak time, but they managed to find themselves a relatively serene spot and he laid out the picnic with exaggerated ceremony. He'd shrugged off her random remark of earlier, and barely glanced at her now as they settled on the large rug his mother had packed along with the food.

'Hot,' Matias said, sprawling on the ground with his hands behind his head, staring up at a cloudless blue sky from behind his designer sunglasses. 'If I'd known it was going to be this hot I would have suggested we come equipped with our swimming gear—although swimming gear in these waters is strictly called a wetsuit. Unless you happen to be extremely hardy? Are you?'

'I've been swimming a few times,' Georgina said politely, gazing off into the distance but very much aware of his loose-limbed elegant body on the rug next to her. She was sitting up, as rigid as a plank of wood. He was sprawled on his back, his body language unspeakably relaxed and sexy.

'Very impressive.'

'You don't have to put on a show when it's just the two of us, Matias. I know the last thing you've ever been when it comes to me is *impressed*.'

'You need to lose your insecurities. Earlier I asked you a question.'

'What question?'

Since when was Matias Silva equipped to talk to her about insecurities? Who did he think he was?

He was looking at her. She could feel the weight of his gaze on her and it made her squirm.

'Why are you still working here? Living here? In your parents' house? I would have thought that after you were let down by that loser this would be the last place you would want to stay.'

Georgina turned to look at him for a few seconds, then looked away. The questions felt invasive, and way too personal. She'd barely talked to anyone in any depth about the break-up all those years ago. She'd just got on with her life and side-stepped the pity and the sympathy.

'There's a big, bad world out there,' he mused, ignoring every *No Entry* sign she was erecting and barging through. 'Maybe you've stayed here because, for all your talk about still being a fan of happy-ever-after fairy tales, it's safer for you to avoid putting it to the test and you can do that by burying yourself in your parents' house and daydreaming about a world of possibilities you have no intention of exploring.'

'This suits me at the moment.' She was holding on to her temper with difficulty, but she wanted to throw something hard and heavy at his beautiful head. 'I can save while I'm here. And, trust me, Matias, if something came up and made me think about leaving then I would.'

'Something like what?'

'I'm finished with this conversation!'

She sprang up and began walking fast in the direction of the car, not looking back to see whether he was following or not. He was making her confront deep-seated insecurities about the direction of her life and she loathed him for it.

Yes, of *course* she knew that there were more adventurous roads she could go down! But he didn't understand and he never would. He had blown off this village when he was a teenager and he had never looked back. He had left as one person and morphed into a completely different one. He had pursued wealth and power and now he thought the way wealthy, powerful people thought. In black and white.

She glanced behind her to see him sweeping up the picnic, hardly touched, and carelessly flinging everything inside the basket which had been provided.

'What I think…what I choose to do with my life…is none of your business!' She turned to him with furious eyes as soon as they were in the car and the engine was switched on.

'You're right.' Matias looked at her levelly—a long, unflinching look that she had difficulty returning. 'But do you want to know something?'

'No!'

'Well, I'll tell you anyway—considering you've made it your life's work to tell *me* what you think of *me* and *my* life choices. You're a coward. You talk the talk, but you don't walk the walk. You're in your parents' house because you're afraid of all the crap that happens out there in the big, bad world. You might have in your head some nonsense about the perfect man, but you won't be looking too hard for him because you don't want to get hurt again.'

'That's not true!'

Her huge green eyes held a mixture of hurt and defiance and Matias knew that he had put that look there. But she'd never been backward at coming forward, and if she couldn't stand the heat, then she had to get out of the kitchen.

'Did he hurt you that much, Georgie?'

'I *hate* you.'

'No, you don't.'

He smoothed his finger over her cheek and this time he let it linger there. And she couldn't push him away because she was mesmerised by his touch and by the *nearness* of him.

She leaned towards him, the palms of her hands flat on the smooth leather of the passenger seat. 'What do *you* think?' she muttered gruffly.

He cupped the side of her face with his hand. 'I think you were probably a lot less hurt than you should have been if you actually loved the guy, but you never loved him.'

'How would *you* know?'

'He was never the one for you,' Matias said gently. 'Which I said to you at the time. But your parents approved of him and that was enough for you to get sucked into something that never had legs in the first place.'

'You think you know it all!'

'I know enough.'

'You've never had a long-standing, successful relationship!'

'Never wanted one.'

'Because...?' Georgina looked at him with mutinous, challenging green eyes.

'Because I prefer to direct my energies into the more tangible business of making money.'

'Why the fixation with money?' Georgina dared to ask, even though his shuttered expression was directing her away from any more personal questions. 'It's not as though that was the sort of thing that ever mattered to your parents.'

He had eased out of the parking slot and they were steadily making their way back to his mother's house. She'd barely noticed because she'd been so wrapped up in him.

How could he be so full of contradictions? How could he be so charming, so lazily persuasive, so charismatic… and yet so coolly remote and untouchable?

'But that's just it,' Matias said, sliding icy grey eyes across at her. 'A bit of farming…a bit of hocus-pocus herbalism…a spot of magic massage here and there… You can pull that off when you're buried deep in a village somewhere, but the real world is slightly more judgemental about that kind of nonsense. I found that out myself when I went to boarding school.'

'What do you mean?'

'I mean,' Matias gritted, his voice hard-edged and unforgiving, 'when you're thirteen and your parents are pulling up to collect you in a camper van and your mother is promising discounted Reiki sessions to the parents of boys you've only known for five minutes… Well, let's just say that's the stuff that learning curves are made from.'

'I never knew…' She only realised that the car had stopped when he killed the engine.

'No need for the tea and sympathy, Georgie. I got exactly what I wanted out of that school. I learnt what needed to be done to get me where I needed to get. Money, *darling*, may be the root of all evil in *your* critical, judgemental eyes, but it's also the greatest passport to freedom. Have enough of it and the world is yours for the taking.'

He opened his door and she scrambled out too, protesting heatedly that the last thing she was, was *judgemental* and fighting off a tug of sympathy for that young boy stuck in a boarding school where he didn't fit in.

She was all hot and bothered, with eyes only for the man striding ahead of her towards the front door.

'Not the right time,' Matias cautioned, barely breaking stride.

'What are you talking about?'

'An angry, ranting girlfriend? What will my mother think?'

He looked down at her. Her colourful hair was everywhere, her bright green eyes were flashing fire, her full mouth was half open. She was the very picture of passion. She was the most tempting creature he had ever seen and he was shocked at how powerful the urge to take her suddenly was.

He drew his breath in sharply, hearing the sound of his mother's footsteps. And then the door opened, and Matias lowered his head and did what he'd wanted to do all day.

He kissed Georgie.

No messing about with anything delicate or gentle or tentative. This was a real kiss, hot and hard and hungry, his tongue probing, meshing with hers.

His erection was rock-hard, throbbing. Her softness was a powerful aphrodisiac and the swell of her generous breasts so close to his chest set up a series of graphic sexual images in his head.

'You two should get a room!'

His mother's voice was amused and warm and it broke the spell. Matias pulled back, raked his fingers through his hair, and realised that he couldn't remember when he had last lost control like that.

CHAPTER FIVE

HOT RED COLOUR surged up into Georgina's cheeks. She sprang back as though she'd been burnt. She couldn't meet Rose's eyes, nor could she risk looking at Matias, so she stared down at the ground instead, wishing it could swallow her up.

'Well done,' Matias murmured.

He urged her into the house, following his mother, who was disappearing off to the sitting room and chatting animatedly and thinking... Heaven only knew what, Georgina worried. Certainly not that these were two people due to break up in under two weeks.

'What are you talking about?'

Still reeling, Georgina stopped dead in her tracks and looked up at him. Ahead, Rose was peppering them with questions about their day, heading for her favourite chair. Georgina cringed at the thought of having to reproduce excited tales of how their day had gone.

'I think we've managed to convince my mother that everything's on track between us. She couldn't have looked happier when she saw me kiss you.' He paused. 'Award-winning performance, Georgie,' he said roughly.

He glanced away for a few seconds, during which time

her mind went completely blank before it cranked back into gear and joined up the dots.

What she'd seen as devastating had been a routine, necessary pretend show of affection for him. He hadn't wanted his mother to open the door to a scowling girl-friend in the throes of a heated argument with her son so he had kissed her to shut her up.

It had worked.

The only problem was that she had returned the kiss as though it had been the real thing. She had thrown herself into it body and soul, never wanting it to end. That kiss had flung open a door to feelings she now shamefully realised were still very much alive and kicking.

Humiliation stiffened her backbone and she clenched her jaw and took a few deep breaths before answering. 'Thanks. Wouldn't have done for your mother to have seen us bickering.'

'When you returned that kiss I almost got the impression that it was more than just a response to keep this charade on the right track…'

Georgina laughed. It sounded brittle to her ears but pride had kicked in. This wasn't real life. This was make-believe. To him she was still the annoying girl next door, and just because she'd had a makeover it didn't mean that she'd suddenly turned into Cinderella…it didn't mean that Prince Charming was going to be falling head over heels in love with her.

She met his eyes and wished that she could see what he was thinking. But his expression was shuttered. Was he desperately trying to contain his impatience? His ap-prehension that she'd been a little too enthusiastic? Was he terrified that he might have to start erecting *No Tres-pass* signs around himself to keep her at bay?

Her mouth was still tingling from the feel of his tongue meshing so erotically with hers. She wanted to touch her lips with her fingers to cool them, and just in case she did that unthinkingly she clenched her fists at her sides.

'Don't be crazy,' she said gruffly. 'Why would you get that idea? I keep telling you that you're not my type...'

'Ever thought that you might be attracted physically to a guy who *isn't* your type?'

'No. I like to believe that I approach relationships with my head and not my body. Especially after the business with Robbie—which you've made sure to remind me was the biggest mistake a girl could ever have made.'

'I was under the impression that he was definitely an *approach with your head* situation...'

Georgina flushed and fidgeted.

Matias shifted uncomfortably and raked his fingers through his hair. He stared down at her, his body rigid with tension.

'You don't have to worry that I'm going to throw myself at you, Matias,' Georgina said impatiently—because how much more obvious could a person make it that he was worried she might start making a play for him?

'What makes you think I would be worried if you threw yourself at me?'

Thick silence settled between them. Georgina had no idea what he was trying to say. Was he actually *flirting* with her?

She stared at him, open-mouthed, and he brushed his finger along her lower lip. Conflicting sensations flooded through her. Shock...unbearable excitement...shameful arousal...and absolute fear. Because this was definitely unknown and unexpected territory.

He didn't take his finger away. Instead he stepped towards her and cupped the side of her face with his hand.

'I don't know…what you're trying to say…' she stammered, for want of anything better.

'Liar. You know *exactly* what I'm trying to say.'

Matias smiled slowly. He took his time. He leaned in to her. It was an easy, slow movement that paralysed her to the spot. This time he kissed her gently and tenderly, and she couldn't stop a sigh of forbidden pleasure as she leaned up and closed her eyes and kissed him back. Because she was lost and she couldn't help herself.

Her arms were doing just what she'd hoped they wouldn't do—winding round his neck and drawing him towards her. Her breasts were squashed against his chest as they unconsciously closed the gap between themselves, and she could feel the scratchy tingle of her nipples against her bra.

She wanted him to touch her so badly that it was a physical ache. And *she* wanted to touch *him*. More than anything else in the world she wanted to take his bigness between her hands and *feel* him.

The craving inside her was so intense that it took her breath away. It terrified her.

She had no idea what was happening because she had never felt anything so powerful in her life before. It carried the force of a tsunami, and some primitive instinct told her that it was a force she had to keep at bay or beware the consequences.

With a gasp, she pushed him away. He immediately stepped back, although he continued to stare down at her, his beautiful eyes unfathomable.

'This isn't part of the deal,' she hissed fiercely.

She wrapped her arms around her body and met his

stare head-on. She wondered if he thought he was so irresistible that she just wouldn't be able to help but melt into his arms like a Victorian maiden.

'This is an…an…*arrangement*… And if I remember correctly it's an arrangement *you* rejected until you decided that you had no option but to accept because you couldn't face letting your mother down. This isn't *real*. Fantasy isn't going to get in the way of *reality*.'

'But that's not what this is about, is it?' Matias purred, infuriatingly calm.

'Then what was…what was…*that*…?'

'You mean our passionate kiss?'

Georgina glowered, her colour high, her whole body aflame with a longing she couldn't quite manage to douse.

'Lust,' Matias murmured succinctly.

One word but it couldn't have been more erotic or more devastating. Because it was stripped of all the pretty packaging that he might have used to soften its naked potency.

'I don't get it,' he continued in a low, lazy, wildly sensual voice, 'but I want you.'

'No,' Georgina whispered, 'you don't. I get on your nerves! How many times have you told me that? You and I have *nothing* in common! We're like chalk and cheese! And don't even *think* about telling me that opposites attract, because we're not just opposites…we're so different we could have come from different planets!'

'Mysterious, isn't it?'

'Is that all you have to say?'

'I'm being honest.' He shrugged. 'So what if we're from different planets? What does that have to do with whether we want to find the nearest bed…or table…or sofa…or patch of ground…and rip one another's clothes off? This isn't about confusing reality with fantasy, Georgie. This isn't about us actually *having* a relationship. No, this is way more elemental than that. I see you and I want to taste you.'

'Matias…*stop!*'

'Why? Am I turning you on?'

'No! I don't want you! You're mistaken!' Georgina heard the pathetic desperation in her voice with dismay. 'Your mother is waiting for us! I… She's going to come out in a minute… She's going to want to know what's going on…'

'She won't come out,' Matias assured her in a deep, velvety voice that was just ever so slightly amused. 'She's leaving the love birds to have fun together without her getting in the way. Why do you think she propelled us off for a session at the beach? Why do you think she insisted on us being together under the same roof while we're here?'

'Well, she won't find us doing anything together! That kiss? It never happened!'

'No?' he drawled, eyebrows raised. 'Why's that?'

'Because I'm not *you*, Matias.' She was relieved that she had regained control over her vocal cords. She wanted to sound cool and dismissive and she wasn't too far away from succeeding. Logic and common sense might have flown through the window for a few seconds, but both were back now. 'I don't do passing-ships-in-the-night relationships.'

'Have you ever tried?'

'I don't need to. I know that kind of thing is not for me.'

'So instead you make a checklist for the perfect guy

and see if reality tallies up with the picture you've got in your head?'

'There's nothing wrong with knowing what you want when it comes to finding a partner.'

'And tell me how that worked for you last time round, Georgie. Tell me how that's been working for you since.'

'That's not fair.'

'I know,' Matias said roughly. 'I apologise. But sometimes you have to jettison the checklist and take what you want.'

'Not me. Robbie wasn't right. I know I got seduced by the fact that my parents approved, and they'd never really approved of any of the boyfriends I'd ever brought back home, And I know that since Robbie I've had a break from men...who wouldn't? but it doesn't mean that I have to do something just because...because...'

'Because it feels good?'

He shrugged and stepped away from her, and suddenly the air between them felt cool, the void too gaping for comfort. She wanted him back, closer to her, and she fought the impulse to step towards him.

'Just because something feels good it doesn't mean that you have to reach out and take it. I'm not a kid in a sweet shop with permission to grab whatever candy takes my fancy before I get bored with the game and move on.'

'So serious...' Matias said, heading towards the sitting room, leaving Georgina to traipse along in his wake. 'So intent on passing up on the fun elements of life.'

Georgina heard the lazy amusement in his voice and realised that he didn't really care one way or another whether she took him up on his offer or not.

He was attracted to her, and he'd probably picked up

similar vibes from her. She could try and argue that he was off target but why waste her time doing that? The man had vast experience when it came to women and he would burst out laughing if she tried to pretend that she didn't find him attractive.

But sleep with him?

No way!

'I am *not* passing up on the fun elements of life just because I've turned you down!' She yanked him to a stop so that she could glare up at him. 'Matias, you… you're the most egotistical man I have ever met in my entire life!'

'Okay.'

'*Okay?* Is that all you have to say?'

'What more do you want me to add to the mix, Georgie?'

'You have *never* been attracted to me in your life before,' she snapped, hands on her hips, one eye on the sitting room door, which was slightly ajar, making sure to keep her voice low because she knew walls had ears.

Matias looked at her, his head tilted to one side in thoughtful contemplation. 'Because you've always taken such pains to be irritating, Georgie. Always on a soap box…always dressed like a hippy with a cause. Why have you never made the most of your looks?'

'How *dare* you…?'

'You opened this conversation. Don't start trying to shut it down because you don't like the direction it's taking. You're sexy as hell, but this is the first time I've ever noticed because you've always kept your voluptuous curves hidden away.'

Sexy as hell? Voluptuous curves? The man was so shallow, Georgina thought weakly. But something inside her was twisting and melting. Her body was letting her down badly, responding to his superficial compliments as though they really mattered.

'You really just have one thing in mind when you look at a woman, don't you?' she threw at him.

He didn't look unduly bothered. 'We could keep going round in circles for ever on this one, Georgie.'

He took her arm and she bristled at his touch, as though she'd been plugged into an electrical socket.

'But, much as my mother is keen on giving us some downtime together, there's only so long she will hang on before curiosity kicks in and she comes out to make sure we haven't dropped dead in the hallway.'

Which left the conversation in mid-air. He'd started something that she somehow hadn't managed to finish, even though she'd tried. She'd made a big deal of telling him that she wasn't interested in any sort of casual sexual relationship with him that would never go anywhere, but she hadn't ended up feeling victorious or satisfied with the stance she had taken.

Georgina spent the remainder of the evening in a state of restless flux. She felt as though she'd been put into a washing machine with the cycle turned to spin. All her preconceived notions about Matias had taken a beating, and so had her precious principles about what made sense when it came to relationships.

He'd come along, a devil in disguise, and she couldn't stop her mind from playing over and over what he had said to her.

His casual touches over the course of the evening burned through her clothing and made her shiver. The deep, sexy timbre of his voice sent chills racing up and down her spin. The proud angle of his head and the star-tling beauty of his lean face made her shiver and think forbidden thoughts.

And soon they would be leaving together. He would be spending the night in her house. In a different room, but still… The thought of them being alone together after what he had said, with the atmosphere so charged be-tween them, brought her out in a cold sweat.

The conversation drifted around her. She participated, but her voice seemed to come from a long way away, barely penetrating the chaos of her thoughts, which were all over the place.

She surfaced to hear Rose asking her about the up-coming shoot.

'How will those pictures of my carrots and aspara-gus come out, do you think?' She was smiling at Matias. 'You wouldn't believe how talented she is,' she confided proudly. 'And always doing her best to promote the pro-duce here.'

'I saw some samples of her work.' His silver-grey eyes settled on Georgina, bringing a pink tinge to her cheeks. 'She's brilliant.'

The pink tinge turned to a deep red—a mixture of pleasure and embarrassment at the flattery. She launched into a jerky speech about the chef who had commis-sioned her for the photo shoot, and heard herself bab-bling on about the procedure for getting just the right shots put together so that everything looked natural, but enhanced.

'Anyway,' she concluded, wanting to feel more re-lieved than she actually did at the thought of having a perfectly valid excuse not to spend the next day with Ma-tias, even if the night ahead lay before her like the threat of the hangman's noose, 'the shoot is tomorrow and then I shall be going to her place in the evening to show her the mark-ups, get her opinions. So...'

She turned to Matias with a phoney smile and he raised both eyebrows, unfazed.

'It'll be a perfect opportunity for you to catch up on all that...er...work you told me you had to do...' she said, and turned to Rose with a woman-to-woman look. 'He's a workaholic... Sometimes I have to drag him away from that computer of his! I shall have to change that or we'll soon find ourselves at loggerheads! That's just the sort of thing that can bring a relationship crashing down. You know how women *love* attention...and a man whose first love is his work...? Well...'

Rose looked at her thoughtfully. 'You could take Matias with you in the evening. I'm sure Melissa wouldn't mind meeting your boyfriend, Georgie, and Matias...? Georgie's right. Relationships are all about compromise. It would do you good to see her in action...'

'But it's going to be baking hot,' Georgina protested, hanging on to her smile by a thread. 'And she lives up a hill! I usually walk up for the exercise! But Matias...' She looked over to him and said, with complete honesty, 'He doesn't do walking...'

'I could start,' Matias returned without batting an eye. 'How steep can a hill be around here? I might not tackle Everest, but I'm as fit as the next man, my darling—as well you know.'

Rose looked delighted. Matias looked highly amused. And Georgina... She felt the pit of her stomach fall away, even though she knew that she was being silly.

Matias wasn't going to chase her like a horny teenager pursuing a hot prom queen. He could have any woman on the planet he wanted. And if he wanted her for a couple of seconds because they'd been thrown together, because he was bored and between women and she happened to be wearing less hippy-like clothes, then the feeling wouldn't last.

'Nice try.' It was the first thing he said on their way to her house. 'I'm a workaholic you're going to come to blows with sooner rather than later because you want romance and I'm too busy staring at my computer to indulge you…'

The night air was humid and still. Georgina was keeping her distance but she could still feel his powerful personality wrapping itself around her, wanting to draw her close.

'It's true. You are a workaholic… I'm not breaking new ground by pointing out the obvious.'

'But there was just a whiff of desperation when you started clutching at that straw…and in your eagerness to make sure I'm not around tomorrow. Are you nervous at the prospect of the both of us in the same house?'

'No! I told you that I don't believe in…in…'

She eyed her house with relief. They had chosen to walk there rather than take the car and it beckoned to her like a port in a storm—because once inside she could flee to her room and shove him into the guest room she had prepared.

'Casual, scintillating sex? Don't worry. I won't come knocking on your door in the middle of the night…'

Which immediately conjured up all the wrong images in her head.

'And I'll leave you alone during the day too, to do what you have to do, because as it happens you're right. I have a lot of work to get through. I shall take myself off to a business in Padstow I've been contemplating buying for the past couple of months. So you can relax. Reluctance in a woman has always been a turn-off for me.'

They'd reached the house and he lounged against the door as she unlocked it and then preceded him into the hallway. When he paused she reluctantly turned and looked at him.

His dark eyes were cool. 'I'll be ready at six for this walk I shouldn't be able to do because the only exercise I'm capable of is getting into the back seat of my chauffeur-driven car.'

'Matias…'

'Goodnight, Georgie. Sleep well in your empty bed.'

With which he vanished in the direction of her father's office at the other end of the house, leaving her to pointlessly mull over the joyless coldness of her empty bed and to spend the night tossing and turning, wondering where he was in the house and whether he was thinking about her at all, before finally falling into a restless sleep at a little after midnight.

She barely looked up from her work the following day. True to his word, Matias had disappeared, but his absence—perversely—did nothing to quell the tumult of her thoughts, and she was keyed up when, at a little after six, he appeared in the doorway of her studio without warning.

She was ready to go and had done away with any girly dress code. There was too much heavy humidity in the air, and the strenuous walk up to Melissa's house would be impossible in something frothy and frivolous.

He, likewise, was in practical gear. Faded jeans, a

dark grey short-sleeved polo shirt and walking boots. For a few seconds she lost herself in just looking at him, because he was drop-dead gorgeous, but then she gathered herself and began collecting everything she had to take with her, stuffing tablet, portfolio and camera in a weatherproof rucksack which he promptly took from her.

'I'll carry it,' he said smoothly. 'I'm stronger than I look.'

He grinned and she reluctantly smiled back, relieved that a truce appeared to have been called. She'd spent a lifetime bickering with him, so how was it that she now felt at odds with herself, unable to function properly, at the thought of him withdrawing from her?

He obediently followed her to her old car, and immediately turned to her once he was inside. 'Tell me about your friend Melissa.'

The sexy teasing was gone, replaced by a genuinely friendly interest—and Georgina hated it. A Pandora's box had been opened but now everything was changing back. How was she going to deal with it? She missed the way those dark, lazy eyes had made her feel like a woman. She missed the way his husky drawl had made her melt and feel restless, as though there was an itch deep inside her that needed to be scratched.

She asked him about his day, returning polite interest with polite interest, but once they'd parked the car and begun trekking up the hill to Melissa's house conversation flagged because it was just too unbearably hot and still to talk.

For once, Georgina felt too puffed to appreciate the undisturbed countryside around her. The winding trek up was usually something to be done slowly, but this time she was relieved when it was over—when the front door was opened and the cool of the house greeted them.

Melissa suited her surroundings. It was something Georgina clearly scarcely registered, but as introductions were made Matias was startled to realise that as little as two months ago he would have had no time for the chef's wildly eccentric dress code. It would have been a little too reminiscent of what he had grown up with, and what he associated with the sort of carefree irresponsibility that never got anyone anywhere.

Now he had to concede that a lot had changed on that front. He'd switched off from the small details of his mother's life, accepting the limitations between them as just the way it was. The further he'd travelled away from his past, the greater the chasm between them had grown. He didn't know when that journey away from his parents had begun. He just knew that it was a journey from which there had been no turning back.

That was life.

Until now, when everything he'd learned to accept had been turned on its head. He and his mother were daily groping their way towards a deeper connection, and that involved him hearing the ins and outs of her life—the small things he had missed from the bigger picture. He could understand now how and why Georgina had taken it upon herself to tell the little lie that had led them to the place they were now, and he wasn't sorry about any of it.

Caught up in the business of cropping images and discussing final layouts, Georgina only noticed the passing of time when Matias appeared in the doorway to the kitchen.

'I think you two might want to come out here and have a look,' he said.

Georgina looked up and blinked. It took her a few seconds to register, but she didn't have to go out to see what was happening and neither did Melissa. They were both accustomed to the swift weather changes in this part of the world and she looked at her friend with dismay.

'I knew it!' Melissa stood up, stretched, and gathered up her long brown hair into an unruly ponytail. 'I spoke to my brother on the phone this afternoon and I *told* him that it was getting way too hot and way too humid for comfort!' She laughed and began moving towards the kitchen door. 'Stay put, you two. I'm going to head upstairs and make sure that all the windows in the house are shut!'

'Melissa…' Georgina sprang upright. 'We need to get going…'

There was the sudden whiteness of lightning and then, a few seconds later, a crack of thunder loud enough to make her jump. She moved to where Matias was hurriedly shutting the kitchen door and closing the window against the pounding of rain that was as sudden as it was fierce.

She raced to the window and peered out. The rain was a sheet of water driving across the horizon. The sky, which had been so bright and blue for weeks, was an angry black. The wind was gathering momentum and howling. There was no way they were going to be able to walk back down that hill to her car.

'There's no point worrying about the weather,' Matias said from behind her.

Their eyes met, reflected in the window pane with the stormy evening an unfolding drama outside. A frisson of apprehension rippled through her and for a few fraught seconds she couldn't break the connection as they both stared at one another in the glass pane.

'Matias, you don't understand...' She edged away, got past him, and then turned round to look at him.

'So it's raining?' He shrugged. 'I'd forgotten how fast this kind of thing happens down here.'

'This is a disaster...' Her voice was barely audible over the pounding of the rain on the roof and against the windows.

Flash flooding.

Matias might stand there looking as though he didn't have a care in the world, but he never came to Cornwall and, despite what he'd just said, he wouldn't remember how brutal these downpours could become. He lived his charmed life in the city, where the weather was a lot more polite.

'You need to revisit your definition of disaster.' Matias dumped his glass in the sink and then turned to her, leaning against the counter just as the kitchen door flew open and Melissa made a dramatic entrance.

'Windows all shut!' she cried gaily, with the joyful satisfaction of someone announcing the winning raffle ticket number. 'I've never seen anything like this before! I should have guessed, though! The heat we've been having over the last couple of weeks... Well, everyone's been saying we're due for a storm!'

'"Storm" is a bit of an understatement, isn't it, Melissa?' Georgina smiled weakly and followed her friend to the fridge, to give her hand getting stuff out for a meal.

'It's wild out there!' Melissa peered past Georgina to where Matias was still lounging against the counter.

'But no matter!' She winked at him. 'You city gents need to experience a little of what this part of the world is all about! Now, scoot—both of you! I shall fix you a gourmet meal and then you can get cosy in the bedroom I've prepared!'

CHAPTER SIX

BEDROOM I'VE PREPARED...

They were supposed to be an item. There was no way Georgina could express to her friend the horror she felt at the prospect of sharing a room with Matias. What young couple, going out with one another, slept in separate bedrooms? Like survivors from the Victorian age?

Melissa would burst out laughing, would think that Georgina was having her on. They lived in a village. How long would it be before gossip did the rounds and someone told someone who told someone else that the 'loved-up' couple were as distant as two strangers?

It was a risk that Georgina was not willing to take—not now that they were in the thick of this ill-thought-out charade.

She could barely enjoy the fabulous meal Melissa had prepared. She heard herself making all the expected appreciative noises at the ingredients that had been used in its preparation—ingredients provided by Rose, produce from her farm.

She knew that Matias was laying on the charm. For all his ruthlessness, his indifference when it came to emotions and his coldness, he could be persuasive, and by the end of the evening, with the rain still slamming against the window panes and no hope at all of risking any kind of trek back down the hill to the car, Melissa had joined his fan club.

'He's brilliant,' she whispered, tugging Georgina back while Matias preceded them up the stairs. 'Honestly, Georgie, I was beginning to despair that you would ever move on after that creep.'

'Brilliant?' Georgina asked weakly. 'He should be the last person you think is *brilliant*.' She laughed to dilute the urgency of what she was saying. 'He's the least laid-back, least relaxed person in the world! He's a workaholic who has no time for much except the business of making money.'

'I know!' Melissa smiled. 'And I love that he doesn't try and gloss over that fact. Honesty in a guy is so refreshing. And besides, aren't we both workaholics in our own way?'

'What do you mean?'

Brilliant? Refreshing? Honest? Suddenly Matias appeared to have attained all the attributes of a saint in waiting.

'Well, I don't know about you,' Melissa said wryly, 'but try tearing me away from the kitchen! Charlie says that I never have time to go to the movies or have days out because I'm always desperate to try some new idea for a dish! Now, if that's not being a workaholic, then what is? And I know you can be a slave to your camera. How many times have you told me that you've spent a Saturday looking at photos and working?'

'That's different,' Georgina said uncomfortably.

'No, it's not. It's fantastic that you've met your soul mate. I can tell there's a real connection there.'

They'd reached the spare bedroom and Melissa pushed

open the door, and Georgina knew in that instant what it felt like to have tunnel vision because all she could see was the double bed.

'I know you love your space…' Georgina turned to Matias, who looked right back at her without revealing anything at all '… I'm sure Melissa won't mind if you want to sleep here on your own. I mean, this bed is really tiny—barely any room for two people to share. Matias likes his space…' She looked at her friend without actually meeting her warm brown eyes, realising, not for the first time, how hard deception could be. 'Don't you? Darling?' She turned to Melissa. 'He's a restless sleeper. Thrashes around.'

Share a bed? Inconceivable. Especially when the atmosphere between them was so…so alive with tension. No way!

'And *you* snore,' he said. 'You don't see *me* complaining.'

'I love it!' Melissa was looking between the two of them with bright-eyed interest and delight. 'I love it that you two are just so comfortable with one another.'

'I wouldn't dream of putting our host out,' Matias said smoothly, nailing the conversation dead.

He strolled towards Georgina and slung his arm over her shoulders. The warm weight of him stirred the melting pot of confusing reactions over which Georgina seemed to have no control. She could feel his skin burning into hers, insistent on making its effect felt.

'I've popped a couple of towels on the bed,' Melissa was saying, moving into the room and doing her best tour guide impression. 'There's lots of hot water—and, Georgie, I know we're not the same size, but I've put a tee shirt in the bathroom and you can use that if you want to…'

Georgina blanched. Matias had moved off to peer out of the window, where the rain continued to launch itself against the panes like bullets.

Her brain was beginning to malfunction. She couldn't take on board any further nightmares. The fact that Matias was as cool as a cucumber enraged her. Did he think that this was somehow going to play into his hands? No, of course he didn't, she told herself, because he would never pursue a reluctant woman—far less one who had shot him down in flames.

The door shut behind Melissa, and as soon as it had Georgina folded her arms and looked at him with undisguised horror. In return, he didn't look in the slightest bit concerned. He wasn't uncomfortable with the situation at all.

'Forget it,' he drawled as he began the process of undressing without so much as a by-your-leave.

'Forget what?' Georgina said tightly. The closer he was, the faster her pulses raced and the higher her colour became.

'Playing the outraged virgin. I didn't conspire to change the weather and your friend is simply being considerate in offering us a room for the night. I've phoned my mother and told her the situation.'

'I didn't see you do that!'

'That's because you were too busy dreading the prospect of sharing a bedroom with me.'

The buttons of his shirt were undone and her hungry eyes were inexorably drawn to the sliver of hard brown chest. Her pulses raced faster. She felt that in a minute she would forget how to breathe.

'Why do you think that is?' Matias murmured conversationally. 'Do you think you can't trust me not to try something because I've told you I fancy you? Didn't you believe me when I told you that I'm not into begging a woman to share my bed?'

Georgina croaked something. She knew what she wanted to say, and the person she wanted to be, but what emerged was nothing like what she had in mind. She wasn't controlled or cool or together. She was a nervous wreck and her body language was saying it all.

'Of course I believed you. That's not what this is about!'

'Maybe you don't trust yourself. Is that it, Georgie? Do you think that if you're too close to me you're not going to be able to help yourself?'

'I don't think I've ever heard anything so egotistical in my life before!'

'But then that's me, isn't it?' Matias told her, his voice cooling and his eyes hardening. 'An egotistical swine. No matter what I say or do, that will *always* be me, won't it?'

Somehow that level self-criticism felt like a slap in the face and Georgina knew that it wasn't true. Maybe once upon a time she had had those preconceived notions about him, but things had changed. He wasn't one-dimensional, he wasn't the cardboard cut-out of a callous son who never visited his poor mother and was only interested in making money.

She had seen the way he interacted with Rose and had glimpsed the vulnerable man beneath the cool mask. He had made her laugh with his quick wit and his sense of humour and had floored her with his intelligence and the breadth of his knowledge.

When she wasn't spoiling for a fight with him he got under her skin and opened her eyes to the man she'd always known existed, deep down. The man who still had the power to enthral her. And then there was his sizzling sex appeal, like nothing she had ever experienced... The last thing he was, was the arrogant egotist she had described him as being.

Honesty compelled her to say, 'You're not that.'

Matias shot her a surprised look and stilled. 'Meaning...?'

'I thought you were one thing,' she told him awkwardly, looking away and licking her lips nervously, but determined that he must know what she really thought. 'I thought you were cold and heartless for not coming down here more often. I thought you were just another arrogant guy wrapped up in making money and being rich, without any depth, but you're not. I can see the way you are with Rose...'

She reddened and stumbled over her words. She felt a bit as if she had thrown herself down a hole without knowing how far she would have to fall, and right now this meandering conversation made her feel that she was falling without a safety net.

'How's that?' Matias questioned gruffly.

'You do small things for her...reach for her if you think she needs help getting to her feet. You're solicitous. I think you feel you're really getting close to her and that you want to try and bridge whatever gap is there between you. Someone arrogant and selfish wouldn't care about bridging gaps.'

Georgina wondered whether she had said too much. His face was cool and remote. It was impossible to gauge what he was thinking.

'And I've seen the way you look around the house, looking for anything that might need replacing, keeping on top of things without Rose even really realising what you're doing. So, no. You're not an egotistical swine. Although…'

'Although…?'

'Although,' she said, bringing herself back on point, 'you're still really full of yourself. And if we're sharing this bedroom then you keep to your side of the bed!'

She folded her arms and tilted her chin.

Matias laughed softly and then disappeared into the bathroom.

No change of clothes—nothing. Georgina eyed the tee shirt Melissa had left for her, and for good measure the pyjama shorts in soft cotton. Both were made for a size eight slightly built woman, but in the absence of anything else they would have to do.

She had no idea how long Matias was going to take, but somehow the thought of following behind him and showering in the shower he had just used made her skin tingle.

She tiptoed out of the bedroom and two doors down found the family bathroom. The cottage was small, but wonderfully equipped and eclectic, but Georgina was in far too much of a rush to admire the mosaic tiles, or the ornate gilt mirror over the old-fashioned sink, or the claw-footed bathtub.

Melissa would be downstairs, experimenting with food. Georgina knew that her friend was a night bird. But she took a very quick shower and was back in the bedroom before Matias was done. Who said that women took their time when it came to their ablutions?

The tee shirt was stretched tightly across her breasts but she had forgone the shorts, which hadn't fitted at all.

She huddled under the quilt on her side, all lights in the room off, her eyes squeezed tightly shut. Her heart almost stopped beating when she heard the bathroom door open and then the soft footsteps of Matias before he slipped under the duvet next to her. The room was in darkness and the torrential rain, still banging against the window panes like angry fists, was strangely cosy and romantic.

She expected him to say something—something sarcastic or teasing or irritating. *Something.* He didn't.

He rolled onto his side, depressing the mattress with his weight. It made her cling further to her side, like a drowning man clinging to a lifebelt. His silence was oppressive. It made her wonder whether he was asleep. She found herself listening to his breathing and was then conscious of her own...

Georgina didn't know quite when she fell asleep, but she did know when she woke up.

The room was still pitch-black and for a short while she was utterly disorientated. The driving force of the rain had softened to a persistent patter, going from sounding like rocks against the windows to pebbles. She needed the toilet, and she cursed under her breath as she tiptoed her way through the bedroom, groping and taking her time because she didn't want to switch any lights on.

She couldn't have tried harder to be quiet, but the flush of the toilet and the sound of running water as she washed her hands resounded like the booming of church bells on a Sunday morning.

Tense as a bowstring, she crept stealthily towards the bed. Intent on making no noise, her narrowed eyes pinned to the inert dark shape on the bed, she took her eye off the ball. While her eyes were as keen as an eagle's, and her breathing as silent as a sigh, her feet were not quite so obliging.

An errant item of clothing on the ground was her

downfall and she stumbled, panicked, reached out and fell with a crash.

She had a second's worth of mindless dismay and then Matias was there. He'd leapt from the bed, slammed on the lights and was kneeling on the ground before she had time to screech that she was perfectly fine.

Mortified, Georgina could barely look at him.

'What's going on?'

'Nothing! Nothing's going on.' She tried to scramble to her feet and winced in discomfort. 'I went to use the bathroom. I'm sorry I woke you up but it was dark and I didn't want to switch the light on.'

'Let me have a look.'

'Go away! Go back to sleep!'

'Don't be an idiot, Georgie.'

Georgina didn't answer. She was miserably conscious of her state of undress and the wretched many-sizes-too-small tee shirt which Melissa had kindly lent her. Not to mention the fact that she was in her underwear because she hadn't been able to squeeze herself into the insanely tiny pyjama shorts. She was aware of her legs on show, her thighs and her breasts, which were bursting out of their over-tight confinement. She was conscious of her body in a way she had never been in her life before.

She jumped up—and subsided just as fast with a little yelp of pain.

She abandoned the struggle as Matias scooped her up in one fluid movement and carried her to the bed, depositing her as carefully as if she were made of china. He was thoughtful enough to switch off the glaring overhead light, but then he immediately switched on the lamp by the bed, which at least had the benefit of being more forgiving.

Georgina kept her eyes tightly shut. Matias examined her foot, gently turning it in his hand, pressing here and there and asking questions that she could barely answer because her mouth was so dry.

'You'll live,' he said drily, straightening, at which point Georgina risked looking at him.

He was wearing a pair of boxers and nothing else. He was so beautiful that she felt faint. Her heart was hammering and she knew that he would be able to suss out perfectly well what it was she was trying so hard not to convey—because there was a watchful stillness about him, an electric awareness of the situation and only a tenuous thread tethering them both to the straight and narrow.

He broke the connection, turned around.

'Matias…' She heard the hitch in her voice. 'What?' He slowly swivelled to look at her, a taut, towering, brooding presence that was all shadows and angles.

'Nothing…'

'Nothing? *Nothing?* In that case I'll go downstairs and work,' he said, not looking at her. 'That way you can sleep in peace and you won't have to try and creep around like a thief if you need to use the toilet.'

He began dressing, and for a few seconds Georgina watched him in tense silence, safely tucked under the duvet, legs drawn up to her chin.

Maybe I don't want you to go downstairs to work… maybe I don't want to sleep in peace…maybe I can't sleep in peace or do anything in peace with you around… maybe, just maybe, I'm sick to death of fighting this thing between us because, for me, it's been there for ever…

Never had she longed so much to say the unthinkable, to risk it all by throwing herself at him. She'd never had time for lust—but, then again, she'd never known what it felt like to be tempted.

Hands balled into fists, she bit down hard on the temptation and remained silent.

He didn't stick around. He got dressed fast and walked out of the room without a backward glance, and when the door was shut Georgina sagged back against the pillows and closed her eyes.

Her mobile phone was telling her that it was still very early in the morning. The sounds outside were reminding her of what awaited when dawn broke—water everywhere and rain turning the landscape into a miserable, sodden grey lake.

She was here.

He was here.

He'd never beg her. Or pursue her. Or even hint. He didn't care about her even if he did have a different take on her now that they'd been flung into one another's company, just as she had a different take on him.

She was a novelty for him. They weren't even *suited*! Could there be any *more* reasons for not doing what she was about to do...?

Her feet began taking her out of the bedroom and down the stairs. Her body was all for it. Her brain was on the back foot and no longer raising any objections. Having ruled the roost for so many years, it was now resigned to obeying stronger commands.

She knew the house and knew where he would be. Either in the office that Melissa used or in the kitchen, with its sprawling weathered pine table and four-door Aga.

She headed straight to the kitchen and hit the jackpot. Because there he was.

Georgina paused in the doorway and her breathing

slowed and her heartbeat accelerated. He was staring out of the kitchen window at the inky black rain-lashed gardens, only visible when lightning flashed, illuminating the bending trees and shrubs.

He was still half naked but had slung on his jeans, which rode low on his lean hips. From behind, he was all muscle and sinew and bronzed streamlined beauty.

She padded towards him and knew exactly when he became aware of her presence, because he stilled and then he turned around, very slowly, and looked at her in silence.

He broke the silence to ask her in a roughened undertone, 'What are you doing here?'

He hadn't been working. Only one light was switched on, over the kitchen table, so that he was enveloped in semi-darkness. Confused, Georgina wondered whether he'd just been staring out of the window and thinking. Thinking about what? *Her?*

She held on to that thought because it gave her the courage to stand there in front of him, back in her jeans just as he was, but with the too-tight top an open invitation—whether he realised that or not.

He realised.

He stepped towards her into the light and his eyes dropped to her breasts, lingered there, lingered on the shape of them, their heavy weight and the prominence of her nipples pushing against the thin stretchy fabric.

When eventually his eyes collided with hers, they registered what she was struggling to vocalise.

'Well?'

He took another step towards her, poetry in motion, his dark, brooding beauty sending shivers through her.

'Did you want something to drink? Water?'

'I couldn't get to sleep,' Georgina whispered, moving towards him.

'No?'

Matias paused, just out of reaching distance. It was going to be up to her to close the gap. He'd laid his cards on the table, told her that he wanted her, and she had turned him away. Now he was in charge, and this was his way of telling her that if she wanted him she was going to have to make the first move.

But what if he'd lost interest in the interim?

Georgina shut down that train of thought immediately. She was here and she was going to take what she'd wanted to have for...*for ever*...

'No. I started to think...'

'Thinking can sometimes be a dangerous luxury.'

'Certainly dangerous...' She stepped towards him, and she was breathing thickly as she placed one flattened palm against his chest. 'Because I was thinking about *you*—thinking about the fact that I want you. Matias, I don't want to play it safe. You're dangerous... I know that...but I want to know... I *need* to know...'

Her voice trailed off and uncertainly she kept her hand where it was, not knowing what the outcome of this was going to be, but knowing that she had to risk possible rejection to find out.

'You need to know what it feels like to take a walk on the wild side...?'

'Something like that,' Georgina muttered inaudibly.

She made to remove her hand, already smelling rejection, but then he took her hand in his and tugged her towards him, a little closer, close enough for her to feel the warmth of his breath on her face.

'You're right about me, Georgie. I'm dangerous. And

what you're doing right now… It's called playing with fire.'

'I know,' she whispered. 'But maybe I've lived too long telling myself that playing it safe is the only way for me. I've been so careful not to take chances as far as guys are involved but you're right. Being careful might make sense, but sometimes making sense can be a joyless exercise. You don't tick any of my boxes…'

'Who's interested in a checklist?'

'I always have been,' she breathed. 'Especially after Robbie. I felt like he slipped through the net. You're right. My parents approved and I suppose I felt at the time that making them proud was important. After all…' She laughed self-consciously. 'I spent my life not living up to their expectations. At least that was what I thought, deep down. Never bright enough. Bit of a disappointment, really. So Robbie came along, and they approved, and that counted for a lot… And then…'

And then there was you…there was always you… And who's to say that Robbie wasn't my way of trying to escape from the stranglehold you'd always seemed to have over me…?

It occurred to her in a revelatory flash that maybe, beyond the whole lust thing, doing this…taking this step… *making love to this man*…would snuff out the hold he'd always seemed to exercise over her. The unknown was so tantalising, wasn't it? Matias had always been her fantasy guy, but as soon as he became a known quantity she would be free of him, in a manner of speaking. He would no longer be a dream inside her head, an untested benchmark against which other men had always been found wanting.

'And then…?' he was asking her now, in that dark

voice, rich as the richest chocolate, that could make the hairs on the back of her neck stand on end.

'And then, when it all fell apart, I sat back and took stock and told myself that I would never make the same mistake again. Next time round I would go out with someone I felt was suited to *me*. Someone who had all the qualities I looked for. Someone on *my* wavelength.'

'But now you like the thought of playing with fire…?'

'Have *you* ever played with fire?'

'Not when it comes to sex,' Matias murmured huskily. 'I've had one or two nail-biting moments with deals that hung in the balance, but I like knowing where I am when it comes to relationships. We need to go upstairs, Georgie. We need a bed…'

Their eyes tangled, and in the soft light, with the steady drumbeat of the rain against the windows, something inside Georgina twisted. This was the point, she knew, when decisions would be made and there would be no going back.

So she would be taking a risk? But where had being careful got her? This fake relationship was the closest thing she'd got to adventure in years. This man standing in front of her was the closest thing she'd got to exciting in even longer. He wasn't right for her and he didn't try and pretend otherwise. He fancied her because… She didn't quite know why, but he seemed to… And, God, did she fancy *him*. He took her breath away. Always had.

She could fight the attraction but this was her moment, her window. If she walked away now then he wouldn't look back, but she would always wonder. *He* wouldn't, but *she* would. He wanted a bed and so did she.

But first…

She ran her hands along his thighs. She couldn't miss

the thick bulge of his erection. A surge of feminine power rushed through her in a wave and she stifled a groan. She laid her hand on it and heard him hiss at the touch, although he kept himself perfectly still.

Eventually he clasped some of her bright, tangled hair in his hand and gently drew her face up so that they were staring at one another.

'Think hard,' he murmured, 'because you'll be stepping out of your comfort zone. My mother thinks we're having a relationship, but we both know the truth…'

'I get it, Matias. This isn't for real. I'm not going to start getting confused and delusional. How many times do you think you have to hint at that before you realise that you're preaching to the converted?' Her voice was strangled, because thinking straight was proving impossible when the evidence of his attraction to her was pulsing against her hand.

'Let's go upstairs,' Matias urged, his breathing ragged. 'The way you're touching me… I need to get these jeans off. I need to feel you…taste you…take you… I want to be inside you, Georgie, hot and hard.'

'Matias…'

'That's nice…'

He kissed her long and hard and deep, until she could scarcely breathe. She just couldn't get enough of that dragging, hungry kiss.

'I like it when you say my name like that… I like the sound of you wanting me as much as I want you… I'd take you right here on this kitchen table, but we'll have to save the adventure for when we have a bit more privacy.'

He drew back, and the hungry darkness in his eyes made her giddy with excitement.

'For now… Let's go upstairs…'

CHAPTER SEVEN

THEY MADE IT up the stairs softly and quickly, any noise drowned out by the pounding of the rain outside. The click of the bedroom door shutting behind them made her shudder with anticipation.

'I need to see you.' Matias moved to switch on one of the lamps, bathing the room in a mellow glow. 'I want to see every inch of your glorious body when I make love to you.'

This felt like tasting forbidden fruit, and now that she had succumbed to temptation her excitement levels were rising fast. Georgina looked at him as he walked towards her. He touched her and she curved into him, and for a few seconds they held one another without saying anything.

Then, 'I'm not the skinny catwalk model type,' she murmured against him.

'You're not.' He propelled her towards the bed without breaking contact.

'You *like* skinny catwalk model types.'

'Is this based on your close observation of me over the years?'

Georgina reddened, and he laughed softly and kissed the side of her mouth.

'You're wondering,' he murmured, 'whether to tell me that I'm an egotistical swine…'

'If the hat fits…' But she smiled nervously, and as the back of her knees came into contact with the mattress she collapsed onto the bed, eyes darkening as he remained standing, began unzipping the jeans.

Her arms were spread wide, her hair a vibrant mane across the pillow. The jeans came off, and then the boxers. and she drew in a sharp breath when he circled his penis with his hand and gently played with himself while he watched her with smouldering intensity.

Drugged with desire, Georgina discovered a side to herself she'd never known existed. A side without inhibition…a side that wanted to touch, to lick, to taste, to feel her own wetness the way he was feeling his own arousal.

Gone was the primness that had held her in check all her life and in its place was a wanton, bold, daring woman who wanted to explore every inch of the man now settling onto the bed next to her.

'Too many clothes,' Matias said thickly, and he undressed her at speed, rearing up as he tugged down her jeans, taking her underwear with them, and then the too-tiny top.

For a long moment he stared at her. He adored her with his eyes and she couldn't breathe for wanting him.

'Good God,' he said in a driven undertone. 'So damned beautiful…so bloody sexy…where have you been all my life?'

It was just a figurative way of speaking, but, oh, how she wanted to shout, *Here… I've always been here…*

It was so erotic, such a turn-on, and the heat pooled wet between her legs. He straddled her and gently swept her hair back, so that he could trail delicate kisses along her neck and enjoy the hitch in her breathing and her soft purrs of pleasure.

His movements were slow, leisurely, intensely arousing. His touch was delicate, but she knew that there was sheathed power behind the light touch. He was taking his time.

He covered her mouth with his and began kissing her, tasting her, probing the inside of her mouth with his tongue while he idly stroked her belly. Her generous breasts begged to be touched, and if by not touching them he intended to ratchet up her frantic desire to have him then he was spot-on.

'So bloody beautiful,' he murmured raggedly.

She laughed with her eyes as they broke apart for a few seconds. 'You don't mean that.'

'I never say anything I don't mean.'

'No, you don't, do you?' Georgina's breathing was shallow and she wriggled sinuously against him, like a cat responding to the bliss of being stroked. 'You don't care how your words affect other people, do you?'

'Life's a tough business.' Matias looked down at her for a few seconds, his dark eyes impenetrable. 'I spent my early life moving away from my parents' hocus-pocus lifestyle choices, and I discovered along the way that focusing on the tangible is all that matters. Caring too much about the abstract is a recipe for disaster.'

'You mean love…?'

'It gets in the way of what's really important in life.'

'Which is what?'

'Too much talk.' Matias neatly sidestepped the question, but then shot her a crooked smile because her questioning green eyes refused to be deflected. 'You don't give up, do you? I don't do *love*, Georgie. My head rules my life. Always been that way and always will be that way. I've seen first-hand what happens when you start thinking with your emotions. You end up with a chaotic, rudderless life. Don't look at me as though I've put out a hit on Father Christmas!' He laughed softly. 'Now, stop talking and let me pleasure you… You don't have to feel nervous with me,' he soothed.

'I'm not,' Georgina lied.

'Now who's telling fibs? You're tensing up. I can feel it.'

'I'm not what you're used to. Physically.'

'So you've already reminded me—and, no, you're not,' Matias responded with honesty. 'But I say that as the greatest of compliments. I like your body…so sexy…a man could lose himself in your curves… I can't begin to tell you just what I want to do to you…'

'I'm not experienced…'

'I'm not looking for experience.'

He couldn't hold off any longer and he covered her breast with his hand, played with her stiffened nipple, rubbing it and feeling it pucker between his fingers. He was so close to having an orgasm just from touching her like this that he was seriously shocked.

'Matias…'

'Shh…'

'I've never done this before,' Georgina said in a rush, and Matias went completely still.

She held her breath and wished that she could yank that admission right back into her mouth and bury it. She wanted him more than she'd ever thought it was possible to want anyone, but was he going to want to make love to a virgin?

She'd never given a huge amount of thought to the fact

that she'd never slept with a man. She'd never been the sort of girl to be seduced by the thought of sleeping around. Then, when she'd met Robbie, she hadn't wanted to rush into bed with him. It had been important to her to take her time. She'd been pleased that he hadn't tried to force her hand. She could see now that he just hadn't been as attracted to her as she'd hoped, and vice versa. They'd both jumped into something for the wrong reasons. But now…

'When you say…?'

'I haven't done this before. Robbie and I…' She faltered in embarrassment and looked away, but Matias gently turned her so that she was looking at him.

He rolled onto his side and manoeuvred her onto hers so that they were facing one another. 'But you were a serious item…'

'I know,' Georgina said in a small voice.

She wished she'd never opened her mouth now. Because would he have *guessed* that she was a virgin? She could have pretended…bitten back any cries of pain if it hurt when he entered her. Judging from what she could see, he was impressive when it came to size. She felt like an idiot.

'No sex… That should have been the writing on the wall for you…'

'It's not *always* about sex,' Georgina protested helplessly.

'Oh, but it really is. And after Robbie…? Was there no one who could tempt you between the sheets?'

Georgina squirmed. 'I've been busy,' she muttered, her face as hot as a furnace and as red as a beetroot. She took a deep breath and gave him an out clause. 'I'll understand if you don't want to proceed any further.'

'What are you talking about?'

'You're used to stunningly beautiful women who would have lost their virginity in their teens…'

'I'd be your first…' Matias said, with a certain amount of wonder. He felt a surge of desire, a naked, raw craving rush through him in a tidal wave. 'I'm going to be honest with you…'

'Of course,' Georgina said miserably.

'I haven't been so turned on in my entire life.'

He was swept by the uncomfortable thought that a woman with no experience, a woman with romantic notions, might likewise be a woman with a heart waiting to be broken. But then he remembered how vehement she had been in her conviction that he wasn't her type, and how readily she had accepted the rules of this game, and the errant moment of unease was gone.

This was a flash in the pan. A really thrilling, rush-of-adrenaline flash in the pan. For *both* of them. It would burn out, they would go their separate ways and that would be that. She would meet her Mr Right in due course. If she lost her virginity to him then she would be in good hands—because he would be gentle with her. Many wouldn't. Furthermore, they *knew* one another. They had history.

'Really?' Georgina asked.

'Really—and enough talking.'

He would do his utmost to slow down, but temptation was like a banquet put in front of a starving beggar.

Georgina luxuriated in the sight of his lean, glorious beauty. In the shadows, his body was all angles and strength, bronzed and powerful. When he straddled her, the feel of his thick, pulsing erection filled her with wonder…with dark excitement…and with sharp apprehension all at the same time.

She was shocked by the graphic direction of her thoughts. Her lack of curiosity before when it came to sex astounded her. Curiosity was tearing her apart now. She felt as though she was waking up and coming alive for the first time in her life.

'Enjoying the sight?' Matias teased.

'You're very big…' she breathed, with honesty, and he burst out laughing and settled alongside her, turning her so that they were facing one another.

He sobered up. 'Don't be afraid. I'll be gentle, and the female body is fashioned to take a man of my size. Relax and you'll enjoy the ride. I promise you.'

He kissed her, kissed every inch of her face—soft kisses that melted her from the inside out. If she was nervous about making love, his touch was dismantling those nerves and sending her inhibitions to the four winds.

She wriggled and fell back as he pinned her hands above her head and then began kissing her again—her shoulders, her neck, her breasts, nibbling and licking, and then, when she could take no more of the rising excitement, he took one throbbing nipple into his mouth. He moistened it with his tongue, teasing the stiffened bud until she wanted to scream. He nipped it gently, suckled, drawing it into his mouth then moving on to pay attention to the other.

He stilled her when all she wanted to do was thrash around, and when she was still he cupped her between her legs, waiting and then slowly insinuating his finger into her, feeling her wetness, gliding over it and finding the tight bud of her clitoris.

Georgina couldn't stand it. Nothing had ever felt so good. She felt a burst of intense pleasure begin rippling through her as his finger glided between her thighs, smoothing the velvety crease there. She parted her legs and moved against his finger. Her body arched up and he continued to lick and tease her protuberant nipples.

There was no question that he knew what to do with a woman's body, how to electrify it on all fronts, how to make it twist and wriggle with pleasure.

With a groan of self-restraint Georgina pulled back from that devastating finger and applied herself to giving *him* some of the pleasure he had been giving her. Inexperience made her hesitate, but the driving need to feel him was greater than any insecurities on that front.

She cupped him in her hands and, kneeling, took his bigness into her mouth. She felt a thrill of delight at his immediate response. She could tell that he couldn't resist what she was doing to him and that gave her a heady sense of pure feminine power.

Every muscle in his body tensed as she continued to lick and suck him, while her own enflamed body had time to cool down a little. Just a little.

His deep moans thrilled her. The way he clasped her hair, guiding her, thrilled her. Everything about this guy thrilled her in ways she couldn't define.

She licked his shaft and he uttered a stifled groan.

'My God, Georgie…' His voice was unsteady, his breathing uneven. 'I can't think straight when you're doing that.'

Georgina broke off to say, 'Good,' before picking up where she'd left off.

'This isn't going according to plan…' He tugged himself free of her exploring mouth and took a few seconds to gather himself before staring down at her with dark amusement. 'Speed wasn't on the agenda.'

Sprawled back on the pillow, arms spread, Georgina

stared at him from under her lashes with drowsy delight, her body moving to its own beat because she just couldn't seem to keep still.

'I'm so desperate for you,' she moaned.

'In case you've missed it,' Matias said roughly, 'the feeling's mutual.'

He began groping for his wallet, cursing softly under his breath until he'd extracted protection.

Where was his fabled cool? Nowhere in evidence, Georgina realised with a rush of satisfaction. His hands were trembling as he donned the condom and his movements were urgent as he settled over her.

He entered her gently, and she knew that he was exercising extreme restraint. Bit by bit he inched his bigness into her wetness, slowing when she tensed, then pushing more firmly as she accommodated his girth.

'So fantastically tight and wet,' he groaned. 'You're driving me crazy, woman.'

Her groans were fast little puffs as he sank deeper into her, and then he was moving fast and hard.

Georgina winced. Then the fierce discomfort of that initial thrust was overwhelmed by the exquisite sensations racing through her as he picked up pace. His girth and size, which she had eyed with some apprehension, was the very thing that felt so good now that he was deep inside her.

Somehow, without their bodies parting an inch, he manoeuvred her so that she was on top of him, her full breasts dangling down to his waiting mouth. Her body knew what to do and it was the most amazing thing. She knew how to move, how to gyrate on him until the need to come was so overpowering that she could no longer resist.

The orgasm that swept her away was shattering. She

heard herself cry out as she arched back—a soft, urgent cry—and she knew that he was coming as well, because she could feel the rigid tension in his powerful body, the stiffening just before release, and then she collapsed against him, utterly and completely replete.

Matias broke the silence. 'That was…amazing.'

Warm and drowsy after the racing fury of her orgasm, Georgina curled against him, enjoying his warmth and the lean, muscular angles of his body. This was a dream come true. It felt that way. Yes, it was dangerous, but it felt so good, so *right*. She wanted to shout from the rooftops that it had been better than amazing for her, that she was now *complete*.

'Lovely,' she said instead, and she felt him grin against her neck.

'Try not to go overboard with enthusiasm,' he said drily, but his voice was amused and teasing, his dark eyes slumberous and warm as he looked at her.

'I won't,' Georgina replied, equally lightly. 'Your ego is big enough, Matias Silva, without me swelling it even further.'

'I'll take that as your quirky way of telling me that the earth moved for you.' He nibbled her ear, then her neck, then smoothed his hand along her warm, soft body, taking his time to feel every glorious inch of her.

Outside, the fierce tempo of the rain had faded into a soft patter. And into this comforting background noise several questions began to raise their tiresome heads. Top of the list was…*what happens now?*

'I'm going to go have a shower…' It was the only thing Georgina could think of to say as her head began to whirl. 'Er…we should get some sleep…and then tomorrow… Well, you never know with the weather round here. You wouldn't believe how long the rain can last. Flooding. Roads under water. But it sounds like it's beginning to fade…'

'Thanks for the weather update.'

Matias grinned, holding her in place next to him, and Georgina was horrified to discover how much she liked that possessive arm pinning her to the spot.

'Why are you going to have a shower?'

'Because…'

'Don't even *think* about getting dressed.' He stroked her thigh and slipped his hand between her legs, so that he could play absently with the soft, fuzzy hair there. 'We're not done yet… How's the foot doing, by the way? I hope things weren't too energetic for you…'

'Foot?'

'Ah, good. You've forgotten. I'm taking that to mean you haven't given it a passing thought. I don't want to tire you, or hurt you if you're sore, but I want you again, Georgie. I don't know what you've done to me…you're a witch.'

'Matias…'

Suddenly she was reading all sorts of things into his carelessly delivered words. *The sex was amazing…where had she been all his life?….she'd cast a spell on him like a witch…*

Like a horse breaking free of its restraints her imagination was playing fast and loose with reality, and even as she tried to rein it in she could feel its perilous temptation towards a fairy tale ending that was never in a million years going to happen.

Heart beating like a sledgehammer, she pulled back from the seductive allure of his caresses to meet his eyes in the darkened room. 'This was never supposed to happen, Matias. We got carried away and one thing led to another. I'm not completely naïve. I know these things happen.'

'You're right when you say that this wasn't on the cards. But it's on the cards now.' He slid his finger into her wet crease and felt her little spasm of delight. 'And don't try and tell me that this is a one-off, that we've got to put the whole thing behind us because "one thing led to another". Your body is telling me that you're as hot for me right now as I am for you.'

'That's not the point...'

'Then what is?'

'Our sleeping together could lead to all sorts of complications.'

'Personally,' Matias returned wryly, 'I think that you ringing on my doorbell and telling me that we're an item was a lot more fraught with complications. I wanted you. I want you now. And I'm not going to have a shower and then pretend that this never happened.'

'So what do you suggest?'

Georgina gasped as he found the stiffened bud of her clitoris and gently began to rub the pad of his finger over it.

'I can't think properly when you're doing that...'

'Good. Because this isn't about thinking. This is about the two of us giving in to something that's bigger than both of us.'

'It doesn't make sense...'

She began to move against his finger, her body disobeying her brain as she'd known it would. She'd barely come down from the splintering high of orgasm and she could already feel little spasms of mounting pleasure as he rubbed her. Her nipples ached and she pictured his dark head nuzzling and suckling at her breasts. That turned her on even more.

'Let's agree not to question this, Georgie. So what if it doesn't make sense? We got on this rollercoaster and I think we should just go along for the ride. When the ride comes to an end we'll deal with it...'

'You should at least think about it,' Rose was saying as she fussed around them.

They had come for breakfast—a routine that had been established ever since they had arrived, a week ago. Their nights were spent together at Georgina's house. Their days were largely spent with Rose. Time was galloping past and Georgina had decided that uncomfortable thoughts were best left unexplored.

She'd made big decisions. She'd chosen to carry on sleeping with Matias instead of doing what her head had told her to do, which was to write off that single night at Melissa's as an anomaly. She'd made loads of excellent arguments to support her decision, but now that the decision had been made what was the point of tormenting herself with pointless speculation about whether she'd done the right thing or not?

Besides, with each passing day Rose seemed to have a renewed lease of life, and Georgina knew that the openly touchy-feely stuff between herself and Matias partially accounted for that.

They were no longer involved in a charade—at least not as far as the physical side of things went—and maybe she had picked up on some intangible vibes and was responding to them. Who knew?

Right now Rose was waiting for a response to a question that had the potential to open up a can of worms.

Sprawled in a chair, long legs stretched out in front of him and crossed loosely at the ankles, Matias was watching Georgie from under luxuriant dark lashes and maintaining an unhelpful silence.

'It wouldn't work,' Georgina said awkwardly as she began to clear the table. 'I mean, Rose, so much of my work is tied up here… I couldn't just ditch all of that and move to…er… London. It's a dog-eat-dog world there and I'm just a minnow. I'd be eaten alive.'

She paused after that bagful of mixed metaphors and tried to garner support from Matias with a meaningful look. He returned her stare without taking the bait.

Rose's face fell. 'But then I just don't see how things are going to work between the two of you.' She looked at Matias with a hint of apology. 'I know you hate talking about things like this, Matias, and I hope you won't be offended…'

Matias waved a casual hand and shifted ever so slightly. 'Feel free, Mother. I don't want you to think that you have to edit your words because of me.'

'Well, I do understand that all those clandestine meetings in London must have been terribly exciting…'

She paused fractionally to look at Georgina, who duly responded, 'Terribly…'

'But after the first excitement relationships have to grow and mature. You're both here now, and I can see with my own eyes just how much enjoyment the pair of you find in one another. You're in one another's company all the time and I think that's giving you so many opportunities to really deepen the connection between you. In fact, I've seen that with my own two eyes! I've seen the way you look at each other!'

Out of the corner of her eye Georgina was aware of Matias's discomfort at this perfectly reasonable observation from his mother and a dart of malicious satisfaction streaked through her.

He was absolutely in favour of them continuing their relationship while he was enjoying the sex, and because of that he had jettisoned all plans to engineer their situation towards an eventual break-up. Was it any wonder that his mother was now beginning to look beyond the present to the future?

'It's going to end up being impractical if you have to conduct a long-distance relationship. Those things seldom work. It's far too easy to be tempted by someone else if the person you love is a thousand miles away.'

'Cornwall isn't a thousand miles away from London,' Georgina pointed out. 'And,' she added for good measure, 'if a guy is tempted just because there's a bit of distance between himself and the woman he's supposed to be madly in love with, then he wasn't madly in love in the first place.'

Rose knew her son, and she knew very well that Matias had always been short on commitment and big on variety when it came to women. Georgina could understand perfectly well why she was worried about the distance between them, but there was no way she was going to pretend that her migrating to London was an option. *No way.*

And wasn't this a good excuse to start sowing the seeds of what might go wrong between the love birds?

It had been so easy over the past few days to be lulled into thinking that there was an element of *reality* about all this—but she and Matias had two very different takes on reality.

For her, reality was a relationship founded in commitment—a relationship that was going somewhere, developing into something that had a future. Something beyond sex.

For Matias, reality was taking what he wanted. It was sex and fun until the sex got boring and the fun began to peter out.

'Some might say that a long-distance relationship really siphons off the flash-in-the-pan romance from the slow burn of something long-lasting. Wouldn't you agree, Matias?'

Matias shrugged and raised his eyebrows.

'Your mother has a point, don't you think? Clandestine is all very well and good, but when the thrill of that is over and done with, what next?'

Silence greeted this provocative remark, and Georgina bit down hard on a hiss of impatience.

The telephone trilled from the hallway, breaking the silence, which had continued to stretch.

Rose scuttled out of the kitchen.

'You're breathing fire,' Matias drawled. 'Care to tell me why?'

'Why do you *think*, Matias?'

'My mother does have a point,' he agreed mildly. 'If you want your career to develop beyond doing a few shoots for the chef down the road, then you're eventually going to have to head for the big, bad city lights.'

'You *know* that's not what she was talking about!'

She clicked her tongue with annoyance. How could he just lounge there, sprawled in that chair with that half-smile on his face, looking so drop-dead gorgeous when he should be taking her seriously? She knew that if he'd already got sick of her, if the sex had run its course, then he would be leaping onto the exit strategy she had tried to set in motion.

'True,' Matias was honest enough to admit.

'We need to prepare the way for your mother to realise that this isn't going to end up where she thinks it is. Matias, read between the lines. Rose is building up to this being more than just a relationship. Why didn't you follow my lead?'

'I've always hated the concept of being a follower.'

'I'm being serious!' Georgina cried with frustration.

Matias pressed his fingers against his eyes, and when he looked at her it was with bone-wrenching gravity. 'I know you are,' he said in a low voice. 'And, trust me, I fully appreciate the wisdom of what you were trying to do. But...'

He raked his fingers through his hair and for the first time since she had known him Georgina could see that he was grappling to express what he wanted to say. In a man as fluent, as lazily sophisticated and utterly controlled and self-assured as Matias Silva, it was a sight that left her temporarily lost for words.

'But...?' she encouraged, when nothing further seemed to be forthcoming.

He straightened in the chair and raked his fingers through his hair. 'But this whole charade has gone down an unexpected route.'

'I don't understand...'

'My mother was depressed. I found myself somehow cajoled into a role I hadn't auditioned for...'

'I *get* that, Matias.' The last thing Georgina felt she needed was a reminder of just how much of an unwilling participant he had been in this whole charade. 'Which is why—'

'Hear me out, Georgie. I thought that once my mother was back in the land of the living—mentally—we could bring this whole game to a timely end. I hadn't banked on my relationship with my mother veering off in unforeseen directions.' He shifted uncomfortably and looked at her broodingly. 'We've spent a lifetime plodding along,' Matias said heavily. 'Always polite, always distant.'

His voice was so low that she had to move close to him to hear what he was saying. Having sat down, she felt her knees almost touching his, and she was leaning into him, her bright hair pulled over one shoulder.

He absently tugged at the curling ends of her hair, twirling strands around his finger while he continued to hold her gaze. It was a gesture of unbearable intimacy and it went straight to the very core of her, even though she knew she was reading way too much into it.

'I spent half a lifetime pulling away from my parents,' he said ruefully. 'In the end we simply inhabited different worlds. My father could never understand it, and my deepest regret is that it became a rift that was never resolved. With my mother... Well, I suppose I tried to heal that rift by making sure no expense was spared. Whatever she wanted, she got.'

He shrugged.

'Now, though, that rift is healing, and it's an unexpected by-product of this little charade of ours. I've never been closer to my mother. That's why I chose not to take you up on the very considerate rescue package you were putting into motion.' He leaned back and shot her a crooked half-smile. 'I can see that you're moved by my uncustomary outpouring of confidences...'

'I think it's brilliant that you and your mother are finding a way forward...' Georgina wanted to tack a diplomatic *but* on the end of that remark, but then she looked at him, at his guarded expression, and her heart twisted.

She gazed back helplessly at him and he pulled her towards him and kissed her.

Conversation closed.

CHAPTER EIGHT

GEORGINA WASN'T SURE what had been resolved by their hurried conversation.

Would the opportunity arise for her to try and get some sort of timeline for their relationship that should never have been? Did Matias even *do* timelines? And if she pushed him…what then?

Thoughts whirled in her head, sparking off one another, one confused thought leading to another.

She didn't want this to end. She wanted a timeline so that she could brace herself for the inevitable, but she didn't want the inevitable to come.

That realisation of weakness snaked through her, terrifying, implacable and revelatory.

This wasn't about lust. Maybe it had started there—although when Georgina thought about it she knew, in her heart, that there had been far more than lust when she had stepped out into the unknown and lost her virginity to Matias.

Yes, he was sexy—and, yes, he had touched her and her whole body had come alive. But she'd never been the sort of girl who was seduced by good looks and a bit of charm. Fact was, Matias had won her heart. And he'd won it, without even trying, a long time ago. Making love to him had been the final stage in a journey that had begun when she had been an impressionable teenager.

For him, she had become just like any one of his other women. Yes, they had history—so maybe not *quite* the same—and, yes, the circumstances behind their relationship were different, but in the end she was sleeping with him on his terms, ceding to something that was going to end because he wasn't into relationships or commitment.

She remembered the towering blonde in the small dress who had been in the process of being dispatched. She remembered rolling her eyes when Matias had said something about her being better off without him.

Here she was. At some point in time he would end up dispatching her in exactly the same way—probably when he thought that the charade they'd begun was no longer required. He'd never guess that she'd fallen in love with him and Georgina shuddered at the thought of him ever finding out.

'Where is she?' Georgina frowned and glanced to the door which Rose had pulled shut behind her when she had gone to pick up the telephone.

Matias looked down at her and then outlined her mouth with his finger, gently tugging at her bottom lip and making her shiver with sudden electric excitement when he inserted his finger into her mouth so that she could suck on it, mimicking what she did to his erection when they were together, naked.

Her mind went blank for a few seconds.

Forgetting to think whenever he touched her was becoming a lifestyle choice.

'We should go and find her.' Georgina managed to draw back and shoot him a stern look from under her lashes.

'If you insist,' Matias drawled, 'although, given this little window, I could think of one or two things I'd rather be doing…'

'Matias!'

'Will you ever stop being shocked at perfectly innocent statements?' He grinned but didn't remove his hand from where it was caressing the side of her neck. 'Or blushing? No, you'll never stop blushing. You've been doing that since you were a kid.'

'I can't help it,' Georgina mumbled. 'It must be a novelty for you, Matias.'

She thought of the Amazonian blonde, so beautiful, so experienced, so *with-it*. She began walking towards the door, her fingers lightly linked with his, as if her body had been programmed to keep touching his whenever and wherever possible.

'You're not kidding.' He tugged her to a stop and stared down at her thoughtfully. 'I haven't had too many dealings with women who blush at the mention of sex.'

'I don't do that!'

'You're doing it now.'

'Do you like it?'

'A change is always as good as a rest…'

Georgina subdued a little dart of pain. *Who wants to be a novelty in someone else's life?* she wondered. *Especially when you're in love with that someone and want nothing more than to be a permanent fixture?*

She plastered a rueful smile on her face and turned away.

'I've never made love to a virgin before, either,' he murmured, pulling her briefly against him and smiling.

'Notch on the bedpost, Matias?'

He frowned. 'Don't say that.'

'Why not? It's true, isn't it?'

'Do you want to start an argument with me?'

'Of course I don't.'

Georgina looked down, but he wouldn't allow that, tipping her chin so that she was forced to meet his gaze.

She looked back at him with a veiled expression, then said, her voice cooler, 'But we're both into being honest about what's going on here.' She shrugged. 'This is all for your mum, and I'm really happy that it's ended up being about more than just bringing her out of her mental slump. I'm really happy that along the way the two of you have finally managed to forge a meaningful connection.'

'What does that have to do with you thinking that you're a notch on my bedpost because you were a virgin when we first made love?'

Georgina wished that he would stop going on about her virginity. It wasn't his intention, but did he have any idea how much the mention of her virginity led her to comparisons with all those women he had bedded who *hadn't* been virgins? She hated thinking of him in bed with other women. She'd never had a jealous bone in her body before, but right now her entire skeletal frame was glued together by the green-eyed monster.

'It was just an expression,' she said lightly.

'I *don't* see women as notches on my bedpost,' Matias persisted.

She could almost smile at his outraged expression. He'd said to her in passing that when it came to women he always laid his cards on the table, was always open and up-front with them. No commitment, no cosy meals in, no meeting the parents. If they chose to ignore those ground rules, then that wasn't his fault. He had a black and white approach to relationships that beggared belief.

'Let's drop this conversation. It's not going anywhere.'

She opened the door to a silent house, but instead of following Matias remained standing behind her, then he leaned down and whispered into her ear.

'You're not a notch on my bedpost—and don't put yourself down by saying something like that.'

'Who says I mind being a notch on your bedpost?' Georgina pointed out calmly.

That deepened his disapproving frown which, in turn, gave her a weird kind of kick. She raised her eyebrows and succumbed to something wicked inside her.

'I mean…' She dragged the syllables out as she looked at him without blinking. 'If I'm going to be a notch on anybody's bedpost, then who's to say that I don't want it to be yours?'

'This conversation is really beginning to get on my nerves, Georgie.'

'Why?'

'Don't give me that *butter-wouldn't-melt-in-my-mouth* expression,' he growled in return.

'I wasn't. I'm just saying…' she paused and tilted her head to one side '…that if I had to lose my virginity then there's no one in the world I'd rather have lost it to.' She said that with heartfelt sincerity. But little did he know just how sincere those words were, and before he started circling the truth and zooming in on it, like a hawk spying a sparrow, she added lightly, 'You're a fantastic lover. You've given me confidence. And when I look ahead…'

'Look ahead?'

'Well, you know…to when this is all over and I move on…'

'I don't speculate about events that have yet to come—so, no, I *don't* know.'

'Well, one day I'll meet the man I'll want to settle down with—a man who's going to love me the way I love him and want to settle down with me the way I want to settle down with him—and when that happens I'm going to think back to—'

'I get the picture,' Matias snapped, flushing darkly. 'No need to expand. And if this isn't the sound of you wanting to start an argument, then I don't know what is.'

'I have no idea why you're angry.'

'Whoever said anything about being angry?'

His dark eyes collided with hers and she swallowed painfully.

'I just don't think that this is the time or the place to start a soul-searching conversation about some man who has yet to appear on your horizon.'

'You're right.'

Matias scowled. 'Yes.' His voice was tight and clipped. 'I am.'

'Let's go and hunt down your mother—but before we do I just want to say that I'm willing to go along with this business of not sowing the seeds of discontent because you feel you're finally building a relationship with your mother. But at some point we're going to have to put a timeline on this...'

'And we will,' Matias inserted smoothly. 'Now, let's drop the subject and find my mother—before she comes looking for us and discovers the love birds in the middle of a row. And don't even *think* of saying that that would be just what the doctor ordered.'

She was whisked out of the sitting room, and before she'd had time to wonder why he was in such a foul mood, when all she'd done was reassure him that she wasn't going to become clingy and needy, even though she blushed and had been a virgin when they'd gone to bed together, they were in the kitchen.

Georgina had thought that they would find Rose doing what she seemed to enjoy doing—namely, preparing something for them to eat, with the television or radio on in the background.

They didn't. Rose was sitting at the kitchen table and staring off into the distance, ashen-faced and as still as a statue.

'I was just about to come and find you two,' she said quietly. 'But I wanted to have a few minutes to myself first.'

'What's going on?' Matias questioned urgently, while Georgina did what seemed to come naturally to people in tense situations…went to make a pot of tea.

Concern made her want to rush and sit next to Rose, hold her hand. Instinct told her that this time it was Matias who needed to do that—as he was doing now.

'That was the consultant on the phone,' Rose was saying, after clearing her throat and breathing deeply. 'Remember those tests I was waiting for results for? Well, it seems that I haven't been given the all-clear after all.'

'I'll get the guy on the phone now. Find out what's going on.'

'Matias, no.' She laid her hand on his and patted it. 'I'm more than capable of handling this situation.'

From where she was standing, Georgina thought that that looked very far from the truth. She met Matias's panicked gaze and her heart went out to him. He was so strong, and yet right now so vulnerable. And she could understand why. His newly burgeoning relationship with his mother was still as delicate as a green shoot finding the sun. He wasn't quite sure how to deal with her obvious distress. He had conditioned his responses for so long to be dispassionate. Would he be able to handle the depth of his emotions?

In a flash, Georgina realised that she seemed to be reading him so thoroughly, and she wondered whether this was a by product of her love.

Was it?

She rested a cup of tea in front of Rose and drew up a chair next to her. 'So, word for word, what did he say?'

'I need an operation,' Rose said flatly. 'And sooner rather than later.'

'You're scared,' Georgina said quietly, 'and I get that. You'd got your hopes up that you'd be given the all-clear. But there's nothing to be afraid of.' She could feel Matias's eyes on her. She took Rose's hand and held it between her own. 'If there was anything truly concerning they would be sending an ambulance over for you right now. *Are* they?'

Rose shook her head and relaxed a little.

'When are you due to go in?'

'He wanted to see me the day after tomorrow, but I managed to persuade him to see me this afternoon.'

'See?' Georgina said reassuringly. 'The day after tomorrow? I'll bet this operation will be as straightforward as pulling out a tooth.'

She heard herself saying all the right things, and in between Matias chipped in, but on this rare occasion, words didn't come easily for him.

'I just worry,' Rose concluded, sighing. 'However straightforward an operation it may or may not be, who knows what will happen? General anaesthetic carries risks—especially for someone like me whose health has been compromised. And there's another thing...'

'What's that?' Matias questioned in a roughened undertone.

'It's been so wonderful seeing the two of you together,' Rose began. Her eyes welled up and she looked away quickly. 'When Georgina told me that you were going out…well, I could hardly believe it.'

Georgina fidgeted, but remained smiling. 'Perhaps you should try and get a little rest?' she murmured. 'You've had a bit of a shock. I can bring your tea up to your bedroom…'

'I thought that it couldn't possibly be true. But I've watched you together and I've hardly been able to credit it. Matias, you're my son, and I love you very much, but I know what you're like with the ladies.'

Matias flushed.

Georgina watched with some amusement as he tried and failed to find a suitable response, resorting to raking his fingers through his hair and squirming ever so slightly in his chair. For the first time in his life he was being openly called out on his behaviour and he didn't know how to deal with it. That was obvious.

'You like variety. Your father and I… Well, we knew we were meant for one another from a very young age, and we never wavered in our conviction or in our love.'

'I… I… We're not all the same…'

Georgina thought that if ever a person had looked as though they were being slowly spit-roasted over an open fire, then that person was Matias. The look he shot her was positively despairing, and it sent his appeal for her shooting into the stratosphere. If her heart hadn't already been handed over to him, then it surely would have been handed over right at that very moment.

'If you intend to toss Georgie aside, Matias, then you

must do it before I go under the knife. I don't think I would be able to make it through if I thought that you were going to break her heart. I've been praying and keeping my fingers crossed that this lovely relationship you have goes the distance, but I'd rather face the worst-case scenario *before* I have the operation than go under general thinking that I might wake up to find that you've decided to break up—'

'Rose!' Georgina interrupted brightly. 'I'm right here! You're talking as though I've left the room! I'm more than capable of taking care of myself should we…should we *both* decide that things aren't working out between us!' She did her best to look as cheerful as possible. 'You really shouldn't be worrying about any of this. You've got enough on your plate.'

'She's right,' Matias said seriously. 'This is the last thing you should be thinking about. Especially when…' His dark eyes roved over Georgina's face. 'Especially when,' he continued gravely, 'we've both been waiting for the right moment to announce our engagement.'

For a few seconds Georgina didn't register what Matias had said. She continued smiling her glassy, soothing smile, but then the smile fell away and hot red colour flooded her cheeks.

It seemed that Rose was congratulating them both… saying something about a ring… And it also seemed that Matias was answering. But their voices were coming from a long way away, and only penetrating her brain the way a very fuzzy light might penetrate dense fog. Her brain certainly felt very foggy.

She was barely aware of Matias escorting his mother upstairs, because somewhere along the line she appeared to have lost the power of speech and of coherent thought in general.

He reappeared after fifteen minutes and stood in the doorway for a few seconds before strolling into the kitchen.

'Not exactly the reaction I was expecting,' he drawled, circling her before dropping into the chair facing hers and promptly leaning forward, arms on his thighs, legs spread apart. 'Where's all the girlish excitable chatter?'

'Matias…' Georgina blinked and then focused on him, still blinking like an owl. '*Engaged?* How could you tell your mother that we're *engaged*?'

Suddenly galvanised into action, she leapt to her feet, sprinted over to make sure that the kitchen door was firmly shut, and then positioned herself in front of Matias, hands on her hips, her green eyes glinting dangerously.

'What choice was there?' Matias countered without batting an eye. 'You heard her. She's terrified of the operation ahead of her—which, as it turns out, is to have a pacemaker fitted. A routine procedure. She's genuinely concerned that things between us are going to go belly-up—that I'm going to revert to my bad old ways, but only after I've well and truly broken your heart. I think she believes that if she's braced for the worst, then she can steel herself to face it.'

'So just like that you decided that you'd expand our relationship into something a thousand times more serious…?'

'I'll admit,' he said grudgingly, 'that I've done what I accused you of doing, when you showed up at my house and informed me that we were a loved-up, starry-eyed couple. I've involved you in something you hadn't anticipated. But this is just a temporary add-on that will take my mother past this hurdle...'

Georgina's mind was in freefall. *Engaged to Matias Silva?* Under normal circumstances it would have been a dream come true. Under these circumstances it was a complication he couldn't begin to understand. It shouldn't make a difference, but somehow it did. It was like being within touching distance of nectar, but knowing that you were never going to reach it.

'What's the problem?' Matias asked. 'You saw how she reacted.' He paused. 'My mother has never discussed my life choices. Naturally, I've always known she disapproves, but to hear that disapproval voiced for the first time...'

He shook his head and turned the full wattage of his attention onto Georgina.

For a few seconds she was lost. This was a Matias she'd never thought she'd see. He was actually confiding in her, telling her things about himself that she knew he would never have told anyone—would probably never have admitted to himself.

A little voice whispered inside her: *A pretend engagement...with a man you're in love with...a man who, for the first time, is opening up about himself...*

It was hard not to feel quietly privileged.

It was also dangerous. And she banked down the seductive little voice that was beginning to question whether Matias perhaps felt more for her than he himself knew.

'It's a sign of how much closer you two have become in a short space of time,' she mused thoughtfully. 'She trusts you enough to say what's on her mind instead of holding it in.'

'So, back to the matter at hand.'

He slapped his thighs and stood up, all business now. That window of emotion had been shut. Georgina wished with all her heart that she could push it open again. Instead, she followed suit and moved to finish tidying the dishes.

'Back to the matter at hand?' she asked.

'Rings.'

'What about them?'

'We need to get one.'

'Why?'

'Come on, Georgie. An engaged woman always wears a rock on her finger.'

He moved to stand next to her and lifted her hand, inspected her finger.

She snatched her hand away. 'Surely that's taking the pretence too far? Has it occurred to you that when it comes to something as serious as an engagement I might actually want to wear a ring on my finger that *means* something? That's a declaration of intent from a guy who wants to go the whole hog and walk up the aisle with me?'

'No,' Matias said, dropping her hand and heading for the door, then spinning round on his heels to look at her before opening it. 'My mother's recommended some jewellers. I, personally, would rather get something in London, but perhaps a ring from somewhere local might carry more significance.'

'Did you hear a word I just said?'

'I heard every word. Are you telling me that you're not willing to go along with this?'

'No… I can see the upsides… I just thought you should know that—'

'Okay. Got it. Then let's go. We can wrap this up in a

couple of hours. My mother's appointment with the consultant is later this afternoon. I'll want to accompany her. If she sees a ring on your finger her spirits will be good enough to deal with the details of the operation.'

He was back to being the Matias of old. Assured, in charge, emotions firmly under lock and key.

Despite spending most of his adult life anywhere other than Cornwall, he still knew the roads and streets like the back of his hand, and they were at the jeweller's within forty-five minutes of leaving the house.

'One of my mother's daughters designs bespoke rings here.' Matias killed the engine outside an exquisite chocolate box house on a side street, sandwiched between a bridal shop and a high-end shoe shop. He looked at her wryly. 'In between her concerns over this upcoming operation, she managed to impart *that* gem of information.'

Georgina was gazing at the shop front. 'Emily Thornton?' she said. 'Have you any idea how expensive her stuff is?'

'Have you any idea how little I care about that?' He reached across her to push open the passenger door, then remained staring at her for a few seconds. 'You look as jumpy as a cat on a hot tin roof. It's just part of this charade we've signed up to.'

'I realise that it doesn't mean anything…'

'So you shouldn't feel anxious. Now, let's go and see what the finest jeweller in the West Country has to offer, shall we?'

Squashing the temptation to attach any significance to the choosing of an engagement ring, and making sure to keep at the forefront of her mind Matias's flat reminder that this was all just a continuation of the game *she* had initiated, Georgina eyed the array of glittering jewels brought out for their inspection.

There were no prices on any of them—which was alarming. The quality was stunning, and her mouth was dry when she casually pointed to the most gaudy of the rings on display.

'Funny...' Matias murmured under his breath. 'That's the last ring I would have pictured you choosing.'

Georgina shrugged, but got the feeling that he knew exactly what was going through her mind—she intended to save choosing a ring she truly loved for a guy she really cared about. It was a twisted version of the truth, but she was determined to play this game as coolly as he was.

When it was slipped onto her finger she stared at it, while the young sales assistant oohed and ahhed and told her that she couldn't have chosen anything more beautiful.

'Why don't you try that one, my darling?' Matias removed the ring and returned it to the girl, his dark, amused eyes firmly fixed on Georgina's face. 'Personally, I think an oversized diamond squatting on a band of gold isn't right for your delicate finger.'

Their eyes tangled—and then he reached out and picked the very ring she would have chosen for herself.

'There, now...' He held her hand up and inspected it from all angles. 'Much better. We'll take it.'

He paid, and Georgina stared at the delicate strands of interwoven rose gold and the small perfect diamonds that followed the strands. When she twisted her hand ever so slightly the strands almost seemed to move, like a thread. of liquid gold flowing over precious gems.

She shoved her hand down to her side, because when she looked at the ring the whole scenario felt way too real.

'Now,' Matias said, as they were leaving the shop, 'we'll collect my mother and take her to see the consultant.'

There was nothing romantic about this occasion. He had switched off the second they had left the jeweller's, and once in the car had promptly engaged himself in a lengthy conference call conducted partly in English, partly in Italian.

Georgina stared ahead, and started when he said, without looking at her, 'That gaudy bauble wouldn't have fooled someone as astute as my mother.'

'I still think we could have held off actually buying a ring. You could have said we wanted to choose something later, in London.'

'And deprive her of the pleasure of knowing that we'd found something locally? You know my mother when it comes to keeping it small and local. I have to admit she has a point when it comes to choosing a ring.' Without taking his eyes off the road he reached for her hand, held it up and glanced at the perfect band of gold. 'Like it?'

'It's fine.'

'You can keep it when this is all over.'

'Why would I want to do that?'

'Call it payment for services rendered.' He shrugged. 'But if you find that offensive, then by all means you can give it back to me. At any rate, we'll cross that bridge when we get to it.'

Georgina thought that he couldn't have succeeded better when it came to keeping things on a strictly business level.

She sat on her hand for the remainder of the journey to the house, staring straight ahead. Then it was all go as they took Rose to the hospital, where her consultant was waiting for her.

Her nerves were palpable, barely concealed under a flurry of questions about their choice of ring.

'It's going to be fine.'

Georgina continued to reassure the older woman and was pleased to notice, when they eventually reached the hospital, that she automatically reached for Matias's arm—a real indication of how much their relationship had progressed and confirmation that this make-believe engagement was the right thing to do.

The last thing Rose needed right now was the additional stress of worrying about Matias walking away. Not just walking away from *her*, Georgina now realised, but, in Rose's mind, walking away from the relationship which had slowly been building between herself and her son.

Did she perhaps think that a Matias returning to his former ways—a Matias whose only goal was making money, whose take on relationships was casual and dismissive—would also be a Matias who would no longer want to forge those filial bonds which had been missing for so many years?

Georgina sighed to herself, because it seemed as though by taking this step she and Matias might well have jumped from the frying pan straight into the fire. And, much as she wanted to adopt his approach to the situation, which was to take things one day at a time and only cross bridges when they got to them, she found herself chewing over all the worst-case scenarios that might arise.

While she waited for Matias and Rose to return from the lengthy consultation, she thought about the dangers inherent in this pretend situation that she so badly wanted to be real. She wondered how long they would continue the pretence…how long they would continue sleeping with one another. She felt helpless to end things. She wanted him so badly that she was willing to take whatever was on offer. And she hated herself for becoming so much like all those women who had preceded her.

And then there was the practical question of how they would conduct a long-distance relationship…

For the first time Georgina gave house room to thoughts of moving to London. Of course it was a nonsense, because she would never leave Cornwall to pursue the dream of being more to Matias than a casual affair. But if she were to be close at hand…

She was staring down at the ring on her finger when she heard footsteps and looked up to see Matias and his mother walking towards her.

'All booked for the day after tomorrow,' Matias said, looking from the engagement ring on her finger to the delicate bloom of colour in her cheeks.

'I thought I might as well get it over and done with.' Rose's voice was brighter than it had been. 'I've never believed in private healthcare, but I have to admit that it's a weight off my shoulders knowing that I don't have to wait weeks to have this operation. And, as Matias says, the sooner it's done, the sooner I can start enjoying wedding plans. That is, Georgie, if you won't find a middle-aged woman too intrusive? Of course your parents will be want to fly over as soon as they can… Alison's going to be beside herself with joy. You'll have to tell me what she says! I expect you'll want to phone her as soon as possible. It's wonderful, isn't it?'

CHAPTER NINE

'I'VE BEEN THINKING…' Georgina didn't look at Matias as she said that. She busied herself sweeping up the suit jacket he had discarded on the kitchen counter and the tie which he had dropped to the ground. The jacket would have cost what most people might earn in six months, and the tie was the softest of silk.

She had discovered that Matias treated his clothes with the casual disregard of someone who knew that he could snap his fingers and replace the lot at a moment's notice. However, it went against the grain for Georgina to accept this cavalier indifference to possessions that cost the earth.

'You've been thinking…?' Matias drawled, sitting on a kitchen chair and swivelling it so that he could stretch his long legs out in front of him.

Summer had abruptly turned into a rainy, bleak autumn, and outside the relentlessly blue skies had become a thing of the past. Now, a fine, persistent drizzle was drumming against the window panes. Nothing like the savage downpour that had accompanied that very first time they had made love, but weedy and insistent and never-ending.

Something smelled good. Georgina not only photographed food but had also proved herself to be more than competent when faced with cooking it.

'You're doing an awful lot of travelling to and from here.' She leaned against the counter and looked at him with clear, level green eyes. 'I've had a lot of interest after my last shoot—from people in London and a publishing house in France, of all places. I feel that it might further my career if I moved to London.'

She could have added that the frequency of his visits to Cornwall was no longer strictly necessary. It was over a month since Rose had had her operation, and she was now back on her feet and wondering why on earth Georgina wasn't thinking about moving to London.

'After all,' Rose had pointed out, 'it's not as though Matias is ever going to contemplate moving down here full time, and commuting can't be a long-term proposition. I'm back to rights, and if I'm going to be moving into something smaller in the village I shall feel quite capable of being on my own. You two need to think about what's going to work for you...'

Georgina thought uneasily about the engagement that had only been put in place as a temporary measure. She'd held off telling her parents, because she knew that involving more people than strictly necessary—especially her parents—would be to start hurtling down a dangerous slope, but the fact of the matter was that she and Matias were lovers, and still no mention had been made of timelines.

That being the case, this didn't seem too dramatic a step forward. Did it...?

'Is my mother behind this sudden decision?'

Something in his voice made the hairs on the back of her neck stand on end, and something in those cool dark eyes was setting alarm bells ringing in her head. However, having put one foot on this road, she now felt obliged to carry on.

'She *has* been wondering why you're continuing to commute. I know you spend a couple of days a week down here, but the rest of the time you're up and down, and she thinks it's weird for a newly engaged couple not to be trying to find a solution so that they can be together a bit more.'

'Is that a fact…?'

Matias stood up and strolled to the window to stare silently outside for a few seconds before turning back to look at her. His expression was shuttered, unreadable.

'I wouldn't normally consider moving as an option but, like I said, I've had a lot of interest from two companies in London and one in France. The Paris one is obviously… You know… Actually, they want to set up a meeting with me…'

She knew that she was stammering and her voice tapered off into a lengthening silence as he continued to look at her for a while without saying anything. Georgina recalled the knotted stomach she had had when she had first gone to his house to tell him of her hare-brained idea to rescue his mother from her downward spiral of depression.

The knotted stomach was there again.

'It's not what you want to hear?' she said flatly.

Matias inclined his head to one side. 'No,' he returned. 'It's not.'

'Why not?' Georgina asked bluntly.

'The fact is, I've been doing some thinking of my own.'

He glanced across to where a pot was simmering on

the stove, to the bottle of wine on the kitchen table, to the jacket and tie which had been neatly tidied away— all trappings of a domesticity he had always shunned.

'My mother is back on her feet. The operation was a success, as I knew it would be. She's now strong enough, in my opinion, to deal with the fact that there isn't going to be any walk down the aisle.'

His fabulous eyes were the colour of wintry seas and his expression was remote—the expression of someone retreating and walking away.

'Of *course* there's not going to be a walk down the aisle.' She felt sick, dizzy, and she was sure that it showed on her face because she could feel her colour draining away. 'That's not what this suggestion is about. Yes, it makes sense if this engagement is going to continue, but also I really have a chance of developing my career if I move out of Cornwall.'

'This is my fault,' Matias breathed with self-condemnation.

'I have no idea what you're talking about.'

'Don't you, Georgie?'

'No. I don't.' She kept her voice cool. 'And I wish I'd never said anything.'

'Look around,' Matias told her quietly. 'You're cooking for me...you're tidying up behind me... Somewhere along the line you've started the business of trying to domesticate me.'

'Matias, I'm doing no such thing! And please don't forget that it was *your* idea to take things one step further by pretending to be engaged! And if I'm cooking, and tidying up your clothes, have you stopped to think that it's because you happen to be staying in *my* house and I don't want to see clothes everywhere? And I have to cook for myself so I might as well cook for you as well.'

She tilted her chin at a defiant angle, and in return Matias looked back at her with appreciation.

'I'm not up for grabs, Georgie. And the reason I blame myself is because you were wet behind the ears and a virgin. I should have known that there was always going to be a danger that you might start confusing fantasy with reality…start thinking about a relationship I'd never have time for. I wanted you—and I took what I wanted because I'm a selfish bastard.'

Georgina's eyes flashed and she held his stare steadily. 'Don't try and take responsibility for this, Matias, and please don't try and make out that I want all this to be real. I might be inexperienced, but I'm not an imbecile. I didn't have to carry on sleeping with you after that first night. If you took what you wanted, then has it occurred to you that I did the same? Took what *I* wanted?'

'Is that your story and you're sticking to it?'

'I *haven't* started confusing reality with fantasy,' she said through gritted teeth.

And she hadn't. She knew that their engagement was a sham, but the truth was that she'd begun to hope… They'd slipped into a comfortable zone, and she'd started hoping that beneath that comfort there was something substantial for him, just as it had become substantial for her. She'd deluded herself into thinking that the sizzling sex and their easy familiarity amounted to more than it obviously did.

He hadn't been lulled into wanting her more because of what they'd ended up sharing. He'd ended up having to deal with just the sort of unwelcome expectations that got on his nerves.

'Okay.'

He shot her a crooked smile, which made her teeth snap together in frustration because of the disbelief he couldn't be bothered to conceal. But she knew that it should come as no surprise. His history with women told its own story, and she had chosen to ignore all the warnings he had put out there at her own peril. He was too astute when it came to the opposite sex not to have noticed those sidelong glances, the tender touches and, yes, that slide into domesticity that said more than words ever could about what they had and what it signified for her.

If, however, he thought that she was going to break down and start getting emotional, then he had another think coming—because no way was she going to do that.

'Perfectly understandable to call off the engagement at this stage,' she informed him. 'You're right. Rose is in a much better place now that the operation is out of the way and she's been given a clean bill of health. Also it suits me, because I can focus exclusively on seeing where my career takes me now that my field is expanding.'

'So you do intend to move to London?'

'Possibly. I don't know.' She fiddled with the ring on her finger, then removed it and slid it over to him. 'I don't want this. The thought of keeping something "for services rendered" makes me feel sick.'

'Georgie…' Matias stared at the ring but didn't pick it up. Instead he raised his eyes to hers and held her gaze. 'This is for the best.'

'I know,' she said sweetly. 'I think I've already heard that speech from you. Remember? When you were getting rid of the Amazonian blonde?'

'This is hardly the same sort of situation.'

Georgina shrugged. 'It is—more or less. It's a break-up… one that was always expected. But there's no need for you to spin the line about you being bad for me.'

'It wouldn't be a lie.'

'Nor would it be relevant.' She looked at him defiantly, challenging him to take her up on that statement. When he didn't, she continued, 'I'll talk to Rose…let her down gently.'

'You can leave that to me,' Matias muttered heavily. 'Like I said—and whether you choose to believe me or not—I blame myself…'

'If you want to be a martyr then I can't stop you. But I'm not blaming you, so there's no need for you to jump in and throw yourself in front of the train. At any rate you're no longer the bad guy in the story. You've built a great relationship with your mother. Don't jeopardise that by being the one to let her down. I don't want her assuming that you're leaving a heartbroken wreck behind because you couldn't resist returning to your revolving door love life.' She tilted her head at an angle, eyes cool.

'What will you say?' Matias asked, recognising the stubborn set of her jaw.

'That things didn't work out in the end but that we're going to remain good friends.'

She stood up and wondered how the rest of the evening was going to play out after this conversation. She couldn't see some cosy chat over the chicken casserole followed by a romp in the sack. What she *could* see was her howling to the four winds because the void opening up in front of her made her feel nauseous and lost and defeated.

'I'll leave now.'

Matias had read her mind and stood up. He hesitated

and Georgina spoke quickly, before pity could cloud his face and before he could reopen the conversation about it all being his fault.

'Good idea. I think that's for the best. Will you take all your stuff? Or I'm quite happy to drop it off to your mum's house.'

'Are you going to be okay?'

'Just go, Matias. The last thing I need is for you to tell me how sorry you feel for me. I always saw this coming and I'm absolutely fine.'

Still he hesitated, before finally turning round and leaving the kitchen—leaving her standing there on her own, unable to move a muscle.

She heard the sound of his footsteps receding, then eventually the sound of him coming down the stairs. She heard him pause and she knew that he was debating whether he should come over…say goodbye…make sure she hadn't stuck her head in the oven. Because she was obviously so pathetic that not only had she fallen for him but now—now that the rug had been pulled from underneath her fragile little feet—she would end up going to pieces and falling apart at the seams unless he produced some bracing words of encouragement.

Okay, so perhaps she *was* going to fall apart at the seams, and perhaps she *would* go to pieces, but she would do it in her own time and then she would start rebuilding her life. Away from Cornwall…away from the memories.

Matias stared moodily out of the window of his plush office on the thirtieth floor of a towering glass building which represented the very summit of what his vast reserves of wealth could achieve. Only the privileged few could afford to breathe the rarefied atmosphere up here.

Someone was saying something, and he registered that it involved making yet more money with yet another deal of even more magnitude than the last one.

Ten days.

Ten days since everything had crashed and burned, leaving behind a restlessness that got on his nerves. He'd always had complete control over his life, but for the first time he was floundering, and it was a sensation that was driving him crazy.

He'd spoken to his mother but hadn't enquired after Georgina's whereabouts. Several times he had begun to dial her number but had terminated the call before it could connect.

True to her word, she had told his mother exactly what she had said she would. His mother, predictably, had been bitterly disappointed, but she had dealt with the disappointment and had reached out to him to console him.

It was only now that he had engaged with her that he realised exactly how much distance he had allowed to settle between them. He had allowed his childhood experiences to dictate the outcome of his relationship with his parents and that had been a mistake. The fact that things were settling into a different place now had given his mother a renewed lease of life.

'If you two found that you couldn't make it work,' she had said sadly, when he had phoned her the day after Georgina had disappeared, 'then it's for the best that you called it a day before you took the next step forward and found yourself married. So much more difficult to unravel a relationship at that point.'

'We did our utmost to make it work, but I'm not the easiest person in the world to…er…to…'

His mother had interrupted him to assure him firmly

that no blame had been put on his shoulders. Since then, even though he had spoken to his mother every day, she had said nothing whatsoever about Georgina and pride had prevented Matias from asking.

She'd made her decision, he thought, and she would get on with her life. She was better off without him, anyway, whether she chose to believe that or not. And he'd had a narrow escape. He'd recognised the signs of her falling for him. She might not have admitted it, but he wasn't blind. Yes, far better that they'd parted company—and if she was still on his mind, it was because he was worried about her.

He was interrupted mid-thought by someone addressing him directly, and he turned round, frowning.

Six people were sitting around the glass and chrome conference table in his office, but for the first time in his high-powered, meteoric career Matias was finding it difficult to focus. With the decisiveness so typical of his forceful, aggressive personality, he told them, without preamble, that the meeting was over.

'My PA will be in touch tomorrow and my CEO Harper will carry on with proceedings from here on in.'

He was feeling better already—because he was doing something…taking charge of this vaguely uncomfortable situation that had been distracting him since she'd gone. He was sick to death of *thinking*.

He watched as everyone began gathering up their belongings after a brief moment of utter confusion. He waited. Not moving. Waited until they had all cleared out of his office then he got his mother on the phone.

Second by second, his mood was lifting.

'Where is she?' he asked, as soon as his mother had answered the phone.

'Darling, it's very nice to hear your voice,' Rose answered with some surprise. 'Would you be talking about Georgie?'

'You know I am, and tell me you're not avoiding my question…' he countered drily, settling into his leather chair and swivelling it so that he was staring out of the window to an uninterrupted view of milky blue sky.

'I feel that if Georgina wanted to get in touch with you then perhaps she would have,' Rose pointed out pragmatically.

'Granted. But…'

'But?'

He cleared his throat. 'I feel we still have some talking to do.'

'After all this time?'

'Ten days. That's not long. I… What is she up to? I… You know what I'm like… I want to make sure that she's…okay. Naturally I would phone myself, but if she wants some time out…' His voice tapered off.

'That's thoughtful of you, and you'll be pleased to hear that she's doing well, Matias. At least, that's what she said when I spoke to her the day before yesterday.'

There was another brief moment's hesitation, during which Matias jumped in, his voice irritable. 'Good! Glad to hear that she's doing well. Excellent!'

'She was very excited before she went,' Rose mused, 'but I could detect a certain nervousness underneath the excitement. Understandable, of course…'

'Went? Went where?' His senses were suddenly on red alert, his brain whirring round and round as he tried to compute what that throwaway remark meant.

'Did she not tell you? No, of course she wouldn't have, if you two haven't been in touch. Such a shame… I would have mentioned it to you, but, as I said, I felt that Georgina would tell you herself if she wanted you to know. Maybe she got the impression that you might not be interested?'

'Mother, where did she go?' Matias paused. Then, 'I just want to make sure that everything's all right with her.'

'Because you usually leave a string of broken hearts behind you, Matias? Not in this case. Georgina made it absolutely clear that *she* was the one with the second thoughts.'

Matias couldn't prevent an appreciative smile. He could just imagine the conversation. 'Where is she? If she's okay, then maybe I'm the one who isn't.' Something punched him in the gut, shaking his foundations.

'Oh, Georgina's taken a wonderful job,' Rose confided. 'She was offered it quite out of the blue… I think she was under the impression that most of the work would be done over here, but it turned out that they were so impressed with what they saw they invited her to go to Paris for a six-month secondment to work on a fabulous new magazine that's about to hit the streets there. Provincial French cooking. She's been asked to be the lead photographer. Such a great opportunity.'

'Paris? *Paris?*'

'I was a bit concerned as well, darling. You know our Georgie hasn't travelled far and wide. But she introduced me to the lovely guy she'll be working with…'

'Lovely guy?'

'Jacques something-or-other. Looks a little unconventional, but absolutely charming.'

'Jacques something-or-other…?' Matias gritted.

'Are you feeling all right?' Rose asked.

'Never been better. Sit tight, Mother. I'm heading down to Cornwall. I'll be there in a few hours.'

He didn't give his mother any time to question the decision. He knew what he had to do and he knew why he had to do it.

Paris?

Jacques something-or-other?

Georgina was in a fragile place. He had turned her away, just as he had turned away every other woman who had dared venture into the forbidden territory of wanting more than he was programmed to give. He'd been too abrupt—had overlooked the fact that she *wasn't* like all those other hard-nosed women he had dated in the past. She wasn't equipped to get past a broken relationship just by hitting the clubbing scene.

She'd been defiant and stood her ground, had denied every insinuation from him that she'd broken the rules of the game and fallen for him, but she had and she would be vulnerable. Vulnerable and in Paris. And that was a very bad combination, because vulnerable women had a way of appealing to just the kind of men they didn't need.

Who the hell was this Jacques character anyway?

He needed to find out exactly where she was! And if she needed to be rescued then, by God, he wasn't going to shy away from the task.

At last he was doing something. And he hadn't felt this good in a while.

It was after ten by the time Georgina stepped out of the taxi. The past week had been a frenetic round of social events, because everyone at the smart Parisian publishing house had wanted to make her feel at home and she couldn't have been more grateful.

She'd really needed this job—had yearned for the distraction it offered. She'd agreed to every term and condition and had been eloquent in persuading them that the sooner she was on board, the better. No sooner had the ink dried on the contract she had signed than she had been in Paris, ready to fling herself head-first into the commission—anything to lessen the pain of no longer having Matias in her life.

Accommodation had been found fast and everyone had gone out of their way to welcome her.

Tonight she had been for a casual meal in a lively bar with three of her colleagues and she was exhausted. Exhaustion was good, though, because the minute her mind stopped working in overdrive the thoughts began kicking in, and when that happened it was like spiralling down a bottomless hole.

Thoughts of Matias…of what it had been like with him and the way she had discovered that you didn't need to spend years finding out about someone to know that you loved them. It could happen in the snap of a finger. She thought about the way he had made her body sing, the things he would murmur when they made love. She hated it, but she was captive to the torment of remembering.

She was a million miles away when she became aware of someone stepping out of the shadows—a looming figure that sent her into a panic.

She didn't think. She acted completely on impulse. Because figures stepping out from the shadows were never going to be pleasant surprises.

She swung her handbag and she swung it hard. She aimed straight for the torso and she struck with perfect timing.

'Georgie!'

Georgina froze. She recognised that low, velvety voice instantly, but it still took her a couple of seconds to react, and then she sprang back and stared up, open-mouthed, as Matias straightened.

'Matias? *What are you doing here?*'

'I…' He shook his head and looked away briefly. 'I've come to talk to you,' he said in a low, driven undertone.

'Is that right? Well, I can't think of anything we have to talk about—and how did you get hold of my address? How did you even know where I was?'

'My mother told me.'

'She had no right.'

'She didn't think it was a state secret. Let me in, Georgie.' Matias paused. 'Please. Remember there was a time when you showed up at my house…did I refuse you entry?'

Georgina eyed him sourly. He was in black jeans and a black tee shirt and some kind of bomber jacket, and he looked utterly and unfairly drop-dead gorgeous.

'Time's moved on since then, wouldn't you say?' She was proud of how she sounded, which was a lot more controlled than she was feeling. 'One cup of coffee, Matias, and then I'm going to have to ask you to leave.'

They rode the elevator in silence, and she opened her front door and preceded him into the apartment without looking at him, although she was aware of his presence with every ounce of her perspiring body.

She dumped her handbag and the backpack holding her camera equipment on the granite counter separating the kitchen from the living room and faced Matias with her arms belligerently folded.

'Why are you here?'

'I had no idea that you'd taken yourself out of the country. Do you have anything to drink?'

Georgina gritted her teeth and glared. 'I have coffee. Like I said.'

'Anything stronger?'

'No.'

'I deserve this…' he muttered.

'You broke off an engagement that wasn't even an engagement.' Georgina shrugged. 'No big deal.'

'Why did you feel that you had to take a job over here?'

She flushed and her eyes skittered away. Her whole body was rigid with tension. Why had he come? She didn't want to *like* the fact that he was here, but she did. She didn't want her body to *feel* like this, hot and flustered and excited, but it did.

Would he ever stop having this sort of effect on her? she wondered despairingly. Would she bump into him in three years' time, when he had another woman hanging like a limpet off his arm, and feel this same surge of unwelcome attraction? Was that her fate?

'They made me an offer I couldn't refuse.' She lowered her eyes and started making a pot of coffee.

The apartment was purpose-built, in a new block, and the gadgets were all brand-new. It was very different from her parents' house, where everything harked back to days gone by, from the crockery to the appliances.

'I thought you were going to take something in London.'

'Does it matter? Is that why you rushed over here? Because you were concerned that I wouldn't be able to cope with a change of country?'

'You don't have much experience of big city living,'

Matias muttered. 'You've lived in a small village all your life.'

'I can't believe I'm hearing this.' Georgina dumped the cup of coffee in front of him and then sprang back and glared at him. 'How incompetent do you think I am, Matias? First you thought that you had to run as fast as you could because I'd made the mistake of falling for you! Did you think that I was daydreaming about actually marrying you and living happily ever after? With a guy who's made a career out of making sure he doesn't get too involved with a woman? Oh, yes, of *course* you did! I mention that I might find it helpful to move to London to progress my career and all of a sudden I've turned into a starry-eyed idiot who wants to settle down with you for real!'

She heard the ring of outrage in her voice and felt the sting of pain in her heart. She'd started deluding herself into thinking about happy-ever-afters. She'd been a fool and he'd run away for a very good reason. She would never admit what she felt for him to his face, but it was something she would never be able to hide from herself, and denying her love, as she was doing now, was an agonising reminder of the truth.

'It's possible you may have got that impression,' Matias muttered, not giving an inch, programmed to defend his choices, whatever the provocation.

'And second—' Georgina had to stop herself from yelling as she overrode his interruption '—to add insult to injury, you storm over here on a mission, I presume, to save me from myself!'

'Did I say that?'

'Pretty much, Matias! I'm a simpleton from Cornwall, who's so accustomed to village life that I couldn't possibly handle the trauma of big city living!'

'You're putting words into my mouth,' he said, but he was uncomfortably aware that that was precisely the impression he had given when he had shown up unannounced. The time had come to set the record straight. But setting records straight had never felt so momentous an uphill climb, and he was so far out of his comfort zone that he could scarcely corral his thoughts.

'I'm doing no such thing, Matias Silva!' She glared. 'That's *exactly* what you said! Did you think that I would find it all too much, living over here? In Paris? Well, for your information, I'm absolutely *loving* it over here!'

'Are you?'

'Yes! The job is invigorating! I'm learning all sorts of new camera techniques! I'm working alongside a talented crew of people and it's fabulous being in a corporate atmosphere instead of doing my own thing!'

'So you don't miss anything about…anything at all…?' Matias inserted roughly.

She tilted her chin at a challenging angle. The thought of him feeling sorry for her was unbearable. Had Rose somehow implied that she was having a miserable time over here? She had made sure to sound as chirpy as a cricket in all her conversations with the older woman! But had Rose heard the unhappiness in her tone of voice and mistakenly assumed it was down to the job rather than down to the fact that her heart had been broken in two?

'Nothing,' she asserted firmly. 'Nothing at all.'

CHAPTER TEN

MATIAS HESITATED. HE wondered if this was what it felt like to have one foot dangling over the edge of a precipice, with no safety net below. He'd become accustomed to exercising complete control over every aspect of his life, so this was a first, sitting here, staring at the woman who had been in his head ever since he had walked away from her, knowing what he had to do and what he had to say and yet fearful of an outcome he couldn't predict.

'I didn't come here because I thought you couldn't cope…with…with life in a big city…'

'That's not what you said.'

'And it's what I told myself when I decided to fly over,' Matias admitted unevenly.

Restless, he sprang to his feet, lean body taut with suppressed tension, and paced the small kitchen before sinking back into the chair. but this time leaning forward towards her, elbows on thighs.

'I told myself that I was worried about you…that it was a perfectly understandable reaction. But that's not why I came, Georgie.'

'Good.'

Something about the uncertain expression on his face was striking a chord inside her, eroding her determination to stand her ground proudly and get rid of him as fast as she could. Since when did Matias Silva ever look uncertain?

'I had to come. I had to talk to you.'

Georgina folded her arms and didn't say anything. Silence, he had once told her, was always a successful ploy when it came to getting other people to say things they might not have banked on saying. What better time to try it out for herself?

'I've been…thinking about you, Georgie… I haven't been able to focus…'

Georgina stiffened. He was a man who was only about sex—it didn't take a genius to figure out why she'd been on his mind. It would certainly explain the hesitancy on his face.

'In that case,' she told him coldly, 'you've had a wasted trip.'

'What do you mean?' He looked at her narrowly, but the ground was slowly giving way under his feet and he couldn't think straight.

'I *mean*,' she said quietly, as the energy for a fight seeped out of her, 'I'm not returning to any sort of relationship with you.'

'You're not?'

'Matias…' She tugged her fingers through her long, unruly hair and sat facing him, chin propped in her hand, green eyes sad and pensive. 'I know what this is about. You tell me that I've been on your mind…that you can't focus? I realise that what you want to say is that you miss the sex. But I won't be coming back to you to pick up where we left off until you get genuinely bored with me. We had a clean break and now I'm moving forward.'

'You can't be.'

Georgina laughed shortly. *How dared he?* 'Really, Matias? And why's that?'

'Maybe because *I'm* not, and I'm desperate enough to hope that I'm not alone in that.'

His voice was a mumble and she had to strain to pick up what he had said.

'I don't know what you're trying to say, Matias,' she told him bluntly, just in case hope started sprouting shoots and staging a takeover.

'I haven't come here because I miss the sex. I haven't come here to rescue you from your decision to leave England. I've come here because I *haven't* moved on.'

He sat back, swept his hands through his hair, his eyes not quite meeting hers, and then he sighed and pressed his fingers against his eyes.

'I never realised it before and maybe I should have,' he muttered in a shaken voice, watching as she inclined her head to one side, wary and attentive at the same time.

'What do you mean? And please don't spin me any stories, Matias. Don't say stuff you don't mean because you think it'll make me feel better or worse, or because you think it might get me back into bed with you. *What* have you never realised before?'

'When you waltzed into my house you were the last person I expected. You'd never been to see me before. You'd never expressed any desire to come to London. You'd never shown any interest in what sort of life I led there, or what sort of place I lived in. And yet...'

'And yet...?'

'And yet I wasn't fazed. I didn't stop to think about that. I should have. If I had, I would have realised that you and I...we have so much history between us. I've known you for ever.'

'And that's a *good* thing?' Georgina asked gruffly. 'Matias, you've always struck me as someone who likes novelty. Even when we embarked on…on the physical side of things, I got the impression that I was…a novelty…a change from your usual type of woman…'

'I deserve that.' He met her gaze evenly and then shook his head with regret. 'My priorities were cemented when I was too young to question them. My parents lived from one day to the next. I hated that…'

His voice was halting as he began to explore emotional territory he had always been loath to cover. He raked his fingers through his hair and realised that they weren't quite as steady as he might have hoped. The weird thing, he thought, was that she *knew* all of this—either by inference or because he had told her in some way, shape or form during the time they had spent together. And yet tension was snaking through him, strangling his vocal cords and blurring his thoughts.

'I don't suppose they ever gave it a moment's thought, but their lifestyle made me realise that the one and only thing I wanted from life was security. Financial security. I'd watched as they bounced from one scheme to another. I stopped focusing on the fact that they were perfectly happy doing that. I stopped focusing on the fact that their choices didn't impede on their responsibility as parents. I only saw…'

Georgina reached out and impulsively rested her hand on his, barely registering that he didn't remove it, that he covered it with his own.

'I suppose,' Matias said pensively, 'that going to boarding school conferred innumerable advantages upon me, but there were also warnings there that I was too young to interpret. I was an impressionable adolescent, and my parents' hippy lifestyle suffered in contrast to the well-ordered lifestyles of the well-heeled kids I was suddenly having to live with. I didn't envy what they had, but bit by bit I knew, whatever their private lives might have been, that financial security was something that *protected* them—like varnish on wood. By the time I left that school my ambitions were in place. And there was no room in that agenda for relationships.'

'So you enjoyed women for a while and then…then you moved on…?'

'Something like that.' He smiled crookedly—a heart-breaking smile that made her jaw tighten. 'But I'm straying off-topic here. I… I think I might need something stronger than coffee.'

'I have some red wine…' Georgina began, standing, but he wouldn't release her hand.

'Maybe not. Georgie, let's sit somewhere more comfortable.' He indicated the sofa in the sitting room of the open-plan apartment. 'Maybe I need to say what I need to say without the help of alcohol but not in an upright metal chair.'

'Am I going to like what I hear?'

'Depends on what you want to hear.'

'I'll withhold judgement until I've listened to what you have to say.'

But she knew that she was losing perspective. He was so…so much a piece of her…so spellbinding…just so beautiful… And right now he was as open as she had ever seen him, and that, in itself, riveted her attention and made her heart beat so fast that she wanted to pass out.

'When you walked through the door of my house that very first time it felt natural. I guess I should start with that. Though it was something that hardly registered with me then. Your scheme was crazy. It was also the most generous thing anyone could have done. Generous and impulsive. I turned you away because I was accustomed to being the one in control, and then, when I did decide to go along with your charade…'

'Your first idea was to get me to dress the part.'

Georgina gave him a tentative smile. She had given up trying to work out where this was leading. It was honest, and that was the main thing. She would deal with wherever it ended up when it got there.

'I couldn't resist you,' Matias said simply. 'Somewhere along the line, on some level I didn't consciously understand, I accepted that a change of wardrobe had nothing to do with the level of sexual pull you had over me. I don't think there was a single minute I didn't look at you without wanting to touch you. You have no idea what a big deal it was for me to make love to you that first time… You trusted me enough to gift me with your virginity and that wasn't just a big deal to you. It was a big deal to me too, even if I didn't appreciate just how big at the time. Didn't appreciate,' he tacked on roughly, 'just how privileged I was.'

Georgina tensed, reluctant to talk about it. She didn't want her emotional vulnerability paraded. She looked around her at the trappings of independence. *This* was the woman she was now, she told herself. She couldn't afford to succumb to the temptation of what he was saying.

'But you still got scared when I mentioned that I might want to see what London held for me,' she reminded him tautly.

'I reacted predictably.' Matias was honest. 'Everything seemed to coalesce in my head all at once. The fake engagement…the trappings of domesticity that had somehow taken over, bit by bit…the situation that suddenly felt like the sort of slippery slope downwards I had always avoided.'

Hot colour stung her cheeks. 'I never meant to try and trap you,' she said stiffly.

'But you had anyway.'

'How so, Matias…?'

She was determined not to wear her heart on her sleeve—not for a second time—but she knew that her voice was betraying that good intention.

'Somehow I'd managed to drift into a pattern of behaviour…commuting to and from London, coming down to Cornwall, taking my jacket off and slinging somewhere, accepting that you would do what you always did and pick it up, hang it up. And…'

He gave her a crooked smile.

'And tell me that I had more money than sense. I'm not sure when I started to accept that level of easy, cosy familiarity without automatically railing against it. I just know that something sparked inside me. Maybe it was the way I noticed you looking at that engagement ring, as though it was the real thing… Maybe it was when it struck me that I *liked* it—that I *liked* returning to your side, looked *forward* to seeing you…touching you…holding you…*talking* to you… But suddenly… I don't know… the shutters slammed down. Old habits die hard. I'd become so accustomed to assuming that love was something other people did that I reacted instinctively. I had to break off the engagement, had to escape, and I told myself that it was for the best.'

'You looked forward to seeing me? Talking to me?'

'You'd managed to tame me, and I couldn't even work

out when it had happened. I just knew that it scared the living daylights out of me, and the only way I could cope with that realisation was to run away from it as fast as I could.'

'I never knew...' she murmured softly.

Her heart was pounding, her pulses were racing and the time for games was over. He'd said so much, and now it was her turn to go the final mile and say what was in her heart.

'Why would you? I barely knew myself,' he said.

'I...' She took a deep breath. 'I never, *ever* thought we would end up in bed together. When we did, it felt so good, Matias, so *right*. Only afterwards, when the dust had settled, it slowly dawned on me that the reason it felt so good—the reason I hadn't had a moment's doubt about losing my virginity to you—was because I *loved* you.'

He moved to speak.

'Please don't say anything. Please let me get this off my chest and finish saying what I have to say. You've come this far to say your piece. Well, I might as well return the favour. Being engaged to you, even though I *knew* that it wasn't a real engagement, felt like a dream come true. I didn't like it that it did, but I couldn't pretend otherwise. And then, somewhere along the line, I started thinking that we got along so well... I fantasised that you might realise that it was more than just the fact that we got along between the sheets. But the weird thing was that even though I *knew* it was all going to end in heartbreak for me, I never regretted a single second of what we had.'

'And now here we are again.'

'I can't believe you've come all the way over here, but I'm glad you have.' *Glad that I've put my heart on the line, whatever the outcome.* It felt as if a weight had been lifted from her shoulders.

'I had to. I'm in love with you.'

Georgina had spun so many daydreams about Matias uttering those very words, and in all those daydreams she had squealed with delight and clapped her hands and smothered him in kisses. But actually, now that he had spoken them, what she felt was a spreading warmth, as though a candle had been lit inside her.

He pulled her towards him, manoeuvred her so that she was sitting on his lap and kissed her—a soft, tender kiss that melted everything inside her...a kiss she never wanted to end.

When, eventually, he drew back from her, she wished that she could bottle the loving expression in his eyes.

'So will you marry me, Georgie?'

'Do you even have to ask? Surely you must know the answer to that? Just try and stop me, Matias Silva.' She linked her fingers behind his neck and smiled. 'Don't forget you've already bought me the engagement ring of my dreams...'

Georgina heard the sound of Matias's car on the gravel outside and her heart leapt, as it always did at the sound of his arrival.

She looked around, making sure everything was just right. Dimmed lights. Candles on the table. The smell of wonderful food.

She had followed three of the fantastic recipes from the French cookery magazine on which she had worked. It had felt strange to look at the photos she had taken and attach them to the recipes she'd so diligently followed.

Her stint in Paris felt like a lifetime ago, but then,

as she'd reflected on more than one occasion, it would, wouldn't it? Because so much had happened since then.

On that dreamy morning after the night when every single wish she'd ever had and a million more she hadn't even been aware of having had all come true, she'd woken up with Matias next to her in bed. In her wonderful apartment in Paris.

'I've been thinking,' he'd drawled, pulling her against him so that their warm, newly awoken bodies were pressed against each other. 'You should stay here and finish what you've started. I have an office in Paris and, coincidentally, I also have an apartment. We could have some fun here together before we return to London.'

They'd had a lot of fun. Her six-month secondment had been absolute bliss. She'd debated whether to remain in her own apartment, but in the end it had seemed silly because she'd spent so much of her time with Matias—who, in fairness, hadn't objected when she'd wanted to go out with work colleagues on her own, and had always been willing to accompany her if she asked.

They'd returned to London and the preparations for their big day had begun in earnest, with Rose having a lot of input—more than Georgie's own mother, who had descended in a flurry of excitement only a month before the big day.

Which, as it happened, had been just the right size sort of day. Friends, family, a handful of her work colleagues—including some of the people she had met in Paris, with whom she was determined to stay in contact. And some of Matias's colleagues as well—a couple of whom had privately confessed to her that they'd never thought they'd see the day.

Nor had he, she'd wanted to say.

They were married in the local church in Cornwall, and then he'd whisked her away to the Maldives for their honeymoon.

It was the first real holiday he had ever had as an adult. Which was just one of those incidental admissions that made her see how much he trusted her by confiding in her.

And as soon as they'd returned the big decision had begun as to where they would live.

Not Cornwall, and Georgina was happy with that—especially after her stint in Paris, where she had tasted life in a big city, and not just in the capacity of tourist. She had made numerous connections while she had been out there.

She'd told Matias she was happy to acquiesce to life in his London house, which was big enough to house a small battalion. But Matias had looked at her thoughtfully and suggested that perhaps London wasn't quite the place for them.

'At least, not central London,' he had mused. 'I think I've become accustomed quite quickly to having peaceful downtime with you. Without the sound of traffic outside my front window.'

'You hardly live on a busy street over a parade of shops, Matias,' Georgina had pointed out wryly, which had made him burst out laughing.

In the end they had decided to move out towards Richmond. Close enough to the city for Matias to commute—although he was fast discovering the joys of flexible working hours which, as the guy who ran the whole show, he could take at the click of a finger.

The house was enormous by London standards, with

a sprawling garden, and the entire transaction had been completed in record time. Money talked.

Now they had been living here for a little over four months and…

Georgina looked around her. Looked at the beautiful kitchen table, the impeccable worktops, the flagstone tiles on the floor which they had chosen together.

Every single little thing had been hand-picked. Having lived under her parents' roof while they were on the other side of the world, Georgina had been able to bring precious little to the table, so Matias had insisted on starting from scratch.

She looked up to see the man of her dreams standing in the doorway. He had shed his coat and was rolling up the sleeves of his white shirt, but he paused, eyebrows raised, taking in the table-setting.

'Tell me I haven't missed an important anniversary,' he drawled, smiling and pulling her towards him so that he could kiss her—a long, lingering, loving kiss.

Georgina breathed in his unique, woody smell, clean and musky at the same time, and as powerful an aphrodisiac as anyone could ever dream up. She wound her hands round his body and slipped her fingers under the waistband of his trousers.

'Nope…' she breathed a little unsteadily. 'My birthday isn't for another few weeks and there's no anniversary yet.'

'In that case…?'

He nodded to the elaborate setting and she smiled and tugged him into the kitchen, fingers linked, where she poured him a glass of wine while he peered into the oven, sniffing the aroma appreciatively.

'I just wanted the right mood board to tell you what I have to tell you.'

'Which is…?' He held her at arm's length and looked her directly in the eye.

'When I showed up on your doorstep and informed you that you were going to be my loving boyfriend,' she said seriously, which made his eyebrows shoot up with rampant amusement, 'I never thought that a year later I would be wearing your ring on my finger and I'd have gone from pretend loved-up girlfriend to wife for real…'

'Tell me about it… One minute I was dispatching a blonde because watching paint dry was turning out to be more fun than being with her, and the next minute my life was being turned upside down by a girl who'd been holding me to account from the day she'd learned to speak her first word…'

Georgina grinned, then stepped towards him and stroked the side of his cheek with the back of her hand. '*Someone* had to hold you to account, Matias Silva. But now that we're happily married it seems a little selfish to keep you all to myself, so I've decided to share you.'

'With…?'

'Gender to be decided. I should tell you that for the first couple of years conversation might be a little limited, but I can guarantee that you'll be in love with him. Or her.'

She patted her still flat stomach gently and then smiled when she saw his reaction, because it was everything she could have hoped for and more.

'My darling…' Matias breathed huskily. 'I love you so much.' He covered her hand with his. 'I don't know how I ever survived before you stormed into my life and took charge, even if you didn't know you were doing it…'

He grinned and nuzzled the side of her neck, and when their eyes met his were so full of love that the breath hitched in her throat and her eyes welled up—which was crazy.

'I'm going to be the best husband it's possible to be, Georgie, and the best father. And now…' He looked over her shoulder to the impeccably laid table. 'I think the food can wait for a bit, because I can think of a few more inventive ways for us to celebrate…'

* * * * *

PREGNANT
BY THE
COMMANDING
GREEK

NATALIE ANDERSON

For Kathleen,
your relentless perseverance and efforts
are such an inspiration to me—you rock!

CHAPTER ONE

'WHAT DO YOU MEAN, he wants us to "get rid of it"?' Antoinette Roberts scooped up the small, greying terrier and clutched him close. 'Doesn't he realise that "it" is a gorgeous, living creature?' She glared at Joel, her junior colleague.

'I don't think he does, Ettie,' Joel answered in an agitated whisper. 'He just stormed in here first thing and demanded access to Harold's apartment and started clearing stuff out.'

'You're kidding?' Disgust surged through Ettie.

Cavendish House, an exclusive apartment building in the heart of London's Mayfair, offered full concierge service to its privacy-loving residents, and, as head concierge, Ettie was used to delivering it for her demanding guests; from everyday mundane queries to the most outrageous, extravagant requests.

She didn't just arrange parcel deliveries and make restaurant bookings, she sourced rare first editions of famous novels and cajoled Michelin chefs to cook in a resident's apartment to help create the perfect proposal... And she was proud of the service she worked hard to provide. Until today there'd been no request she hadn't been able to fulfil.

But she drew the line at the euthanasia of a perfectly healthy, beloved pet on a total stranger's *whim*.

'I suppose George let him in?' she growled.

Joel nodded.

That'd be right. George, the building manager, was obsequious to clients, pernickety with petty rules while sloppy with what was actually crucial, and a belligerent bully to the personnel. Ettie spent half her time fixing his blunders and soothing staff resentment when he'd blamed them.

It was her fault it had got this far with the dog. She'd arrived late for the first time in years because she'd been up most of the night counselling her stressed-out sister, Ophelia, who was panicking that she'd flunked her latest physics test. Not that Ophelia had flunked a test in her life. Fiendishly academic, she was away at boarding school on a partial scholarship. Ettie was paying the rest of the fees and Ophelia was desperate to secure a university place. That meant another scholarship, which in turn meant outstanding results in every assessment in this last year of her schooling. As amazing as Ophelia was, Ettie worried the pressure was too intense. But she wouldn't let Ophelia give up her dream. Ettie had sacrificed too much herself to allow that. So, after calming Ophelia, she'd lain awake fretting about how she could better financially support her. Since their mother's death two years ago, it fell to Ettie to make it happen.

But making things happen was what Ettie did. She'd learned and worked for it, making miles-long lists and instituting systems so her sometimes impulsive and distraction-prone self wouldn't forget anything. But today she'd lapsed into her natural disorder. She'd overslept, in her mad scurry she'd missed breakfast, lost her last hair tie and resorted to using an old rubber band, and still missed her train.

When she'd finally raced into Cavendish House this morning, it was to the shocking news that her favourite long-term resident, Harold Clarke, had been rushed to hospital in the small hours of the night. While his passing had been quick and peaceful, his family—the family Ettie hadn't seen visit once in the five years she'd been working there—was already on the premises and clearing out his treasures. Apparently they didn't regard Toby, Harold's small terrier, as a treasure. They'd sent him down for Joel, her junior concierge, to "get rid of".

If Ettie had been at work on time, that nephew would never have made it into the apartment, let alone cast his callous instructions for Toby.

'Ettie, there's something else...' Joel called after her.

Not now there wasn't.

Shock, grief and sheer fury overrode the caution and calm she'd schooled within herself over the years. Ettie tightened her hold on the small dog and impulsively swept to the lift. Appalled by that uncaring request, she'd no time for niceties or other distractions. The family were monsters.

At the slide of the doors, Ettie stepped out onto Harold's floor. His apartment door was open and curt voices echoed along the corridor. She stalked the length of it, unconsciously stroking the soft fur of the small dog. A quick glance into the room showed George on the far side looking as smarmy as ever, next to an older-looking couple. All three were facing a tall man who had his back to her but, given the sullen looks on the faces of the others and the iceberg-thick atmosphere, he wielded the power. His immaculate appearance and crisply clipped hair enraged her all the more. He was obviously loaded because the impeccably tailored suit was clearly bespoke. No off-the-rack number ever fitted so perfectly—lovingly emphasising his height and strength. Though most men didn't have perfect physiques either. One look and she knew he was fit, healthy and wealthy. So why did he need to be so greedy over Harold's assets? Why be so *cruel*?

'You shouldn't be in here.' Ettie didn't hesitate stepping into the room.

How could he not have visited Harold in all this time and yet turn up the second he thought there were valuable possessions to be claimed?

'You don't storm in here and start stripping out Harry's assets and condemning his dog to instant death.' She barely paused to draw breath. 'You want to us to "get rid of" Toby?' Her voice quivered but she stood straight, not letting the tremble in her knees spread to the rest of her.

Because the man had turned around and Ettie was rendered breathless. He was much taller than her and younger than she expected. No older than thirty. But it was his face that stopped her—he had the sharpest, most handsome face she'd ever seen. High cheekbones, a straight nose, a full mouth, a cleft in his chin and a square, relentlessly masculine jaw…and to cap it off, deep brown, unbearably intense eyes. Brown eyes usually held some warmth, right? Not his. She'd never encountered either such beauty or such coldness. He was totally intimidating.

But it seemed he wasn't left as much breathless as speechless. Good. It was obviously time someone challenged him and his appalling instructions. Inhaling sharply, Ettie recovered enough to continue her attack.

'Toby is the sweetest little dog ever, not that you'd know because you never visited him or Harold in all this time…' Her voice trembled as she thought of the quiet elderly man who'd been gentle. And so alone. 'Now it's barely five minutes after…and you want Toby put down? Are you even human?'

George cleared his throat. 'Ettie—'

'You're not going to get away with it,' she carried on passionately, too steamed up to let George and his lack of spine stop her from telling this jerk some home truths. 'I won't let you.'

She became aware Joel had arrived and was breathlessly standing beside her, an appalled but fascinated expression on his face. The older couple present didn't look at her at all but stared at the tall stranger with silent, seething resistance. She knew how they felt.

The man's arctic glare sharpened on her, pinning her with almost visceral force. 'Who are you?'

She refused to quake. 'I think that's my question. You're the one trespassing.'

'I think not,' he said softly. There was a faint foreign tone to his cutting, cold accent.

George was frantically doing some kind of dance behind the arrogant ass's back. But she paid no attention—she was too incensed. The guy needed to be schooled. Tired and strung out and sad, Ettie couldn't hold back her contempt. 'You've never once set foot in this place before now.'

'No.' His quiet confirmation sounded stronger than George's audible gasp.

'You're despicable,' Ettie told him.

'Despicable?' He glanced behind him and caught George midway through miming self-strangulation. He turned back to face her. 'I think what your colleague is trying to convey is that you've made a mistake.'

There was the slightest curl to the man's lips—as if he was deriving some small, hideous pleasure from this moment.

Ettie frowned, not comprehending. She was still puffed from the force of her emotions and her furious dash up to the apartment. 'I'm not Mr Clarke's nephew,' he informed her with brutally cold precision. 'In fact, I'm no relation whatsoever to Mr Clarke.'

Nonplussed, Ettie blinked. Now she took a moment to study him, he didn't look anything like Harold. This man's hair was dark and thick and his eyes were that wintry brown, not blue, and his bronze complexion was more than a summer tan. A wave of relief so strong it was shocking rippled through her. He wasn't an animal-murdering brute?

Then she was hit with a wave of something else altogether. Something from deep inside, so hot and intense that she refused to acknowledge, let alone define it. Because it was *shocking*.

'Then what are you doing in here?' she snapped uncharacteristically. But she was determined to halt the appallingly inappropriate, *intimate* direction of her thoughts. Why was everyone looking at him as if he was ridiculously important? Why was George turning greener by the second?

'You've made a mistake.' His gaze drifted over her uniform in an inspection so quick it was almost insulting. 'And yet I think you're this star concierge I've heard about. Cavendish House's very own Girl Friday.'

She had a sudden prickling sensation that a giant black hole had opened up before her, but that she'd already taken the fatal step. It was too late to stop—the fall was in play and there was no way to backpedal and stop herself tumbling into a bottomless pit.

'My name is Leon Kariakis. And as of close of business last night, I own this building.'

Leon Kariakis? *The* Leon Kariakis? Serious, publicity-averse, wealthier-than-most-small-countries Leon Kariakis?

Ettie stared at him, slack-jawed. Oh, yeah, she'd fallen into one never-ending crevasse. All she could do was comment stupidly, 'You own…' she drew in a breath and tried to regroup '…and you're not—'

'No relative. This man is Mr Clarke's nephew and I've

already spoken to him and his wife about Mr Clarke's belongings. Nothing will leave this building until the executor of his will has been to the premises and itemised everything.'

The other man began to bluster but Leon Kariakis turned and quelled him with a filthy look. 'Is it true you instructed the staff to get rid of the dog?'

The nephew didn't respond.

'Is it true?' Leon Kariakis demanded an answer.

'I didn't mean—'

'Evidently it was very clear what you meant.' Leon cut the man off. 'You will leave immediately.'

'You can't throw us out.'

'I think you'll find I can,' Leon Kariakis replied softly. The atmosphere chilled even more, his physical threat apparent even though he didn't move an inch. If Leon Kariakis wanted to manhandle this guy out of the apartment, he'd do so with ease. And the sorry excuse for Harold's family knew it.

Ettie's heart raced faster than a puppy chasing a pigeon. Since when was Cavendish House even on the market? And to be bought by Leon Kariakis? Even she'd heard of the serious son of the incredibly rich Kariakis holiday empire. His parents owned a number of swanky five-star hotels on the continent, but sole heir Leon had gone into finance, making even more eye-watering amounts of money in an unseemly short amount of time. Apparently buying up exclusive residential apartment buildings was his new hobby. And she'd just called him out—accusing him of animal cruelty and disgusting greed.

'This isn't over, Kariakis,' the nephew blustered. 'You'll be hearing from our lawyers.'

'I look forward to it,' Leon replied tersely. 'I imagine they'll be much more pleasant to deal with than you.'

Ettie bit down on her lip to stop her unbidden smile as the nephew and his wife stomped out of Harold's apartment. They didn't so much as look at her, or the small dog she was still cuddling. But neither she nor Toby were out of the woods yet. All-powerful, super-serious, still scowling, Leon Kariakis wouldn't have appreciated her shouting at him in public like that.

'Everyone else, please leave as well.' He seared her with an icy glance. 'Except you.'

Yeah, she'd just lost her job.

George stepped in. 'Mr Kariakis, I'm terribly sorry for this misunderstanding. Ettie is always—'

'I'll meet with you later.' Leon Kariakis's snappy dismissal brooked no argument.

George shot her an irritated look that she ignored, even though she knew he'd been about to throw her even further under the bus. She was fine. She could handle it. But her heart thudded as her Joel reluctantly left too.

She turned to face the music, disconcerted to discover Leon Kariakis was still watching her and still wasn't smiling. Indignation surged and she lifted her chin at him. She'd been doing her job—protecting her client's pet—and she wasn't going to apologise for that. The silence echoed in the apartment. Even Toby, the dog, didn't stir in her arms, but she stroked him regardless.

'You're Antoinette Roberts,' he said quietly. 'Cavendish's Girl Friday. I've heard much about you and yet…'

She'd disappointed him?

Too bad. Even though she knew she was about to lose her job, she felt a small flush of pride that he'd been told about her. What had he said before—star concierge? Yet she couldn't claim any praise as entirely her own. Joel and the other guys were always willing to help.

'I have a very good team,' she said.

He kept regarding her steadily, but no warmth soft-ened his eyes.

She should probably apologise for mistaking him for one of Harry's mean relatives, but suddenly she couldn't get her voice to work. Awareness trickled down her spine as the tension within her transformed. She'd loathed him on sight, only now…it was another emotion stiffening her spine. And it was just insane. Ettie Roberts did *not* lust after anyone. Ettie Roberts was far too sensible.

But Leon Kariakis was abnormally handsome and the way he was looking at her right now was unbearably in-tense. It was only that, mixed with relief that he wasn't a cruel tyrant out to murder an innocent animal, that made him all the more attractive in this moment, right? It wasn't *real*. Leon Kariakis wasn't someone she'd ever be inter-ested in and he'd certainly never be interested in her.

A sudden wave of defensiveness let her mouth slip the leash. 'If you're going to sack me, just get it over with.'

There was another moment of profound silence. She burned with a horrible mix of embarrassment, nerves and resentment. She hated how calm and in control he was. Even when she'd shouted at him he hadn't lost his ice-cool composure.

'You don't like uncertainty?' He watched her steadily.

'I don't like being kept waiting.'

His eyebrows shot up. 'I'm taking the time to think.'

'Does it usually take you this long?' She didn't mean to be rude, but it surprised her. He was incredibly successful and she bet he hadn't become so by mulling over trivial decisions about low-level staff.

But wasn't she was doing him a disservice? He'd already stood up to those horrible, grasping relatives before she'd even arrived and he'd had no hesitation in showing them the door. She was finally about to offer a shamefaced, be-lated apology when he spoke.

'I've found that giving a problem my full consideration, rather than making a snap judgment, results in a better night's sleep for me.' He offered the slightest sarcastic curve to his lips in lieu of an actual smile.

She'd made a snap judgment that he was Harold's nephew, and this was an unsubtle rebuke for that. Yet it wasn't his reprimand that bothered her. It was another rip-ple of that forbidden feeling slithering down her spine. She did not need to be thinking about sleeping—specifically *him* sleeping—at this moment. And she did not need to be wondering what he'd look like with an actual, genuine smile on his face when he was already this attractive.

He studied her for another long moment and his gaze lowered to the resting creature in her arms. 'The dog is old,' he said bluntly.

'So that means we should just put him down?' she asked scornfully, her outrage torched again. The debate was on and she was fighting for Toby.

'He'll miss his owner,' Leon answered with surprising softness. 'He'll fret.'

The note of compassion from him oddly made her more uncomfortable.

'So we find him someone who can be with him all the time so he has the companionship he needs while he grieves.'

He reached out and petted the dog's head gently. Ettie froze, stunned by the illicit surge in her body at his close-ness…the craving.

'He can't go to a shelter,' she added.

She couldn't help staring at Leon. She'd never seen someone as handsome, or as serious, and suddenly he felt more of a danger to her than when she'd thought him to be a heartless brute or when she'd thought he was going to fire her. The unaccustomed response within her to his fierce masculinity was shocking.

She whipped up her resistance. She didn't want to *like* him. Of all the moments for her stagnant sensuality to spark up…

'Would you take him?' Curiosity burned in his eyes.

'I would,' she answered without hesitation. 'Except I'm at work all hours and he'd be lonely. And I'm not allowed pets in my building.'

'Pets aren't allowed in these apartments either,' he muttered. 'Isn't that the rule the previous owner implemented?'

'No resident ever minded Toby. He's lovely and he was around before that petty rule came into force.' She looked down at the dog protectively. She'd disliked that owner who'd wanted to charge more but offer less. He'd employed the awful George to enforce the 'new way'—most of which involved paying the staff less for more onerous rules and rosters, which had led to that festering resentment and feeling as if they couldn't be trusted. Ironically, the rumour was that the absent owner had got into money trouble… and now she was faced with this guy.

'You aided and abetted Mr Clarke in keeping Toby a secret, didn't you?'

They all had. But Ettie lifted her chin; she wasn't about to offer excuses or drag her friends under with her. 'Are you going to sack me for it?'

He remained impassive but she sensed his assessment. And his judgment. 'That depends. What other rules do you break?'

'Just the stupid ones.'

He watched, waiting for her to expand on her answer, but she refused. She was not going to desperately fill the awkward silence he was deliberately leaving. And she was not going to let his stunning looks have a stupefying effect on her brain any longer either. She was here for Toby—for the last thing she could do for old Harold Clarke.

'He needs to be in a familiar environment,' she said. 'Given he's not a nuisance to anyone, you should allow Toby to remain in Cavendish House, don't you think?' she asked with more defiance than deference in her voice.

Because more than anger bubbled within her at his silent appraisal and that stern stare beneath those slightly pulled strong eyebrows.

She tore her gaze from him and desperately looked around Harold's apartment to remind herself of her mission. The old man had been their longest resident. He'd mostly kept to himself, but he'd been kind and his dog had been his world. He'd protected the vulnerable even when he was vulnerable himself. 'We owe it to Harold to take care of Toby.'

'We?'

'Yes.' She lifted her chin pointedly and looked back at him. 'Why can't you take him?' she challenged directly.

There was another moment of total silence, but as she gazed into his eyes, the amber light within them flared. 'No reason that I can see,' he muttered.

She blinked. 'Pardon?'

'Toby will move to my penthouse. You'll take him for fresh air.'

Her jaw dropped. He wanted her to go to his penthouse? 'You want him to sleep in your apartment?'

'It's a temporary arrangement,' he said brusquely. 'On the condition that you walk him. You feed him. I do nothing but provide the space.'

The sizzle she felt was just her, right? She gave herself a mental shake. Just because he was insanely good-looking didn't mean she had to turn into a twittering ditz. She'd pull herself together and get the job done. 'You want me to—'

'Morning and night obviously. Yes.' He turned that cool demeanour on her and dared her to object.

Ettie was so stunned, she couldn't help questioning him. 'Why can't you walk him?'

The coldness that entered his expression now stunned her. 'We'll find a more permanent solution in a few days. In the meantime, there'll be no disturbance to the other residents.'

She was shocked. 'You really want me to—'

'Do I really need to repeat myself?'

'No. Of course not.' She stilled, annoyed with his superciliousness. Usually she'd say 'sir', but she was struggling to suppress her rebellion and tell this guy what for again. He couldn't walk or feed the dog himself? Was he for real?

And yet he'd just offered up his own space to ensure Toby's safety and security, so that the vulnerable little dog could stay.

What the hell had forced that foolish suggestion from him? Leon Kariakis smothered his growl and gritted his teeth. He didn't want anything to do with the dog. The ancient, arthritic creature was most probably incontinent and most definitely going to be a pain. Except he was a sweet-looking thing with the saddest eyes Leon had ever seen, and there was no way he could resist reaching out again to soothe the boy with a gentle pat. As he pulled back, he inadvertently brushed his fingers on Antoinette's arm. He glanced up to her face. Sea-green, luminous, emotion-drenched eyes glared back at him.

Why was she looking so angry again now?

He was the one who ought to be put out. And truthfully he was still oddly angered by her assumption he was the selfish bastard who'd issued the instruction to destroy the innocent creature. Somehow he wanted to make her pay for the conclusion she'd so swiftly, and unjustly, leapt to.

Not *somehow*.

His body knew *exactly* how he wanted her to pay. He wanted her to keep looking at him with those overly emotional green eyes, but not with anger and judgment. He wanted to see hunger and willingness. *Desire*.

Basic instinct roared. Because he knew it was there within her too. She'd studied him anew once she'd realised her error. And she'd responded on the same basic level as he had—the sparkle of awareness in her eyes, the flush in her face, had given her away.

He wanted her beneath and about him. His primal response to her passion shocked him. He wanted her in the most animal, basic of ways.

It was the most inappropriate thought of his life. Lusting after her was wrong. He was staying in the building for only a week or so to understand its processes first-hand before deciding on what changes needed to be made. The last thing he should do was flirt with one of the staff who was literally in his firing line. She was off-limits and he was never that out of control. Ever. This was a situation that required a swift conclusion. Yet he couldn't resist getting involved directly.

'You'll need to bring the dog and all his accoutrements.' He checked his watch and then glanced back at her.

'Yes, of course.' She lifted her chin.

The action didn't make her any taller. She remained a smidgeon shorter than the average woman and slight through the shoulders. Her dark blonde hair was swept off her face into a loose, messy ponytail and her wide green eyes offered unusually clear reflections of her feelings.

She wasn't the sleek automaton he'd envisaged when

he'd been told about her. She wore barely any make-up—as far as he could tell, there was little more than a slick of lip gloss. Yet her skin was smooth, unblemished and glowing. The uniform black trousers and monogrammed T-shirt she wore did little to reveal much of her figure, but what they did show was slim and the suggestion of fit. His overall impression was of supple, fresh femininity. He'd been accosted by another of the more elderly residents in the lift this morning who'd been at pains to tell him that Antoinette Roberts was the only reason he'd remained at Cavendish House in recent years.

One look at her and Leon understood why.

But she wasn't his type. She'd spoken to him in a way no one else dared to. Tearing strips off him with blunt, brutal honesty, not stopping to censor herself or having the slightest hesitation in telling him what she really thought. Her heart wasn't just on her sleeve, she was waving it on a flag in front of him.

It was extremely novel. In his life, communicating emotions had not only been discouraged, but also punished. As his parents had ruthlessly taught him, any kind of emotional display was a weak loss of self-control.

Yet he didn't want Antoinette to start picking her words with care now. He liked knowing, without any uncertainty, exactly what she was feeling. And it was her fierce protectiveness that riveted him. Like a lioness protecting a lone cub, she'd held her corner and not given an inch, no matter the possible personal cost to herself. She'd fully expected him to fire her. But Leon knew people made mistakes. He'd give her one chance to redeem herself.

'Be on time. Always. I don't like to be disturbed,' he said roughly.

'I can be discreet,' she answered defiantly.

He simply stared at her. As if she could come into his

apartment unseen? Unheard? As if she could ever be anything but disruptive?

A thread of wicked amusement trickled through him as she stilled in the face of his silence. He knew the exact moment she mentally replayed her words and realised an alternative innuendo. The same intimacy-drenched scenario he was imagining. A deep rose burnished her creamy skin—her cheeks, her neck, even the small hint of skin he could see at the vee of her high-collared T-shirt. But then he registered the rebellion in her gaze again—together with her less than subtle attempts to suppress it.

He didn't want her to suppress anything.

The urge to haul this petite emotional tornado close and kiss her into a frenzy of desire almost felled him. Grimly he fought the need to provoke her into taking everything else she might want from him. He knew he could. He saw the awareness in her eyes. Women found him attractive and sex was a fun relaxant. But he'd bet that sex with Girl Friday here wouldn't be as much fun as mind-blowing. If the incandescence of her anger was anything to go by, in bed she'd be unrestrained and utterly responsive.

Sex of the best kind. The kind that was irresistible.

He knew she felt the sparks. They were why she'd flushed over her choice of words. Why she'd trembled at his inadvertent touch before. Why she was looking at him with unrestrained rebellion now. Because she didn't want this chemistry either. And that irritating rejection was precisely why he couldn't resist making what he knew would be a massive mistake.

He roughly pushed the request past the tightness in his throat. 'I want you in my apartment in one hour.'

CHAPTER TWO

'WHY DIDN'T YOU tell me?' Ettie groaned to Joel as soon as she safely got back into the small concierge office, Toby still in her arms.

'I didn't have the chance...'

Of course he hadn't. Ettie shook her head and stopped him, regretting her unfair question. 'Sorry, I know you didn't.'

'Don't you think he's out of this world?' Jess, one of the housemaids, leaned over her desk. 'Chloe saw a model-type leaving his penthouse late last night. She was in the lift. Really dishevelled.' She waggled her eyebrows in a suggestive gesture. 'First night in and he's already—'

'No gossip,' Ettie whispered loudly, but softened her rebuke with a smile at the maid.

The news didn't surprise her. Of course he'd bed models. He was as striking as a model himself. He'd have no trouble getting any woman he wanted into bed. Even she'd responded to him on a purely primal level. He was so handsome it was almost painful. He was extraordinarily uptight, though, and he had a way of looking as if he could see right through her, while at the same time revealing nothing of his own thoughts.

Unabashed by Ettie's warning, Jess just laughed. 'Well, I think he's gorgeous. I'd do him.'

'He's an unsmiling ogre,' Joel grumbled. 'An arrogant jerk who thinks he's special.'

Well, with his obvious physical strength as well as his business success, he was a bit special. He had it all—looks, wealth, women…success.

'He was unfairly harsh with you, Ettie,' Joel added. 'And as for George…'

Yeah, it was no surprise that her boss was nowhere to be seen—hiding out until the dust had settled, no doubt. But she smiled at the hint of protectiveness in Joel's voice. 'He'll be even harsher if I don't get all that stuff up to his apartment within the hour.'

'Do you want help?'

She shook her head. 'We're behind down here already—you get on top of this for me and I'll deal with the ogre.'

She had to go into his apartment. Repeatedly. Her heart beat stupidly quickly at the thought. The range of inappropriate images that rioted through her head at the prospect of turning up to his apartment early tomorrow morning… Would he be awake or sleepy? She'd bet her life he didn't bother with pyjamas…but what if he had another dishevelled model-type with him? Ugh.

Get a grip and act like a professional.

Somehow she had less than fifteen minutes until the hour he'd given her was up, and she was not being late a second time today. With the dog in one arm and pushing a trolley with all his other stuff, she took the lift. She knocked but got no answer, so keyed in the security code.

'Hello? Mr Kariakis?' She walked into the apartment, but the room was silent.

Was she supposed to leave Toby alone in here or wait with him? Gritting back a frustrated sigh, she popped the dog down and turned to lift all his paraphernalia from the trolley. As she struggled with full arms, she noticed

Toby wandering off towards a bedroom. She called to him quickly, dropping his water bowl as she hurried to catch him. And at that worst possible moment the ancient rubber band securing her ponytail snapped, sending her hair flying about her face in a mess of half-curls and straggle. She dumped the dog's gear down in the middle of the room and glanced about for something to use. She spied a pen lying on the nearest table and quickly swiped it up. She twisted her unruly hair into a knot on top of her head and secured it with the pen. Thank heavens perfect Leon Kariakis wasn't there to see her in such a debacle with the dog, basket, blankets and bowls all in a muddle at her feet.

'Ms Roberts.'

She froze. And wasn't that just her luck?

She swivelled to face him as he strode through from the bedroom. Usually it was at this point that she'd offer her first name to a new resident. Something held her back from doing so with Leon Kariakis, however. The grim look of disapproval on his face perhaps?

He still looked impeccable in that charcoal suit. She quelled the smidgeon of disappointment that he might've relaxed a little in his own space; it wasn't to be.

'You're late,' he said.

'Actually, I'm right on time.' She held up her watch and then walked further into the lounge, trying not to let her confidence plummet. Remote and controlled, he relentlessly watched her progress as she self-consciously set up Toby's basket in a corner of the room with a stunning view of the city out of the floor-to-ceiling windows.

'Is that my pen in your hair?'

She froze. Could his voice be any more arctic?

'Sorry, my hair tie broke.' She looked at him and registered the astonishment in his eyes. 'It's a special pen?'

'It can write upside down.'

Was he kidding? She couldn't contain an impish grin at his perennial solemnity. 'You do handstands and take notes?'

Was that an answering glint of humour in his eyes now?

'It's my pen.' He ignored her little joke. 'You stole it.'

'I *borrowed* it.' So much for any chance of a sexy librarian look with the whole hair-tied-in-a-bun thing. The man didn't soften an inch. She sighed. 'You'd like it back right away?'

'If you wouldn't mind.'

Seriously? He was that uptight about a *pen*?

As she took it out her hair tumbled into chaos. She was too aware of his gaze lingering on the unruly mess and then he returned to look at her eyes. Suddenly she felt hotter than when she'd been furious about what was going to happen to Toby.

She held the pen out to him. Wordlessly he took it and put it into the breast pocket of his jacket. Over his heart.

She quickly turned away, wishing he'd just leave her to it. Instead he watched the fall of her hair, and her every other move as she set out Toby's blanket and bowl. Toby padded straight into his basket and curled into a small ball.

Leon leaned against the wall, still watching intently as she gave the dog a couple of soothing pats.

'Is there nothing you can't do?' he asked.

She was unwilling but unable to resist looking up at him. She wasn't sure if he was being sarcastic or not, but she resolved to treat him as she did any other difficult client— with respect and *distance*.

'There's plenty I can't do,' she muttered softly. Keep her hair under control for one thing.

'You've thought of everything.'

She straightened. 'It's my job to think of everything.'

'And you're very good at your job,' he drawled.

She looked him directly in the eyes at that. 'Yes, I am.'

Which was why he wasn't going to sack her for her earlier mistake. Which was why she was going to maintain a professional distance from him now.

Ophelia needed her to keep this job. She needed to remember that. She'd ignore the silent, magnetic pull.

'I assume Security has given you your own access code so it doesn't matter if I'm here or not.' His huskiness somehow built that sense of intimacy in the moment.

She nodded, momentarily fascinated by the discovery that his eyes weren't completely wintry; there were almost amber lights in them. Warm ones.

'This is a short-term solution,' he said. 'Until we can get him rehomed in a more suitable environment.'

'Of course.'

Focus, Ettie.

She looked around the room and then sent him a sideways look. 'Though this environment seems pretty suitable.'

Leon walked over to her and hunched down by Toby's basket. 'Is he always this subdued?' He patted the dog gently again. 'I wondered if he wasn't well.'

Ettie smiled at him, pleased he was concerned. 'He's old and quiet and missing Harold. He's probably wondering what on earth is going on...'

Leon absently scratched the dog's ears.

'His quality of life is good, though.' Ettie looked at him earnestly.

'Don't worry. I'm not about to summon the vet.'

For a split-second Ettie relaxed, but she was then hit by a flood of intense pleasure at seeing this powerful man almost kneeling at her feet. It was dizzying. 'I'll leave you two to get to know each other, then.' On an irresistible impulse, she teased him. 'Perhaps you could smile at him? Make him feel welcome?' That stupid suggestion had popped out before she'd thought better of it.

He suddenly stood. She'd not realised how near he was. Now he towered over her.

Don't prod a grumpy beast.

'Bare my teeth at him, you mean?' he muttered quietly. 'I'm not sure it's wise to do that to a wolf.'

That low pull tugged deep in her belly—purely physical, animal magnetism that set off a melting sensation deep within. Restless, inappropriate desire. With it came recklessness.

'One wolf to another?' she nudged dangerously. 'Don't you ever just smile?'

Oh, yes, she'd crossed a line now.

He didn't answer other than to stare down at her as if he couldn't believe what he'd heard. As if he was contemplating what kind of retribution he was about to mete out...

He liked to take the time to think, right?

Ettie had forgotten how to think. Or move. Or even breathe. She just stared right back at him for an endless moment. He really was far too handsome. And far too serious. She was utterly mesmerised. 'Thank you for taking care of him,' she whispered.

Something fierce flared in his eyes. 'Contrary to what you thought earlier, I'm not a monster.'

No, he wasn't. And she guessed he was allowed to be as serious as he liked, in his own home and all.

'I'm sorry for that mistake,' she finally apologised. Flushing with heat, she brushed a lock of her rebellious hair back from her face. Again.

He watched her movement as intently and inscrutably as ever. 'Thank you.'

She didn't feel forgiven, she felt flayed.

She didn't know if he stepped closer, or if she swayed,

but suddenly there seemed to be no space at all between them. Her breath stalled in her lungs. He was so very close. But he was also utterly, inhumanly, still. He had such intensity of focus—expressionless, but not remote—and having that focus solely on her was more than dizzying, it was like being in the path of a lightning strike. She was going to get burned, but the chance to get lit up…?

Another long moment passed before her brain kicked back into operational mode. Oh, heaven, he probably thought she was waiting for him to make a move. He must get so many women throwing themselves at him. *Models* in the lift, remember? He'd never look twice at her. Mortified, she desperately clawed back her sanity and her dignity.

'I'd better get back downstairs,' she croaked, turned tail and fled.

Leon was hanging on to his control by the thinnest of threads. He'd spent the day determined to forget Antoinette Roberts. And for the first time in a very long time he'd spent a day failing.

She kept appearing in his thoughts—gorgeously fresh, her beautiful, wavy hair shimmering with every turn of her head. He never should have made her give his pen back because now he was beset with the fantasy of having that glorious hair spread across his pillows as the rest of her arched up to…

Leon stalked out of Cavendish House, his body aching. It was late in the evening but he'd not bother with dinner, he'd walk and wear himself out that way. Toby was fast asleep in his basket and too old to keep pace with him. He knew Antoinette had returned earlier to walk the dog and given him food. Leon had deliberately stayed away at the time, but the scent of her lingered in his rooms, sending his brain back into the direction he'd been trying to avoid all day.

Since when did he lose control over his own damn pulse? Ice-cool control was the one thing he always maintained. Antoinette Roberts threatened it with one fiery glance. Maybe it had been too long since he'd taken a lover. He should've taken up that offer last night.

Grimacing, he walked along the footpaths. The shops were open late and crowds milled about. He glanced sightlessly into the windows as he threaded through the masses. But through one immaculate window display he swore he recognised the gleaming rich hair of the petite woman standing with her back to him.

Great. Now he was seeing her everywhere.

But then he heard her voice as well—her lilting humour as she asked a customer if she needed help. He stared into the store, listening through the open door. Either Antoinette Roberts had a doppelgänger, or she'd come straight here after her shift at Cavendish and was now helping some woman choose a set of thank-you cards.

He walked in, quickly taking in the high-end stationery supplies the shop was stocked with. A couple of minutes later the female customer walked past him on her way out carrying a beautifully wrapped parcel and a satisfied smile on her face.

Leon walked up to the woman behind the counter. 'Ms Roberts?'

It was definitely her. And he definitely couldn't stop staring. Gone was the utilitarian, practical Cavendish concierge uniform and now she was in a lithe little black dress. He could finally see something of her legs and, just as he'd suspected, they were smooth, shapely and gorgeous. He'd known that if she could make those black trousers look sexy, she'd be dynamite in a dress. This one had a

slightly scooped neckline, which meant there wasn't anywhere near enough cleavage, but there was skin—creamy,
silken-looking skin and the suggestion of sweet curves beneath the fabric. And her glorious hair was freed from that
bouncing mess of a ponytail and now cascaded in glossy
wild waves down her back. It looked lush, as if it'd be soft
to touch and he'd bind it around his wrists—

'Oh.' A blush flooded her smooth cheeks and she licked
her lips. 'Mr Kariakis?' Then her wide-eyed gaze narrowed. 'You left Toby alone?'

The beseeching reproach in her eyes made him feel
guilty even when he shouldn't. 'You know he ate a good
dinner; now he's fast asleep. He's not missing me.'

The inward tension he'd been trying to settle tightened
again. He'd needed to get out of that soulless apartment.
He'd wanted to exorcise the ghost of her standing there,
challenging him with that sassy look in her eyes as she'd
flicked his stupid pen back at him. He'd been hopelessly
distracted by the memory—but he was thrown back into
that whirling web of desire again now.

'What are you doing here?' he asked irritably.

'What do you think I'm doing?' Her tone cooled to
match his.

His tension spiked, he released it on her insane work-
load. 'You've worked all day already.'

She stiffened. 'Lots of people work more than one job.
I'm sure you work long hours too.'

But there was a hint of tiredness in the backs of her
eyes.

'You're tired.' He refused to believe she wanted to work
fourteen or more hours a day.

'Oh, no,' she answered airily. 'Actually as soon as I'm
done here, I'm going clubbing.'

'Are you?' He fired with her challenge. 'Excellent. Take

me with you—I'm new to town and don't know all the cool places.'

A disconcerted expression crossed her face and he inwardly laughed. He couldn't lie to himself any more. His offer to care for the dog was based in selfish motivation: to see more of Antoinette. He wanted her in his bed. Ideally tonight. It had hit in that first second—lust at first sight. Lust that was only increasing the longer he spent in her company. Perhaps if he satisfied the urge, it'd disappear as swiftly as it had come.

And her reaction to him? He could tempt her.

'I…' She glanced at her watch and that flush across her delicate, high cheekbones built.

It was five minutes until closing and he wasn't planning on leaving. 'You like working here?'

He made conversation to ease her embarrassment. Despite those delicious feisty flashes, she displayed hints of shyness. He found the combination unbelievably tantalising.

'It's nice.' She nodded.

He tensed. 'Nicer than Cavendish?'

Was she thinking of leaving her concierge job? In some ways that would be good—it would free them of any messiness, given their positions there.

'It's quieter than Cavendish, but I don't build the same relationship with my customers as I do there. I only work the late nights here.' She glanced at the counter display. 'It's beautiful stationery.'

'That's why you work here—because you like the product?'

A bubble of laughter burst from her shimmering lips. 'No, if I just liked the product, I'd buy it.'

'So it's money.' He frowned, unhappy at the thought that she was forced to work two jobs. 'We don't pay you enough.'

A wary expression crossed her face. 'It's fine. I have commitments. Most of us do, right?'

He shouldn't pry further but he couldn't help watching intently, waiting to see if she'd say more. Her clear eyes dimmed with faint shadows.

'Saving,' she muttered, unable to help herself.

Unusually for him, his curiosity deepened. But it wasn't his business. He had no right to press further. 'Good for you.'

She nodded awkwardly. 'So did you want anything in particular?'

He bit back the blunt answer of what he particularly *wanted* and made himself breathe first. 'I wanted to see if it was really you.'

'Well.' That impish smile flashed on her lips, flicking away the shadows in her eyes. 'It is.'

'In another uniform.' He couldn't help noticing that damned demure neckline again.

'Black again.' She bit her lip as she quickly glanced down as if afraid she'd spilled something. 'Always ready for a funeral, that's me,' she quipped. 'But it's discreet. Unobtrusive.'

'I would never describe you as unobtrusive,' he muttered quietly.

She'd burst into his life in a blaze of passion and fury.

She met his gaze, silently questioning just how he'd describe her. Unspoken awareness flickered between them, like a gravitational pull.

Her blush returned full force, a ruby tide over her creamy complexion. 'I should get back to work. It's almost time to close.'

She was flustered again. He was fascinated by her unconscious dance—she advanced closer with those challenges, then retreated in shyness. He glanced around the shop, pleased to discover it had emptied completely of other customers. 'Show me the biggest seller.'

'Seriously?' The droll scepticism on her face was a picture.

Entertained by her expressiveness, he leaned closer. 'Why not? You don't think I can afford it?'

She sent him another look. 'Well, I know you don't need a new *pen*.' She lifted an item from the counter and met his gaze with a prim, shop-girl pose. 'But we have an exquisite range of journals.'

'Exquisite,' he echoed dryly.

'Incredibly so,' she emphasised, refusing to acknowledge his soft sarcasm.

'What is it about girls and diaries?' He reached out and traced the smooth leather cover with his finger. 'Do you pour out your soul into one of these every night?'

'What if I do?' She lifted her chin in that irresistibly defiant gesture.

'Would it make for fascinating reading?' He was appallingly curious now. For the first time intrigued enough to want to know all a woman's thoughts, all her wishes, every last secret and deepest desire.

'Sadly, no. I only keep lists in mine.' She reached across the counter and flipped an open book around to show him. 'See?'

'This is yours?' His pulse rate lifted.

'I work on it in quiet moments,' she said. 'I have permission from my boss—it's good to see our products in use.'

Her defensiveness amused him. Was she as discomforted by him as much as he was by her? He leaned closer to read the scrawled list.

'I forget things,' she added nervously. 'I'm naturally disorganised, so I work hard to get it together and nail my job. Lists are the only thing that work for me.' She tried to pull the journal back but he planted his hand down to keep it there. His fingers brushed against her for the second time that day. Skin touched skin. She stilled, as did he.

A millisecond later she snatched her hand back. But he knew she'd felt that current of electricity flow between them.

He turned the pages of her journal, refusing to feel any remorse—she was the one who'd offered it for his viewing. But to his disappointment there were no deepest desires on show inside. Only ruthless organisation, as she'd said.

'Everything in your life is dictated by a list?' There were reminders, shopping lists, ticked-off tasks, pros and cons for other things... 'It's a lot of lists.' He flicked through more pages, wishing there were something far more personal in it. 'And in a rainbow of colours.'

'It doesn't need to be boring. Right? But I'm no artist, so I just choose a different colour for each...'

'I have a planner,' he offered idly. 'But it's online.'

'Online?' She shuddered theatrically. 'I couldn't get all these lists on the one screen. And what if it got deleted?'

'What if you lost your journal?' he countered with the obvious. 'What if someone you don't want to read it gets hold of it?'

Her impish grin darted back. 'That's why there are only lists and reminders.'

'So, nothing too personal or incriminating?' He sighed with genuine disappointment. 'You're not a risk-taker, then.'

Her eyes widened.

'You won't run the risk of someone discovering your secrets,' he explained.

'Perhaps I don't have any,' she muttered.

'Everyone has secrets.' *And desires.*

Silent, she just gazed back at him.

'And I'll bet you're not really going clubbing,' he added quietly.

This time her smile was more sheepish than impish, and she shook her head.

'Have you had dinner?' He didn't give her time to answer. 'I don't think you've had time if you came straight from your shift at Cavendish. You must be hungry.'

He saw her hesitate and spoke again before she could deny it. 'Have dinner with me.'

'No thanks,' she instantly answered.

'Am I that awful?' he shot back, unafraid to challenge her directly. He knew what he wanted. He knew what she wanted too. He was just more honest about it.

She stared at him for a moment, shocked. 'No, I—'

'Well, don't let me down so roughly. It's only dinner.'

Roughly? Ettie narrowed her eyes on him. He was pulling her leg, right? Behind that serious facade there was some humour. 'It's not a wise idea. You're my boss.'

'It's not a date, just dinner. If it makes you feel better, you can tell me about life on the concierge desk. I need to know how the whole operation works. There'll be no repercussions for complete honesty.' He paused. 'Anyway, I'm not really your boss.'

Yeah, right. 'You own the building I work in.'

'But a management company employs the staff.'

'Do you own the management company?' She wouldn't have been surprised if he did.

'They're contracted... I don't own them.'

'So that makes it okay?' Her heart was pounding unnaturally fast.

'I think it creates a technicality we can take advantage of.' He looked right at her. Those amber flecks in his eyes lit up with every word. 'And you like breaking the stupid rules, right? This is a stupid one. Besides, I'm only living in the penthouse while I get my head around the building. Then I'll lease it to a client and move to my next investment, so you won't see me much.'

His message couldn't be clearer. He was saying he'd stay out of her way. That his presence was temporary. That this was just dinner. Just one night.

But Ettie needed a moment.

'You don't ever want to stay in one of your buildings?' She was intrigued by his transitory lifestyle.

'I like projects. I like the excitement and unique challenge of each one, and once I've overcome that challenge it's time to move on to another.'

She suspected he wasn't just talking building acquisition. It was lovers as well. 'You get bored easily?'

A speculative gleam heated his eyes even more. Yeah, he was talking on more than one level. But he answered with that customary seriousness. 'I like to keep busy. I like having problems to grapple with.'

'You don't ever want to just blob out on the beach?'

He cocked his head and considered it briefly. 'It's not something I've ever done.'

'Seriously?' She frowned. 'Not ever?' Didn't his parents own all those hotels in Greece? Wasn't that the ultimate holiday destination? 'You never have holidays?'

'Do you?' he countered.

'I don't have much choice.' She grimaced. 'I work hard but I don't have the same financial rewards, and I have obligations...' Which she didn't want to go into with him right now. 'What's the point in all your success if you don't stop and celebrate it every so often?'

'The point is the success itself,' he answered.

'You don't get tired?' She was flummoxed. If she could take a break somewhere warm and beautiful, she'd be there in a heartbeat.

'Don't worry,' he murmured. 'I know how to relax.'

Yeah, she bet he did. She sent him a reproachful glare and he suddenly laughed. Ettie gaped, stunned at his instant transformation from unsmiling autocrat to hot, buttered hunk. She dragged oxygen into her tight lungs. It wasn't right that a man should be *so* gorgeous.

'It's not what you're thinking,' he said. 'Well, not entirely.'

'How do you know what I'm thinking?'

'It's written all over your face.'

Hopefully not *everything* she was thinking. And hopefully it wasn't obvious how her innards were positively melting. 'So you don't do this often? Pick up women and take them to dinner?'

'No, not often, actually. Does that surprise you?' His expression returned to serious as he studied her. 'You don't believe me?'

'You've been seen with other women,' she said.

His eyebrows shot up. 'When?'

'Last night, apparently.' She tried to play it cool but she was already regretting bringing it up. 'A woman leaving your apartment.'

He'd probably been celebrating his first night in Cavendish House.

Now Leon studied her for another long moment. She knew he was thinking. She just wished she knew *what*.

'You were talking about me.' His lips curved ever so slightly. 'You were curious.'

Before she had the chance to deny it, or to apologise, or to melt in a swelter of embarrassment, he continued softly.

'Was she seen in my company?' he asked. 'I don't think so. The woman who left my apartment late last night had arrived only minutes earlier. She's an acquaintance who'd heard I'd moved in. She came to see me as a surprise but it wasn't something I wished to pursue.'

'You don't like surprises like that?'

What red-blooded man wouldn't want to be surprised by some model-type turning up at midnight with a booty call on her mind?

'I already told you,' he replied. 'I like challenges.'

Surely he didn't see *her* as a challenge?

But she was pleased somehow, that he didn't dally with anyone and everyone who offered.

Leon picked up her journal from the counter and opened it again to look at the long columns of her lists. 'You could write a list about whether or not to have dinner with me.' He shook his head and snapped her book shut. 'Or you could just trust your instincts.'

Ettie regarded him warily. Her very basic instincts were hell-bent on leading her into trouble and her instincts had let her down before. Leon Kariakis was pure temptation and he knew it. Unfortunately for him, she was determined to remain in control of herself.

But this was a dare and he didn't scare her.

'All right, then,' she decided with spirit. 'Only to tell you all about the Cavendish.'

'Wonderful.'

He waited while she closed up the shop and set the security alarm. She grabbed her coat, but despite the chill in the air she didn't put it on. The thing was ancient and the zip was broken and she didn't want him seeing how worn it was.

'What do you usually have for dinner?' he asked as they walked along the crowded footpath.

Usually on the nights she'd worked late she grabbed a chocolate bar from the tube station on the way home or didn't bother. Tonight had been going to be a not-bother night. But she wasn't about to admit that. 'I might cook a quick stir-fry.'

'But if you were to dine out?'

She shrugged as nonchalantly as possible. Truth? She *never* dined out.

He sent her a sideways look. 'I know a good place.'

'I thought you were new to the area and didn't know any of the cool places.' She couldn't help smiling.

'I asked one of the concierges at my apartment building,' he replied smoothly. 'They offer a superb service.'

She rolled her eyes and kept pace with him along the busy footpath. A couple of corners later he paused outside a beautiful brick mansion.

She shook her head at him. 'No chance. You have to have a booking.'

He shrugged as if he wasn't fazed. 'We won't take up much space.'

It was a celebrity chef's place—the kind you had to make a reservation for six months in advance, which was actually a good thing, as it then gave you the time to save the small fortune you needed just to enjoy an appetiser, let alone sample the full menu. Ettie made bookings all the time on behalf of her Cavendish residents.

But Leon simply walked up to the door, which the discreet security guard immediately opened. The maître d' swept towards them, his wide gaze fixed firmly on Leon and his smile welcoming and wide. Leon didn't even need to utter a word.

'May I have five minutes, sir, if you'd like a drink first?'

'Thank you,' Leon answered with the ease of one born to privilege. 'Champagne?' He turned to Ettie.

'Lemonade,' she replied firmly and caught a gleam of pure amusement in his eyes.

'Definitely not a risk-taker,' he murmured.

'Fine, then,' she breathed. 'Champagne.'

One glass wouldn't do any harm.

They'd barely been given their drinks when the maître d' reappeared to lead them through the busy dining room. Ettie tried not to stare. Several faces were familiar to her but not through personal acquaintance. These were publicly led lives—an actress, a politician. Possibly a minor royal? They stopped at a secluded table in an alcove near the rear of the restaurant. It was quieter than the main dining room, more intimate and far more private.

'You like it?' Leon asked as she took her seat.

'You know the owner?' She hazarded a guess as she tried not to stare at the gleaming lighting and sumptuous décor, but she couldn't hold back her smile. The place was amazing. 'This is really kind of you.'

'No, I'm not really kind,' he corrected bluntly. 'This is pure self-interest. I get a pretty companion for dinner to take my mind off my misery.'

'Misery?' She quirked an eyebrow while battling the warmth she felt at his compliment. He didn't really mean it. He was just adding 'charming' to his repertoire, which was very unfair of him. 'Because your life's so terrible?' Curious, she watched him keenly for his answer.

But he turned the conversation back on her. 'Was it really going to be a stir-fry?'

'No,' she admitted with a chuckle. 'I hate cooking. Generally I exist on grilled cheese sandwiches.'

'There's a place in the world for a good grilled cheese sandwich.' He nodded. 'But not here.'

'Then what do you suggest?'

'I suggest we leave it to the experts.' He nodded at the maître d', who, with a slight bow, left for the kitchen. 'So, why are you working such intense hours?' Leon sipped his champagne. 'Do we not pay you enough to live on?'

She too took a sip and savoured the fizz of bubbles before replying. 'I'm saving.'

'For travel? A house?'

She laughed and shook her head. Was she really here to *entertain* him and take his mind off whatever torments he thought he had? 'I've a younger sister who aspires to go to university.'

'It's just the two of you?'

She nodded and took another sip.

'How old is she?' His gaze narrowed.

'Seventeen. She's away at boarding school up north.'

'You support her financially?'

'She's on a partial scholarship.'

'And you pay the rest?' His mouth tightened. 'But you're not that far out of school yourself.'

'I'm twenty-three, so a few years out. It's her last year, so it really counts.'

'And she's obviously talented.'

'Top of her school.' Ettie beamed with unashamed pride. 'She's amazing. She wants to study medicine. So.' She inhaled deeply. 'A lot of study.' And a lot of tuition and living fees. But Ophelia was worth it and she'd do anything to see her achieve her dreams.

'What happened to your parents?'

'Twenty questions, huh?' She sent him a look but answered anyway. 'My father was never around. My mother passed away a couple of years ago.'

'That must have been hard.'

It had been but she didn't want to dwell on her mother's slow decline with cancer. Not tonight. Not here. She smiled softly. 'We've survived.'

She didn't tell him about the huge mistake that she'd made not long after her mother's death either. The total car crash that had been her love life.

'What's your sister's name?'

'Ophelia.'

'Antoinette and Ophelia,' he said quietly. 'But you're "Ettie"?'

'Yes, fingers crossed neither of us suffers the delusions or disappointment of our namesakes.' She sat back as the waiter appeared and placed dishes on the table. 'My mother was a romantic.' Not that she'd had any kind of romantic luck. Like mother, like daughter. 'This looks amazing.'

She was pleased to have the interruption to the topic. And she realised she was absolutely *starving*.

He waited for her to take a bite, amusement softening his innate seriousness. 'What do you think? Better than a grilled cheese sandwich?'

Ettie couldn't answer, she was too busy salivating. But she finally swallowed her mouthful. 'I've never eaten anything like it. It's to die for.'

And that was all she could say, because she needed more this instant. He probably thought she was an idiot, but right this second she didn't care. This was one of those rare experiences in life that had to be luxuriated in.

'Here, try this.' He pushed another plate towards her.

Ettie tasted what was, frankly, the food of the gods. Conversation turned to flavours and textures. Leon was animated, knowledgeable and entertaining as they debated which dish was the most delicious.

'Do you have room for dessert?' he teased her almost an hour later as she sat back with a satisfied sigh.

'I should say no, because I'm not remotely hungry now…' She trailed off.

When was she ever going to be in a restaurant like this again? With a man like this? It was a once-in-a-lifetime fantasy night and she didn't want it to end.

'What if we share?' He offered her pure temptation.

She flashed a huge grin at him. 'I get to pick, right?' she said impulsively. 'Because you can come here any time.'

He laughed a little beneath his breath. 'Sure.'

'Or maybe you should pick.' She suddenly backpedalled, remembering the guy was all but her boss. 'You probably know what's good…'

There was a quizzical light in his eye and his eyebrows twitched. 'I'm sure they're all good.' He turned and said something softly to the waiter who'd magically appeared with his impeccable service-required senses on full alert.

Ettie narrowed her gaze on Leon. 'You did not just order every dessert on the menu.'

'You don't have to eat them all, just taste.'

Her jaw dropped at the decadence of the suggestion and she shook her head. 'That's wasteful.'

'Then we can take the rest home for later,' he said softly.

Ettie stilled, swamped with heat at the suggestion of intimacy that throwaway comment inferred. Was he assuming she'd go home with him tonight?

Images burned in her brain—of her licking a decadent chocolate dessert while in bed with him. Even better, licking said chocolate dessert *off* him.

'Ettie?' He was watching her closely as if he could read her mind. 'You can take them home and have them for breakfast,' he clarified in a slightly husky voice.

The less than subtle undercurrents between them were unbearably strong and gaining power with every passing second. She licked her suddenly dry lips and decided it was his turn to answer twenty questions. 'Do you have any brothers or sisters?'

He hesitated and for a moment she thought he wasn't going to answer.

But his mouth twisted. 'I'm an only child. Spoilt little

rich boy.' His tone was mocking, but the edge of bitterness ran deeper than a mere joke.

'But you built your own business, right?' She knew his parents had that Greek hotel empire, but he'd gone into finance on his own. That was according to the official bio in his 'most eligible bachelor' blurb in the magazine Jess the housemaid had been flashing around this afternoon at work.

He shook his head. 'I had every advantage—education, health, wealthy parents. While my business success is my own, I can't rightly claim to have done it all by myself when I came from that starting point. Most people don't get that privilege to begin with.'

'But you made the most of your opportunities.'

Of course those schools, those contacts—sure they helped. But in the end, he had to do the work himself. And there were plenty of heirs to vast fortunes who'd frittered their lives away.

A lick of something indefinable flickered in his eyes. 'I like to extract every possible success from every possible scenario. Yes.'

Again that undercurrent swept over her like a blanket of wild dizziness—sensuality of a kind she'd never encountered or imagined. Sexual tension so intense…but it was also teasing, almost fun. Which was surprising, given he was so very serious…and she so very inept at banter.

Two waiters appeared and set six dishes on the table. Six decadent desserts that were miniature works of culinary art.

'They're only small portions,' she said softly, as if that made it better. 'I imagine they're rich.'

'Why don't you take a bite and find out?' That tone was back—dry on the surface, but wicked beneath—daring her to take the risk, to take a bite of something so far out of her league. To taste something miles away from her realm of experience.

She picked up the silver fork and forced herself to focus on the glorious-looking *food*, rather than the man across the table mesmerising her. She took a moment to mentally debate which she should taste first—it was a three-way contest between the chocolate nirvana, the caramel or the raspberry heaven. In the end the chocolate won.

Ettie closed her eyes as she sucked the rich mousse from the spoon.

'Good?'

It was impossible to answer him—the deliciousness too much to express. It was like all the good things in the world had been put together in the one flavour bomb and it had just burst on her tongue.

'Have you tried this?' she mumbled with her mouth full. 'Because I'm not sure I can share after all. And there aren't going to be any leftovers, sorry.'

Leon covered his mouth but she could see deep laughter dancing in his eyes.

'Don't hide your smile,' she scolded recklessly, cross with him for hiding that spark from her. She just knew that had been a gorgeous smile and she wanted to bask in the full impact of it.

'You have great teeth,' she added dizzily as she swallowed more of the silken chocolate. 'Are you afraid I might think you're human? Because don't worry, we all know you're...' She trailed off, suddenly aware she shouldn't complete that rambling sentence.

'I didn't want you to think I was laughing at you,' he said with mock-defensiveness. 'Some women get sensitive about being seen enjoying food.'

Who? Those model-types he hung out with?

'I'm not bothered,' she said honestly. 'I'm utterly un-

ashamed about enjoying this…' She breathed out and sur-
veyed the luscious desserts still before her.

'Well, *I'm* the one offended,' he muttered. 'You don't
think I'm human?'

Hmm, unfortunately she had said that. 'I also said you
have great teeth.' Which was even more mortifying, but
she smiled at him anyway.

'All the better to bite you with,' he answered severely,
but she saw the sparkle in those amber-lit eyes of his. No,
he wasn't anywhere near as serious as she'd first thought.
He was *guarded.* So guarded he'd been wary of letting
her see him relax. Why was he so defensive when he had
everything?

'Perhaps I deserve a bite,' she acknowledged with a
chuckle. 'But you were laughing at me.'

His expression turned sly. 'So are you offended?'

'I'm not that precious. You suit a smile. You should do
it more often. If I lived in Cavendish House I'd be smiling
all the time.' And if she owned the place, she'd be doing
back-flips.

'It's not bricks and mortar that make people happy.'

'Oh, they help.' She laughed openly at that. 'Here, taste
this. It'll help too.'

'Oh, am I allowed some now?' Sending her a speaking
look, he picked up his fork.

Ettie's pulse skidded all over the place as Leon escorted
her out of the restaurant. She shrugged on her coat just
for something to do and turned, ready to walk to the train
station. She refused to let her spirits lower now the night
was over.

He caught her hand in his. Electricity surged at the firm
clasp of his fingers over hers and a new level of intimacy
seared. She knew it had been building between them, yet

she was suddenly shy, but overwhelmingly she wanted everything she probably shouldn't.

He turned her to face him.

'So, clubbing?' he asked.

She couldn't seem to speak, so she just shook her head.

'You don't want to dance with me?' he asked quietly.

Oh, she wanted to dance with him. Just the two of them. Intuitively she knew he was asking for just that—an *intimate* dance. It was fantastical. But ever since he'd walked into the stationery shop, it was as though she'd stepped into another dimension—an alternative reality where the truths of tomorrow really didn't matter and where the past was irrelevant and where for one crazy night this way-out-of-her-league guy was paying her attention.

He stepped closer, his expression intensifying—even more serious, and *hungry*.

'This is a very bad idea,' he said softly.

'Yes,' she agreed softly. She couldn't quite believe he even wanted to get closer to her, but here he was, leaning in with so much intent.

She'd been working so hard for so long. She'd been let down too many times. She'd been alone for what felt like for ever. What did it matter if there was no future in this? She'd pinned her hopes on a future with a man before, only to be heartbroken. With no hopes, no expectations…there would be no heartbreak, right?

'Terrible.' He lifted his hand and gently framed her face.

She quivered at that lightest of touches. 'Yes.'

She read the sultry promise in his eyes as those pros and cons swirled in her head. What was the worst that could happen? She'd have an amazing experience with a god-like man. And whether he enjoyed it as much as she…well, that was up to him, wasn't it? Couldn't she let that fear go?

'But I want to do it anyway.'

He did? He really did? She smiled and her tummy swarmed with butterflies…but below that, molten heat swirled. 'Yes.'

There was only now. Only this sensation. Only this one chance. And she wanted it.

'And so do you?' His gaze searched hers intently.

'Yes.' *Of course.*

She might be inexperienced, but she wasn't stupid.

'And that's all you're going to say tonight?' His lips twitched.

She stared at him, willing him to smile. 'Yes.'

'To anything I ask?'

She'd not taken a moment purely for herself in such a long time. 'Um…yes.'

His mouth didn't curve into a smile; instead it moved closer. He brushed a light kiss on her lips. Ettie remained still, her face upturned to his, not quite sure this was actually happening. He too was immobile, watching her with that ultra-serious, inscrutable intensity. She didn't want him to watch, she wanted him to *act*.

And then he did.

He cupped her head, threading his fingers through her hair to draw her closer so he could kiss her properly. Not a gentle brush of the lips, but a devastating, can't-get-enough kiss that mirrored the desire clawing deep in her body. That deliciousness in the restaurant was nothing on the sensations shivering through her body now. He devoured her as if she were the best of all those award-winning desserts. She lost track of time and place, there was no more thought, no more doubt as sensation transcended—and overwhelmed—everything. There was only one destination for her tonight and that was right here in his arms, with his mouth sealed on hers and his lips, hands, tongue and heat all working that dizzying magic. He made her tremble, made her want more than she'd ever wanted *anything*.

She moaned, totally overcome. 'Leon—'

He stepped back so suddenly she nearly stumbled. He quickly clamped an arm about her but somehow walked her forward at the same time. He waved and hailed a taxi. Of course one pulled over immediately—he had that way about him. People instantly recognised power, influence, money, and moved the minute he asked.

He thrust a couple of large notes to the driver through the window. 'Just drive.'

He hustled her into the cab ahead of him, then joined her on the back seat and pulled her in as if he'd been starved of kisses for aeons and was now making up for it. A famished, demanding man now feasting. She was okay with that. So okay. Because she'd discovered her own hunger— her own pleasure in exploring him too. She ran light fingers along his jaw, feeling that hot, sexy stubble—still unable to believe that she was really touching him and he was touching her. She was suddenly super-hot, although neediness made her shiver.

His hand skated over the hem of her dress. His teasing fingers circled, finding bare skin, seeking out more. Ettie quivered but he kept kissing her, and excitement thrummed throughout her body. Who knew kissing could be this erotic? This intense? This incredibly awesome?

She never wanted it to end. Time needed to stop. Because this was *it*. This was her moment—just for her. And he knew—he kept kissing her, increasing the dizzying intensity and turning up the heat with every luscious lick and slide. His teasing fingers skimmed her thigh so lightly it was only a slight tickle. Yet powerful waves of heat rolled over her. Her mouth parted more as she moaned and lifted her hips to quicker meet the delicious, unpredictable stroke of his fingertips. The tease was intolerable. She wanted a firmer touch. She wanted *more*.

He deepened the kiss further still, his tongue wickedly caressing inside her mouth until she was dizzy on the delight of it. He'd unleashed a hunger, a driving need she'd never known. She soared on the sensation, strung higher with that exquisite tension he drew her along with. She couldn't stop the rock of her hips now, instinctively enticing him to touch further, touch harder. His teeth nipped her lower lip just as he skimmed his fingertips higher— all the way to her soft, simple cotton panties. She gasped at the caress. He stilled and lifted his lips a mere millimetre from hers. Then those trespassing fingers stroked once more—so intimately that she violently squirmed, unable to hold back a moan as her fingers curled into fists. *Yes*. That was what she wanted. But he suddenly broke the kiss. Breathlessly she stared up at him. His gaze ensnared hers—his eyes were dark with promise, with satisfaction, with *hunger*.

He growled the address for Cavendish House to the taxi driver, their gazes still locked. Dazed, she read the determination in his eyes, felt the possessiveness of his hand cupping her so intimately, and understood exactly. He wanted e*verything*.

If she was going to stop this, to say no, the time to do it was now. But it was also the time to say yes. Was she really going to be another of Leon Kariakis's conquests? His challenge for the night?

Yes.

Now she was in this other world of touch and light and scorching sensation, nothing could stop her from having this. Having him.

Just once.

She'd worked hard to rein in her natural impulsiveness.

She'd had too much responsibility to be reckless…but this was only one night.

'Yes?' he prompted in a gruff undertone.

She nodded. She wanted the experience she knew he could give her. He swooped and kissed her again—pure reward, pure promise, invoking that breathless restlessness all over again. But he slipped his hand from beneath her dress and rested it on her breast instead, almost holding her captive. She acquiesced to everything, to the kiss, to the utterly foregone conclusion of this night—and simply drowned in the flood of pleasure his exquisite passion pulled from her.

But as they neared the building she suddenly clutched his wrist and whispered with panic, 'No one can see me.'

'In my company?' He half laughed at her drama and discomfort. 'I've already thought of that, don't worry.' He leaned forward and spoke to the taxi driver again. Moments later the gate to the underground garage slid open, letting them escape the cab unseen.

In the lift Leon pushed a series of buttons on the security pad. 'The lift will go straight to the penthouse. It won't stop on any other floor.'

Even so, she stood as far from him as possible because there was still a security camera in there. She wasn't ashamed but she was protective of her privacy and she didn't want her colleagues knowing that she'd… Embarrassed warmth flooded her and she fixed her gaze to the floor and let her hair fall forward, hoping her face couldn't be seen. At the ding of the bell, the doors slid open to his penthouse suite.

Leon led the way, keeping a little distance as he swiftly shrugged off his jacket and tie and tossed them onto the nearest sofa. 'Toby's asleep,' he said easily.

Ettie took the moment to pause and settle her heart-rate. The elderly dog was comfortably curled in his basket and she could see he'd drunk some of his water. She breathed out a little of her tension as she glanced back at Leon. 'Why'd you take him?'

'Same reason you would have if you could,' he answered. 'Why did it surprise you so much that I did? Why think I'm such an ogre?'

Was there a hint of hurt in his eyes?

'I don't think you're an ogre,' she said softly. 'You can just come across as a bit stern.'

'You want me to smile?' He sounded sardonic.

'Yes.'

But he remained as still and as serious as ever. 'Come here.'

His request—command really—was impossible to ignore. She was drawn to him; she had been from the first moment she'd seen him. So she went to him, her heart thundering faster with every step.

'You're sure about this, Ettie?' he asked.

'Just this once,' she whispered. 'Only this once, okay?'

Leon didn't reply. He was so very still, so very serious. She knew he was thinking, she just didn't know what. But she sensed his tension, some kind of warring within. Instinctively she reached out and placed her hand on his chest.

His heart echoed hers—beating with a fierce gallop. The pace reverberated through her palm, up her arm and into her own tightly wired body. His enigmatic gaze glittered down at her.

And then he smiled.

CHAPTER THREE

ETTIE BLINKED, STUNNED again by his instant transformation from moody male model to sinfully arrogant tease. Oh, she was in such trouble. 'What are you thinking about?'

'The best way to begin.'

She swallowed as her poor heart raced even more. But lower down she melted with anticipation. 'Did you need some help with that?' she asked weakly. 'Should we list the options?'

He laughed, which made him all the more heart-stoppingly handsome. But just as she gaped—beyond dazzled—he swooped. He caught her gasp in his kiss, sending Ettie straight back into that intense desire she'd felt in the taxi. Oh, the man could *kiss*. He was playful and teasing—alternating deep, luscious licks with light nibbles that were designed to provoke her to madness. She had more freedom now than in the car, so she wound her arms around his neck and pushed closer, revelling in the press of his hard, masculine body against hers. He was tall and taut and she felt the strength in his core stillness. But his wicked hands wandered again, back to the hem of her dress, back to the silky skin of her inner thigh. She moaned, collapsing against him and letting her feet slide further apart as he trailed those fingertips to the top of her leg, teasing so, so close to where she ached to be teased.

Oh, yes. Please, yes.

But she didn't say it, didn't chant the plea circling in her head. She couldn't—she was too busy being kissed to glorious dizziness. But he must have read her mind, because then he went there—skilfully circling that tight bundle of pure sensitivity. She gasped, breaking the seal of the kiss as pleasure rushed upon her.

'*Oh...*'

He clamped her to him with his other arm, supporting her as the orgasm sent her body into spasms of blissful sensation. Never had she come so quickly with a man. Well, never had she actually *come* with a man.

Panting and suddenly so self-conscious, she pressed her forehead against his chest. He stroked her back but kept that other hand gently cupping her so intimately, soft touches easing her down yet keeping her hyper-aware of him.

'I've been imagining that all day,' he muttered low in her ear.

Really? Breathlessly she laughed as he suddenly switched his hold and lifted her off her feet to carry her through to the master bedroom.

'Me too,' she muttered shyly as he lowered her to stand at the foot of the big bed. So much.

His smile flashed again and it was like being concussed—all circling stars and dizziness, and she really didn't think she could stand for too much longer. She didn't think she could ever get enough of those smiles. But he stepped close and her eyes drifted shut as he kissed her all over again. Vaguely she heard the slide of her zip and before she realised it her dress had slithered to the floor in a sleek heap at her feet.

'Multitasking?' she mumbled in a moment of embarrassment at the simplicity of her exposed underwear. It was black, cotton—no lace or fancy silk and nothing like what any of those models would wear.

But he was still and staring again, erotic hunger stark upon his face. 'You're even more gorgeous than I imagined.'

She crossed her arms and shook her head.

He smiled again but there was an edge of craving to it. 'You don't believe me?' He stepped forward. 'Never mind.' He caught her in a kiss again and then pushed her so she fell back onto the bed. He moved onto the bed too, braced above her, kissing not just her yearning mouth but also down her neck and then lower still. She wriggled but he put a firm hand on her.

'Let me,' he ordered with a low mutter. 'I've wanted to for hours.'

He removed her bra with the skill of a man who'd undone many women. Frankly Ettie was glad as he then kissed his way from one breast to the other, teasing each nipple to a stiff peak of yearning. She quivered as he trailed teasing hands down her ribs to her hips. What was she supposed to do? How could she possibly resist? Her legs had a will of their own and simply spread—earning her a burning glance and then another of those soul-searing smiles. And then he put those lips to even better use.

'*Oh, my, oh, my, oh, my.*' This time she muttered the chant over and over as he teased her. As those hands pulled the panties from her body and his fingers sought out even more secrets. He was kissing her where no one had bothered to kiss her before. It was so shockingly intimate. So incredibly good.

'Leon,' she moaned, half drawing her knees up in rejection as his tongue swirled to even greater intimacy.

She felt the hot breath of his laughter. It tickled and she wriggled a little—half escaping, a whole lot eager.

'You didn't think you were done, did you?' he said, putting a hand on her hip and holding her still.

But what about him? She'd already…she'd already…

But that swirl of his tongue made any more thought impossible. And then his fingers pushed right into her slick heat. She arched taut, locking those talented fingers in place. But even then he teased. His mouth kept up that magic, sucking hard, while his tongue added rough slicks of pleasure. Unstoppable waves of heat rolled over her in a torrent of ecstasy. He growled against her in appreciative hunger as the convulsions started, applying more pressure with his fingers—pumping deeper, pressing harder against her inner walls, and he ate at her like she was the sweetest treat imaginable. Unbearable pleasure tore through her, harder this time as she squeezed on his hold and rode out the crest he'd conjured for her.

'Leon!'

It was a long moment before he answered, sliding up the bed, licking his lips and sending her a smug smile. 'Better now?'

He didn't seriously expect an answer, did he? Because she was still struggling to return to reality, still catching her breath and still desperate for what more that was to come. She wanted *all* of him.

'This is you making the most of opportunities?' she eventually sighed, trying to keep it light even when she was almost buried in need for him.

His gaze turned smoky. 'Yes.'

'Please,' she muttered in total, helpless surrender.

That smokiness flared to fire—pure, burning lust. He thrust back off the bed and pretty much shredded his clothes. He reached into the drawer of the bedside cabinet and retrieved a condom.

'Don't worry,' he muttered. 'I have plenty.'

She trembled with anticipation—her mouth drying as she watched him. He was very…*well built*, and so highly aroused the sight of him made other parts of her moisten. He knelt on the bed and looked at her. He was a hot, experienced, sexually demanding man and right now he was motionless again—*thinking*.

The sexual suspense was almost killing her.

'How do you want…?' She trailed off. She had such little experience, she had no idea what to suggest.

'You have a list in mind?' he teased with a half-smile. ''Cos I do.'

'You go first, then,' she muttered in a low voice, blushing—and then blushing harder as she realised she blushed all over.

'Oh, *glykia mou*,' he chuckled. 'This first time I'm watching every moment flicker over your beautiful face.' He braced himself over her, running his hand down her side in a manner both soothing and stirring as he looked into her eyes. 'I want to see everything, feel everything…'

She felt a flash of vulnerability but he pressed closer and she could see him too—into those brown eyes that she knew had such depths. Right now, she saw desire and humour and the sharp bite of hunger.

'Then do what you want,' she whispered.

He kissed her into softness and stirring heat again. She couldn't believe this was happening. He overwhelmed her—his size, his heat, his musky scent.

'Breathe,' he muttered, gently probing her tightness. At the catch of her breath he hesitated and gave her a searching look.

'It's been a while,' she mumbled, burning with both desire and insecurity.

Another emotion flared in his eyes—hotter than ever. 'I know.'

He knew? How—because she was so desperate? Because she barely knew what she was doing?

'Relax. Kiss me.'

He lifted her, nudging her legs further apart so she could take him more easily. Then in one smooth movement he kissed her and thrust deep at the same time. She cried out with the shocking pleasure of it and clutched his hips to keep him there.

'Okay?' he growled.

'Mmm-hmm.' She was almost delirious with the delight of it—he felt so heavy, she so full.

And it didn't just feel good, it also felt *right*. For the first time she actually understood why people liked this so much. He muttered something she didn't understand and crushed her closer.

And *this* was what she'd wanted most of all—him with her as completely as anyone could be. He moved, watching her, kissing her, riding her swiftly to that point beyond thought. It was unbearably awesome. She gave herself up to complete hedonism, not caring about anything but the demands of her body—driving her hips in the way instinct dictated she must. His breathing roughened, the glitter in his eyes sharpened.

'Ettie.' He huffed her name harshly and pumped harder.

She curled about him more tightly still, screaming as she came harder and longer than she could bear. She heard his roar of need and felt the sudden, full force of his lust unleashed. He slammed into her. Again, then again and again until they collided, interlocked, shaking together for a sublime moment of eternity, lost in that realm of total ecstasy.

She couldn't breathe. Couldn't believe.

'We're doing that again,' he muttered rawly. 'Now.'

* * *

The dog was gone. Rubbing his sleep-fuzzed head, Leon glanced at the empty basket with a frown. Ettie must have woken early and taken him for a walk. Leon wished she'd woken him—he'd have gone with her. Or better still, delayed her a little longer. His body was hard and ready—despite the aches from the full-on, all-night best sex of his life. His curiosity was fully aroused too. For the first time in a long time, he wanted to know more about a woman.

He paced the penthouse, running his hand through his hair again, aching for her return. One night wasn't going to be enough. He'd guessed they'd be good together, but he'd not imagined quite how hot. He grimaced wryly at the condom wrappers littering the bedroom floor. They'd barely bothered with sleep. After that first intense experience, he'd lifted her into the shower and taken his time to soap her up—easing away the last of her shyness and exposing the sly humour he'd seen fleeting snatches of. He'd held off letting her get off until she whispered something she wanted him to do and learned she knew a few curse words too. Hell, in that moment he'd have done anything she asked. She was generous and sweet and funny and he wanted nothing more than to kiss her everywhere until she came all over again.

Half an hour passed and still she didn't return. A prickle of foreboding slid down his spine. Why hadn't she come back? The full quota of staff would be on shift by now and she hadn't wanted to be seen by any of them.

He stilled, irritated. Was he actually worried about her? And the damn dog?

Disliking the uncertainty, he showered and dressed, but once downstairs he stopped some distance from the concierge desk. Ettie was in her uniform—filling out that crisp monogrammed T-shirt and parading the prim black trousers that on her embodied sexiness. She hadn't seen him; she was too busy pacifying a puce-faced resident.

'I'm so sorry that happened.' She sent the resident her most charming smile. 'Don't you worry, I'll straighten it out with George—he doesn't need to know most of it.' She picked up the box on the desk. 'How about we get Joel to come up and help you lift the dresser back into place?'

It was Saturday. Was she supposed to be working? Even if she was, why hadn't she bothered to wake him and say goodbye? Anger burned beneath his skin, but he turned to leave, fishing out his phone as it pinged with a message.

At the sound of an almighty clatter he glanced back. She'd dropped whatever it was in that box. Now she was flushed in the face and completely avoiding looking in his direction. Which meant she'd seen him. Her obvious discomfort eased the chill in his bones. So she felt awkward? Good. So she should.

She'd sneaked out early this morning and was now attempting to act as if *nothing* had happened. While he could respect her need to keep her private life private, he wasn't going to ignore her. And where was Toby? He almost missed the sleepy thing.

Ettie wasn't butter-fingered. Ever. Yet she'd just dropped an entire box of old cutlery, creating the loudest crash ever heard in the lobby. And Leon Kariakis was here to witness it. Of course he was.

Perspiration slicked over her skin. She couldn't look at him, but she could still see him from the corner of her eye and apparently he was busy scrolling through some vitally important message on his phone. At least he wasn't laughing at her openly.

She'd woken up stupidly early this morning and got hit right in the head with the reality hammer. He was fast asleep beside her—a vision of hot, sleepy sex-god—and she instantly realised how completely out of her depth she was. The one and only other time she'd woken next to a man, it had turned into one of the worst days of her life. Her ex had rejected her in the most humiliating, personal of ways the morning after. And then he'd done it all over again in public. The last thing she needed was to hear even any of that horror again from Leon.

She'd lain there frozen, becoming more and more terrified of the moment when he'd wake and see her in the cold light of day and realise his mistake. Sleeping with the sexually clueless concierge girl?

Her blood had iced at the prospect of the inevitably awkward—*or worse*—goodbye that would ensue. She couldn't bear to have any discussion or polite platitudes.

In the end she hadn't been able to stand the anxious torture. She'd slipped from the bed, wriggled into her dress and run—taking Toby with her before he barked his need to go outside. She'd been terrified of bumping into someone she knew in the lift. Of course, it stopped before the basement, ending her chance to escape to the staff locker room unseen. Jess had entered with her trolley. She'd stared at Toby and then at her.

'You should wear your hair loose more often.' Jess had smiled brightly after a horribly silent moment. 'It looks lovely. I didn't realise how long it had got.'

That was because Ettie couldn't afford to get it cut. And Jess had been lying—it didn't look lovely, it hadn't even been its usual wavy mess, but totally tangled, mussed-up bed-hair. That model had been seen exiting Leon's apartment only the other day in that supposed lift-ride of shame...and now she was doing the same? She pushed away the public humiliation. It wasn't worse than the horror she'd escaped years ago.

But she just couldn't face Leon. Her skin almost blistered with embarrassment at the thought of awkwardly extricating herself from his apartment. Because the last thing she could remember from the night before was his throaty laughter as he'd taken her apart again at some insane hour of the morning and now she couldn't work out if he'd been laughing *with* her or *at* her. She'd been his light relief for the night. And hardly his toughest challenge… in fact she'd been so *easy* she'd almost come in the taxi.

He wouldn't want a repeat. He'd probably been feigning sleep and just hoping she'd leave quietly, right?

But with every step she took, the tenderness between her thighs reminded her of his skilful passion, as did the sensitivity of her skin at her collar from the gentle grazes from his evening shadow…

One night only.

And she was not letting anyone know. Ever.

And she was not going to be able to look him in the eye again either. Ever.

Naturally, it was at that exact moment that he walked up to her desk.

'Where's Toby?' he asked briskly.

She fiddled with the box of cutlery the earlier resident had wanted her to return to the shop he'd purchased it from and just knew the man was *not* smiling.

'Harold's neighbour was away yesterday and only learned about what happened this morning. She's asked to take Toby. She cares for him very much.'

'That makes sense.' His reply was clipped.

'Actually, a number of the residents offered to take Toby when they heard what had happened,' she said meaningfully. 'I think a lot would like the "no pets" rule to be lifted.'

She glanced up then and saw winter had returned to his deep brown eyes. There was no hint of the intimacies they'd shared in his expression. There was nothing at all but cool control.

'Why are you on duty? It's Saturday. Haven't you been working all week?' He fired the questions like bullets.

So that was a no to pets, then. And a no to any kind of smile.

'One of the others called in sick and, as I was here early to check on Toby…' She glanced at Joel, working near by, concerned he could hear them.

'Of course.' Leon nodded. 'Thank you.'

'It really is the best thing, I think,' she babbled anxiously because he had such a remote expression in his eyes and she felt him distancing himself even as he stood there. 'He'll be well cared for. She knows him and…' She licked her lips, dying of mortification, and tried to smile. 'I'll have his things cleared from your apartment shortly.'

He shot her an ice-cool look. 'You'll send one of the porters?'

'Of course.' Nervously she nodded. Because he didn't want her back up there?

Of course he didn't. Could the earth just open up and swallow her whole? *Now?* She'd made the right decision to run.

The second Leon left, Ettie leaned against the desk and breathed out, appallingly weak at the knees. That was it. There'd been no real goodbye. Nor was there any glow of amusement in his eyes—no sense of shared intimacy. If anything she had the odd feeling she'd somehow let him down. But that was impossible, wasn't it? He'd had what he wanted. So had she. And now there was no need to have to talk about it or anything mortifying like that. They could just pretend it had never happened.

It was over.

CHAPTER FOUR

'WHERE'S ETTIE?' THE beautifully clad woman demanded an answer from the youngest concierge. *Joel*—according to his monogrammed shirt.

Leon paused at a distance, unable to resist listening in for the answer.

'I'm sorry, Ms Welby, Ettie is away sick.' Joel offered an apologetic smile.

The woman laughed. 'Ettie is never sick. Just as Ettie never takes holidays. Ettie is simply always here. That's her job.'

'Well, she's not here now,' Joel said firmly.

No, she wasn't. She hadn't been at the desk for the last two days. Leon had noticed. He'd more than noticed; he'd *missed* her—missed seeing her smile and hearing her lovely chat with the residents.

He'd tried to avoid the concierge desk as much as possible initially. Unfortunately, he'd soon discovered that it was the heart of the operation. He'd pushed back—spending long hours at his office headquarters, taking more meetings. But he'd always glanced over when he'd walked in. And as the weeks passed, he'd walked through the lobby a little more often than was really required. But she still didn't look at him.

And now, even though it had been over three weeks,

even though he knew all he needed to, he couldn't bring himself to move out of the penthouse and go home. Ettie still irritated him—rather, the way he kept *thinking* about her still irritated him—and that was a problem, given what he'd discovered about the way Cavendish House was run.

Awareness of her absence—*two days running*—sharpened his curiosity. And a chill of warning slithered down his spine because he saw the protectiveness in Joel's eyes as he referred to Ettie being ill. The young guy was concerned about his colleague. So what was wrong with her exactly, if Ettie was never ill?

'May I help instead?' Joel asked the resident awkwardly. 'Ettie's been schooling me in sorting dry-cleaning, you know.'

But the woman dropped her bundle of clothing on the desk and leaned towards Joel. 'Is Ettie actually okay?'

She'd gone from demanding customer to concerned busybody in a flash. That the woman genuinely was concerned for Ettie underlined everything Leon had learned: that everyone adored Ettie and relied on her completely.

'She should be back tomorrow.' Joel's smile wasn't reassuring enough. 'Let me take this for you in the meantime.'

The woman scooped up the dresses with a laugh. 'Thanks, but I don't trust *anyone* except Ettie. I'll wait for her to return.'

'If you're sure, madam.'

'You know I am.' She turned and caught sight of Leon watching her and her expression lit up with a huge smile. 'Oh, Mr Kariakis, it's lovely to finally meet you. My name's Autumn; I'm in apartment twenty-three.'

Leon nodded. 'Is everything okay for you, Autumn?'

'Well, apparently Ettie is away sick, which is hopeless, because she runs this place, Mr Kariakis; I hope you're aware of that.'

He nodded. He'd rapidly become aware of the fact, as it happened. In every conversation he had with either resident or management, it was Ettie to whom they referred for fixing problems. Which was why the fact that he'd taken her to bed was more of a problem than he'd expected it would be. That and the fact that he still couldn't get her out of his head. 'I'm glad you appreciate the service the Cavendish offers.'

'I appreciate *Ettie*,' she said firmly. 'Ettie is simply the best.'

Yes, she was. He never should have slept with her.

'How long has she been away?' Leon asked Joel as idly as he could after Autumn had headed towards the lift.

'I'm sure she'll be back tomorrow,' Joel said with a valiant defence. 'Ettie's never sick.'

That didn't answer his question, but Leon let it slide. He'd give her until tomorrow to return; if she didn't, then he was going to have to investigate.

He couldn't stop thinking about her. It had only been one night and he'd had many one nights with many women, so why was he stuck thinking about *her*?

Was it simply because she now seemed to be missing? Why wasn't she at work? He disliked unanswered questions. Just as he disliked messy endings and tearful women. They were why he stuck to one night.

Ettie was the first woman who'd left *him*. No tears, no mess, no reference to it at all, in fact. If it hadn't been for the sweet scent of her lingering in the air, he might have imagined the whole thing. Except he dreamed of it every night too.

Not turning up to work wasn't something she often did. Nor were one-night stands. When he'd approached her in front of her colleagues that next day she'd been dying of mortification; he'd just been too annoyed to pay attention to it properly at the time. She was shy. Inexperienced. Sweet. And he was a fool for having lost his head and seducing her. Especially now it had become clear she was the main asset of this entire enterprise and he needed her to take more of a leading role.

A horrible thought hit him: was *he* the reason she was away now? Was she so embarrassed by what had happened she was off hunting for another job? Or had he hurt her in some way and not realised—was that why she'd run off so early that next morning? And how was it possible he felt the loss of that damn dog when he'd had custody over it for less than twenty-four hours?

A sharp memory impinged on his mind. A memory he'd blocked for years—of a tiny puppy he'd adored more than anything else in his life. Only it had been snatched away from him just as everything important had then. He'd been betrayed again by the most important person in his life. He swiftly, curtly reminded himself that pets, like people, were not permanent. The loss of them hurt. Which was why he kept them at a distance.

Emotions—all emotions—were a weakness. He'd learned that lesson long ago and he'd remember it well now. Never admit to them, never show them.

It was barely eight in the morning when he went down to the concierge desk the next day. He'd hardly slept. He wasn't going to rest properly until he knew. That fact irritated him. He didn't allow other people's problems to affect him. He didn't let his *own* problems affect him. He just fixed them.

'Still no Ettie?' he asked Joel bluntly.

'No, sir,' the concierge answered awkwardly. 'But she's never had a day off before in the entire time I've been here.'

Leon spied the battered book open on the desk and recognised Ettie's handwriting. He reached across and spun it round to flick through the pages.

'They're Ettie's lists,' Joel hurriedly explained. 'She designed the systems for us. This is our bible.'

Leon knew exactly what it was. She was insanely over-competent. But basic details were all he needed. A phone number, an address. And, as he'd suspected, Ettie had the staff roster in the back of her book. And, with the roster, full contact details. Feeling like some gumshoe detective— *or stalker*—he employed his photographic memory and left.

The drive took longer than he'd guessed it would. She had to spend a while on the trains in the mornings and evenings, which meant that on those nights she worked her other job she got home horribly late. He climbed the stairs of the rundown housing block, trying not to judge the grime and smell. He knew he was from a privileged background. He was luckier than almost every other damn person in the world. Quelling his concerns for her personal security, he knocked on the door. A few moments later, he heard the locks being pulled back.

'Mr Kariakis?'

Leon tensed. He hadn't been Mr Kariakis when she'd been screaming her pleasure beneath him. But he shoved the resentment aside, because she looked horribly unwell.

'What are you doing here?' She peered past him as if expecting to see someone else. 'Has something happened?'

'What's wrong?' He pushed the words out.

It was a searing pleasure to see her, but he was also hit with a sharp pain at how fragile she looked… Her eyes were huge in her pale face and she was swamped in an ancient woollen jumper, black leggings beneath, warm wool socks on her feet.

'Do you need me back at work?' She looked so guilty and anxious, he felt bad.

'Of course not,' he said curtly, keen to dismiss her guilt. 'Not when you're clearly ill.'

Her eyes widened. 'Did you think I wasn't?'

He drew in a sharp breath. 'Ettie,' he growled. 'Invite me in.'

She didn't want to—that truth was written all over her beautifully expressive face. But she stepped to the side. The atmosphere intensified as she closed the door behind him. Something was bundled up inside him too tightly and he had to turn away from her.

She lived in a small, dingy apartment. There was no television, just books, and an old laptop on the dining table. He noticed an instrument case on the bookshelf together with a pile of sheet music. The sofa looked old and lumpy. But she'd tried to brighten the place up with a throw and cushions and three little pot plants on the narrow window-sill. It was immaculately clean and tidy. That made sense.

He'd seen the organisation and management systems she'd put in place for the concierge desk. Everything was written up neatly—processes and information. Perfection. No wonder every resident had been asking where she was these past few days.

'You noticed my absence?' she asked huskily.

He'd noticed her absence when he'd woken that morning and found her gone. He'd been noticing it ever since. 'I was concerned you might have been embarrassed about what happened between us. I didn't want that affecting your ability or desire to remain at Cavendish House.'

Her chin lifted. 'I'm not ashamed. And I'm not pining after you, if that's what you were thinking.'

'No.' He almost smiled because hadn't that been one little wish? 'So you're not planning on leaving Cavendish?'

Her brow furrowed. 'Did you think I was off having

interviews or something?' She shook her head. 'Of course not. I love my residents.'

He stilled. He should have remembered that about her— loyalty, *passion*. That tension soared. It took everything he had not to take two steps and haul her into his arms.

'How did you find out where I live?' she asked, wrapping her arms around herself in a self-conscious gesture.

'I might've looked at your personnel roster.' He glanced at her.

She still looked shell-shocked and paler than he could've imagined. He had the urge to scoop her off her feet and abduct her. He'd take her back to his apartment, he'd...*what*?

Leon gritted his teeth. Not appropriate. Not allowed.

Ettie swallowed hard, still unable to believe Leon Kariakis was standing in the middle of her tiny flat. It was mortifying. Worse than that, it was...*exciting* in an appalling, illicit way. She'd wondered if she was hallucinating when she'd first answered the door. Now adrenaline surged and she fought not to be driven towards his innate sensuality, fought to settle the sizzle stirring in her blood. Yet her heart beat with more vigour than it had in weeks.

It's not why he's here.

'It was nice of you to be concerned, but it's just a stomach bug,' she said unevenly. 'I think the worst is over now, but you don't want to catch it.'

Please leave. Please leave.

Before she did something stupid like throw herself at him.

'You're sure you shouldn't see a doctor?' He frowned at her.

'No, truly. I just need a little more sleep.'

That customary stillness settled over him as he stared at her. 'Ettie.' His voice was little more than a whisper.

She froze, mentally replaying that soft call to her. Had

she heard what she so desperately wanted to hear in his voice? Had there been something more than concern? Had there been longing?

Because of the size of her flat, he was delightfully—dangerously—close. She dragged in a sharp breath, straining to resist. It would be so easy to reach up and kiss him.

You can't.

If she did, she'd be lost. She wasn't cut out to cope with an affair with a man like him. What he'd made her feel that night? She'd be an addict in no time—desperate to have her fix even at the expense of her own well-being. She couldn't afford to be a stupid romantic like her mother—always falling for the wrong guy. The guy who'd never love her back. Leon Kariakis didn't do relationships, he did challenges. Regret swamped her.

If only…

She'd written down the pros and cons and lit a match to send the paper up in smoke. Even so, that lopsided list was burned on her brain. She knew the reality and her responsibility.

'I *need* my job…' She was reminding herself more than telling him. 'I'm sorry to have troubled you. You didn't need to come all the way out here.' Her words were at odds with her secret want. She wanted him to have come here because *he'd* needed—*her*.

'No trouble,' he said stiffly, distance evident in his stance again. 'And you don't need to worry. I'm not about to ask for anything…*inappropriate*.'

He wasn't? Great. Now she was even more mortified by her slight assumption that there'd been any *personal* element to this visit. He valued her more as a concierge than as a concubine. He had no 'best lover ever' award for her—though he'd certainly won hers.

Now he strode to the door, his long pace leashed. He

almost looked angry. 'I'll be implementing some changes at Cavendish House. We can discuss them when you get back.'

She nodded, unable to speak because a stupidly large lump had sprung up in her throat.

'But you're not to return until you're fully fit,' he added as an afterthought. 'Everything can wait until then.'

But it couldn't wait.

Because she'd missed her shift at the stationery shop, her boss had released her from all duties there—dismissing her with immediate effect. As she wasn't on contract, just a relief worker, she had little recourse but to suck it up. The tummy bug had eased—she'd stopped vomiting, though she still felt horrible and horrendously tired. That was too bad. She had to get back to work. Three days off had been an indulgence too far.

She needed the money. And she needed the distraction.

'What's been happening?' she quickly asked Joel as she stepped behind the Cavendish House concierge desk first thing the next morning.

Joel didn't have the chance to reply because Leon Kariakis was bearing down on them both, his expression shockingly thunderous. Oddly his jaw was shadowed, as if he'd not shaved for a day.

'What are you doing here?' His cold, furious gaze sliced right through her.

'What does it look like I'm doing?' Ettie summoned the biggest fake smile she could muster. She was keeping things professional. Maintaining distance. Doing her job.

'You're not working today,' Leon snapped. 'Turn around and go home. I'll hail a taxi.'

Ettie gaped, then glared at him. Had he *no* thought for

privacy? And as if she could ever afford to go all the way home in a cab!

'Excuse me a moment, please, Joel.' She stalked into the small office, not bothering to see if Leon followed her. Because of course he did.

'What are *you* doing?' she threw at him the second he'd closed the door.

'Ettie.' It was a soft growl.

It was the almost irritated look of concern in his eyes that devastated her. She had to turn away from it. But he grabbed her shoulders and turned her back, tilting her chin up. Not so he could steal a kiss, but to subject her to his disapproving inspection. His frown deepened. 'You've lost weight. You shouldn't be here at all today. Not for the rest of the week.'

'I'm fine,' she argued, burning at his touch, at the tension tearing her apart every time she so much as thought about him. Which was insanely often. And to see him? To be this close to him? She was going to have to find a new job after all.

'You're pale. Have you had breakfast?' He interrogated her grimly.

'I need to be here. I need to work.'

'You still look awful.'

'And thank you for that,' she muttered. 'I'm *fine*. It's my decision, Leon. Not your concern.'

An indefinable emotion whipped across his face and then he froze. 'Not my concern?' he echoed with lethal softness.

'You value your independence as much as I do and don't try to argue otherwise,' she said. 'If you needed to work, you would. And I need to work.'

'Not today—'

'I have no sick leave left,' she snapped. 'The stationery

shop has given me the boot because I missed shifts this week, and I need the money because Ophelia has unforeseen expenses. I *am* working today and you are *not* stopping me. Nor are you offering to help me,' she burst out, rejecting his offer before he could make it. Because she just knew he would make it now she'd told him all that. 'I don't want any help from you.'

His mouth opened and shut again as he visibly sought for control. But then he lost it. 'Damn your pride, Ettie,' he ground out in a low voice.

He ran a frustrated hand through his hair, his customary coolness evaporating in a swirl of motion. 'There's independent. And then there's stubborn and pig-headed. You're the latter.'

The guy had no concept of talking quietly. He was all orders and commands and shouting. Joel could probably hear him on the other side of the door, and it would be around the staff that she and Leon Kariakis and were alone in the office, arguing like…like…*lovers*.

'Shush,' she whispered furiously.

'Did you just shush me?' His gaze glittered.

'I have to get on with my job. Please, Leon,' she suddenly broke and begged, her voice catching. 'Leave me alone.'

Leon was silenced. And furious. She couldn't be any clearer. She didn't want him around. But he knew she did. He could see the desperation in her eyes now—she was positively drinking him in.

'What are you doing?' Her voice wavered as he stalked nearer.

Behaving badly. Doing what they both wanted. What they both needed. He hadn't slept a wink since seeing her yesterday, his temper was ragged and he'd been under extreme restraint for too long. Her chin was stuck in the air and her 'leave me alone' vibes couldn't hum louder. He wasn't going to linger where he wasn't wanted.

Except he knew he *was* wanted. Very much. He could see it in her luminous, emotion-laden green eyes, and those vibes had a strong bass thrum of desire. But she had irritatingly strong willpower. She didn't want to want him any more. Well, that made two of them. Because he'd never wanted to be held hostage to desire like this. Never wanted to feel this need to know she was okay. To be so shockingly concerned about her appearance.

She was so beautiful. But right now she looked unbearably fragile. Pale and interesting didn't suit Ettie—she was meant to be full of vitality and radiance.

'Leon.' Her whisper wasn't one of rejection. It was a plea.

He was desperate to get her out of his head, the want for her out of his blood. Never before had he wasted time thinking about anything other than work. He'd never let himself want something so much it became a complete distraction. He controlled all his emotions—even desire.

So now he didn't kiss her. He couldn't. Not when she'd asked him not to. But he'd allow himself just the smallest, gentlest of touches. As he spanned her waist, he heard not just a hitch in her breathing, but also a stifled moan. He felt the ripple of yearning arch through her body and he pulled her closer into his embrace. A hug, right?

But desire burgeoned between them. He gazed into her eyes, watching the searing craving build. Neither could hide it. Nor deny it.

'You don't want any help from me?' he growled at her. 'But you still want me.'

Her soft mouth parted, her lips full and reddened. But her eyes pleaded with him—tormenting him with two vastly different requests. 'That's different.'

It was. And it complicated everything.

She didn't want to want him. Well, *ditto*. With every ounce of willpower he could summon, he released her and stalked out of the room.

Ettie's heart plummeted as the door slammed behind him. She'd *craved* more contact with him. That need had been constant since that first night. No matter how hard she'd fought against it the want simply grew. And now?

She'd banished him for good.

She breathed in and out, trying to steady her pulse and ignore the sharp pain high in her chest. Eventually the adrenaline burst vanished, leaving her overwhelmingly exhausted.

It was so stupid to still feel so tired. She'd not lied to Leon, she'd slept like a log last night, but she just couldn't seem to get enough rest despite turning in as early as she could. She had no idea how she was going to rearrange Autumn Welby's massive walk-in wardrobe right now. Autumn liked her to do it every month and usually it was fine—enjoyable even—to see the dazzling dresses. But this morning the thought of sorting out all those evening gowns made her arms ache and the prospect of Autumn's perfume collection made her gag even more.

'You okay, Ettie?' Joel frowned as she walked from the concierge office to the lift. 'Need a coffee?' He held out a mug.

'No, thanks. I'm fine,' she lied.

In truth she was hot, cold and queasy and the strong smell of coffee almost made her retch. The lift dinged and the doors slid open but Ettie didn't step in. She'd never felt so awful in her life.

'Ettie?' Joel called to her again.

She turned her head to answer him, but then she heard someone else.

'Ettie? *Ettie!*' Leon was shouting.

Blindly she reeled as her body pulsed with regret and *longing.* She opened her mouth to reply but it was too late; nothing came out.

CHAPTER FIVE

'ETTIE…'

It was the merest whisper, but it was that same voice she'd heard in the moment before everything went black.

Leon.

Blinking rapidly, she tried to sit up, but he firmly pushed her back down onto the plush sofa. She shivered at the contact, goose bumps lifting all over her skin. It was appalling how much she wanted that touch.

'Stay still,' he ordered tightly.

He was leaning so close, he was all she could see. Bossy as ever. He'd taken off his jacket, and in his crisp white shirt and dark tie he looked stunning. But it was his eyes that made her all but limp—the potency and depth of the brown and the heat in the amber lights. How had she ever thought his gaze was cool?

It wasn't a ripple of forbidden desire that slithered down her spine now, it was a tsunami. Her body was a disgrace to her—a confused mess. Unwell one moment, racked with feverish lust the next.

'Leon…' She murmured the all too obvious like some brainless devotee. She'd ached to see him again. Then she remembered. She'd fainted at his feet. What an *idiot*.

He looked more serious than ever, which ought to have been impossible. 'I told you, you're still unwell.'

'I've just…' She trailed off.

'It's gone on too long, Ettie,' Leon said decisively.

She struggled against the sneaking desire to lean against him. Instead she made herself look past him. Where was she? Not the concierge office because there was no sofa in there.

'I'm in your penthouse.' Her pulse spiked as she realised.

'Yes.'

'Why?'

'Because you fainted in the lobby.'

'No, I meant… I could have gone into the office.' She moistened her dry lips with her tongue. He hadn't needed to bring her up here. *How* had she got up here? Her heart sank and soared at the same time. He'd carried her. She just knew it.

'Too bad for you.' His tone was cool.

It was too bad, because she still wanted him even when it was impossible. And so damn embarrassing. She shut her eyes to block out the intensity of his impact on her, but somehow it just made it worse. She could *feel* his heat and strength. 'I don't mean to be ungrateful.'

'Leave it, Ettie,' he said softly. 'The doctor's on her way.'

Her eyes flashed open. 'A doctor? I don't need a doctor. I just need another day in bed…'

He was so very near and at her words something stirred in his eyes. Physical weakness sapped her willpower. *His* bed was very near. His bed, where he'd made her feel *everything*.

Her mouth dried as her skin sizzled. Her yearning multiplied to the point of madness. And he knew her thoughts, didn't he? Because he leaned closer, his hand sliding through her hair as he cupped her head and searched her eyes.

'I'm probably infectious,' she mumbled, a final, hopeless defence.

She'd become a little challenge for him again, that was all.

'Too late. I think I've already got it,' he replied grimly. 'Feverish. Sleepless. Loss of appetite…'

Her heart pounded so hard it was a wonder it didn't snap her ribs. 'Leon—'

A loud knock on the door dragged his attention from her and his too rare smile flashed even as he groaned. 'Just in time…'

Ettie pulled herself into a sitting position while Leon answered the door. She heard a concise conversation in Greek and didn't understand a word.

'Ettie, this is Dr Notaras,' Leon said briskly, returning to the lounge followed by a tall, glamorous brunette. 'I'll just be in the study. Call me when you're done.' He said that last to the doctor.

Ettie smiled wanly at the terrifyingly skilled woman and tried to tell her she was fine, but the doctor wasn't all that interested in what Ettie had to say initially. She was too busy taking her temperature and looking in her ears and mouth.

'You've not got any fever,' the doctor noted with a cautious expression. 'And there's no sign of any ear or throat infection. Nothing in the chest. Your pulse is strong, blood pressure good.' She then asked a few questions about her background—no diabetes or history of heart problems?

Ettie shook her head. But what about the nausea? And her sensitivity to some smells?

'Is there any chance you could be pregnant?' the doctor asked blandly.

'N…' She broke off.

There was only one, impossible chance. Although…

She pressed her lips together to stop herself stuttering. There'd been more than one *chance* in that one magical night. Her brain kickstarted into frantic overdrive—desperately searching her memory for dates, signs, *denial*. Finally she seized on the only important fact she could bear to consider. They'd used protection. Every time, right?

'I have a home test in my bag and I can take bloods right now...' the doctor said with quiet efficiency after Ettie's lengthy silence had spoken volumes.

'I can investigate that possibility on my own,' Ettie whispered with a shake of her head. She needed to get away from Leon and find out for herself.

But the doctor searched in her bag for a second and then handed Ettie a slim foil package. She gave Ettie her contact card as well.

'Get in touch if you'd like to see me again. It's truly no problem.' The doctor gave her a professional, but sincere smile.

Ettie had the horrendous feeling it was a huge problem.

'I can come to wherever you are,' the doctor said encouragingly. 'Any time. Leon said—'

'This is just between us, right?' Ettie interrupted swiftly. This woman wasn't about to tell Leon pregnancy was even a possibility, was she?

'Of course.' The doctor nodded and stood.

'Thank you.'

Dr Notaras called something in Greek and Ettie quickly put the slim package into her pocket. She wasn't discussing this with Leon; there was no need. Because it *was* impossible, wasn't it?

She heard more rapid Greek and the lift chime. A few moments later Leon walked back into the lounge alone. He didn't look any less serious, or any more relieved.

'I should get back downstairs.' She couldn't look him in the eye.

'You're staying here,' he replied curtly.

'Leon—'

'If you go back down, I'll cart you straight back up here again even if you scream at me to stop. I don't care who stares.'

Furious at his high-handedness, she determinedly stood in a swift movement. 'I have a job to do and I'm perfectly capable of doing it.'

'What's this?'

Ettie glanced down. The pregnancy test had fallen from her pocket and with his damn panther-like reflexes he'd picked it up before she'd even registered it had tumbled.

'It was just something the doctor...' She trailed off, clenching her fists tightly as he read the print on the packet.

He looked from the test to her. His face had actually whitened beneath his olive-toned skin and his eyes narrowed. 'Is this a possibility?'

She couldn't reply; she was too shocked to see him looking so *appalled*. Her pulse skittered. He didn't want this. He really, *really* didn't want this. Well, nor did she. She breathed in and out, but couldn't think for the noise of her blood pounding in her ears.

'Ettie?' he snapped.

She shook her head. 'We used protection.'

Leon's breath hissed out between his gritted teeth. Her plea granted the smallest peace in his sea of panic. It revealed she'd only him to consider, only that one night. There was no other man in her life and she'd not slept with anyone else in a long time. But then he'd known that the night he'd been with her. She'd been shy and sweet and definitely not especially experienced. The expression of rapture and amazement on her face when she'd come in his arms haunted him. He wanted to make her respond like that again; he'd been aching to do that for weeks.

But now?

The fear in her eyes only grew. 'I just can't be pregnant. Not to—'

'Me?' He frowned. Yeah, even she instinctively knew he wasn't father material. His blood chilled. 'Sorry, Ettie. I know there aren't any other possibilities for the baby's paternity.'

She swallowed but didn't deny it.

'Go and do the pregnancy test,' he ordered. He needed to know. Now.

Her hand shook as she took the package from him. He could all but see her brain processing, frantically remembering dates, the dawning realisation that it might be real. That maybe the reason she'd been feeling rotten wasn't from any infection.

Why hadn't she told him just now? What would have happened had he still been away? If he hadn't been here to see her faint? Would she have told him once she knew? Horror burned. This was everything he didn't want. Flickering memories stirred—of the childhood he'd hated. Of loneliness and lack of power. Everything he didn't want.

He paced the room as he waited. He had to get on top of this situation. *Now.*

She couldn't look at him when she returned from the bathroom. She didn't speak either. She just sat back down on the sofa and drew her feet up until she was in a small ball. An intense pressure built in his chest. But he leaned against the wall and waited, even though he already knew.

'It can't be right,' she said in a whisper. 'We used protection.'

He stared at her fixedly. 'Nothing is one hundred per cent fail-proof.'

'Abstinence is,' she muttered grimly.

Her answer offered a wisp of amusement. 'You know that wasn't an option that night.'

She lifted her lashes, her eyes revealing her distress. 'We're talking lifelong consequences, Leon.'

So she was going to have the baby. One swirling chunk of unease settled within him.

'What are you thinking?' he asked as calmly as he was able. Which was frankly nothing on his usual impassive façade.

She shied away from looking at him again.

'Ettie?' His almost customary cool rose a few degrees. This was so personal, so deeply troubling, he couldn't keep his equanimity. Because it wasn't quite up to him any more.

'I need some space.' She tried to stand up but her face turned grey.

'Sit down.' He was furious with her.

'It'll pass,' she snapped.

And just like that the atmosphere flared, leaping right into dangerous. *Emotional.*

'Most probably. But until it does, you stay right where you are.' He huffed out a tight breath. 'You're not going back to work today.' He threw out a gesture to close down the immediate argument in her eyes. 'Give this today at least, damn it.'

They both breathed out harshly. And then she sank back down to sit on the sofa again.

'It was a night for me,' she muttered fiercely. 'Just for *me*. Just one night. And now this.'

'I'm sorry.' And he truly was. He knew she didn't do one-night stands. He knew she wasn't all that experienced. And the one time she'd let herself go? 'You've got to tell me what you're thinking.'

Because she was thinking—overthinking—if the tight

expression on her face was anything to go by. A myriad of emotions flickered in her eyes, but mostly misery.

Finally she turned towards him, squaring her slim shoulders. 'I'm going to have the baby.'

Yes, he'd known that she would.

But then she spoke some more. 'You don't have to...'

A fierce fury enveloped him as she started to negate his input. 'I don't have to *what*?'

Her lack of answer sent him on the attack. 'You doubt I'd want to be involved?'

'You can't even bring yourself to take a dog for a walk,' she flared up. 'How are you going to meet a baby's needs?'

'I only said I couldn't walk the dog because I wanted to see more of you,' he ground out. 'You know it was my excuse to get you up to my penthouse.'

Her eyes widened and her mouth opened. But she remained speechless. He glared right back at her. She really *hadn't* known that?

He muttered something unprintable beneath his breath. 'I wanted you the second I laid eyes on you, Ettie. And it was the same for you. Frankly, I still want you. Isn't that a good place for us to begin this?'

Her mouth hung open for another moment. Then she snapped it shut and vehemently shook her head. 'There is no *this*. And *that* doesn't last.'

Didn't it? Because it had already lasted longer for her than for any other woman in his life.

He stilled, rapidly reassessing his strategy. He had a highly developed capacity to think through all possible problems, combinations, options in a situation...and he was equally swift to sift and find solutions. An unplanned pregnancy was the antithesis of his life's ambition. He'd never wanted a child. Never wanted a long-term relationship. He'd never even considered it. But fate in the form of a failed condom was forcing both upon him.

He could barely bring himself to think of an actual baby. It was too tiny, too vulnerable. He wouldn't even know how to hold the thing. He ran a hand through his hair and dragged back his focus. He'd do what he was good at— *management*.

While he could provide many important things— wealth, home, an elite education…those things weren't what really mattered. But he'd ensure it had everything he hadn't had. Safety. Security…

He glanced back up and saw her sitting on that sofa— her arm already curved across her flat belly in an instinctive, unconsciously protective maternal gesture as she watched him with a very wary expression on her face.

For only a second did he brood on those old, darkest of memories. The fear, the pain, the isolation. His mother had hated him and she'd shown it in almost every action of almost every day.

But Ettie would be a good mother. Probably too good, given that she put everyone else ahead of herself. She did everything within her power for those she loved.

But it was a shame that it had happened so soon for her and with him of all people. Guilt sucked the strength from his bones. He never should have seduced her. He'd been selfish and greedy and now changed her life irrevocably. Because that baby she was carrying was his.

His inner animal wanted to beat his chest and roar. He'd not stopped wanting her in these past few weeks but he'd been determined to do the right thing. He'd kept his distance, respected her wishes…not messed more personally with his latest business acquisition. He'd tried to restore his own control and not break those rules all over again. But this changed everything.

It was very simple now. The baby would have Ettie. And Ettie would have him.

And there was only one tolerable course of action to ensure that: *marriage*.

It would be an amicable, workable arrangement—basically an acquisition like any other. They just needed to hammer out the terms, come to an agreement and settle it.

But, given the way she was freaking out in front of him, she was going to resist. He was going to have to go gently with her. One thing he'd learned in his business dealings was that in a takeover the acquisition generally loathed being ordered to do something.

'I want to go home.' She glanced at him and defiance shone in her eyes. 'I need some space.'

Leon bit his tongue. Hard. She wasn't staying in that hellhole of an apartment a moment longer.

'This is a shock,' he said after a moment. 'But we're going to figure a way through it. I am trying really hard here not to…'

'Take total control?' she guessed coldly. 'Keep trying.'

He glared at her and made himself draw in another steadying breath. 'I'd like you to live with me,' he said. 'I'd like not to have to worry about you when you're not here.'

'You'd worry that I wasn't doing a good enough job alone?' She got defensive.

He bit back a growl and tried to take even more care over his words. 'You're very good at taking care of other people. Yourself, not so much.'

'I've looked after Ophelia all my life. And myself. I can take care of it,' she said defiantly. 'It's my baby.'

Her statement of claim sent sparks through his blood. There was the fierce tigress—all passion and protectiveness—but he was every bit as protective.

'Mine too,' he shot back. Screw gentle. 'And *we* will take care of it.'

The look she sent him was pure mistrust and it was so damn unwarranted, it riled him more. 'We're equally responsible, so we'll handle this together.'

She looked away.

He got it. He did. Or he tried to. She was used to taking care of everything by herself. He didn't know much about her mother, but he got that Ettie, the child, had been the responsible one. She'd been the primary carer for her whole little family. But she needed to understand that he wasn't going anywhere.

'I will not abandon you,' he ground edgily through gritted teeth. 'And you're not staying in that damp apartment. That's not happening.'

'It's my home.'

Not any more. 'You'll move in with me. Immediately.'

'You're not even asking now,' she said in an accusatory tone. 'You're dictating.'

'Yeah.'

She stared at him, clearly shocked by his unashamed affirmation of the fact.

'I'm not tiptoeing around, Ettie. Be where you need to be.' He shrugged. 'I'm not going anywhere and nor are you.'

Her fragility frightened him, her resistance frustrated him. His own wants made him grouchiest of all. He wanted her in his bed but he couldn't have that now. He'd have this sorted instead. It was an easy enough fix if they could both keep their cool. He'd tried to reassure her and take it slow, but he was used to giving orders and having them instantly obeyed. 'You're not going to wake up in the morning and find me gone.'

Her skin flooded with colour. Because yeah, that

was exactly what she'd done to him. He strode over and hunched down in front of her, striking while he had the advantage. 'We'll get engaged.'

'We'll *what*?' She actually shrank back from him.

'I don't want everyone thinking you're just my live-in lover or latest affair; I want you to have more status than that.' He drew in another deep breath but it did little to take the edge off the irritation that was festering with her refusal.

'Oh,' she said poisonously. 'Because as your fiancée I'd have *so* much *status*.' Her words simply dripped with sarcasm.

'Ettie,' he couldn't help a half-laugh, 'don't be a witch.' He leaned closer. 'I want this child to be legitimate. It should have its rightful inheritance. This is *my* reputation as well as yours.'

She wrinkled her nose. 'You care about your reputation?'

'I keep my personal life discreet.' His personal life generally consisted of pleasurable screws with swift conclusions. 'I'm seen as reliable for my investors. That matters to my business.'

And he was certain it mattered to her. She was afraid he'd abandon her—well, this was one way of showing he wasn't about to. 'We'll get a ring and announce our engagement—'

'I'm *not* getting engaged again,' she blurted, before blushing beetroot.

'Again?' Leon stilled as her words sank in and a balloon of outrage burst in his gut. 'You've been engaged before?'

CHAPTER SIX

ETTIE SEEMED TO have frozen in place on the sofa. 'We don't know each other at all, Leon. This just can't work.'

'Tell me what happened,' Leon said grimly.

'It doesn't matter what happened,' she snapped.

'Obviously it does, because it's rendering you irrational now.'

'Me irrational? You're the crazy one—insisting on marriage when it's completely unnecessary.'

Actually, it was imperative. The more he thought about it, the more crucial the concept had become.

But she leapt up from the sofa and paced away from him. 'I'm not going through that humiliation again,' she muttered. 'I'm no longer that stupid, naive girl who believed in happy-ever-after.'

Her vehemence drew a smile from him. 'You believed in happy-ever-after?'

She lifted her chin in the face of his amusement. 'Why shouldn't I have?' But then she blushed again and turned away as some bitter memory made her face fall. 'Forget it.'

He considered her words quickly—*humiliation, naivety.* 'He broke up with you?'

She nodded.

He didn't press for more details. Now wasn't the time. 'I'm not promising you moon dust,' he said with simple clarity. 'I'm not declaring undying devotion. We'll have no lies. No false promises.' He drew in a breath as the perfect plan crystallised in his mind. 'Don't think of this as a traditional marriage proposal. This isn't romantic love, rainbows and unicorns, this is a real solution to a real issue,' he said. 'Obviously I'll financially support both you and the baby one hundred per cent. That's a given. But here's my offer. If you marry me, I will pay for all of Ophelia's schooling. Not just the rest of this year, but all her university studies as well. She wants to do medicine, correct? So a decade or thereabouts of training and specialisation? Paid for. She doesn't have to stress about getting a scholarship, she just needs to be accepted onto the course. She can choose any university—hell, any country; if she wants to do some parts of it in the States, Europe…that's fine. All fees, all accommodation costs, living costs, everything. I have it covered. She only has to get the grades.'

He paused, watching intently for her response.

She was motionless, her clear-eyed gaze fixed upon him. 'You can't possibly—'

'Say the word and I'll have my lawyer draw up the contract. I do not enter contracts lightly, Ettie. And I do not break them. This is a legitimate offer. All you have to do is accept it.'

'By marrying you.' Her focus wavered.

'Yes.'

'But we don't love each other.'

'That's irrelevant.' He dismissed the concern with ruthless efficiency. This wasn't about anything emotional, this was about security, practicality, plain common sense.

She swallowed. 'You would expect us to remain married…for good?'

Something stirred low in his gut at her question. He ignored it. 'I don't see why it shouldn't work out long-term.

However, if things became difficult between us personally, then we'd find an alternative solution. My financial commitment to your sister wouldn't be broken, however. Nor to you. As the mother of my child, you will always have a home.'

Ettie reeled. He made it sound like she'd won the lottery. 'Why can't we find that alternative solution now?'

'Because I will not allow my child to be born illegitimately,' he reiterated sharply. 'However, I don't imagine that things would become difficult. We work together well, Ettie.'

Work together? He really saw this as an emotionless, uncomplicated resolution? Obviously for him it was exactly that. Because apparently it wouldn't be the 'done thing' for him to have an illegitimate child with a service worker…

And he was playing on her loyalty and love for her sister to get what he wanted. It was ruthless of him. But she suddenly realised that that was what he did—targeted an acquisition and did what it took to make the deal happen. And he did it damn fast. No wonder he'd made all that money by such a young age.

'You know I can support you, Ettie. I have the finances and the wherewithal to ensure both you and the baby have everything you need,' he said firmly.

The shutters on Ettie's bruised heart closed. 'The baby will need more than financial security.'

She needed more too. Because she knew happiness came from something other than money. But she had the feeling she wasn't about to get it.

'Of course, but the basics in life also matter. Food, clothing, decent accommodation.'

His cold emphasis on the latter irked her enough to spell it out. 'What about emotional security?'

'You already love the baby.'

His simple, swift assertion silenced her and to her horror tears sprang to her eyes. Because in that instant she realised she did. As shockingly unexpected, as inconvenient, as *new* as it all was…it was wonderful. Raw emotion swept over her at the thought of that tiny little being growing inside her. Their baby. Her imagination sprang into overtime, sending her images of a beautiful child—a female Leon, or maybe a mini-me little boy… If this baby had half Leon's looks, it was going to melt every heart.

'Write the list, Ettie.' He was watching her coolly as if analysing her every word, every expression. 'All the reasons for, all the reasons against. Make your decision from there.'

There was no 'decision' and he knew it. The arrangement he'd offered was impossible for her to refuse. Because it wasn't about her. It was about this tiny baby. And it was about Ophelia. Leon was offering complete security for them both. Ophelia could just relax and focus on her studies without the added pressure of trying to get a scholarship. He'd said she could apply to any university and Ettie knew he meant it. It was incredibly generous…

But Leon didn't really want *her*. It had been a one-night-stand—that was all he'd wanted. And she'd lived with the consequences of a one-night stand. Her sister, Ophelia.

She and Ophelia had both been unwanted by their fathers. She'd watched her mother become embittered by the betrayal of the men she'd wanted to love…to the point where she no longer coped with the normal demands of life. And Ettie had been a fool for love too, hadn't she? Flattered by the first man to pay her attention… She'd been such an idiot. And now?

Leon Kariakis didn't actually want anything from her. He had more money than he knew what to do with and he had an endless stream of willing women. He was simply stuck with her and being honourable about it—saying all the right things, attempting to do the right things. But wasn't that only going to lead to resentment in the end? He'd never want to be trapped together for good with her. And his 'contract' was too unbalanced. He was offering a ring and room in his penthouse…and what did she bring to the party? Her overly efficient womb.

'You're offering all this…paying for so much,' she said awkwardly. 'It doesn't seem fair. What do you get out of it?'

His expression smouldered. 'I get what I want.'

Something heavy shifted within her. That low drag deep in her belly that pulled her towards him. But he meant the baby, right?

'Ettie.' That low, irresistible growl sounded.

'Yes.' It whispered out before she'd even thought it.

He was the one who moved, walking towards her until there was too little space between them. 'Let's go and get your things from your flat.' His voice was husky.

She couldn't move.

'Ettie…' He put his hand on her waist. The amber lights glowed in his deep brown eyes. But he didn't smile. He looked edgier than ever as he applied pressure and pulled her against him until she was in no doubt of his physical response to her.

'Will this be…part of the contract?' She flung her chin up, determined to hold her own with him. Because if she couldn't do that now, she had no chance of keeping him in check.

Something flashed in his eyes. 'I'll be faithful to you and I expect the same in return. But I'm not going to demand sexual favours. There won't be a clause detailing a minimum number of intimacies each week.'

She opened her mouth, shocked at the suggestion. At

the appallingly hot response of her treacherous body to such a requirement.

'If anything happens, it's up to us in that moment. Just like normal,' he said. 'No expectations, no repercussions… regardless of what we do in private.'

No repercussions? It was so ironic, but she couldn't laugh. Right now she couldn't even breathe.

He ran his hand down her spine, coming to rest his palm on the curve of her hip. 'Maybe we should stop negotiating…'

Her body melted. He was seducing her into saying yes. And she knew he could, so easily. Abruptly she pulled out from his hold. 'Maybe you don't try to distract me like that.'

'Maybe that kind of distraction would be good for you,' he countered with a small smile.

Sensation rippled down her spine. 'Maybe we should just go and get my stuff.'

She heard his low laugh as she walked away. She realised too late that he'd manipulated her into doing what he wanted. He'd easily played her…because he knew she was weak with want for him still. She screwed her eyes shut; that was *so* mortifying. Echoes of her ex-fiancé's callousness circled in her head—building her demons of insecurity. She *hated* her inexperience.

'Come on, *glykia mou*. Let's get moving.'

'What does it mean?' she asked. 'That expression?'

Another flicker of a smile curved his lips. 'My sweet.'

'You think that's going to get you extra points?' she asked tartly. But she was breathless beneath the weak sarcasm. It was *really* unfair of him because he didn't mean it.

'I think it's only a matter of time,' he murmured wryly. 'And I think you know it as well as I do.'

'You weren't interested in a repeat,' she said stiffly.

'Because you shut me down.' He shot her an astounded look. 'I was respecting *your* wishes.' And he didn't look all that happy about it.

Her heart thundered. He'd thought she'd shut him down? 'And now?'

'All bets are off.'

Craving curled through her body. Intense, shocking, explicit want. It was desire for contact, right? Physical closeness because she felt alone. It was just an instinctive, basic need that she was determined to suppress.

'The situation is what it is, Ettie,' he added. 'We might as well make the most of it.'

'And in your world "making the most of it" is us sleeping together again?' she jeered bitterly.

'We do it pretty well.'

Pretty well? Great. For him it had been just as average as she'd feared and he was just using *her* weakness for him to get what he wanted.

He suddenly chuckled. 'Oh, Ettie, you're so transparent.'

Before she could argue he turned her to face him and brushed his lips over hers in the lightest whisper of a kiss. Her breathing faltered—all that tantalising promise was only a breath away. But he didn't mean any of it.

'It's not fair of you to tease me this way.' She valiantly defended her heart when he lifted his head from hers.

Because he knew, didn't he, just how overwhelmed she was by his sensuality?

But at her words he stilled. A second after the lift door opened, she found herself with her back against the wall of the lift and he was right there in front of her. Hot, fierce fury unfurled deep and low in her belly at the smoking expression in his eyes.

'I'm not teasing,' he muttered.

Leon slammed his mouth over hers—determined to

draw out her spark even if it was only because she was aggravated with him. He wanted her fire. He kissed her hard and deep, plundering her softness with a flick of his tongue. The flare within her was instant. Her hunger took him by surprise and unleashed his own. Hell, he'd wanted this and he'd been too long denied. He curled her arms around his neck so he could haul her closer and grind her against the wall. Her fingers twisted and locked in his hair.

The heady relief at having her in his arms again contrasted with the burning desire tightening his body to the point of pain. He was angry she'd held him at bay when she so clearly craved his touch the way he ached for hers. Now he was mad with her. Now he wanted to torment her. To please her.

She moaned as he cupped her breast with a firm, greedy hand. Her nipple strained against her shirt. Her fingers tightened in his hair. She was so hot he lost his head completely, rushing straight back into that insane intensity of all-consuming lust. He'd suffered weeks of being without this. He didn't know how he'd stood it.

A bell pinged somewhere in the distance. It took him a moment to realise that the lift door had slid open.

'Oh, excuse me.'

Leon froze and glanced down at Ettie, amused to see her turn bright pink. She hurriedly disentangled her fingers from his hair and craned her head to see who it was talking.

It turned out the lift hadn't stopped at the basement. He hadn't even had the brains to push the damn buttons in his haste to touch her. The lift had been summoned by another resident. As a result it had stopped halfway down the building and right now Autumn Welby was staring at them with frank fascination.

'I'll wait for the lift to return. Nice to see you're back, Ettie,' she said breezily. 'I'm so glad you're feeling better.'

Leon glanced again at Ettie, but now she'd gone pale. He tightened one arm around her waist and reached out with the other to push the button on the lift.

'Ettie won't be back on the concierge desk for the foreseeable future,' he said briskly, sending Autumn a dismissive smile.

'Oh.' Autumn nodded. 'Lovely for you, terrible for me.'

The lift doors slid shut again and he looked back into Ettie's face to see nothing but fury.

'For the foreseeable future?' she repeated in a frigid voice. 'Just like that, Leon?'

Yeah, just like that. He wasn't about to apologise and he didn't have the brain to explain it all just yet.

She extricated herself from his arm and folded her own across her chest, all but tapping her foot as the lift swept down to the basement.

'Everyone will know now.' She threw him an appalled look as she stomped out into the garage. 'Everyone will know in minutes.'

'Ettie, we're getting married. You're having my baby.' He followed her slowly, determined to remain calm and get his head around her response to that kiss. 'They're going to find out some time anyway; it might as well be now.'

She drew herself up short and whirled to face him. 'But it's so early…'

A horrible thought hit. Was she worried about miscarrying the baby? Was that even a possibility? A surge of protectiveness—and self-condemnation—welled in him. He shouldn't be pawing her when she needed rest.

'Everything will be fine.' He pushed past the hoarseness in his voice and led her to his roadster. He didn't want his driver for this ride. He needed his own hands on the wheel. 'You're fit, healthy, strong.'

And so damn beautiful that all he wanted to do was

scoop her into his arms, toss her onto the nearest bed and pick up where they'd left off before they'd been so brutally interrupted. But he couldn't exhaust her with his selfish lust. He had to put both her and the baby ahead of his own desire. Ettie needed certainty and security. She had too many worries, too many responsibilities. But he'd lift them from her. And while lust might not last, it would get them through this phase until they settled into a long-term arrangement. He could provide her with a lifestyle she'd only ever dreamed about. She'd never have to worry about paying for her own groceries or heating again. She didn't have to scrimp and save for her sister's education. She could care for their baby and breathe easily for the rest of her life. Those key points she could never argue against and never beat. He had this situation won and she knew it.

'You'll have to get another car.' She glanced at the Italian two-seater.

He nodded.

'What about Ophelia's holidays?'

'I have plenty of space.' He didn't tell her he meant his London home. They weren't staying at Cavendish House another night. She was too uncomfortable and he understood that. They needed privacy. She needed the space to let go of her inhibitions—to scream his name as she came.

Cool it, Romeo. He mocked himself. She was exhausted and overwhelmed and the last thing she needed was him making physical demands on her. He'd won already. He could wait a little longer.

CHAPTER SEVEN

IT TOOK ETTIE only five minutes later to fill a small case with clothes and a few very personal effects from her flat. She went to fetch her coat from where it hung over the back of a chair.

'Leave it,' he said. 'We'll get you a new one.'

She stiffened, saddened that he'd noticed how worn it was. She cast a last glance around the room. How was it possible that such a tiny apartment could feel so empty? She'd helped her sister learn to read here. She'd made Ophelia's lunches and cleaned her uniforms. For so long it had been the two of them against the world…

And she wasn't telling Ophelia about this yet. Not until she'd got control of everything—mostly her emotions.

'I'll get the rest of your things boxed up; don't worry about any of it.'

Don't worry?

Her mother had fallen for the wrong man more than once. Ettie had made an almighty mistake putting her faith in a guy already… But maybe Leon's way was right? Maybe it was as simple as writing up the list—the pros and the cons and being cool-headed about it.

He wanted the baby. She came with it. So he'd keep her happy to keep her onside—give her a home, help support her sister. He might even have sex with her if she played her cards right. But even that for him wasn't *emotional*. It was a relaxant—a satisfying physical release. An added bonus to the deal they'd made.

Maybe it could be just fun for her too? Maybe she could be more like Leon? He seemed to have it so completely together…

The irony was that everything had been pretty fine—better than it had in ages actually. She'd been making it work in this final stretch of Ophelia's schooling. But now it felt as if her life had fragmented and all the elements were slipping from her control. She was furious with herself. But she couldn't quite regret it completely.

She watched Leon drive them back into the heart of London. He seemed to enjoy controlling the powerful machine. He appeared as calm as ever. Certain of his place in the world and the decisions he made. It was as if his handsome face had been carved from marble by a master craftsman. Expressionless. Emotionless, he'd locked back into business focus easily. So he really had only been teasing moments ago, while she'd been almost *desperate* for his touch. Now she shivered with a horrible fear she was going to feel even more alone living in his apartment.

'Where are we going?' She sat up and twisted to read the road sign. 'We just went past Cavendish House.'

'We're going home.'

'The penthouse there is your home.'

'No, that's where I was staying for a few weeks while I studied my new investment. *This* is my home.'

They'd turned into a quiet side street in the heart of Mayfair. Her heart ceased beating. It wasn't an apartment in a building, but the *whole* building. She'd known he was wealthy, but this wasn't a millionaire's penthouse; this property was worth multi-multi-millions—a billionaire's mansion in one of the most expensive streets on the planet.

'How many bedrooms?' she muttered.

'Only six.' He walked ahead of her. 'Four bathrooms.'

Oh, was that all? She shook her head after him as he led the way. There was a gleaming kitchen—light, airy, equipped with appliances Ettie wouldn't know how to turn on...

'There's a catering kitchen and staff quarters downstairs.'

She blinked. 'You have a lot of staff?'

'I have a housekeeper; she doesn't live on site but she comes every other day. She'll prep food for us if we want. My executive assistant sometimes uses it if we're working late on a deal.'

'Oh?' She tried not to imagine his beautiful assistant. 'I expect she's very efficient.'

Leon sent her a sideways, all too knowing look. 'He is.'

Ettie stared, overwhelmed by the trio of reception rooms. The home gym and pool and cinema room almost gave her conniptions. It was all beautifully furnished in muted greys and neutrals, with pops of colour—shades of blue in a few rooms, green in another. The curved wrought-iron balustrade of the staircase revealed snippets of the delights of each level. There were both polished wooden floors and plush carpets, and the light fittings sparkled like works of art themselves...speaking of which, striking paintings adorned the walls. The bathrooms were lined with vast marble and gleaming chrome...the entire house was a simply exquisite, designer's wet dream.

Yeah, he'd really been slumming it at Cavendish House. She'd thought *that* was exclusive, but this was a whole new level of luxury.

'Why did you buy it?' she asked out of complete curiosity. What did he need such a big home for?

He looked surprised by her question. 'I liked it.' He glanced around the recreation room. 'Don't you like it?'

She'd have to be mad not to adore it. She thought of the inviting crystal-clear blue of his indoor pool and the spa alongside it. 'You use the beauty treatment room often?'

Grinning, he shook his head. 'No, nor the bar and home cinema much either. You're welcome to it all, of course; this is your home now.'

She didn't think she'd ever feel at home in such an immaculate, luxurious space. It seemed every item in it was unique and priceless.

'Where are the bedrooms?'

He led her up the curving staircase. 'There are a couple of bedrooms on each of these floors. The study up on the top floor opens onto a rooftop terrace; it's nice on sunny days. But this is my room.'

His bedroom alone was larger than her entire flat. An enormous bed was the centrepiece, but the room was large enough to hold a sofa and an armchair as well as a beautiful wooden cabinet. A wide doorway offered a glimpse of the gleaming marble and black finish of his bathroom.

She cleared her throat. 'Which is my room?'

He sent her a glinting look. 'If you don't want to be in mine, you can choose any of the others. Though I'd prefer it if you were on the same floor as me. For later in the pregnancy.'

No, she did not want to be in his room, or even on his *floor*. He wasn't having everything his own way.

Ettie snatched up her bag and marched to the bedroom furthest from his, knowing damn well she was spiting herself as much as him in this small act of defiance.

'I'm going to run a couple of errands,' he said coolly, following her to the room she chose. 'I'll be back in an hour or so. You take your time and settle in.'

'Okay,' she said.

'Fancy anything in particular to eat?'

She shook her head. 'Whatever you think will be nice.'

He nodded and left.

It took only a moment for Ettie to hang her few clothes—they really didn't suit the designer walk-in wardrobe. With a rueful grimace, she walked around the house again—taking in more details now Leon wasn't here to distract her. It really was incredible. It even had its own garden, which in this space-at-a-premium part of London was almost unheard-of. The whole place was impeccably maintained—that housekeeper clearly had fun keeping it pristine and photo-spread-worthy, with perfectly folded towels at the ready and vases of fresh flowers to give the place vibrancy. All this for one guy?

He came from a completely different world to hers.

But what struck her even more was the lack of anything particularly personal of Leon's on display. There were no family photos, or holiday snaps. The only vaguely personal images were some arty black and white shots of some buildings—buildings he owned, including this one. It seemed his property empire was everything he cared about.

She returned to the bedroom she'd chosen and walked into the stunning white and grey marble bathroom. She simply couldn't resist that deep-set bath. Not when there was that selection of French perfumed soaps and salts to add to it. Not when she needed to relax so badly. A few minutes later she sank into the gloriously scented, warm depths.

But her raging thoughts wouldn't quieten. That was impossible when her world had been totally turned upside down. Leon Kariakis was insisting they marry. Offering a *contract*, not his heart. But she was going to be okay with that because she was *not* going to make the mistakes of her own past, or of her mother's. She was going to learn from Leon—be businesslike and efficient.

She slipped lower, appreciating the silken slide of the water on her bare skin, and her mind wandered to less *businesslike* imaginings. This bath was definitely built big enough for two.

All thoughts of efficiency fled as sexual frustration suddenly flared. Why hadn't he touched her again since they were interrupted in that lift? That kiss had been incendiary and she ached for more. The nausea that had plagued her for days had dissipated as arousal replaced it. She wanted him to send her into that place where thoughts couldn't impinge, where there was only feeling and pleasure and so much *touch*...

'Ettie?'

She almost jumped right out of the bath.

'Sorry, I won't be a minute,' she gasped. 'I'm just in the bath.'

There was a moment's silence on the other side of the door. 'You must be hungry.' He sounded a little huskier.

Absolutely. But not for what he meant. 'Sure. I won't be long.'

She levered herself out of the bath, wrapped her body in one of the enormous plush towels and quickly dressed.

He was waiting for her in the kitchen. 'I got this for you,' he said without preamble, pushing a small box across the counter to her.

Ettie's heart stopped. Reluctantly, but unable to refuse, she opened the box. She blinked a couple of times, almost blinded. 'Where'd you get it from?'

'Christmas cracker, where do you think?'

'You bought it?'

'Well, I didn't steal it.' He rolled his eyes.

She didn't ask if it was synthetic. She didn't want to give him another chance to look smug.

'You can't just buy what you want,' she muttered, her resistance to him building in a wave of heat and fury. Because it was such a beautiful ring and there was that weak, romantic, *foolish* part of her that would've loved to be given this in another time, another circumstance, with other words… 'You can't buy me,' she added ferociously.

'I know that,' he said softly. 'If there's anyone who knows money can't buy happiness, it's me.'

His reply struck her silent. Unexpected and revealing—had he not been happy? When? She waited, willing him to say more. Instead she watched that expressionless veil slide across the flare in his eyes.

'Just put it on, Ettie.'

It was a flawless square-cut emerald set in a platinum band. A large diamond sat either side of the pale green stone. Simple yet sublime, and so very stunning.

She stalled for time because she was shaking inside. She'd never touched anything like it in her life. 'You often go out to get takeaways and come back with precious jewels?'

'Every Wednesday. You can set your watch by me.'

Smart Alec. 'I thought this was business.'

'It's personal business.' But there was a glint flicking in his eyes again. 'And it is straightforward.'

How could it be? He didn't think this was complicated?

Was this really just another acquisition for him—a fiancée and a baby? He was so in control and unconcerned and capable. Didn't he feel fear? Didn't he feel anything? Was he really as emotionless as he appeared?

'Stop overthinking. It'll work out.' He walked around the counter, took the ring out of the box and reached out to hold her cold hand. 'For the baby, okay? You want your child to have two actively involved parents. Here you go. A united front. A team, Ettie.'

She sent him a baleful look. She did want that, very much. Because it was what she hadn't had and he knew it. He was counting on that as he slid the ring down.

But people co-parented the world over with perfectly amicable arrangements and weren't married or even engaged. They made it work. There was no reason why she and Leon couldn't work out something just as successful.

Except his argument for marriage was compelling. She too wanted her child to have the security Leon was offering. And she'd nailed being practical at work, so why couldn't she apply the same to her personal life?

Intuition sent a tinge of unease down her spine. The problem was *his* magnetism. He only needed to stand this close, to hold her hand like this, and her heart was racing, sending excitement through every vein, to every cell. Ettie could fall far and fast—make the mistake of believing that, rather than being his "for the practicalities" fiancée, she was his match for real. And that wasn't fair on him. Or on her. Because the same was so not happening for him. He was *only* about the practicalities.

So she had to focus on the same. Keep her guard up, warn off her weak, blind heart.

She hauled together all her emotional strength and pulled her hand from his, tore her gaze from his. She'd accept this for what it was.

She smiled down at the ring. 'It's beautiful, thank you.' Then she turned, desperately commenting on the first thing she saw. 'I didn't know you already had a dog.' She was determined to make things easy and casual between them.

Blinking, he sent her a mystified look.

'The dog bowl on the bench behind you?'

'Oh?' His eyebrows snapped down, forming a frown. 'I ordered those when I thought that Toby might stay.'

Really?

'I'm sorry I said yes to that resident taking him without talking to you first,' she muttered thoughtfully. The sense she'd wronged him somehow in making that choice had been nagging her for these last couple of days.

'Don't apologise; it was best for the dog,' he said crisply.

So he hadn't really wanted him? But she'd sent Toby to that other resident the very next day, so Leon had been super-quick off the mark getting in bowls for him. But that was just his hyper-efficiency, wasn't it? Just as he'd convinced her to agree to marrying him and ensconced her in his home within two hours of learning she was pregnant. It was how he was a billionaire before thirty. Leon Kariakis got stuff done with single-minded, ruthless efficiency and there was nothing emotional about it.

Yet she couldn't look away from him—aware once more of that simmering intensity that his stillness masked. He'd loosened his tie and his shirtsleeves were rolled back and a tuft of hair was still ruffled. She suspected it was from when she'd run her fingers through his hair in the lift earlier. Did he know how tormenting he was?

'You're feeling better.' He changed the subject.

Yes. With every step closer she was to him unfortunately. And she was incredibly curious. He wasn't just a closed book. He was padlocked-and-sealed-in-an-underground-vault private. But they were having a baby together. Getting married. Even in business arrangements, people did due diligence, didn't they? Maybe if she offered information first—broke the ice—he might feel a gentle obligation to reciprocate?

'My father wasn't there for me. Ever,' she said quietly.

He paused and glanced at her.

'So thank you for wanting to stick around.'

He tensed. 'I'm not like him.'

'I know.' The guy was already a better father than what her own had been and what Ophelia's had been by the simple fact he was actually interested. 'My mother got her heart broken a couple of times. It hurt her badly.' She was quiet a moment before summoning courage. 'What about your parents?'

'Absent, mostly.'

Really? She was surprised. 'Didn't they turn up to sports day?'

'No. Are you ready to eat? You must be hungry.'

She frowned, irritated that he'd shut that conversation down so quickly. 'We can't just…start living together and being engaged. We need to get to know each other, Leon.'

He blinked at her again. 'What do you want to know?'

'I don't know. Anything.' Everything. She glanced at those empty bowls on the far bench. 'Did you have a dog when you were a kid?'

'No.' To her amazement his expression became like blank granite. 'Come on, dinner is on the table.'

'Which one?' she asked tartly.

Leon knew he'd been abrupt, but some things she didn't need to know. Life was for living in *now*, not remembering the miseries of the past. He tried to ignore the prickling at the base of his spine. He was satisfied she was in his house finally, yet he was unbearably aware of her in his space. The mansion was large but her presence seemed to permeate every inch…the scent of her, the soft sounds as she moved about.

He'd had to get out just to clear his head. Sort out the ring as consideration for the contract. Decide on dinner. Check in with his assistant and ensure everything at the office was under control…but he'd listened with only half-concentration and in the end he'd not been able to get back fast enough to check on her.

Stupid to be so concerned. He knew emotions weakened a man—muddying the mind and making decision-making difficult. Isolation and independence brought clarity. There were mergers and acquisitions, splits and divisions, and this was just another. It should be simple.

'Oh.'

He suppressed a chuckle as Ettie came to a halt at the entrance to the formal dining room.

'When did you do this?' She gaped at the table laden with dishes.

'It was delivered while you were in the bath.'

She gazed from the table to the discreet trolley in the corner. 'It's from a restaurant.'

Yeah, as concierge to an exclusive apartment building, she knew how it worked. He paid, the staff delivered. And it was worth it for the privacy.

She lifted the silver cover of the nearest dish and her eyebrows lifted. 'Do you only dine from award-winning restaurants?'

He took a seat and stared at her with all the lazy arrogance he could muster. 'I like savouring perfection,' he drawled.

She rolled her eyes and he laughed in delight.

'You asked for it,' he ribbed her. 'You think I'm pompous? I can eat a wrap on the street from a food van like anyone else, but tonight I want to sit in comfort and privacy and let *all* my senses feast.' He sent her a meaningful look. 'I have a pretty companion to ogle. Besides which, you're tired and you need a decent meal.'

And frankly, her enjoyment of decent food increased his own pleasure in it.

She sighed and sank into the chair opposite his. 'You're so used to doing everything your own way, aren't you?'

'Isn't everyone?'

She laughed aloud, a bubble of genuine amusement. 'The fate of the only child,' she teased. 'You've never had to learn to compromise.'

He tried to smile but his mouth had swiftly dried. It wasn't her fault. She simply didn't know.

'You're very serious,' she continued her judgement. 'Hard-working.'

'It's how I became successful.' He tried not to sound like a stiff-necked ass, but it was true.

'So,' she angled her head to study him, that teasing light brightening her eyes even more, 'not a wild playboy…at least not publicly. You were never the spoilt heir to a fortune who fritters it all away on women and wine and destructive vices…'

'No, that's not me.'

'But why not?' She seemed quite fascinated. 'It's the trap lots of people in your position fall into, isn't it? Stories like that fill the news… Playboy heirs. Dissolute, depraved, who end up broke—'

'Or dying of an overdose; I get the picture,' he finished coldly. 'I guess that's not the way I was raised.'

'So how were you raised?'

He eyed her across the table and she met his censuring look with a radiant smile of utter innocence. Yeah, she knew what she was doing and he knew she wasn't about to let up.

'Strictly,' he muttered.

'You said they were absent.' She looked thoughtful. 'Do you see them now?'

He didn't think of his parents much and he certainly never discussed them. Why would he? But he had to give her something—she was like a dog with a bone. The bald facts would do. 'We have dinner once every six months. It's scheduled—the full year in advance. We discuss returns, hotel occupancy rates, the stock market.'

Her eyes widened. 'Twice a year?'

'Yes.'

'And that's it?'

'Yes.' He could see her mind working overtime.

'Do you ever take a date?'

'Never. It's an obligation on both sides. They never doubted I would do anything other than succeed. And they ensured I was never spoiled by the wealth I was born into.'

He pointedly stabbed a chunk of steak and shoved it into his mouth. That was enough, surely? She was more curious than a barn full of cats. And the meat tasted like sawdust and glue. He made it go down with a hard swallow. 'Look, I know you're worried about how little we know of each other, but it isn't something that can be forced, or hurried,' he said, closing off the conversation. 'Time will take care of it.'

She still looked thoughtful. And utterly unconvinced. 'Most people wouldn't work as hard as you if they didn't have to.'

'Why not? Don't we all need a purpose? A sense of dignity from a job well done? What makes you think I wouldn't need that too?'

'But to be so driven... When is it enough?' She gestured at the furnishings in the large room. 'What is it you have to prove?'

'I don't need to prove anything,' he growled. 'Perhaps it's just that the goalposts shift. I make a plan to achieve one thing, when it's knocked off I feel like a challenge for something more. Isn't that human nature?'

A shadow crossed her eyes. 'So you're never satisfied with what you have?'

His chest tightened and he laughed and groaned at the same time because her effervescent curiosity was going to be the death of him. But she was irresistible. It was that manner that made her so popular with the residents at Cavendish House. She made you feel like you could confide everything in her and she'd sort it all out for you. 'I'm satisfied,' he growled. 'I just want *more.*'

Right now he was greedy for *her.* She was wearing a thin old T-shirt and jeans that hung a little loose. But she was still flushed from that bath and her skin looked luminous and silky soft. She smelled tantalising and her hair was a wild, damp mess down her back and he just wanted to thrust his hands into the gorgeous length of it and bind her close beneath him.

'I'll tell you something, Ettie,' he said bluntly, shoving those X-rated thoughts to the back of his mind, 'when you come from a background like mine, you swiftly learn that people only stick around because they want something from you.'

She perked up. 'Is that true, really?' She looked at him keenly, a teasing smile flicking at her mouth. 'Aren't there any uncomplicated, nice people out there who just want to be friends?'

He couldn't help but laugh. 'Perhaps I'm too prejudiced to be able to spot them.' He leaned closer and called her out on it. 'Even you wanted something from me.'

'But you wanted the same thing from me.' She wagged a finger at him. 'So that makes us even.'

'I'm as bad as you?' he asked in mock-outrage.

'Possibly worse. Because you took advantage of everything you have to seduce me.'

'And you didn't?' He scoffed. 'With your wild ponytail and passionate eyes?'

'My what?' She looked astounded.

'All the emotions.' He pointed to her eyes, suddenly quite serious. 'Here.'

'What are my eyes expressing now?' she asked, still but breathless.

He stared at her intently—searching those beautifully clear eyes for the signal he'd wanted for so long. And then it was there.

'Your desire for me to take you to bed.' He simply snapped. He didn't want to think any more. Didn't want to try to solve unworkable problems. Damn well didn't want to talk around the issues or, heaven forbid, his freaking past. He didn't want to think of her being hurt by some jerk and her mum dying and leaving her to raise her sister alone. He wanted to relax, damn it. Eat good food and kiss the beautiful woman in front of him over every inch of her delectable body until she arched and begged him to finish her hard and fast. Everything else be blowed.

Her mouth opened, then shut and he could see her deciding how to handle her reply.

'Wow. Impressive.' But her sass was all bluff because what he'd said was true.

He clocked her rising colour, her quickening breath, her widening eyes. And he really didn't want to talk any more. Talking wasn't anywhere near as effective as action. He'd thought he should back off, especially after she'd been so mortified about that woman catching them in the lift. But they needed to clear the air of this tension that kept building. There was only here and now. Together they'd find oblivion.

He pushed back from the table and stalked around to where she now sat bolt upright. He grabbed her hand and tugged her to her feet.

She thought he'd seduced her that night? That was nothing on what he was about to do. He wasn't waiting. He wasn't taking this slow. He wanted her beneath him, about him. He craved the welcome of her soft heat. He pulled her against his body and gazed into her green eyes. For a moment it was as if they'd romped back to that first night—soft laughter, whispered desire, sensual freedom. It didn't need to be anything more than that.

But there was no time for whispered words and soft laughter tonight. His need was too raw. He kissed her, and in that moment it was all over.

Unrestrained, ruthless, he stripped her bare right there in the formal dining room, boldly touching every spot he revealed. The emerald and diamond ring caught the light, sending small, sparking chinks of light onto the ceiling. His pleasure intensified at seeing her wearing it—the time-worn signal that she was taken. For a second he stilled, paralysed by the sudden ferocious anticipation of seeing her belly swell with her pregnancy over the coming months. She'd be softened and ripe with his child. His mark. He wanted to mark her all over—suddenly possessed by a primal, appalling need to stamp her as his. And he gave way to it in that instant, curling his arm around her waist to lift her up and carry her to his bed.

He wasn't making her come in five different ways before filling her this time. He wasn't letting her come at all. Not until she was unable to bear it a second longer. Not until she begged for mercy. Not until they were both at the end of their sanity. In the cage of his arms he caressed her, alternating with licks, love bites, kisses—he teased and tasted every inch of her glorious body. She was pregnant. She was hot. And she was his.

He laughed roughly as she moaned, her hips circling, her hands seeking to touch him too. He suffered the tormenting slide of her fingertips, the delight of her hard grip, and moved to retaliate. He relished the way her muscles quivered under his onslaught. But nothing pleased him more than the look of hunger in her eyes. She was as willing, as craving, as he.

'Leon, please. *Please.*'

He paused above her, soaking in the moment he'd been aching for.

'Why have you stopped?' she asked, her expression edged with desperation.

'I don't want this over too soon,' he answered with rough honesty.

'I've wanted this for weeks,' she moaned. 'So much.'

Satisfaction and frustration split him. Fire and fury. 'Then why did you deny us?' Why had she put up those barriers? He was making her pay for that. '*Why* did you resist?'

How had she? But he couldn't wait for her answer—the demand of his own body, his own need, was too strong. She moaned in soft, earthy surrender as he thrust hard, fiercely claiming his possession. He arched, his eyes closing as pleasure sent sharp bursts down his back. His body tightened more, wanted more—deeper, harder, for *longer*. But she lost it beneath him, about him, crying out as her sweet body was wracked with the feral convulsions of one hell of an orgasm. But this wasn't over yet. He simply *refused* to let it be over yet. So he held still, his will stretched to the point of pain.

'Leon, it's so intense,' she gasped. 'So intense.'

'All the more reason to embrace it,' he growled, still furious with her for making them wait all these weeks.

'Please,' she begged, breathless and twisting and fierce beneath him. 'Please, Leon.'

It was as much a desperate plea as a forceful command. And now he could do nothing but surrender to both. He felt torn in two by the fierce, unrelenting urges to both master and worship her body.

'Ettie,' he growled. Demanding. Devoted.

The give and take, the push and pull was mirrored in his hard thrusts, in the buck of her fiery hips. He roared as his shy lover responded with that fight. She was that desperate for him. Which he adored because he couldn't get enough of her either. She made him both weak and strong. He was almost rendered unconscious by the ferocity of the pleasure as he pushed her to climax again. Yet her scream was silent, her body so taut with tension, shaking with intense delight, it couldn't render it vocally. The sight of her in that moment stopped his heart. His release came, instant and savage and so intense he all but blacked out.

When he returned to reality and summoned the energy to lift his head, he was horrified to find her face pale, her eyes simply huge and—glistening with tears?

'Are you okay?' he asked warily. Guilt hit him anew.

She was *exhausted* and he'd just subjected her to the roughest of rides. 'Sleep.' He drew the coverings over her, partly to hide the resurgence of his own desire, impossible as it ought to have been. He'd wanted her too much for too long. But surely he could wait until tomorrow before having her again?

Shadows crept into her beautiful, clear eyes. 'I can go back to my room.'

An ice-cold storm brewed in his belly. 'You want that?'

She licked her lips and glanced away from him. 'If that's what you'd prefer.'

Of course he wouldn't. 'What's going on, Ettie? Was I too rough?'

'No.' She wiped her eyes and turned away.

Not good enough. He turned her back towards him and gazed into her eyes. 'Then what?'

Her colour mounted and she seemed to be holding her breath. 'That other night you couldn't seem to get enough…but if you don't really want me any more, we don't have to…'

If he didn't really want her?

'Ettie,' he huffed out a relieved laugh, 'I thought you were exhausted. I didn't want to be too demanding…' He lost his train of thought as he saw the shadows shift to smoke in her eyes. '*Glykia mou.*'

'Sorry,' she muttered, colour flooding her face.

'Why?' He pulled her closer. 'I'm not sorry that my new fiancée is a nymphomaniac.'

He laughed at her gasp of outrage and thrust back the coverings so he could satisfy his need to see her naked beauty all over again.

'We *do* have to, Ettie.' He bent over her uncompromisingly. 'We damned well do.'

He angled her so he could see right into her eyes as he swept his hands over her soft curves and watched the ebb and flow of her tension. To his relief and pleasure, her smile returned. A more feminine, more feline one than he'd ever seen on her. He growled and surged into her—slower this time, tormenting them both to the point of madness. And it was utter bliss.

'I didn't know it could be this much fun.' She almost laughed a long while later.

Fun? Had she thought that was *fun*?

He'd thought it was devastating. But he cleared his throat and pulled his brain back from its fanciful, post-orgasmic superlatives. 'It's supposed to be fun.' And now he was looking, he couldn't tear his eyes from the satisfied glow enveloping her. 'You look better than you have in days.'

'I feel better.' Her cheeks were rosy and there was a relaxed softness in her expression. She was stunning.

But he cocked his head and aimed to tease them both back to lightness. 'Orgasms for medicinal purposes?'

'Who knew, right?' She giggled.

'What happened with your ex?' The question just slipped out at that most appalling moment. He hadn't meant to ask it—not ever. But the idea that she'd cared for another man enough to want to marry him had grated on his deepest-set nerves. What had been so special about the jerk? Why had he let her go?

Leon gritted his teeth—why did he even want to know? But he did. Desperately.

Ettie was too quiet. He rolled to his side and propped his head up on his hand, studying the return of those shadows. They flickered across her face—resistance, sadness. He hated that some guy had hurt her. He didn't mean to hurt her more by asking about it now. Were the memories that painful? Had the bastard mattered so much she could barely bring herself to speak about him?

'He jilted me just before our wedding,' she finally answered.

'At the altar?' His skin tightened.

'Almost.' She seemed to shrink deeper into the mattress. 'His family had arrived. My friends. Ophelia was so excited about being bridesmaid…it was so humiliating…'

'Why did he do it? Was there someone else?' He couldn't fathom it. What man wouldn't want Ettie in his life? She was sexy, she was funny, she was sweet.

She looked away from him.

'We hadn't been intimate,' she said huskily. 'I'd wanted to wait.'

Leon's brain malfunctioned for a moment. *Not intimate? Wait?* 'You hadn't been intimate at all?'

She shook her head. 'We'd kissed but…' She shrivelled lower into the mattress and tugged the sheet higher. 'I wanted to wait.'

'For your wedding night?' He stilled as a bubble of something hot and fierce and frankly savage bubbled in his gut. That she'd wanted to do that—gift the guy her virginity—made his innards twist.

'I know, it's quaint, right?' She wouldn't look at him.

He shook his head. 'Sweet,' he corrected gruffly.

'I should have known it wasn't right.'

'What do you mean?'

'It wasn't hard for me to want to wait.' She lowered her chin and all but talked into the sheet covering her. 'I thought I had a low sex drive. That it was just me.'

His eyes widened. The woman didn't have a low sex drive. She was the hottest, most insatiable lover of his life. 'But your fiancé didn't want to wait any more?'

'He said it was so close to the wedding…that we should.'

He'd applied pressure and manipulated her innate desire to please. Leon tensed. 'And how was it?'

Her face burned red again. 'He didn't stick around for the wedding, so I guess it wasn't that good.'

So it had been just the once? He had to snap his mouth to keep his jaw from hitting the floor. 'And there's been no one since?'

Her blush built to beetroot, making it easy to read the deep embarrassment and insecurity all over her expressive face. She thought she wasn't sexy, that she didn't know what she was doing. That she'd not been able to satisfy her selfish ass of a fiancé. So there'd been that one let-down of an experience followed by appalling betrayal and rejection after.

And then there'd been him.

'That's why I was so reckless when you… It was so

different…' She fell silent, that mottled rosy pink slowly washed from her skin.

He was savagely proud it had been so *different*. 'Poor Ettie. You finally let go enough to have some fun, and then—'

'I end up pregnant,' she mumbled.

One night. Massive consequences. It wasn't exactly fair.

'I guess mindless, meaningless, fantastic sex just isn't for me,' she attempted to joke.

'No, it is,' he replied, utterly serious. 'It just needs to be with me.'

She flushed deeper and her smile faded. 'Is it good for you?'

Was she seriously worried about that? He couldn't keep his hands off her. But that jerk had hurt her, striking an insecurity within.

'There's nothing wrong with you,' he whispered. 'Nothing wrong with what you do, how you respond…' He ripped back the sheet from them both. 'Look at what you do to me.'

She turned her face away but he tenderly cupped her chin and made her look. And then he kissed her—long, deep and lush—and felt that fire between them crackle.

'He was a jerk, Ettie,' Leon muttered, filled with protectiveness.

'He was. I just wanted to please him.'

He hated the bastard who'd had no idea of the treasure he'd had in his hands. He hated the damage he'd done to her. But he had to ease up on releasing that rage. She was more vulnerable than her ultra-efficient, all-smiling concierge persona revealed. 'You left school early and had to work?' He talked, trying to contain his anger and ease the tension gripping his muscles.

'Initially I left because Mum got sick. I needed to care for her and Ophelia.'

But she'd been a kid herself—just a teen. He hadn't wanted to listen earlier, but now he wanted to know everything. 'There was no one else?'

'She was young when she got pregnant with me. She was estranged from her parents—I never had a relationship with them or my father. Ophelia was the result of another doomed-to-failure fling. She'd wanted it to work out with him…'

'But that didn't happen either.'

She shook her head. 'Relationships never worked out for her.'

A chill swept over his skin. 'And you held off having boyfriends.'

'I was too busy to meet anyone,' she said softly.

'No,' he contradicted her. 'You shied away from them.' He understood why—she'd seen her mother's heartache and it had put her off. She'd seen the consequences—she'd lived them. He couldn't resist asking the question that burned in his gut. 'What did he give you that others didn't?' Why had she said yes to that guy?

'I met him not long after Mum died. It was very quick and I was vulnerable, I guess. He flattered me. He made me think I was special.'

Leon hardened inside. 'So he should've done—he was your boyfriend.'

'I wanted someone to love me. I thought he did. But he didn't.'

Leon didn't believe in love. He didn't believe anyone had it—they had habits and pleasant arrangements. But he could offer Ettie loyalty. 'I'll never betray you like that.'

She looked at him sombrely. Didn't she trust him yet?

'Can we always be honest with each other?' she asked

softly. 'Like you said, we're not talking stardust and promises. Don't flatter me. Don't try to soften any blows. Let's just be grounded and honest.'

That fierce savagery clawed at his insides and he finally lost his grip on it. 'Okay, here's some honesty for you: I crave your body, Ettie. I've dreamed about having you again every night for these last three weeks. I adore having sex with you and I want to do it all the damn time.'

Now her smile blossomed. 'Okay.'

She leaned in close and did more than let him. She met him—stroke for stroke, moan for groan. He denied the edge of desperation in his own need for physical fulfilment. He refused to face the fact that he couldn't seem to get enough of her.

All that mattered was that she was here. He'd free her of financial responsibility, he'd give her physical satisfaction, he'd offer her a lifestyle only he could provide...and she'd stay. His child would be safe. As would she.

His plan was perfectly falling into place.

CHAPTER EIGHT

She shouldn't have told him about her ex-fiancé. Leon must think she was such a naive fool. She'd done *all* the talking last night—exposed herself and all her embarrassing history. He'd shared virtually nothing, except his fantastic bedroom skills. Had he never been embarrassed? Never been rejected?

Of course not.

He couldn't reciprocate with any humanising stories of his own humiliations, because he didn't have any. And right this second she completely resented him for that. And because he was blocking her from making her own choices. Again.

'You're *not* going to work today.' He was furious.

It was almost nine the next morning. She'd slept in and he was late heading to his office because they were arguing about her plans for the day. As it was, she was feeling unsettled. She wasn't used to having a personal life, let alone everyone knowing about it. Her colleagues, her clients would all know she was sleeping with him. And the massive rocks on her finger were only going to make them even more curious. So she was tense enough without him telling her what she could and couldn't do. Again.

'Are you ashamed of what I do?' she spat sullenly.

'Do you think I'm that much of an ass?' He rolled his

eyes. 'Thanks so much. You do honest work. You're good at your job. But do I want a pregnant woman carrying deliveries upstairs? No. I do not.'

'Joel would help me and it's not like I'm huge and uncomfortable already—I'm not even showing. This baby is months away, Leon. What do you want me to do all day?'

The flicker in his eyes irritated her.

'Be your concubine?' she asked tartly. '*Really?*'

'That's your fantasy, not mine.' He practically purred. 'I don't want you working as head concierge of the Cavendish any more. I want you as building manager.'

'What?' His statement undercut her argument and completely derailed her train of thought. She stared at him. 'You *what*?'

'Building manager. I want you to take over from George. It's obvious who does the work. It's Ettie. Who fixes the orders? Ettie. Who does all the rosters? Ettie. Who do the residents rely on? Ettie. You're doing it all already anyway—you might as well get paid for it.'

She simply sat there, her jaw dropped.

'I can't understand how you've not been promoted already. Actually I can: George has been claiming credit for most of your work. And then tried to blame his mistakes on you.'

Ettie did her best impersonation of a goldfish.

'I've already spoken with the management company,' he continued. 'George has agreed it's time for him to move on to a smaller establishment. And the residents committee have approved it as well.'

'Were you ever going to actually ask me if I wanted the job, or did you just expect me to jump at the chance?'

'I knew you'd jump.' He smirked. But then held up his hands. 'It's no more than deserved, Ettie.'

But she couldn't accept any promotion—not now she'd slept with the new owner.

'What's wrong now?' He released an exaggerated sigh.

'They'll think it's nepotism.'

'Why should you care what they think? The proof is in your ability to do the job. No one who knows you would ever think you *slept* your way into it.'

'Thank you *so* much.' Her blush burned.

He laughed. 'Enough. We've banished that insecurity already.'

She scowled at him. 'If it's more money, then—'

'You're already wearing my ring, Ettie. You're not backing out now. And your "more money" isn't anywhere near enough to cover Ophelia's fees for the next decade.' He brutally shut down her thinking. 'All I ask is that you take the rest of the week to recuperate from the stress of the last few days; you didn't get a lot of sleep last night. Take time to get to know this place. Then go back next week and take over fully from then.'

'You have it all mapped out,' she said stiffly.

Why did that surprise her? She swung her legs out of the bed, determined to do *something* in defiance of him.

'No. Stay there and rest.' He braced one arm either side of her and leaned over her until she fell back onto the mattress.

Quick and furious and so damned easily he proved his point, leaving her breathless and so relaxed her fight fled and all she could do was moan her approval.

'You keep distracting me with sex,' she muttered when she could breathe again.

'I'm distracting myself with sex too.' He stretched and stood, apparently energised. 'It's a good distraction.'

'But we're not solving this problem.'

'There isn't a problem,' he replied with stubborn simplicity. 'You're making a problem where there isn't one. You don't need to work today, Ettie. You've worked all your life. You've been responsible all your life. Why not take a day to have a break? You're still working—you're growing a little human.'

'I can't sit around doing nothing,' she argued. 'I've never done that.'

'So learn how to relax. Read a book. Watch TV. Sleep. Anonymously blog about your misfortunes. Whatever, just *rest*.'

She glared at him and then couldn't help laughing, as she knew he'd intended. 'Anonymously blog?'

'Yeah.' He put his hands on his hips, warming to the idea. '*My life as a billionaire's bought bride…*'

She giggled again, but then realised what she actually wanted more than anything was for him to *stay* with her today. She enjoyed his company. But he was off to maintain that millionaire income and she had to keep this as light and 'easy' as he was.

Stay in your lane, Ettie.

'I promise I'll be here for when you return, oh, lord and master,' she cooed. 'In bed,' she added on an impish urge. 'Naked.'

'Hot and wet and ready for me.' He slammed a scorching kiss onto her lips. 'Perfect.'

'I'm getting rid of all the stupid rules,' she informed him when he lifted his head. 'Starting with pets.'

'Oh, I knew that already.'

With a wriggle that was more sexual restlessness than resentment, she threw a pillow as he laughed and left the room.

No way was Ettie spending the day sitting about doing nothing. Not when her brain was fizzing with ideas for

Cavendish House. She fossicked through Leon's study, marvelling at his sleek, luxurious stationery supplies. The guy had a thing for fancy fine-liner pens. Smirking, she twisted her hair into a bun and secured it in place with one and grabbed a handful of others. In the kitchen she collected some crackers, cheese and juice. She spread sheets of thick paper over the dining table to brainstorm on. It took her a while to work out the fancy 'smart house' sound system, but she got music playing eventually. Sunlight streamed through the window. She stared at the room for a moment, stunned anew. It was a gorgeous place to work. Then, energised and excited, she got down to it.

'Wow—could you make your lists any longer?'

'Oh!' Startled, Ettie glanced up to see Leon standing on the other side of the table. Her heart pounded faster at the sight of him than from the initial fright. It was impossible not to react to his presence. 'I didn't hear you come in,' she muttered, trying to regulate her breathlessness. 'What time is it?'

'After six,' he said, amusement quirking his lips.

'*No.*' She looked out of the window and saw the changing sky. 'Where'd the day go?'

'Into all those lists,' he answered drily. 'Is there any paper left?'

'Uh, some.' She glanced down. She'd smothered the table in papers, which in turn were smothered in her scribblings. 'What do you think?'

'I think you haven't rested at all today. Have you eaten?'

His concern warmed her as much as it irritated her.

'Actually I've been snacking all day and this *is* restful. I've been perched on this stool the whole time.' She saw him read through her most recent, refined list. 'You like what I've planned?'

'Yeah.' He quickly scanned her bullet points. 'You

should set up a meeting with the residents' group. They'll be excited.'

'I've already emailed invitations from my phone.'

'Of course you have,' he murmured. 'That's why you got the job.'

'I can't change everything all at once,' she said earnestly. 'I know I'll need to go slow so they have time to adjust…' She trailed off as his gaze narrowed on her.

She flushed at being the focus of his intensity all over again. Every time, even though he outwardly appeared expressionless, he wasn't remote. It felt as if he was so attuned to her needs, her desires, before she was even aware of them herself. Dizzying, dazzling…*confusing.*

'Sometimes an acute, complete change is a good thing,' he said, his gaze laser-sharp on her.

'Rapid change can also be scary,' she responded pointedly. 'The staff might feel overwhelmed or defensive if they feel it's a criticism of the way things were…'

He considered it for a moment and his rare smile suddenly flashed. 'Go with your instincts; they're good.'

Excitement for her work flooded back. 'I can't wait to get started.'

'On your not-rapid changes.' He laughed and reached out, plucking the pen from her hair. '*Mine.*'

She ran her hand through her messy tangle of waves with a grimace. 'Possessive about your pens, aren't you?'

'You think I was talking about the pen?' That wicked smile flashed on his face again as he fished in his pocket for his phone. 'You okay with Italian for dinner?'

She needed a moment to catch her breath. He was just teasing, keeping it playful. Light and easy. So she'd do the same. 'Are you talking pizza or fancy?'

'How about fancy pizza?'

'Perfect.' She hopped off the stool and stretched out the

cricks in her back from leaning over the table all day while he tapped a message on his phone. 'It's Friday tomorrow, then the weekend. Do you actually take weekends off or do you work through as if every day's Monday?'

'You know already.' His answering grin was rueful. 'But we could go to a recital on Saturday night if you like?' He flipped his phone around to show her the promotional information for a concert on at a nearby concert hall.

She read the headliner and stilled. It was an oboe soloist. That was *her* instrument. She looked up and saw his expectant expression. 'How did you know?'

'Saw the instrument case in your flat,' he replied. 'The music book had your name on the front. Why didn't you mention it? You've told me all about Ophelia, but you're reticent about your own dreams, Ettie.'

'*You're* calling *me* reticent?' Her jaw dropped at his temerity. 'I've told you about my ex-fiancé, my mother—'

'But not about your music. Why?'

Because it had been her secret, childish dream and she'd had to bury it. How had he picked up that it had been important—was he some kind of mind-reader? But that was impossible because she *never* thought of it now—it hurt to remember. What he'd exposed was a skeleton shipwreck of a dream that couldn't be resurrected.

'Do you wish you played now?' he asked, still intently watching her.

Her heart ached. Did he have to discover all her secrets? 'It's too late.'

'We could convert one of the lounges into a music room. You could play again.'

'No.' She chuckled softly to hide her sadness and embarrassment. Truthfully she'd been a fool to think she could've made a go of it once. 'I was never that good. I stopped when I took on a part-time job when Mum got ill. I haven't played in years. I never play now.'

'But you were good.' He looked sombre. 'That music was extremely complex.'

'You read music?'

'Sure.' He nodded.

Of course. He probably spoke more than two languages as well, only she didn't yet know it. It wasn't fair that he knew everything about her and she knew so little about him. He hadn't even left clues in his own home—nothing here told her anything more about him.

'So what instrument do you play?' she asked, determined to get an answer.

'Piano. It was compulsory to learn an instrument at school.'

'Boarding school?' She glanced at him sideways, almost afraid that if she faced him he'd fall silent again.

'Yes.'

'For your teen years?' Her curiosity burned. She wondered about everything. What were his parents really like? He had no photos of them at all here. Were they really not close? Did they really only see each other every six months or so? Had he always been this isolated?

'I went there when I was eight,' he said brusquely. 'It was good.'

She waited hopefully but he didn't add anything more.

'It's good for Ophelia too,' she said after a while. 'She gets an education and opportunities she just wouldn't otherwise.' But Ettie missed her sister hugely. If she'd won a scholarship from a day school in town, that would have been so much better. She nibbled her lower lip, thinking about her own child's future education. 'I don't want our baby going to boarding school though,' she realised with quiet conviction. It was too bad if Leon had some schooling tradition going back generations. 'I won't send him or her away. I don't care how good the school might be, there'll be schools just as good here.'

Increasing ferocity fired colour into Ettie's expression, reminding Leon of her passion and protectiveness over the dog the day they'd met. His skin seemed to tighten. He understood why she had mixed feelings about boarding school—she obviously missed her sister. But she didn't know that for him boarding school had been a blessed escape. It had been so much safer and happier than his own home.

'Okay,' he said, needing to draw a line beneath the subject. 'School here.'

He didn't want to think about the years ahead. Right now was tough enough. She'd guessed correctly: he usually worked every day as if it were Monday. But now she was here and yeah, rapid change could be unsettling. His home was altered. Not because she'd brought in a lot of stuff, but because she'd recast the entire atmosphere—with her scent, her laughter, her smile…

Leon hadn't lived with anyone since school. He had no idea how to live with someone. No idea what he was going to do with her all weekend. He could hardly keep her tied to his bed the whole time, as appealing as that thought was. The oboe recital had been a random grasp and mainly he'd been keen to see her reaction because he was insatiably curious about her now. She fascinated him.

He gazed at the colour washing her cheeks and the sparkle shimmering in her eyes. She still glowed with the vivacity and enthusiasm that she'd worked hard all day with. Even when he'd told her not to, he'd known she would. And now that vivacity was enhanced by the filter of pure passion as she fought for something so far in the future it didn't even matter yet. She was so spirited, and so protective of their child's future.

That curling tension tightened—constricting his throat, his chest. He couldn't resist the need to get nearer to her. He wanted her heat, her willingness, her total surrender to his touch. There was something deeper too, something so powerful that he couldn't examine it too closely.

Just want.

He reassured himself. But it was strong.

The weekend plans were irrelevant. Suddenly he had no spare thought for the past, or the future. His immediate need was too intense.

He pulled her against him. He didn't know how else to release the heavy pressure crushing his chest, threatening to cleave him open. He didn't want to be torn apart and have any of this emotion *exposed*. Not memories. Not pain. He wanted nothing but pleasure with her. *Now.*

He slid his hand into her glossy hair and tilted her head back to expose her pretty neck. Her soft lips parted and emotion glittered in her eyes. Emotion he refused to analyse. He didn't know how. He certainly didn't stop to examine his own. He was only seeking her consent—to lose them both in that fiery desire. And he got it—there in her crystal, cloudless eyes.

She might appear vulnerable, but she was strong. He could see her energy pulsing in that soft space at the base of her neck. He bent his head and kissed her hard and deep, releasing all the passion and lust into her, until that weight blocking his chest eased and heat swirled in its place. She was so intoxicating, he sank to his knees, determined to gift her every ounce of pleasure he could. Nothing else mattered. Nothing but now. Here. Her pleasure. Her sighs.

He cupped her full breasts, knowing they were tender and more sensitive, teasing until he felt her need deepening, until he heard her breathy little pleas. Then it was that sweet, wet, secret part of her that he couldn't resist baring, touching, *tasting*.

'Lean on me,' he muttered as he felt her trembling response.

She was hot and lush and he craved every inch, every lick of her. She pressed her hands on his shoulders for balance, her legs spread as wide as they could against the constraints of the panties he'd pulled halfway down her thighs. He revelled in her quivering, in her desperate cries. His blood flowed freely now—warming him, releasing him from that tight, painful pressure. This was what he wanted. He pressed closer still and destroyed her.

Ettie woke late and saw the fresh juice, plain crackers and sliced fruit on a tray beside the bed. She smiled ruefully. Leon was unfailingly attentive and good at anticipating almost every one of her needs. She could hardly bear to think of those insane moments last night when he'd knelt at her feet and made her mad with desire. In that dangerously seductive stance, she'd felt like his queen, as if he couldn't exist in that moment without touching her. He'd made her feel *wanted* in a way she'd never felt wanted before. And he'd made her feel such thrilling, intense pleasure, such total exhilaration, that she'd screamed until she was hoarse.

In the aftermath she'd been so dazed she could barely stand. Her wits had been too scrambled for her to be able to lighten it at all, to even think of *reciprocating*. He'd straightened her clothing and told her to go and tidy herself quick-smart, because their restaurant booking was soon.

Once more, it wasn't just any restaurant and it wasn't pizza. It was award-winning, exclusive and so expensive they didn't bother putting the prices on the menu. There was no choice as to what they got to eat either. That was because the food the world-renowned chef prepared was so exquisite, no one sane would ever think to complain or argue with the selection. Pure perfection. And absolute decadence.

She'd been so tired she'd fallen asleep on the drive home. She'd woken as he'd carried her up to his bed. And once there, she'd realised she wasn't *quite* as sleepy as all that. He'd laughed, indulging her again in that searing, soul-destroying sex. Again. And then again.

Just sex, Ettie. Good sex. Stupendous. But just sex.

But thank goodness he seemed to be as hungry for it as she.

Now he'd gone to work and she had another day to herself before the weekend. Another day to come to terms with the fragile future they were building.

But there was imbalance between them and it wasn't their bank balances. He knew *everything*. Her stupid mistakes of the past. Even her sorry childhood dream of becoming a musician. Every little secret. Furthermore, he'd done so much for her—the ring, the home, the job…and things so much more intimate than that. He turned her inside out, made her mindless with pleasure. He'd given her pretty much everything.

But what had she given *him*? What had he *let* her give him—other than her body? He didn't open up, didn't let her in. She breathed out and reminded herself it was very early days. He didn't trust her yet and he had a thing about people always wanting things from him—he'd joked about it but there'd been a tiny truth there.

What if she was to give *him* something?

Problem was, it wasn't as if he needed her to *buy* him anything and it wasn't as if she had vast amounts of money to splash out either. And it wasn't about a *thing*, it was about doing something thoughtful, to show that she was invested in making this work the same way he was. That she could be attentive too. But she knew so little, she couldn't think of what to do or get, and she was good at getting things for privileged people.

With a sigh, she got out of bed and returned the plate and glass to the gleaming kitchen. She caught sight of the shiny new dog bowls sitting uselessly on the counter. She paused, her gaze fixed on them. Leon said he'd never had a puppy, but he'd been surprisingly willing to take Toby. She'd had a feeling that he'd been more keen on that than he'd expressed. It hadn't all been about getting her up to that penthouse in Cavendish House. She remembered how he'd gently patted the dog.

Her heart pounded as she turned over the wisp of an idea in her mind. It would be a huge risk. But instinct told her it would be worth it. It would be right.

Go with your instincts; they're good.

She turned her back on the lists she'd left on the table and ran back upstairs to get dressed.

Ettie Roberts had a mission.

CHAPTER NINE

LEON TRIED TO stay at work. Tried to concentrate. Tried not to think about the weekend ahead. It wasn't that he didn't want her there, he did, but it felt as if the ground was shifting and he couldn't quite hold his balance. In the end he gave up resisting and let the weight coiling within push him home.

'Ettie?' He rolled his shoulders, trying to ease that tension as he shucked off his jacket and shoes.

'Leon?' Her answering call was pitched high.

'Who else?' he asked drily, following the direction of her voice to the kitchen.

He fought to restrain the urge to go straight up and kiss her until the tightness in his chest eased again. Not two nights running—he had more control than that, right? But in the doorway he paused to draw breath. She looked amazing to his hungry eyes—jeans, T-shirt, hair twisted out of the way and secured with a pen again. His again.

'I wasn't sure what time you'd be home… You're early.' Her face was flushed but it wasn't that usual blush of sensuality.

And she couldn't quite maintain eye contact, which initially intrigued, then concerned him. He strolled closer, trying to take it easy, but his instincts were firing. Something was off. 'What've you been up to today?' he asked. 'No more lists?'

The table was scrupulously tidy.

His pulse began to pound. Why couldn't she look at him? Why was she so flushed? Why so silent?

At that exact moment, he heard a strange scratching coming from behind him. Ettie froze, her eyes wide. He cocked his head and narrowed his gaze on her. 'What's that?'

'Hmm?' she mumbled.

'Ettie?'

The noise sounded again and there was no hiding the guilty look in her eyes—her face was far too expressive.

Now she pressed her lips together in an oddly nervous manner. 'I've done something,' she blurted. 'I got you a present.'

He stilled. 'You what?'

'I got you a present. I hope you don't mind.'

Why would he mind? He actually couldn't remember the last time anyone had got him a present. He didn't have a bunch of friends he did birthday celebrations with and his parents definitely didn't send him anything. Not at Christmas either.

There was another scratching sound. And then a high-pitched yelp. Not Ettie. Not *human*.

Leon spun around. 'Ettie?'

She scuttled past him and he watched her hunch down by a box he'd not noticed before because he'd only had eyes for her. Leon couldn't move. It was a big box.

Then Ettie stood and walked towards him and she was holding—

'He was the runt,' she said all in a rush. 'I don't know quite what breed he is…a mix of many, and I know he's not handsome like Toby, but he wasn't going to have a chance otherwise.'

Leon stared at the creature in Ettie's arms. 'You got me a puppy?'

His heart beat too fast; his lungs felt as if they were in a swiftly tightening vice.

'You have space here.' She sounded as breathless as he felt. 'You could train him to go to the office with you, or he can stay here and play in the garden, or he could come to the Cavendish with me...we can make it work. I just thought you'd like him.' She stepped closer and literally shoved the puppy into his arms.

Leon instinctively grabbed the animal but inside he'd frozen.

'You said you'd not had a dog, but I thought you'd quite wanted Toby. I thought...' She trailed off as she finally looked up at him. 'I don't really know what I thought.' She stared into his eyes, her own growing more concerned by the second. 'Do you mind?' It was a whisper.

Leon couldn't move. He couldn't actually breathe. That pressure crushing his chest was too heavy on his lungs.

'He's about four months old, they think,' she said. 'All vaccinated. If they couldn't rehome him they were going to—'

'He's a rescue puppy?' he croaked, determinedly pushing past the immobility to glance down at the puppy who'd settled so quickly in his arms. Small, with bottomless brown eyes that had a heart-wrenching hint of sadness, mostly black hair but with patches of silvery white...he was ridiculously cute.

'Yes.'

Leon cleared his throat. 'Does he have a name?'

She shook her head. 'You'll have to give him one.'

He didn't want to do that. He couldn't.

Memory washed over him. He'd held a tiny puppy like this only once before years ago. It had been small and fragile like this one. It had been his...but only for a little while.

He stilled as past and present blurred and the reality of

their future hit hard. He didn't know if he could do this. *Any* of this.

'Leon? Don't you like him?'

He huffed out a hard-caught breath. Of course he liked him. How could he not?

'What is it?' she asked softly. 'Leon?' Her eyes suddenly filled. 'Did I do the wrong thing?'

'No,' he muttered quickly. She was so sweet, she didn't realise. 'No.'

'Then what is it?' She wasn't just sweet, she was astute. She saw right through him.

And he couldn't bear that. 'It's not important,' he snapped, needing to shut her down.

'If it's not important, it won't matter if you tell me, will it?'

He almost smiled at her simple logic, but he was stuck, unable to escape the most painful of memories. 'You don't want my poor-little-rich-boy sob story.'

'Yes—'

'It is what it is,' he interrupted awkwardly. 'I can't change it.'

He didn't want questions, didn't want to remember. His mouth was dry and he felt too big to be holding something so small. He didn't want to hold it close. He didn't want to feel. He needed time to think. But Ettie kept looking at him with those beseeching sea-green eyes and when she did that he couldn't seem to think at all.

'Leon—'

'My neighbour gave me a puppy,' he growled before she could say anything else in that husky, sweet voice. She was so frustratingly curious. 'But my mother got rid of it after a few weeks.'

'Got rid of it?' Ettie frowned. 'You don't mean—'

'Yeah, I do mean.' The words just fell out. A bald, uncontrollable burn of memory. The disappearance. The shocking silence and the absolute emptiness inside him. 'They weren't interested in me—I was their tick-the-box baby. They were busy with their careers. Their affairs. They just wanted a trophy and heir. They didn't want the actual *child*. The actual child was…' He broke off, tearing his gaze from Ettie to focus on the small dog that had nestled so easily into his arms. It was so trusting. But he hadn't been able to protect that first puppy…

He dragged in a harsh breath. He shouldn't have said anything, but now he'd started, ripping open that old wound so it oozed poison and pus. He couldn't stop the truth of it spewing out.

'One child was more than enough for my mother to handle and, as I was a child of privilege, it was her duty to educate me on my duty and ensure I wasn't spoiled.'

'Not spoiled?' Ettie echoed softly.

He looked back into her expressive face and watched as understanding dawned.

'She was cruel?' she said.

Leon couldn't bear the sympathy in her eyes. Why had he said anything? He hated remembering how weak he'd once been. He never wanted anyone to have power over him again. Not physical. Not emotional. Not contractual. Never again would he be that vulnerable. That powerless.

'Leon…'

'I was extremely fortunate.' He tried to plug the information leak, tried to squash all that horror back in the depths of his ribcage. 'I had the best education.'

Never show weakness. Never admit to failure. Always fight.

'But she hurt you. Not just your puppy. She hurt *you*.'

So many times, in so many small ways. He froze but

was still unable to think, unable to hold back that pressure bursting within him.

Ettie stepped closer. 'She hit you?'

'Too obvious.' The words escaped, heedless of his battle to keep silent. 'She'd force me to shower in freezing water. Five minutes. Reciting equations, verbs, some poem. Whatever lesson I needed to be drilled in. I had to say it aloud over and over again. That was one of the many...' He paused, drawing in a hard breath. 'Just little things she did to...'

'Torture you.'

'Toughen me up.' He grimaced. 'Cold showers, barefoot runs in the frost, two hours locked in a dark cupboard if I answered back or worse...all things that left no physical mark, but would teach me to control myself. Not cry. Not show weakness.'

Not anger. Not love either. Not any emotions. He'd learned calm instead—to close down, stay still, breathe, *think*. Except he couldn't do any of that now with the way Ettie was looking at him.

'It worked,' he said, stubbornly rejecting what he saw in her eyes. 'I grew resilience. Definitely gained independence. Didn't rely on anyone else for anything.'

'You couldn't tell your father?'

The last sliver of Leon's heart shrivelled. 'He knew.' And he'd done nothing.

'You couldn't tell anyone else?'

There hadn't been anyone else. There'd never been any physical marks left on him. But he had the feeling his old neighbour at their summer house suspected. That was why she'd given him that puppy. Calix had been the runt of the litter, just like this little guy.

His mother had relented too easily—said yes to that nice old neighbour. She'd said yes so swiftly, bubbling with faux gratitude. He should've known it was too good to last. He was to perform. He was to lead. He was to remain in charge of everything. The loss she then subjected him to was to build his fight—the puppy was a mere tool for him to learn pain and to protect himself from feeling it again. Never to lose again.

It hurts when important things are taken from you. The dog isn't important. Our company is.

He'd never trusted again either.

'That's why you were happy to go away to school,' Ettie whispered.

'It was a relief.' Leon wanted nothing more than to freeze back up inside. 'But she'd hit me in other ways. When you're told something over and over and over, you begin to believe it, especially when the person telling you is supposed to be your protector.' She'd shut him off from everyone. Her words echoed in his head.

'They only want to be friends because of your money. They want to use you. But you haven't done anything to deserve what you have. You don't deserve it.'

He realised far too late that he'd said it all aloud. Ettie's expression was appalled. He turned away, unable to look at her any more. If he didn't look at her he might get himself back under control.

'My mother was determined to make me strong enough, good enough to take over the specific challenges of a multi-million-dollar empire. To become the tough, decisive boss I'd need to be. I tried hard to please her.' To please both his parents. He'd tried for so long. 'Eventually I realised I was never going to. Nothing would make her happy. So I decided that I'd never be the heir they'd worked so *diligently* to raise. Not by going off the rails—that would have pleased her, I think. It would have proven that I was as "weak" as she'd said I was. So no drugs, no booze-fuelled parties, no threesomes…' He almost smiled. 'I turned my back on that "duty" and rejected the inheritance they offered. I'll never work for the company, or take charge of it. Instead I worked alone and earned more, just to spite her. I worked every holiday and left home the second I was old enough.'

'To make your own way.'

He'd pushed to the top relentlessly—taken huge risks, worked insane hours. Because he didn't want a cent of his parents' money. Didn't want the 'glory' of running their empire. After all, he'd not *deserved* it—so he'd built his own.

He didn't need them. He didn't need *anyone*.

Now he carried the sleeping puppy back to the box and saw the small bed Ettie had got for it inside. He carefully put the puppy in. Why had he said anything? He never talked to anyone about this. Bracing himself against the silence, he turned back and saw her face. His body tightened.

'I don't want your pity.' All that emotion emptied again. He couldn't stand to see the sympathy in her eyes. 'I cannot be pitied. Look at everything I have, everything I've done.'

'Yeah, you're amazing,' she whispered. 'But you don't let people in.'

'Why would I want to?' He turned to look back at the sleeping dog.

Yet he knew he had to—his own child was the game changer. And it was happening *too soon*. He'd never wanted one, but now one was on the way and he wanted it to have everything he hadn't and still didn't have. Self-sufficiency was key to his own existence, yet he was human enough not to want that for his own child. Thank goodness the baby had Ettie.

He tried to be calm, to breathe, to think. But his heart thundered and his lungs hurt. His whole chest was still bound in tension.

Leon stood so still, Ettie almost believed he wasn't breathing. But as she neared, she could feel the vibrations rolling off him. She sensed the power he was exerting to hold back and press everything back down deep. He'd been appallingly hurt and she'd had absolutely no idea. He'd hidden it so well, for so long.

She might not have had a father, but she'd had a mother who'd loved her, who'd at least wanted the best for her. And she'd had her sister.

Leon had been utterly isolated. The witch hadn't even let him keep his dog. His father hadn't stood up for him. The horror of it broke her heart. That he'd been treated as a project, not a person.

While she'd grown up with nothing but love, he'd grown up with everything but. No wonder he was remote and controlled and untrusting. And right now she knew he regretted saying anything at all. While there mightn't have been physical marks, there were definitely emotional scars. Five minutes beneath a frigid torrent of water must've felt like an eternity. Two hours in a dark cupboard for a small boy must've been pure hell.

'Leon—'

'Don't.'

She knew he was withdrawing. Rebuilding his walls to shut her out again. She couldn't let that happen. Not yet.

'Don't think that this is going to change everything just because you've told me a few things,' she said, trying to reach him. 'We're just getting to know each other, that's all. That helps build trust.'

'Don't actions speak louder than words, Ettie?' The strain was evident in his hoarseness. 'Can't you trust me already? I'm not your dad or your ex. I haven't left you.'

Not physically. But emotionally he was walking out of

that door. And he was turning the focus from himself to her, to help his escape.

'Leon—'

'Have I betrayed you?' he flared.

'No.' She welcomed the resurgence of his emotion and stepped closer. 'But there's action and there's *action*.'

His default response was to close down all intimacy other than the physical. It was the only way she could think to keep him here *with* her.

'Look,' he cleared his throat, 'you're going to make a wonderful mother, Ettie. I know you'll care for this child in a way I was never cared for. But I can only do what I do.' He frowned as if he was struggling to think. 'I'm good at taking control in a crisis.'

Yes. Because his whole life had been a crisis. He'd been locked for ever in a fight for survival, to win, to be free. When had he last taken the time to just breathe? When had he ever let someone else make the calls and shoulder even a little bit of his burden?

'You have to take control because you've never had anyone you could count on.' She placed her hand on his chest.

He didn't reply. The agony churning in his eyes, the blistering beat of his heart beneath her fingers, said it all. He didn't trust anyone. She didn't blame him; she had trust issues of her own. But maybe in time he could learn to trust *her*? Maybe—eventually—they could be a true team?

'Can't you relinquish control to me?' she asked softly, spreading her hand wider and slowly sliding it down his chest. 'Just once?' She felt his muscles tighten beneath her touch, saw awareness flare in his eyes.

'Are you still feeling insecure about your sexual experience?' he asked gruffly.

No. This wasn't about *her*. But this was the language

she knew he understood and it could be their starting point, right?

'Don't you know what you do to me?' he asked harshly as she slid her hand to his belt and twisted her fingers to release the buckle.

She shook her head. That was what she wanted most of all—to see him. To know him. 'Let me see.' She lifted her chin and dared him, unfastening the buttons of his shirt without hesitation. 'Let me do it.'

He didn't stop her. But he didn't help. Like a statue ablaze—the tension thrummed from him as she pushed back the two halves of his shirt so she could see—touch—his burning skin.

'Just let me,' she whispered.

She reached up on tiptoe and kissed along his jaw, aching for the years of sufferance and isolation he'd endured. He didn't lower his chin to meet her lips with his.

'I don't want your sympathy,' he growled, rigid and angry.

'Just as I don't want your money,' she answered.

He pulled back his head to look down at her then. 'This isn't about money.'

'It isn't about sympathy either. This is about *caring*, Leon.' She cupped his jaw with one hand, and slid her other over his chest, tracing the strength and heat. Skin on skin. 'This is about you opening up and letting me in. Let me in.'

'You don't need to take care of me.'

'But you get to take care of me? Next you'll try telling me not to breathe,' she muttered back at him. 'Screw your control, Leon.'

With a sudden forceful push, she pressed him against the wall. His eyes widened and his hands automatically spanned her waist.

'I'm taking control.' She kissed her way down his chest.

Her own passion was unleashed. She wanted to *truly* touch him. She wanted to show him—

'You think?' He hauled her back up to kiss her hard and deep, his anger igniting.

'I *know*,' she said when she tore her lips free.

A crazy kind of confidence she'd never before felt fired through her veins. She knew what to do. What she wanted. She showered his body with kisses, with light, teasing touches of her fingertips, with swirls of her tongue, before letting her lips slide closer.

Her own heat increased the more she heard his uneven breathing, the more she felt his tension build. She stepped back for a moment to slide her own clothes off. Slowing when she saw the way he was leaning back against the wall, his feet planted wide apart, watching her strip. She was no real beauty, definitely no model-type, but clearly it didn't matter.

Only when she was fully naked did she step forward again. She unzipped his trousers, pulled them and his boxers down. She knelt in front of him as he'd knelt before her only last night.

She heard his growl—of warning, of *want*. She smiled and kissed closer, closer, but she didn't take him in her mouth. Not yet. It was enough to let him enjoy looking. She saw his hands curl into fists, his knuckles whitening. He liked what she was doing. But he was still holding back. She didn't want him to hold back.

She licked up the length of him and then looked up. 'Lie down.'

He shot her a look but complied with her request.

Ettie simply stared for a moment at the sheer magnificence of him outstretched on the floor before her. He still said nothing but his raging erection and ragged breathing were all the encouragement she needed. Her mouth watered and that confidence flooded her again.

She straddled him and ran her hands over his body. He was so still. Letting her. Yet resisting her inwardly. He'd learned such control. He needed to unlearn it.

And she just needed to touch him. She was firm. Gentle. Reverent. Then rougher. As she released her grip on her own desire, her pace picked up, her intentions deepened, her need coiled. Her breathing shallowed, her heat spiked.

He was so strong. So alone. So worthy of so much more. And now she was angry. He should have had everything. She would give him everything *she* could right now. With a blind kind of fury, she ached to make him feel the way he made her feel—*wanted*. So. Damn. Much.

She slid up the length of his body, desperately kissing him, stroking, sucking him hard and then grinding her heat on him, until he flipped—literally holding her to him and flipping them both so he was above her...within her.

'*Yes*,' she cried out as he thrust to the hilt.

But he stopped—straining—his eyes closed, his jaw clenched as he fought to regain his control.

'Don't stop,' she ordered, gazing up at him. 'Don't shut me out.'

His hands gripped her thighs deliciously hard. She knew he couldn't resist this for much longer. He shuddered as she moved beneath him sinuously, easing her own ache, enticing him to complete abandonment.

His eyes opened. 'I don't like losing control of my emotions, Ettie,' he grated.

'Is it losing control of them?' she challenged him. 'Or is it just expressing them?'

He was still for a searing moment more. Then she saw the flare and felt his sudden shift. He snatched the pen securing her hair—freeing it into a wild tumble around her shoulders. He wound thick hanks of it around his wrists—literally binding her to him and cradling her head in his fingers so he could see into her eyes, so he could devour her mouth. The tug was strong, but not painful as her head tilted back at his pull—exposing her mouth, her neck, her breasts to his ravenous, rough kisses.

'I like it,' she admitted with low, savage hunger. 'I like touching you. I like seeing you like this. I want you like this.'

'On the edge?' he growled, twisting his hands again to shorten the tie between them.

'Over it,' she said brazenly. 'With me.'

He swore bluntly and drove into her, again and again. Ruthlessly, out of control, he claimed his place in her very core—pushing harder, faster, deeper. This wasn't fun or easy or light. It was the most bared, the most touched she'd ever been. The lump in her throat ached. She'd been alone too. She'd been alone so long, but right now—he was here, right here, literally bound to her. Inside her *totally*. Her eyes stung because she was exposed—vulnerable and shaking and so damn needy of *this*. His kiss, his possession. She felt the wild emotion storming through him and into her, only to transform again into something wonderful that they then rode together. He growled again as she arched, pressing herself closer still, wrapping her legs and arms tightly around him, holding him so they were utterly inseparable. His kiss devastated her. Unleashed emotion rippled between them like electricity—a power surge energising them both into frantic, clawing creatures seeking oblivion in this dark, magic world they made together. She gasped as he thrust harder and harder. He was so powerful. And she so complete. All thought was gone, all words. There was only animal sensation, animal sounds...and then screaming, orgasmic agony.

* * *

Leon flinched, suddenly wide awake. It was completely dark. Despite the warmth of the soft woman curled next to him, he was freezing. His heart was pounding as if he'd been sprinting for his life. He'd woken like this so many times in his youth and he hated it.

Despite the pleasure he'd had with Ettie tonight, he was now tossed back into that old torment. That stupid talk had stirred up thoughts. Memories. Feelings.

Fear.

He should have kept it in, resisted his own damn temptation. But that gift, Ettie's sweetness, cracked him open. Now he tried to empty his mind again but those malevolent memories swirled, relentless. They'd been woken.

He'd kept it all buried for so long—had hidden that dark, incomplete side of himself from everyone. Living alone it didn't matter, it was easy. But in marriage?

He didn't want to poison her with it. He wished he'd never told her. To complain of a little punishment? Of loneliness? He'd been as weak as his mother had warned. What he needed was his control back.

He slid out of bed silently so he didn't wake Ettie and quickly checked the small puppy. It was fast asleep and warm in its little bed. Leon opened up his laptop in the lounge and tried to work. But his mind was fragmented and he'd achieved little by the time dawn finally began to lighten the dark.

He showered, standing for a long time under the steaming jet—trying to relax. He'd get through the weekend, he'd fall back into bed with her...

But he hadn't even made it to Saturday before falling apart. Having her this close was confusing, constricting... those stirred-up memories still prickled like thorns in a blood-splattered bouquet in a damn low-budget horror film. Reaching out, he flicked the faucet to cold and suffered the pelting icy droplets. They were like little knives, pinkening up soft skin. Those memories surged.

He braced. He'd beaten them a long time ago. Banished them. And he'd banish them again now because he was not that boy any more. He had control. He flicked the faucet back to warm. Yeah. He had *power*. And he would make this work.

He'd talked about it with Ettie—told her far more than he'd ever intended. Surely he'd satisfied her infernal curiosity at last? So now it was done and behind them for ever.

He'd get this back to the practical, responsible arrangement he needed it to be.

He breathed in and quietly walked to the bedroom to grab some clothes. Then he got back to his computer. Focused. Calm. Ready.

But Ettie walked into the lounge an hour later, looking like sunshine in a simple denim skirt and white T-shirt. One look and he felt that hard-wrestled-for control slip again. Every time he so much as looked at her it was like that thing bound tightly within him was loosened. But it was something he didn't want released. Not ever.

'You're working already?' she asked.

He nodded, fighting the urge to reach out and touch her. To use sex as his distraction again, as she'd teased the other day...

But last night—how good she'd felt, how intense that had been with her...that hadn't just been distraction. It had been much more than simple, mindless fun. And it couldn't be like that again.

'I've fed the puppy; he's asleep again,' he said after clearing his throat. 'We'll take him for a walk later.'

She nodded and sauntered through to the kitchen looking like the sexiest, sweetest thing he'd ever seen.

He breathed out as she left. See? He could resist. She'd claimed control, but he had it back. Just.

Oh, who was he kidding?

Only now he realised the troubling truth: *she* was his weakness—Ettie Roberts herself. His slide into addiction had already started and he hadn't realised because she felt so good. But *she* was what he craved—*all* the time. But he couldn't use her in that way, as if she were his personal opiate. He had to dial it back. He *had* lost control last night and he'd not expressed anything other than pure, selfish greed.

He refused to be all over her. Sure, they'd sleep together and they'd have this baby, but he'd pull himself together properly and remind them *both* that this was just another business arrangement. That was all it could ever be.

CHAPTER TEN

ETTIE WAS ACUTELY relieved when Monday finally arrived. It wasn't that the weekend had been awful… She and Leon had walked the puppy, wandered around the markets, watched a movie rather than go to that concert—her pick. He'd driven her out of town specially to dine at another amazing restaurant… It was as if he was determined they'd be a normal couple—albeit one with luxurious experiences. She knew he wanted to make this work and she knew he'd be loyal. He had his own brand of duty and honour burned in him. He had everything else too—humour, looks, a bank balance big enough to make anyone's eyes water. And he was so attentive, always ensuring she had what she needed.

Almost all she needed.

But there'd been no more mad, unrestrained sex on the floor, in the kitchen, in the lounge…in fact there'd been no touching at all until darkness fell. But then when it did…?

They'd come together with a wordless intensity that neither of them had addressed afterwards. Neither Saturday nor Sunday. But all through both nights that raw, unrestrained passion had been unleashed. That genie was well out of the bottle now. Leon had made her moan and shake, he'd stripped her back to pure nerves and he'd roared with her, riding her hard. Again. Again. Again. Through the darkness they'd clung to each other, almost crazed with need. Neither of them could get enough and neither of them denied it. Until daylight. Then they were returned to that beautifully curated lifestyle of breakfast at a cute deli, a walk in the park, pondering his next art selection at an elite auction house…but no argument or discussion of anything *deep*. And that was why she was relieved by the prospect of work. She needed the time away from him so she could *think*. Because it wasn't quite right—not since that acutely profound moment on Friday night.

Now she shimmied into her uniform and brushed her hair into submission, ready to face her first day in her new position.

'Here…' Leon was in the kitchen, dressed in a charcoal suit, looking more remote and businesslike than ever. 'Something for your first day as manager.'

She picked up the beautiful business satchel he'd pushed across the counter towards her. She saw the gold insignia and drew in a steadying breath. This wasn't some knock-off from the street markets, this was real leather, from a real luxury label. 'You didn't have to—'

'Look inside.' He sipped his coffee and watched her.

She suddenly felt nervous, because his gaze seemed especially dark this morning—the amber glow was absent. She reached for the slim box tucked inside. Pressing her lips together, she lifted the lid.

It was a pen, but not just any pen. The distinctive white star on the cap told her that, as did the intricately engraved gold nib. 'Leon—'

'Now you don't need to steal mine.' His gaze drifted to her hair and seemed to darken some more. 'You can keep your hair up with it.'

She shook her head. 'I'd be too afraid I'd lose it.' She knew it was worth a crazy amount of money. And it was beautiful—feminine and perfect. But she didn't know if she could keep accepting these kinds of gifts.

'Well,' he set the coffee cup down with a slight bang, 'you can use it to sign the contract in the folder.'

'Contract?'

'The sooner it's signed off, the sooner I can organise the accounts.'

Accounts? With a growing sense of foreboding Ettie looked into the soft leather case again and drew out the slim Manila folder. She opened it and saw several pages of neat type. She stilled as she read the title—it was the prenuptial contract between her and Leon. Their *arrangement* in all its ugly glory.

'I'll need to take time to read it properly,' she muttered, feeling a hit of dizziness as she saw the lists of numbers—*remuneration*. She'd forgotten about their 'deal' over the weekend. She'd been too busy trying to breach his defences again the way she had on Friday night. Too busy trying to restore her own inner equilibrium. And she'd failed on both counts.

His lips twisted. 'Sure. Get it back to me later today.'

She frowned as she studied one page more carefully— the itemised list of her *benefits*. 'This monthly allowance… is for groceries and everything?'

'No, it's your personal allowance.'

But it was more than what she was paid for her job at Cavendish House! She looked up to glare at him.

'You need new clothes and things…'

Her fury mounted and he fell silent at the expression in her eyes. Yeah, he knew she was insulted. But what was worse was that she knew he'd done this deliberately to engender such a reaction in her. Well, it had worked.

'And I get an annual bonus each year for remaining married to you?' she clarified with barely disguised rage.

He lifted that damned coffee cup to his lips again.

'You think I'll respond to that kind of financial incentive?'

'Doesn't everyone?' he asked coolly.

After she'd opened up to him so completely? After what they'd shared on Friday night? Hurt swept over her in a violent wave. Yet immediately after it followed a deep resignation—and *regret*. Because she remembered she'd *already* responded to a financial inducement. It was why she'd agreed to marry him in the first place. This was just the painful reminder of that reality—in cold black and white print.

She shuffled the odious pages together and shoved them into the damned gorgeous bag, tossing the pen in too, not bothering with the perfect little presentation box. 'I'd better get to work; I don't want to be late.'

'I'll drop you.'

'No need.' She turned a huge smile on him as she marched out of the room. 'I'm happy to walk.'

To her enormous relief—and no small amount of regret—he didn't follow her. She breathed quick, steadying breaths all the way to Cavendish House but her nausea had returned. And all her horror.

Yet why should she be so angry about it? Shouldn't she take this as the business opportunity it was? He was giving her everything she could ever want, right?

Because he didn't really want this. Not with her.

He'd lifted that curtain and told her about his life and he regretted it. Not just a wince of embarrassment, but an excoriating extent of regret. He'd pretended he didn't, he didn't show any outward emotion, but she'd seen it eating him, she'd sensed his withdrawal as he sought to rebuild walls he thought were weakened. All weekend she'd hoped—but he hadn't opened up again. Instead he'd made it all about *her*. As if he was determined to make her *happy*—as if it was another job for him to entertain her. Despite their intimacy, the distance she'd felt between them wasn't breached. And she knew the effort he'd made was unsustainable. If it was this hard for him now, she couldn't see how it was going to work for long in the future.

And he'd been busy in the background, hadn't he? Working out his damned clinical contract to seal them both into nothing but a seedy money-for-marriage transaction.

To think she'd actually thought for a moment that they might've become something *more*. To think she'd actually had that fantasy of happy-ever-after. That she'd actually had hope that with time...

One look at that contract and she knew there was no chance. His regret was all-consuming. She'd feel sorry for him if she wasn't so hurt. Did he really think so little of her? Think she'd accept money to make their marriage last month by month?

Now she'd never felt as exposed or as insecure in all her life. Not when her mother had got her diagnosis, or when her ex had texted to tell her the wedding was off. Neither compared to the uncertainty she felt now. Her heart raced as if she'd sprinted her way to work. And now she had to maintain the lie in front of her friends—act ecstatic and in love and all that...it was too hard and all she wanted to do was cry.

Work. Be like Leon. Get it done.

She *had* to get it done. She couldn't let that contract ruin her career as well. She'd worked too hard for it. She just needed to find the time to work out what she was going to do about Leon next. She'd have to do that later.

So she smiled with pure determination as Joel held the door to the concierge office open for her when she arrived, and when he bowed as she walked through.

'Stop it.' She tried to laugh it off.

'You're the boss now… I have to bow and scrape.'

'Ettie,' Jess squealed and leapt up from the seat she'd been sitting on, obviously waiting for her arrival. 'You should *hear* the rumours about you.' She pounced on her and grabbed Ettie's hand, her eyes bugging as she inspected the emerald and diamonds. 'OMG, it's true. I'm *so* thrilled for you.' Jess swept her up in a giant hug. 'When you fainted and he carried you up to the penthouse, it was the most *romantic* thing I've ever seen.'

Ettie hid her face in Jess's shoulder. Her friend's congratulations were heartfelt but she felt hideously awkward. Her engagement wasn't romantic at all, but a business arrangement with benefits.

'And you've worked so hard, you deserve your promotion,' Joel said a little gruffly.

'He's pleased because he gets promoted too,' Jess teased Joel with sparkling eyes. 'What you deserve, Ettie, is *happiness.*'

Ettie blinked back the shockingly sudden surge of tears. She'd worked alongside these guys for years and seeing them this happy for her was…overwhelming. And awkward. So awkward. She blew out a quick breath and smiled as Joel and Jess left the office to get on with their jobs. She could hold it together. It was just hormones and tiredness and the horror of that awful agreement that she couldn't think about right now…

The morning went swiftly because it was perfectly, blessedly busy. But just as she'd finally settled into the swing of it, someone called her to the front desk.

'Hey!'

Ettie's legs suddenly weakened. 'Ophelia?'

'Yes!' Her little sister rushed over and pulled her into a huge hug, managing to dance a small jig at the same time.

'Why are you here? Is everything okay?' Ettie's heart thudded.

'Everything is fabulous.'

Ophelia leaned back and Ettie got a good look at her. Her sister, taller than Ettie, was stunning even in her slightly faded second-hand blazer. Her hair was chestnut and shining and her skin and smile just glowed with health.

'I'm in London for a debating tournament.'

'Of course you are.' Ettie laughed at her gorgeous, geeky sister. 'Why didn't you tell me you were coming?'

'I wasn't sure I could get here. I only have an hour and then I have to get back for the next round.'

'You sneaked out?'

'Well, *duh*.' Ophelia laughed. 'Because I'm so excited for you. I couldn't come to London and not *see* you.'

'Come into the office.' Ettie bit her lip and led her sister into a private space.

She'd phoned Ophelia at Friday lunchtime, after her trip to the dog shelter. She'd told her about moving in with Leon and the baby and *almost* everything.

But not quite all. She could never tell her sister the deal she'd struck with Leon. She could never explain the intricacies of that.

'Is he here?' Ophelia asked as soon as the door was closed, her eyes shining so brightly that Ettie couldn't hold her gaze.

'No, he's in his office. He has meetings.' Right now Ettie was so glad he'd moved out of Cavendish House.

'When can I meet him?' Ophelia bounced on her toes. 'I can't wait to meet him.'

Churning hot acid burned up Ettie's throat. This was so much worse than the lie to Jess and Joel. 'He's a busy guy.'

'You have to come up and see me and bring him. Please! You have to come soon.'

Ettie nodded. But she didn't want Ophelia to meet him. She didn't want this to become that real.

'What's wrong?' Ophelia paused, a slight frown forming on her face.

'Nothing, I'm just…surprised to see you.' Ettie summoned a bright smile, but she and Ophelia were close. Too close—because right now Ophelia saw right through her. She had to act as if it were perfect. It was perfect, wasn't it?

'Good surprised or bad surprised?'

'Good—but if you get into trouble for sneaking out from debating, I won't be happy.'

Ophelia smiled but her gaze was still too watchful. 'Do you love him, Ettie?'

Ettie's throat constricted. She couldn't answer that question. She couldn't answer that one even to herself. But her face burned with a blush.

'Are you happy?' Ophelia's smile was so sweet, so caring, so concerned.

This was the moment to lie. The moment she *had* to lie. But she still couldn't get her voice to work. She made herself nod even as a tear spilled over.

'*Ettie.*' Ophelia wrapped her arms around her. 'I'm worried.'

'Hormones,' she croaked and then laughed to cover it all up. 'I'm fine.'

'You're sure?'

'So sure. Come on, let's have a hot chocolate.'

Half an hour later she kissed her sister goodbye and saw her into a cab to get her back to her debating hall. She stood on the pavement and watched until the cab went round the corner, relieved that it had only been a fleeting visit. It should have been such a treat; instead it had been harder than she'd ever have imagined.

Being that uncomfortable about seeing her beloved sister shattered her. Wrong. It was just *wrong*. It should've been nothing but wonderful, but it had been a nightmare. She couldn't maintain lying to her sister—not for more than the few minutes she'd seen her for just now. She certainly couldn't lie to her sister for the rest of her life. She couldn't lie to her child. She couldn't lie to herself.

Her heart ached.

You've worked so hard for so long.

Yes, and she deserved that promotion. She'd known she did a good job.

You deserve happiness… Are you happy?

She should be happy, right? But she wasn't.

She felt trapped and increasingly afraid that her heart was Leon's prisoner. There had to be another way. She couldn't live this lie. She couldn't lie to those she loved—to *none* of those she loved. Not even him.

'Ettie, are you okay?'

She turned to find Joel on the pavement next to her, concern on his face. 'I'm fine, thanks, Joel. I'm just going to take a walk.'

She needed time to think about how things were going to work. She didn't know what the answer was yet, but something had to change. She walked through the streets and saw the station in the distance. On automatic pilot, she caught the train, letting the familiar route soothe her. She'd not intended to go there, but when she arrived she knew it was what she needed.

Her apartment was colder than usual. Almost empty. He'd had professionals in, because all her stuff was in a few boxes. The furniture was being left for the next person who moved in. She glanced at the windowsill. Not even her herbs needed her any more. They'd already died from the few days of neglect. But it was her home. And in it she'd been honest. And happy.

She needed to be honest again and take back some control. She'd let Leon dictate everything until now. She'd been tired and overwhelmed and confused. But she wasn't now. And she knew what had to happen.

She couldn't sign that contract. She couldn't stay with him. She couldn't live that lie for the rest of her life.

It would slowly tear her apart and she couldn't do that to herself. Because her intuitive, immediate answer to Ophelia's question had hit her hard.

Yes, she loved him.

She'd fallen in love with Leon. In love with a man who didn't love her. Again.

But this wasn't like it was with her ex. She'd never loved *him*. She'd not known what love was until Leon. Not love, nor lust, nor laughter and true companionship…for just a moment she'd had a glimpse of what might've been possible if he loved her too.

Now she looked at the emerald on her finger. It was so beautiful, but without heart. It should have heart with it— it was too stunning to be empty. She took it off and put it on the table, turning away to curl up on the old lumpy sofa. She needed to think through how she was going to be able to live with Leon in her life, but without ever having him in the way she ached for. And she was suddenly so tired, so heartsore, she just had to close her eyes and hide.

The knock on her door an hour later startled her. She checked the peephole and got even more of a shock.

'What are you doing here?' She stepped back after letting Leon in, nervously tugging her shirt when she saw his grim expression.

'Joel called. He was concerned about you.'

Why? 'How did you know where to find me?'

'Seeing as you left your phone at Cavendish, I made a

lucky guess,' he said in a chilled voice. 'Joel said Ophelia visited you. Is she okay?'

'She's great. Really. So happy.'

'I'm glad.'

Ettie pressed her lips together. He didn't sound glad.

'I'm sorry if I worried you,' she said.

He didn't answer. He'd seen the ring on the table and he didn't lift his gaze from it.

'I'm not signing that contract, Leon,' she blurted, unable to hide her hurt from him any more. 'I don't expect you to pay for Ophelia's fees. I never should have accepted that offer. I can make it work some other way.'

'What are you saying, Ettie?' His expression had frozen.

She clenched her fists and tried to hold herself together. 'I allowed you to make all the decisions. It all happened so fast, I wasn't feeling well…we got carried away on a tsunami of panic and some of this wasn't necessary.'

'Wasn't necessary?' he repeated in cool disbelief, and turned to look at her hard. 'Ettie, you're pregnant.'

'Yes, and we need to make rational decisions.'

'You call walking out of work and coming back to this dump a rational decision?'

She drew in a sharp breath. He was angry with her, unused to being challenged. 'This is my home. I was happy here.'

'You're not happy at my home?'

'You swept in and took command—'

'You were *ill*,' he pointed out icily.

'You tipped my life upside down,' she shouted back. 'It's just been so quick and I haven't had the chance to think everything through.' She needed to slow down because her alarm bells were ringing.

'What do you want?' he exploded. 'I was *trying*—'

'Yes,' she interrupted harshly. 'Trying too hard.'

He sent her a wrathful look. 'I *what*?' he muttered, outraged.

'You don't want to marry me any more than I want to marry you.'

That silenced him.

'You don't, Leon.' She rubbed her arms, suddenly cold. 'It's a calculated decision you think you have to live with. But you don't. And I can't live a lie for the rest of my life. I can't pretend to be happy when I'm not.'

'You've given us less than a week.' He was livid.

'Isn't it better to realise the mistake sooner rather than later?'

'Or maybe you should give us more time. I might be trying too hard, but you're bailing out at the first chance you've got. You've been betrayed in the past and you're letting your fears get in the way of a perfectly fine future. You think I'll walk out on you,' he added coldly. 'So you've left before I can.'

His accusation stole her breath.

'I can't do this,' she whispered. 'I can't marry you.'

She was his choice by default. They were forced together purely by the fate of a failed condom. Sure, he was offering security for her baby. Their child would want for nothing—it would have the adoration of both parents.

'You're a good guy, Leon, okay?' she said unevenly. 'You win the honourable prize. You're a man who steps up and does the right thing. But you don't have to take it this far, okay?'

'This far?'

'I can't marry you. I can't live with you. I certainly can't sign that horrible contract and be *paid* to like you. We can just co-parent. We can make some better arrangement.'

He glared at her. 'You're saying you don't want to sleep with me any more?'

'We're only back together because of the baby. You don't really want me.'

'How can you say I don't want you when I can't keep my hands off you?' he roared and shoved those hands into his trouser pockets.

She gritted her teeth. 'That's just sex. And frankly, we're using it to paper over the cracks in this arrangement.'

'We what?' He dragged in a sharp breath. Then another. 'You're complaining about our sex life?'

'You use it to avoid emotional intimacy.'

He froze. 'And what do you use it for?'

She couldn't answer that. She just couldn't.

He stared at her. 'You read too much into everything. You attach meaning to memories that don't actually matter.'

'Don't they matter? Don't you think they impact how we both choose to live?' She stepped closer, suddenly shaking with emotion, with how important it was to cut through to what was vitally important. And honest.

'Yes, I've been hurt before and I don't want to be hurt again,' she admitted. 'And if I stay with you, I will be. I've tried to treat this like an arrangement, but I can't. I'm not like you, I can't keep my emotions "under control", and I don't want to.' She inhaled a deep breath and forced herself to finish. 'We'll work together to take care of the baby, but being together in an empty relationship isn't right. I can't keep sleeping with you, Leon. It's destroying me.' It hurt her so much to say it, but it had to be done. 'You deserve more than this…facade. You deserve love. And so do I.'

She wanted him to find love. He deserved it after everything he'd missed out on. And she wanted to find real love for herself too. To *be* loved. While she could be everything *but* the one he truly wanted, that wasn't enough for her. She wasn't going to put herself through the heartache of being with a man who didn't really want her. Her child needed to see both its mother and its father, loved and loving. If not to each other, then to significant others when and if they appeared.

She'd tried, but she couldn't be like him. Nor was she the one for him. Because if she was he'd have recognised it already—he would have *felt* it. He would have known he didn't need that contract to bind her to him. He was a smart guy, not slow.

'Love?' he scoffed. 'There's no such thing as love. That's the rubbish of fairy tales and films. There's just reality and practicality. There's lust and there are contracts.'

And that just proved her point completely. Because for her there *was* love. She felt it for *him*. She ached to give him everything she possibly could, but he didn't feel that way for her. She braced tightly against the painful intensity of rejection.

This is the right decision, Ettie. Right, right, right.

Leon stared at Ettie's expression in the silence that followed his outburst. Dread surged in his belly, a hideous whirlpool of horror and regret. He shouldn't have said that. He shouldn't have crushed her dreams with his icy reality. She hadn't deserved that. Yet he'd had to be honest with her.

He cleared his throat. 'We can make this work, Ettie. We *will* make it work.'

'Yes,' she nodded curtly, 'but not the way you want it to.'

He glared, waiting for her to explain.

'You might be prepared to settle, but I'm not.' She straightened. In a blink the distress was gone from her eyes. There was only determination there now.

'Settle?' The chill spread from his gut to his limbs and then—blessedly—up to his brain. Finally he could think clearly.

'I do believe in that kind of love, Leon.' She looked up at him. Emotion shadowed her eyes, but dignity shone clearly from within them. There were no tears, only resolution. 'I've fallen in love with you,' she said. 'That's why I can't stay and why I won't marry you.'

He stared, dumbstruck, as his brain short-circuited. She *what*?

'How can that possibly surprise you?' she asked with a shake of her head. 'How could I not…? But you don't love me and that's okay.'

'You're not in love with me,' he blurted mechanically.

She was confusing it with gratitude. He was the first person to do things for her. Not betray her. Not abandon her. Not take and take and take. And she had such little experience with sex, she didn't realise it was just physical pleasure. He'd rubbed her up the right way, that was all.

'It's the lifestyle,' he said roughly.

Now her expressive eyes flashed—all anger. 'I don't fall in love with *things*, Leon. You insult me. Your contract insulted me. I'd still love you even if you were poor and lived in a cardboard box. That you felt I needed some reward for staying with you…' She shook her head.

That feeling inside roiled and burned but still he rejected what she was saying.

Her expression hardened in the face of his silence. 'You don't get to deny my feelings or my wishes. You don't get to make all the decisions.' She drew in a deep breath. 'You've found out all my other secrets—you might as well know everything. I fell in love with you probably that very first night. But you don't feel the same. You're trying to do the right thing, but it's too much to ask of you—it's obvious you don't really want to when you can't bear to reveal anything of yourself and you can't trust me for more than five minutes. And I get why, I do. You shouldn't have to open up to someone you don't care about. But don't deny what's true for me. It's painful enough. You don't want emotional intimacy with me. Fine, don't have it. But you don't get physical either. You don't get to have the cake and eat it too. You want too much from me. I can't separate it the way you do.'

She did *not* love him. He could deny that and he would. 'You barely know me.'

'I know all I need to know. Who you are is what you do. And you do loyal. Kind. Funny. Determined. Stubborn to the point of—' She broke off as her breathing hitched.

Yet it wasn't enough, was it? He'd given her everything he could and it still wasn't enough.

'You don't have to feel bad,' she added, her clear-eyed gaze narrowing on him. 'You don't have to pretend any more. You can find someone else.'

Is that what *she* wanted?

'How bloody generous of you, Ettie,' he said scathingly. 'You haven't even given this a chance. You say you love me but you can walk out just like that?' He snapped his fingers as his anger flared. 'Not much of a love really.'

Her face whitened. 'I also love *myself*. I am worthy of that job promotion. I deserve the great sex life you've shown me is possible. *You're* the one who's taught me I deserve more. Not to expect less or settle for worse. And thank you for that. But now I have to protect myself.' She lifted her chin. 'You don't love me.'

'That's not the point.' He dismissed the statement.

'It is.'

He was so furious he couldn't look at her any more. Wildly he glanced around and saw the herbs on the windowsill had become little more than a collection of musty leaves in the pots. Without her presence and care they hadn't taken long to wither and die. So typical. He felt his grip on himself slip as that monstrous crushing inside threatened to kill every last brain cell he had and render him only capable of...*what*?

Oh, his body knew what it wanted—to prove to her that she couldn't resist him again. Hell, he needed to get away before he totally lost it.

She'd completely rejected everything he'd offered. She'd rejected him.

'At the very least I can house you,' he said icily. 'Not here.' He retrieved the ring from the table. It burned his palm and he shoved it into his pocket. He stalked to the door, needing to leave before he said or did something he'd regret. 'I'll be in touch to make new arrangements.'

CHAPTER ELEVEN

LOVE? SHE WANTED *LOVE*?

Leon was living in a perpetual state of frustration. With every breath he whipped from fury to wrath and back again.

Let her go. Let her stay in her horrible, small apartment. Let her be alone and miserable if that was what she was determined to do. He was happy to have his house back to himself, right? He'd found it hard sharing with someone for the first time in his life. He'd go back to how it had been—how he liked it. Alone, independent, strong, easy.

But he paced the vast, empty space until the puppy got too tired to follow his every step. He sank onto the sofa and scooped the little guy up. The pup immediately curled into a ball on his stomach and began to snooze.

Leon had no such respite. He'd done everything he could for Ettie. He'd given her a far better home. He'd looked after her health and freed her from that financial burden, he'd recognised her worth at work. He'd had her well-being foremost in his mind. What more did she want?

But he hadn't done everything.

The inner voice repeated it—over and over. From a whisper it strengthened in volume and insistence until it was ringing incessantly in his head.

The void she'd left was huge. She'd taken more than he'd realised.

The baby. Right? It was just the baby. He reasoned his way through the bereft sensation. She was taking away his *child*. And with that recognition his anger returned in full force. He railed inwardly at her stubborn selfishness.

He'd been told so often that people would only want *things* from him. Money, mostly. Money and the kind of "doors open" access his privilege engendered. And that wisdom had proven true often enough in the past. But not this time.

He'd given everything to *her*. At least everything that was easy to give—his money, his success, his home. What was harder was what was hidden. What he didn't even want to face himself. The security she craved wasn't financial. What she'd said she wanted—needed—was emotional. And that was impossible. He didn't believe in love. He didn't even know what it was. Yet with every day that dragged, that bereft feeling only built a bigger and bigger hole inside. It wasn't the thought of the baby at all.

He put a security team back on her. He initiated all the paperwork he could think of to secure both her rights and his, ditching that damned contract he'd drawn up over that weekend to try to hold the complications at bay. But three interminable days later, he still couldn't sleep at night. Worry nagged.

He hated thinking of her being alone. He hated remembering her words. But they echoed relentlessly—a melody to his own berating beat—dragging in loss, lust, unbearable loneliness…and at the heart of that hideous mix grew an intolerable, impossible yearning.

I love you, Leon.

It was the first time in his life someone had said that to him and actually meant it. He knew, to his bones, how much she thought she'd meant it. She barely knew him but she believed her words. He'd been unable to. And he'd been right because in the next second she'd snatched them back again by rejecting everything he'd offered. By rejecting *him*. She didn't love him enough to stay. She didn't even want his damn money. She was so determined to be independent, all because he couldn't what—wail on about his past? Open up to her? Love her?

Didn't she understand that he couldn't? He didn't know how.

He knew she wouldn't deny him access to his child. She'd just denied him access to *her*. She'd taken her company, her attention, her presence from him. And somehow that was the worst. He couldn't stand it. Nor could he fathom *why* it was so horrendous.

So he did what he'd always done: he fought for control. He isolated himself. He worked round the clock. And he avoided all contact with anyone at Cavendish House. They'd be Team Ettie all the way. He didn't blame them. He understood their loyalty.

He also knew Ettie needed to be loved. That was why she worked for everyone—she ached for any kind of affection. She didn't realise that all those people cared about her without her having to work for it; it was because of the person she was—sunny, generous, interested, enthusiastic about everything in life…

And he'd been stupid enough to tell her he didn't believe in love.

He sat on the floor of his home and rubbed the puppy's ears and finally admitted to himself that he was a coward. More than that, he was a jerk. He'd not accepted what she'd offered. He'd not even acknowledged the truth of it.

The fourth morning it was worse. He couldn't stand it any more. The isolation and gaping hole inside widened with every angry second that ticked by and today it was an actual physical pain. And that was when it finally hit—it wasn't *rage* he felt. It was *hurt*.

Deep, incurable hurt. He was so vulnerable. She'd prised layers of protection and defence open and then she'd struck him hard.

Not even the unconditional trust of the little puppy soothed him. The dog just made it worse, because he made caring—adoration—seem easy. Not to Leon it wasn't. He closed his eyes and leaned against the cool window overlooking his immaculate garden.

Ettie had given him the smallest, tantalising glimpse of something he'd never imagined. When she'd said she was in love with him, he'd had that heart-busting vision of a small family filled with fun and laughter and passion. A family that was *together*. The kind of family he'd never had.

In his childhood family there'd been no honesty. No laughter. No love. Nothing but cold cruelty from his mother. And when he'd tried to talk to his father, the older man had shut down. Dismissed his truth. Silenced him.

But hadn't Leon just done the exact same thing to Ettie? Hadn't he shut down and closed off contact? He'd refused to even acknowledge the problem, let alone try to resolve it.

While he'd silenced her, Ettie had never silenced him. She'd let him speak. She'd wanted him to speak more. She hadn't judged him for his words, she'd just accepted him.

Bile rose in his throat. He did not want to be like his father. And he sure as hell refused to be like his mother. Why had he thought any of what that woman had wanted was okay?

Never show weakness. Not anger. Not fear. No tears. No laughter.

Even when he'd learned to bury his emotions, his

mother hadn't loved him. Nothing he could've done could have changed that. She'd taught him all the wrong things. And he'd been so busy fighting for those tangible signs of success, he'd not stopped to see how much he was missing. How much his mother had actually *won*—because here he was, living a life so isolated, he might as well be back in that cupboard she'd locked him in.

Ettie was the one who was right. Expressing emotions *wasn't* the same as losing control of them. And even if he did lose control? What then? What was the worst that could happen? The worst had *already* happened.

Ettie had left him.

And now here he was in his huge house—isolated, cold and stuck in the emotional stunting of his past. He'd thought he was over it, that he was free of that pain. But he wasn't beyond it at all. His own beautiful big house offered no more comfort or companionship than that dark, hideous cupboard of his childhood torment.

That constriction inside—the tight-bound hard knot inside him—finally loosened. And it hurt like hell. But he would *not* be an absent father to this child—physically or emotionally. He had to make more of an effort because he didn't want his child turning out like him. He gazed sightlessly over the garden as he fully realised the painful, amazing truth. That knot inside—he'd hardened it, tried to cover it up, because it was more than a crusted nugget of hope. It was his heart.

Ettie had breathed life into it, blowing on old embers to bring back a flame. His inner fire was flickering now but it needed more fuel.

While he'd do anything to protect his baby, what was even more incredible—wonderful and terrifying—was that he'd fallen so completely in love with its mother. It wasn't just the physical contact, but everything she brought with her. Her smile had put sparkle into his life. He simply wanted to put his battered heart into her hands and be with her. And he wanted to care for her in *all* ways. Her words hadn't just unsettled him, they'd also left him raw. She had a power he'd never have believed it would be possible for anyone to have over him. He was still a little angry with her for that. And yet he knew he too had the power to gravely hurt her. He already had. But he'd never do that again.

He thought back to that very first night—to the way she'd run away the next morning, too scared to even look him in the eye. Braced for rejection, for betrayal, she'd been so certain she was going to be hurt. She'd run because he'd not given her what she needed.

But in order to get her back he had to open up in the way he'd told himself he never would, that he'd never thought he *could*. Heartache forced him forward. There was no alternative, no getting over this. The gap she'd left in his life was crippling.

He'd thought he had it all. He'd thought he was invincible. But he had nothing of real value. Now he'd finally realised, he knew he had to do something about it.

There was action and there was *action*.

CHAPTER TWELVE

IT WAS MOVING DAY.

Ettie looked around her little flat. Not much had changed in the days since she'd left Leon and come back to live alone.

He'd been in touch as promised, but only via paperwork. Formal, bloodless documentation offering her an apartment in Cavendish House to make it easy for her to work and be near to his home. It didn't matter how near or far from her he was, he still killed her heart, but she couldn't be under the same roof as him, couldn't sleep with him any more, and that would happen if she stayed at his house. He didn't love her and that was fine, but to remain and give everything of herself would slowly destroy her.

At least Leon travelled for work. She'd have moments of pure respite. Those urges in the smallest hours of the morning, to run to him, to tell him again that she loved him, to try to convince him to love her…she could ignore those. If she ignored them for long enough, surely they'd disappear. Surely she'd done the right thing?

But doubts niggled. Should she have fought harder for him?

Only then she remembered her past. Hadn't she been humiliated enough? The man didn't love her. No man had ever loved her. Not her father. Not her ex. Not Leon.

Snap out of it, Ettie.

The removal van was due in five minutes. She'd had very little to do—just repacked those few belongings she'd got out.

Someone knocked on the door. She checked the peephole. The guy's cap was pulled low but had the removal logo on it. He was early. Of course, anyone hired by Leon would be efficient in the extreme.

She opened the door, knowing the security guard stationed along from her flat would have already vetted him. But it wasn't the removal man. It was Leon himself.

She stared, her tongue stuck to the roof of her mouth. She'd never seen him this casually dressed. She'd pretty much only seen him either in a suit or naked. Now he was in black jeans, black T-shirt—and both fitted him lovingly. The effect of his outfit was…*appallingly inappropriate.* She clenched her jaw and her fists, furious for her basic reaction to him. *Every time.*

He totalled her senses.

'I need to be able to help you, Ettie.' He shifted on his feet and broke the silence. 'Don't you think?'

That's all he wanted to do?

Unable to speak, she nodded and stood aside so he could enter. She had to be stronger than this.

He was holding a tray she'd not seen through the peephole. 'I brought you these.'

A trio of little plants in pretty pots. Fresh herbs to replace the ones that had died.

'Housewarming present for your new apartment,' he explained in her silence. 'I noticed your other ones hadn't survived your absence.'

Of course. He noticed everything. He'd even got the exact right herbs—thyme, chives, basil. Her battered heart burst apart that little bit more. But it was a peace offering and she could be adult enough to accept it, couldn't she?

'Thank you,' she said awkwardly as he put the plants on the old dining table.

He didn't pick up one of the stacked boxes. Instead he looked across the small space to her, his expression more serious than ever. It should have been impossible.

'I'm sorry.' His words spilled suddenly into the taut silence. Uneven and harsh, like sharp pebbles tossed with piercing aim.

Was that what he'd come to offer? An apology? Her heart cranked open again, seeping pain and pure disappointment. She should appreciate the gesture, but she found she wasn't quite ready to be *friends* with him yet. Too soon. Too sore.

She blinked rapidly, tried to pull herself together enough to offer a polite smile. Could he just shift the boxes now? But he was standing there—as still as still, his expression unreadable, his eyes as dark as his T-shirt.

'I don't know what love really is, Ettie. I only know what it isn't and I couldn't let that happen to you. It's why I thought I should—could—let you go. I never wanted you to be unhappy.'

Yes, she knew he hadn't meant to hurt her. He'd only tried to do the right thing. Now, could he *please* pick up a box?

'Ettie?' He paused. 'Please look at me.'

He asked so softly and she couldn't resist. This was the problem; she didn't think she could *ever* resist. Not for long. She wasn't ready for this yet.

He was paler than usual. Intense. Rigid. Her eyes filled because he was trying to open up and be honest and she could see the cost of that effort. She could see the desperation in him. Because he knew he'd hurt her and he didn't like that. He might be bossy, but he was kind, and that broke her heart all over again. 'Leon—'

'No. Let me finish. Hell, start. I'm making a mess of it.' He rubbed his hand through his hair, frustration leaping from him. 'It's taken me a bit to realise you weren't rejecting *me*. You thought you were doing the right thing for me. For the baby. And for you. Because you wanted more than what I was offering. You were right to want that.'

Not the money, the lifestyle, the security. No, she'd wanted something far more precious from him.

'I've always been unwilling to share space with anyone, share anything much. I didn't know how.'

He stood still but Ettie could see the faint trembling of his fingers and she waited. She couldn't have spoken if she'd tried.

'I have that massive house because it made me feel free. I thought we'd hardly be aware of each other in there, but somehow you filled it,' he said. 'I didn't know it at the time, but I've never been as scared in all my life as those few days when you were living with me. And then you left.' He puffed out a long, pained breath. 'And now I've finally worked out what it was I'd been so afraid of. It was that. You *leaving*.' He paused. 'Having you with me was like a dream, and I didn't want to wake up and find you gone. Not again.'

Ettie couldn't move, couldn't open her mouth, not even to release the moan building in her chest. She hurt so much—for him, for her. And the fragile hope that was mounting within was too much to bear.

'I didn't recognise what I was feeling,' he said. 'I just didn't know, Ettie. I've never had it before. Never felt it.' He stepped nearer to her, his eyes blazing almost black with intensity. 'You were right. I buried myself—us— in sex. I had this driving need to get closer to you. It's so good, but that's because it's *not* just physical, Ettie.' His voice lifted. 'It never was. I think back to that first day. I've never been as intrigued by anyone. You were passionate and fiery and sweet and kind. But the thing is, you do lovely things for everyone and I doubted that I was all that special—'

'I don't sleep with just anyone,' she interrupted harshly.

'I know.' He lifted his shoulders and then let them fall in a slight, helpless movement of concession. 'You slipped under my armour without my even realising I had armour on. And then I was vulnerable. I didn't like that, Ettie. Uncertainty is hideous.' He dragged in another breath. 'The trouble is, I don't know *how* to give you what's in here.' He pressed his fist to his chest. 'All I knew was that I wanted you to be free and happy, to fly and have all the things I thought you hadn't had… Before these last few days, I never stopped to wonder *why* I wanted that for you but it's since become obvious. I wanted what's best for you, because I've fallen in love with you. I wanted you to have everything…' His voice petered out and he stood there, alone and exposed.

'I just wanted *you*.' Ettie's throat was so tight she could only whisper as her hope overflowed her wounded heart. '*You* were my pick, my special thing just for me. That first night and ever since, all I've ever wanted was *you*.'

The expression on his face crumbled her defences. He looked torn—somewhere between touched and hopeful and terrified.

'I love you and I'm not going to stop loving you.' Her voice shook. 'But—'

'You think I'm only here because of the baby.' He gazed at her, reading her own vulnerability, her own limiting fears. 'No. Our future was set the second I clapped eyes on you. One night was never going to be enough. But you worked for me and you were shy and I was processing how to get around that when we found out…you were pregnant. That changed everything and I think I just went on auto—instinct telling me what needed to happen and what I really wanted… And that's you—*all* of you and *all* the love you have to give.' He paused. His voice was strained. 'I'm so greedy, Ettie. I want you in my life. I don't want to let you go. I'm *not* going to let you go. And I refuse to regret the circumstances that brought us back together. I can't wait until we meet our baby. I love you.' He shook his head as he repeated it beneath his breath.

She put her hand on his lips and stopped him. 'You deserve to have all the love.' Her eyes watered.

'But how do I show you? How do I make you happy?'

His admission—letting her see his vulnerability—touched her more than anything.

She shook her head. 'You just do—just *you*. Listening to me, laughing with me, loving me. It's not pity. It's compassion. It's understanding.'

He gazed so hard into her eyes it was as though he was drinking her words in and was desperately trying to understand, to believe…

'You don't even realise you're doing it,' she muttered, half marvelling. 'Why do you think I fell in love with you? I took one look and wanted you. Even when I thought you were a heartless brute about to condemn Toby, I still felt that physical pull. But I fell in love with you that night—you let me see your smile, you let me in enough to laugh with me, and it was just magic. You were funny and smart and you noticed what I needed before I realised it myself. You *see* me. You know how to care, Leon. It's innate in you.'

The stark emotion in his eyes melted her.

'You're also completely bossy,' she couldn't help teasing.

He didn't hide his smile then. 'What, you mean I'm not perfect?'

'How boring would that be?' She cupped his jaw, reading the tension lingering in his eyes. 'Just talk to me— about anything. Nothing. Everything. I don't need grand gestures, Leon, or fancy dates. It's the everyday things you already do so well.' She pointed at the herbs. 'See? You notice. You care.'

He frowned and put out a dismissive hand. 'That was just—'

'Thoughtful,' she interrupted. 'You did it because you were thinking of me.'

'I think of you all the time,' he muttered huskily.

She stilled because in that moment she truly, finally, completely believed him. It had been the simplest, most heartfelt declaration she'd ever heard.

'Why are you crying?' He pulled her against his chest as her face crumpled and she sobbed.

'Because I'm happy.' She clung to him, needing to feel his heat and strength. 'I love you, Leon.'

He was here. And he was hers.

'I love you too.' He cradled her gently, stroking his hand down her back as she cried out the days of loneliness and heartache. 'I want everything with you—laughter, love, babies, puppies.'

She gurgled with watery laughter but hugged him hard. 'You were right too,' she said softly. 'I was afraid of going for what I wanted—of making a mistake again—so I ran. It's been so awful. All I wanted was you. And I was terrified that you didn't want me.'

Despite all the kisses that had gone before, this felt like their first. In that magical moment just before contact, when breath mingled and eyes locked, that was nerves and excitement, happiness and wonder. Ettie understood his stillness for what it was—the remnants of fear, anxiety and loss leaving them both. This time their sensuality wasn't to avoid emotional intimacy, but to enhance it. And so swiftly, it flared. Incandescently.

'*Glykia mou.*'

He pushed her clothes aside. Kisses touched skin the second it was bared. When she couldn't stand any more he took her down to the floor, into his embrace. He lifted her onto his lap so she straddled him. Face to face, eye to eye. Back in the light where there was no hiding anything. He held her, helped her slide on him until he was buried as deep as possible. More tears trickled at the sudden, exquisite fulfilment. Sealed tightly to him, staring deep into his eyes, she'd never felt this close to anyone. Never as secure...

And never as *hot*.

A glint of amusement sparked in his eye as he slid his hand down to lightly stroke right where she was most sensitive.

'I'm trying to slow down,' she complained with a moan of delight, and leaned closer to kiss his gorgeous mouth.

'Why?' he muttered against her with pure temptation. 'We can always do it again. We can love each other like this every day for the rest of our lives.'

Every nerve curled in unendurable elation. She trembled in his arms as her physical and emotional reaction to his promise consumed her. He loved her so hard and she loved him right back.

For a long time, they remained breathless in the blissful safety of that loving embrace.

He reached out a long arm and grabbed his jeans from the heap of clothes on the floor and pulled something sparkly out of his pocket. 'Is it too soon to put this back where it belongs?'

She stared at the ring and then back up at him. Her heart galloped faster than it had only moments ago when she'd been recovering from the most intense orgasm of her life.

'We can always get another if you don't like it, but I thought the emerald matched your eyes…you probably didn't notice.' His voice trailed off and he fell silent.

She felt the acceleration of his heart beneath her hand. 'I noticed,' she breathed.

'You did?' His face lit up.

Heart overflowing, she lifted her hand so he could slide the ring back on her finger.

'Will you marry me, Ettie Roberts?' he asked unevenly.

'Yes,' she whispered as she stared into his eyes. 'It's beautiful.' And now it had heart; now it glittered even more brilliantly than before.

'It's for real, Ettie,' he promised, husky and true. 'It's for always.'

Bathed in love, she laced her fingers through his.

'Let's go home,' he said. 'Basil will be wondering where we are.'

'You named the puppy Basil?' She leaned against him and laughed with pure, infectious joy. 'Yes. Let's go home to him.'

Together.

* * * * *

MILLS & BOON

Coming next month

UNTOUCHED UNTIL HER ULTRA-RICH HUSBAND
Dani Collins

You told me what you were worth, Luli. Act like you believe it.

She *had* been acting. The whole time. Still was, especially as a handful of designers whose names she knew from Mae's glossy magazines behaved with deference as they welcomed her to a private showroom complete with catwalk.

She had to fight back laughing with incredulity as they offered her champagne, caviar, even a pedicure.

"I—" She glanced at Gabriel, expecting him to tell them she aspired to model and should be treated like a clothes horse, not royalty.

"A full wardrobe," he said. "Top to bottom, morning to night, office to evening. Do what you can overnight, send the rest to my address in New York."

"*Mais bien sûr, monsieur*," the couturier said without a hint of falter in her smile. "Our pleasure."

"Gabriel—" Luli started to protest as the women scattered.

"You remember what I said about this?" he tapped the wallet that held her phone. "I need you to stay on-brand."

"Reflect who you are?"

"Yes."

"Who are you?" she asked ruefully. "I only met you ten minutes ago."

"I'm a man who doesn't settle for anything less than the best." He touched her chin. "The world is going to have a lot of questions about why we married. Give them an answer."

His words roused the competitor who still lurked inside her. She wanted to prove to the world she was *worthy* to be his wife. Maybe she wanted to prove her worth to him, too. Definitely she longed to prove something to herself.

Either way, she made sure those long-ago years of preparation paid off. She had always been ruthless in evaluating her own shortcomings and knew how to play to her strengths. She might not be trying to win a crown today, but she hadn't been then, either. She'd been trying to win the approval of a woman who hadn't deserved her idolatry.

She pushed aside those dark memories and clung instead to the education she had gained in those difficult years.

"That neckline will make my shoulders look narrow," she said, making quick up-down choices. "The sweetheart style is better, but no ruffles at my hips. Don't show me yellow. Tangerine is better. A more verdant green. That one is too pale." In her head, she was sectioning out the building blocks of a cohesive stage presence. Youthful, but not too trendy. Sensual, but not overtly sexual. Charismatic without being showy.

"Something tells me I'm not needed," Gabriel said twenty minutes in and rose to leave. "We'll go for dinner in three hours." He glanced to the couturier. "And return in the morning for another fitting."

"*Parfait. Merci, monsieur.*" Her smile was calm, but the way people were bustling told Luli how big a deal this was. How big a deal *Gabriel* was.

The women took her measurements while showing her unfinished pieces that only needed hemming or minimal tailoring so she could take them immediately.

"You'll be up all night," Luli murmured to one of the seamstresses.

The young woman moved quickly, but not fast enough for her boss who kept crying, *"Vite! Vite!"*

"I'm sorry to put you through this," Luli added.

"*Pas de problème.* Monsieur Dean is a treasured client. It's our honor to provide your trousseau." She clamped her teeth on a pin between words. "Do you know where he's taking you for dinner? We should choose that dress next, so I can work on the alterations while you have your hair and makeup done. It must be fabulous. The world will be watching."

She would be presented publicly as his wife, Luli realized with a hard thump in her heart.

Continue reading
UNTOUCHED UNTIL HER ULTRA-RICH HUSBAND
Dani Collins

Available next month
www.millsandboon.co.uk

COMING SOON!

We really hope you enjoyed reading this book. If you're looking for more romance, be sure to head to the shops when new books are available on

Thursday 16th May

To see which titles are coming soon, please visit

millsandboon.co.uk/nextmonth

LET'S TALK Romance

For exclusive extracts, competitions
and special offers, find us online:

 facebook.com/millsandboon

@MillsandBoon

@MillsandBoonUK

Get in touch on 01413 063232

For all the latest titles coming soon, visit
millsandboon.co.uk/nextmonth